CRYSTAL LAKE PUBLIC LIBRARY
P9-BZT-332

MARATHON

MARATHON

A Novel By

W. WILLIAM WINOKUR

Published by
Kissena Park Press
5 Union Square West, 4th floor
New York, NY 10003

The cover painting is based on the photograph "Nun in Prayer" taken by Father Sava Janjic at the Visoki Decani Serbian Orthodox Monastery. The Monastery was damaged but not destroyed in the Kosovo War (1998-2000), thanks to the protection of Italian forces, which have blocked every access to the monastery. The original photograph can be found at Father Sava's web site, www.kosovo.com. The author and the publisher are grateful for his permission to adapt the image.

Front Jacket design: Chrysoula Artemis
"The Quest," "The Golden Mean," and "Nike" graphics by Chrysoula Artemis
Back Jacket design & mechanical: Two Red Shoes Design Inc.
Jacket art painting: Jeff Raum
Book design and layout: Scott Friedlander
Printer: Berryville Graphics
Printed in the United States of America

Library of Congress Cataloging-in-Publication "Data"
Winokur, W. William, 1960
Marathon

ISBN 0-9768508-0-X

First Edition
1 2 3 4 5 6 7 8 9 10

To my father, Herbert, thank you for having faith through all of my foibles.

In loving memory of my mother, Cynthia. A brighter star has never shone. Mom, the only thing that eases my fear of mortality is the solitary thought that I will see you again.

Be ashamed to die until you have won some victory for humanity.
—Horace Mann

My dear — Life is never final, and Death will only be a new journey in my Life.
—Ion Theodore

Marathon would not exist were it not for the help and inspiration of many people. I owe my gratitude to: Professor Robert M. Faggen, fellow Horace Mann alum, for his editing and literary guidance—he was truly present at the creation; to Jodee Blanco and Kent Carroll, who sensed the story's magic early on; to Jeff Gomez, Mark Pensavalle, David Zeichner, Chrysoula Artemis, Scott Friedlander, Fiona Serpa, Judy Eda and Lana Ayers—the tireless staff of Kissena Park Press who believed in me as well as in this work; to Les Steinmetz, my brother from another mother, who gave me unswerving moral support. And finally, to my wife Maggie and our three children—Leonardo, Emma and Ian—living proof that the only really important thing in the world is family.

PROLOGUE
RESURRECTION

One day, I became suddenly and frighteningly aware of having lived without knowing the first thing about myself. I hadn't been in a coma, nor was I suffering from disease—it was a veil of a more obscure nature. Now, my eyes are open and I see the world as a blank slate upon which I can press the sharp edge of my soul.

I am called Marianna, but I was born Maria Anastasia. Maria is in remembrance of the Blessed Virgin; Anastasia is Greek for *one who will be resurrected.*

As Marianna, I never thought of myself as being susceptible to flights of mysticism or prone to believing in things hoped for. I was brought up in a secular world whose pendulum had swung away from spirituality. And until now, *destiny* sounded like an ideal embraced only by young poets and tortured romantics.

For years, I wandered through cultural clichés—the free love of the 60's and the decadence of the 70's. Then I grew tired of the banal and traded it in for the corner office and the comforts of a Long Island suburb. *Brotherly love* and *making a difference* were beautifully selfless mantras but they didn't pay my mortgage, let alone a summer rental in the Hamptons. Everything had become an economic equation: how could I accumulate the greatest amount of anything with as little sacrifice as possible. Even the concept of my fellow man had become another cliché. I found myself amid a heap of souls too preoccupied with themselves to achieve anything for humanity—and I had neither the courage nor the imagination to dig myself out of the ruins of beautiful ideas gone awry.

I tried to maintain a separation between what I did for a living and what I did for a life. I had even lost the ability to feel for those closest to me, failing the last one when he needed me the most.

In one's lifetime, the chance to choose the right path rarely visits more than once. About a decade and a half ago, I was given a second opportunity to rise and in doing so I learned an invaluable lesson: to *find* the truth you must first *seek* it—*if* you seek it you must be *willing* to find it.

There are moments in each person's life that mark turning points, choices by which we alter our fate to degrees great and small. What we see of the world, with whom we bond, how we speak to another human being—all these decisions determine who we are, both in our eyes and to those around us. Do we realize the significance as they happen, or is it only in hindsight that their import becomes recognizable? I do not know the answer, but I do know that such an event has irrevocably changed my life. But what intrigues me more is how I perceived life the instant before the event. An entire potential existence was eradicated as a new life course was suddenly plotted. I have abandoned regret of roads not taken.

I am Maria Anastasia.

Much has transpired in my new life since then, but I will now try to set down the story before my memories fade into chaos. It is a journey of salvation and redemption that began thousands of years ago in the sun-drenched mountains of Greece—the birthplace of the Gods.

PART ONE
THE QUEST

1 THE LONE RUNNER

Fiery-robed Helios began his ascent over the end of the eastern world, the same as he has done since the beginning of time. It was the morning of September 9th, 490 B.C., though to those witnessing this glorious sunrise, the date was Metageitnion 18 in the third quarter of the 72nd Olympiad.

The Sun's rays cascaded over the crests of Mount Pentelicus. Its golden hues stood in contrast to the darkness that shrouded the dusty valley below. Night's icy chill gripped the morning air, not wanting to yield her throne to the Goddess of the Dawn. But Eos would win her daily battle.

Over these empyrean towers the Gods command, but below, a lone runner makes his way.

He races against the rising sun with lips parched, limbs numb, and no more sweat to yield. Though tempted to rest, he dares not, for all he holds sacred relies on his swift and tireless feet.

His was the Young Pupil's most beloved story and the Ancient Narrator would tell it once more.

The journey had just begun.

"What the hell difference would it make? He's dead."

"I'd heard them call you the ice woman, but damn—that's cold!" Jack said, frowning at me.

I wasn't cold. I was an attorney, and a damned good one. So was Jack, which was why I was surprised he was second-guessing me.

"By the time I found out, he was already gone. I can't help it if it happened right before the most important case of my career goes to trial. That's all there is to it. I'm not going."

"But..."

"But nothing. I'm not going to make partner at Schroeder, Wilkes & Barron by being sentimental."

"We could request a continuance," he suggested.

"Are you crazy? Momentum is everything and we've got them on the ropes. Didn't they teach you anything at that school? Harvard, was it? I've bust-ed my ass on this case for too long to let some other fifth year associate walk in and fuck it up. So let's you and I get something straight—no continuance, no tears, and no funeral."

The funeral I was so willing to miss was my father's.

It wasn't that I didn't care; it was that it didn't matter. Flying to Florida for his cremation wasn't going to change anything. My father wouldn't know if I was there or not, but my client would. I'm sure Father would have understood—at least I told myself he would. But that masked the more awful truth that I didn't really know how my father felt about many things.

Besides, I had hated Florida since I was nine. I had just celebrated that birthday when my parents joined the migration of North Easterners who went south for the winter, but that year my parents chose not to return with the com-ing of spring. The warm weather and ease of life had bewitched them. For me, the warmth was purgatorial, the ease meant boredom. I eventually escaped back to my natural habitat, moving to New York to attend Columbia University and then Fordham Law School.

My father, Abraham, was a Lithuanian Jew from a small village called *Panamunya*. It doesn't exist on a map any more, having been eradicated during the *pogroms*. My father was the only member of his family to escape—riding north on horseback to pick up the Western terminus of the Trans-Siberian Railroad, which he hid on for its long journey east to Kamchatka. He stowed aboard a ship to Osaka, then another to San Francisco, and finally rode the cross-country rails to New York to find a boyhood friend of his father's who had emigrated years earlier. Considering the times and his background, Abraham did very well for himself, working for and then eventually purchasing his own wholesale candy business.

We lived comfortably but never extravagantly. We had a Chrysler station wagon and took family vacations in the Catskills or Atlantic City. Never owing anyone money and always having plenty of food on the table were his obsessions and the fastest way to solicit a lecture was to scrape half a plate of food into the garbage.

My mother, Christine, was a mongrel of Irish, Scots, German and Polish—hers was a mix that spelled poverty. She was Catholic, so we observed the rituals of two religions in the home. We lit the menorah for Chanukah, and then attended a midnight Christmas mass a week later. I don't recall eating meat on Fridays and there was no bread in the house during the eight days of Pesach.

Christine passed away in her early sixties. She was never one to own up to illness, so no one was surprised that she paid no heed to the fatigue, the shortness of breath or unusual cramps. By the time she was diagnosed with ovarian cancer, it had spread throughout her body and she was beyond any hope of treatment.

When my father became a widower, the idea of his moving north to live with me was never discussed. I didn't think that he would have wanted to anyway, but I never bothered asking him. He lived out the remainder of his life alone, into his late seventies, before succumbing to a fatal stroke. So now, I have no family except for a few distant aunts and uncles who I never see.

My best friend and college roommate moved to Seattle when her husband was recruited by Boeing. We'll always be great friends, but the distance combined with her marriage and two children have altered the intensity and frequency of our contact. Unlike her, I'm divorced, though I prefer to check the box marked "Single" under marital status. I got the house in Old Westbury, where I live alone. I've thought about moving back into Manhattan, but once you get used to lots of rooms and a back yard, cookie-cutter New York apartments look less appealing. Besides, I'm in the heart of the city most of my waking hours, and have a few girlfriends who are usually up for a spontaneous movie, cocktails or an excursion to Barneys.

Jack left me alone to finish my conversation with the funeral director of the Glades Memorial Home. "Yes, the best urn. I don't care about the price," I insisted. "Great. Let me give you my credit card number... No, I can't pick it up… Just ship it." I hung up the receiver.

Ordering my own father's funeral, I felt for a moment as though I were making a dinner reservation. You expect me to be independent and tough? Well, here I am, the smartest, toughest, bitch in the room, fellas! I can blow off my father's funeral! Like that! Like that!

I opened my handbag and pulled out a mirror. After wiping the little bit of mascara that had run from eyes, I threw the mirror back into my purse and clasped the handbag shut. Then I grabbed the folder I needed from my briefcase, straightened my skirt, and headed out the door and down the hallway to the battle awaiting me in Conference Room A.

By 5:30 it was over. I had done what my clients paid me a lot of money to do; I went at their adversary with a legal scalpel as a surgeon might attack a diseased organ. Afterwards, my colleagues and I met across the street at the bar in Smith & Wollensky's.

"Well, you did it again," came the congratulations from Jack. Victory meant more money for the client, and more for us.

"To the woman of ice!" another colleague said, as all raised their glasses. As I drew the glass of wine nearer to my lips, I noticed my hand tremor slightly. I excused myself to the temporary sanctuary of the ladies room where I stared at myself in the mirror and tried to steady my nerves. It hurt when they called me that, but I could never let them know it.

I looked at my watch. The service at Glades, brief as it was, was certainly over. The finality of my father's once animated body now turned to ashes hit me like a white-hot dagger. I knew I loved him, but I had left so much unsaid over the past few years that I had shut my feelings out. My solution was to sink myself deeper into my work, the thing that gave me a sense of instant gratification and the illusion that I controlled it. Winning, after all, was respected… more importantly, it's what got you promoted. The more successful I became, the more it anesthetized any remorse and the discomfiture of conscience.

When I returned to the bar, fortunately the topic of conversation had turned to the election the week earlier. It was November, 1989 and David Dinkins had just become New York City's first African American mayor.

A month after my father's cremation, I had to fly to Miami on SWB business. Afterwards, I went to the Roney Plaza on Collins Avenue where he had lived with my mother in a one-bedroom apartment on the sixteenth floor. I opened the door and was struck with the smell of age—musty and stagnant. It was as if time had stopped somewhere in the 1970's—pink and brown tile in the bathrooms, linoleum kitchen floor, thick shag carpeting that only served as a receptacle for dust and the stains of an old man living alone with no woman to notice them. Some decorative plates that my mother had collected were hanging on the wall, and my father's intricately made ceramic beer steins were still filled with Indian Head pennies and Buffalo nickels.

The only thing the apartment had to recommend itself was a decent view of the ocean. I sat on the small balcony for a few minutes to escape the stale air. Even when Dad was alive, I never liked visiting. Now, the thought that life would end in a one-bedroom box haunted me.

My father was a decent provider. He worked hard and never drank, swore or raised his voice. He just wasn't very communicative in ways I needed as a young girl. To say he kept his emotions to himself would have been a humorous understatement had it not been the source of so many unresolved conflicts in our relationship. In his defense, some of that was due to his limited mastery of the English language. Even though he lived in the United States for nearly half a century, he still spoke with a heavy Russian accent; something that I assumed made him particularly self-conscious—though the Canasta and Gin Rummy tables of the Roney Plaza were a sanctuary for dialects from the old country.

Mom was a more sensitive creature, talking more about feelings, even when it was clear that her life experiences were very different than mine. In many ways, she was the glue that held me and Dad together. It was as if she was his emotional translator, telling Dad and I was proud of me though I longed, just once, to hear it from his own lips. When she died, the glue dissolved.

A sense of missing him was tinged with memories of what had been left unsaid. I didn't want to think of that time when he and I sat in Joyce Kantrowitz's office. She was a counselor at Jewish Family Services in Fort Lauderdale. I was sixteen, and my parents were worried about what I was doing when I came home late at night with no alibi except that I was *nowhere* and had been doing *nothing* while hanging out with *no one*. I remember when Dr.

Kantrowitz asked my father if he loved me. He managed an almost imperceptible nod, all the while looking down at his hands that lay folded in his lap.

"Then tell her."

Silence.

"Abraham, tell her… Tell her you love her," she prodded him.

He couldn't.

Afterwards, she talked to me alone, assuring me that the problem was his, not mine—and that he loved me very much.

"He's lived a tough life," and "it's hard for him to confront his feelings," and more stuff like that. She seemed sincere and had a lot of impressive degrees on her wall—I really wanted to believe her.

As I sat in his Miami Beach apartment packing his few belongings into cardboard boxes, it no longer seemed to matter whether she had been right. This was what was left of my father and yet nothing in his home held meaning for me. I would have thrown it all away, but I wasn't ready to admit that a life could amount to so little.

I'd get to it eventually.

2
ILLIUM'S DISTANT SHORES

The sky's sapphire canvas was interrupted by traces of cirrus clouds whose whirling white plumes faded over the horizon. Hours earlier, before the lone runner had left Marathon, a special offering was made to Athena.

Neotolemus, whose name meant "Son of Achilles," silently ladled a helping from his own meager portion into Pheidippides' bowl. One by one, each of his comrades did the same. Pheidippides knew they would feel the sting of hunger today, so he ate heartily to honor their sacrifice for him and for Athens.

Eventually I did get to it, but not before my father's boxes had gathered dust in my attic for almost two years.

The year was 1991. Another Gandhi was assassinated in India, Kuwait was liberated in operation Desert Storm, the Soviet Union was dissolved and most importantly, I had made partner at Schroeder, Wilkes & Barron. Maybe I should have gone to his funeral, I don't know. I do know that we won that case and I was the only associate in my year to be offered that coveted position.

One Saturday afternoon in late September, I was in my attic putting away some summer clothes. I rarely ventured beyond the area I could reach from the top of the pull-down stairs. But my load that day was so great that I had to make more than one trip and I was forced to push my boxes deeper into its recesses. I noticed the dust and cobwebs covering a box in the far corner, the one filled with my father's memories and keepsakes. I was overwhelmed with guilt and moved to take a closer look. Suddenly, I felt a searing pain as my ankle struck an upturned two-by-four. The pain was made worse by a small ankle chain that had been pressed into my flesh by the blunt side of the wood. I sat and removed the anklet to massage the spot that I knew would be bruised.

I looked at the chain in my open hand. It had been given to me by my mother when I was a little girl. I rarely took it off and even less often thought about it. It wasn't a beautiful piece of jewelry—not made of gold or silver—but it was one of the only tangible connections I had to my departed parents. These thoughts drew me deeper into the attic and toward that dusty box in the corner. It left a clean rectangle on the plywood as I lifted it.

Back in the light of my kitchen, I carefully opened its overlapping cover. The first thing I pulled out was an old book that my father had cherished. It was a leather bound edition of *Mutiny on the Bounty*. He loved stories about the sea, which was odd since he never sailed or swam. The closest he came to water was a chaise lounge by the Roney Plaza pool.

I was placing the book aside when I spotted a gap in its pages. Hidden there was an envelope addressed to my parents. Inside was a card, the cover depicted a sculpture of a woman cradling her child. It read, "To my dear friends, Abraham and Christine, I hope you enjoyed the exhibit. Remember, *where there is love of man, there is also love of the art*. I am enclosing a small gift for

Marianna. I know that in years to come, she will be very glad to have it. Your eternal friend, Ion Theodore."

There was also a black and white photograph. Along its border was written the date, April 28th, 1957. There were my parents standing in front of an ivy-covered building holding hands. It was the first time in years I had thought of "Uncle" Ion—I called him that even though we weren't related by blood. He used to take a subway and a bus out to our apartment in Brooklyn from somewhere in the Bronx. In so many ways, he was the antithesis of my father. Where Abraham seemed reserved, almost shy, Ion had a story about everything. I recalled sitting on the ground before him, listening for hours to his myths and stories. Abraham always viewed things in terms of how practical they were, as if there was only one criteria for any decision—did it help put food on the table or didn't it? Ion, on the other hand, seemed to judge something more worthy the more fantastic the creation—thoughts that clearly weren't going to put food on anyone's table. He would encourage me to create worlds of fantasy, and worse, to share them.

"My dear, fill a canvas for me with your dreams and be ashamed only for not making use of the full array of your palette," he would say in a melodic voice.

The flood of memories continued, at first causing a swelling in my throat. Before I knew it, I was weeping at my kitchen table. It seemed ridiculous, but suddenly I wanted to find him—hoping I might recapture some of the life that I had lost now that both my parents were dead. This was my nostalgia for family, something I had allowed to dissipate, returning with a vengeance.

I could tell Ion about all the visits I never made to Florida, especially the last one, and if nothing else, he would accept my confession of how badly I had let my relationship with my father slip away. He had to; he was the closest thing to family I had left.

There was no return address and the envelope's postmark was too blurry to read. I spent the better part of that afternoon trying to find a telephone number for him, but there was no listing in any of the five boroughs. My frustration grew as I expanded my search to Long Island, New Jersey and Westchester County—all to no avail. I tried to recall personal information, any details that might narrow my search, but what little I had known about him was lost in the decades that had passed since I had last seen him.

My desire to find him was becoming a crusade. In my profession, losing was not an option, but right now I had a feeling of helplessness.

Weeks passed and I resigned myself to the fact that Ion Theodore was going to remain only a curious memory. The invitation to a friend's art exhibit inadvertently pointed me to my next step. Reminded of the card that Ion had sent my parents exhibiting his sculpture, I raced upstairs to find the photo that had come with it.

I couldn't believe I had missed it before. In the shot, my parents were standing in front of an arched doorway. Above and behind Abraham and Christine, carved in the granite wall, were the words:

Tillinghast Hall
Horace Mann School for Boys

The more likely a problem can only be solved during business hours, the higher the odds that you will learn of its existence at 5:01 P.M. on Friday evening. The Horace Mann switchboard wouldn't open until Monday morning so there was nothing I could do until then. Maybe Ion wasn't worth all that anticipation, but I was winning out over the unknown and enjoying defying the odds by finding something that had appeared lost.

I awoke before my alarm clock that Monday. My office is at One Battery Park Plaza; a couple of blocks south of the Whitehall Street Station exit. Not far, but anyone who has ever walked around the Battery on a brisk January day has a good idea of how Ernest Shackleton felt in Antarctica. Winds cooled by frigid Atlantic waters funnel through the Verrazano Narrows and rip through the labyrinth of downtown skyscrapers desperate to escape. I watched as steam from subway vents shot into the icy air above. By the time I reached my building, my face was stinging. Before ducking inside, I braved the elements for one final ritual—a hot cup of coffee from a street vendor.

It was 7:45 A.M.

With hundreds of attorneys in New York, and hundreds more in seven major cities, Schroeder, Wilkes & Barron is one of the country's premiere law firms. Hopeful law school graduates from Harvard to Stanford vie to be one of SWB's new hires, rewarded with ninety-hour workweeks and the carrot of a partnership. After seven years of grueling work, one out of ten is invited to a life of power and prestige.

As the elevator raced upwards and I felt the effects of its speed in my stomach, I thought of my own ascension at Schroeder, Wilkes & Barron and how it had come at the expense of any personal life. Sadder was the fact that I had bought into this tolerable inferno—seduced by the perks and benefits of the *kill or be killed* culture of corporate law. I had gone to law school because I thought I cared for justice—justice for those who were oppressed. Justice was not what we practiced at SWB. The poor and oppressed passed thirty stories below, and that's as close as they would ever get.

The doors opened to a huge marbled reception area lined with expensive hardwood paneling and plush-carpeted floors. No expense was spared in this display of corporate power. My office was cluttered from wall to wall with files and loose papers. In the corner opposite my desk was a small round table; it too was used as a receptacle for paperwork. Over the mocha-colored fabric on my walls hung red-framed degrees. The décor was decidedly masculine—I had no say over it—everything, from plants to prints, had to be approved by our in-house decorating department. My windows faced east, which afforded me a spectacular view of the Brooklyn Bridge. In the morning, the sun's glare is invasive; I closed my blinds to shut out the world.

"You have reached the Horace Mann School located at 231 West 246th Street. Our switchboard is open from 8:30 A.M. until 4:30 P.M. Monday through Friday. If you wish to leave a message..." I hung up the receiver.

It amazed me how disappointed I was by this thirty-minute setback when I have spent so many hours, even weeks, getting the runaround in truly important cases. At half-past eight, I tried again. This time, I got through. Unfortunately, the switchboard operator's news was not as sweet as her voice. She informed me that Ion had retired several years earlier, and had left his residence on the campus. She had no further information about him. However, my persistence got me transferred to a Mr. Alexander, the Head of the Upper School. Mr. Alexander sounded genuinely concerned.

"I'll try to get a last known address for you from personnel," he said as I gave him my number. I didn't have to wait long for his call.

"That's the Queens Community Elder Care Facility," he said, as I scribbled it on my blotter. "But I don't know whether he's still there."

"I understand. You've been more than helpful."

I thought our conversation had concluded when he added, "Do you know how long I've known Mr. Theodore?" He continued without waiting for my answer. "When I met him, I wasn't the Head of the Upper School—I was a seventh grader in his Studio Arts class. Even though I was all thumbs, he made me believe in myself." I was touched that he still called Ion "Mr. Theodore" as though he were back in Seventh grade still in awe of his teacher. "If you find him, please tell him that *Danny* Alexander sends his regards. Oh, and I almost forgot, let him know that our Varsity team won the Track and Field championships this fall."

Finally, I felt like I had some real hope of us being reunited.

"Remember, our visiting hours are only from eleven to six on Sundays," said Charlene of Patient Records.

"Thanks for your help. You've made my day," I said, cradling the receiver. As I looked down, I could see my right hand shaking.

It was probably inconsiderate of me to visit Ion without warning but I was determined to see him no matter what. Questions raced through my mind on a current of nerves. Was my memory just an exaggerated childhood fantasy? How much had he changed? Then I realized that it was not a changed Ion that frightened me. All at once, I understood that seeing him would shine a revealing light on my passage from youth into middle age. I was no longer the young, innocent girl who had sat at his feet asking questions, never tiring of his answers.

Would he recognize me now? At five foot seven, I had a runner's lean figure and I kept my sandy brown hair up at the office and in court. But, even pushing forty, I was the kind of woman who still attracted the attention of men. Would he be able to see that girl in me now, after all my work burying her?

From the outside, the Queens Community Elder Care Facility looks like most other commercial structures that dot the Queens landscape. It is made of white brick—the material of choice during the building boom of the 1950's and '60's. With heavy iron bars on the windows at street level and thick mesh grates over those on the floors above, I wasn't sure if they were meant to keep intruders out, or the patients in.

The interior was no more welcoming. Everything was decorated in varying shades of institutional gray. Adorning the painted cinder block walls were tacky paintings that looked as though they were procured at a flea market, and the floors were linoleum—much easier to clean in the event of an 'accident' during a walk.

The main receptionist sat behind sliding glass windows. She looked up at me, the telephone receiver appearing glued to her jaw. "May I help you?" came in a pleasant but firm tone.

"I'm here to visit Mr. Ion Theodore."

"And your name?" After I answered, she pulled out a file and I realized that she was checking my name against a master list of proscribed visitors.

"I doubt I'm on that..."

"Actually," she interrupted me with a slight tone of surprise and sympathy, "no one is."

"He doesn't wish to see…"

"No. No. He has no regulars, he expects no one."

My relief in learning that he didn't refuse visitors was overcome by the news that he had none to refuse. No family? And what of the hundreds of students and dozens of colleagues from Horace Mann? Perhaps they could not bear to witness their once vigorous mentor in this state.

"Is it all right if I see him? I'm his attorney," I said with all the presumption I could muster.

"I'll call the nurse's station." She picked up the phone again. "Trish, there's a visitor for Theodore. Says she's his lawyer." She paused. "Okay, you can go up, but please see that he puts your name on the list for next time."

"I will."

"Take the elevator to the second floor, turn right, and it's about half way down the hall on your left—Room 231."

The smell of disinfectant filled the hall, barely disguising the acrid odors it was intended to mask. As I side-stepped several residents who shuffled down the hall, I was unnerved by a vague and troubling sense of recognition—here were the poor and oppressed, lonely and abandoned. But was it recognition, or a premonition of what lay at the end of life's rainbow? I feared it was one reason I had distanced myself from my father. When I had watched him and his cronies in Miami Beach, I had trouble seeing beyond the decaying flesh and incontinence of age.

The plate marked "231" lay before me. The door was open, like all the others—privacy taking a back seat to the convenience of the monitoring staff. I reached up to knock on the frame, but stopped as my eye caught the figure of a man lying face up on a single bed; his eyes were either slightly open or unable to close fully.

Opened and twisted, his mouth appeared frozen in mid-groan. His head was bald, wrinkled and pale. Hollowed eyes had sunk deep in their sockets, and the angles of his jawbone protruded from skin that clung to him like cellophane. Was becoming unrecognizable the last metamorphosis of man before dying? I strained to find something I remembered of Ion in these features, but there was nothing. I hovered at the doorway, too ashamed to withdraw and too frightened to advance.

As I stepped closer a flash of white caught my eye. On the other side of the room was another bed, and next to it a burgundy vinyl chair. In it, facing away from me, sat a man with long flowing white locks. I could not see his face, but I knew instantly that he was the man I sought.

Rows of books filled the case that sat across from this second bed. I perused their spines. Rubbing dust jackets were Homer, Milton, Virgil, Plato, Tolstoy, Shakespeare and Cellini. A portable Victrola sat on top with its lid open. A stack of records, some of them with the thick cardboard sleeves, were pressed against the wall behind the phonograph. Next to the old record player was a mahogany sculpture of a woman cradling a child into her bosom; it was the sculpture on the card he had sent my parents. I also noticed a scarred case that appeared to house a musical instrument.

Any notion of a "Kodak moment" was quickly dispelled. The man sat, almost catatonically, staring out the window. It was a literal tragedy that so expansive a life had been made to resign itself to sharing a fourteen by eighteen foot room. There were two small windows, but it was a depressing view, made all the worse by the wire mesh and the gray drizzle that blanketed the cityscape beyond. Eyes that had seen so much of the world now looked upon an urban collage of AC condensers, rusting water tanks and cluttered antennae rising from dilapidated rooftops. I found myself frightened again and diverted my attention to the rest of his things.

A few black and white photographs hung on the wall next to Ion's bed. I was drawn to one in particular. A barefoot young man, whose chiseled countenance was framed by jet black curls, was running at an angle past a camera that had captured him in mid-stride. It was a young Ion—swift-footed and triumphant. His almond-shaped eyes were fixed with confidence, though neither strain nor effort appeared in his face. The muscles of his thighs and shoulders glided in perfect unison to propel his body through the air—a poetic paradox of fluidity frozen in time. Elevated in his right hand was a torch, its flame slightly blurred. I glanced at Ion, still staring out the window, and shuddered at the beauty that he had commanded.

Ion's bed was covered by starched white sheets and navy blue blankets—

hospital standard issue. Next to it was a nightstand on which sat an empty bottle of *ouzo* with a half-melted candle wedged in its mouth. There was a wind-up clock whose time was incorrect, even the minutes were off. Ion had obviously kept up the ritual of winding it—though without regard for its actual time. It struck me that Ion was now content to dwell in the amorphous whirl of unstructured time, waiting for his sands to run out. His absence of schedule starkly contrasted with mine. From my 6:00 alarm, to my 7:42 train, to my 9:15 second cup of coffee, to my entire day broken into fifteen minute segments of meetings and phone calls, until the forty-five minutes with my personal trainer on Tuesdays and Thursdays, the 6:54 train home, the ten o'clock news—my life was demarcated by a rigid grid of time.

Under Ion's bed, I could see an old suitcase. It may have given him the vain hope that this was but a temporary habitat, and that one day he might pack and leave.

"Uncle Ion?"

"Uncle Ion," I repeated. Still, no response. I was becoming nervous. He would not look up at me, continuing to stare blankly out the window. Outside, a torrent of freezing rain and buffeting wind hurled sheets of water against the windows, rattling them in their sashes. I began to wonder if I should have come at all. For an instant, he turned his head as if to see where my voice was coming from, but then retreated into his vacant reverie.

A book on Ion's shelf caught my attention. It was an old edition of *The Odyssey*. Bound in leather, it had turned a faded light brown. The title on the cover and spine were embossed in gold leaf, but most of it had rubbed off. Its binding was unusually supple from having been opened hundreds of times. The pages had frayed and yellowed, and most were so brittle that I had to turn them carefully so as not to tear them. There was a handwritten inscription on the first page.

> *My fellow marathoner,*
> *As you carry our Olympic torch, do not forget the valiant ancestors who have preceded you—and the heroes yet to come, to whom you will pass the eternal flame. Your teacher and friend…*
>
> *Spyridon L. 1st August 1936*

Suddenly, the meaning of the photo on the wall registered. Ion Theodore had carried the Olympic Torch at the Berlin Games of 1936.

Ion was still looking out the window as I sat on the edge of his bed. I opened the book to where he had last left a bookmark. The passage was the reunion between Penelope and Odysseus after their twenty-year separation. I studied the elegant lines and then began to read the scene aloud for my own gratification.

"Then Odysseus in his turn melted, and wept as he clasped his dear and faithful wife to his bosom. As the sight of land is welcome to men who are swimming towards the shore, when Poseidon has wrecked their ship with the fury of his winds and waves—a few alone reach the land, and these, covered with brine, are thankful when they find themselves on firm ground and out of danger—even so was her husband welcome to her as she looked upon him, and she could not tear her two fair arms from about his neck."

I stopped and was startled to hear the passage continue through another voice.

"Indeed they would have gone on indulging their sorrow till rosy-fingered morn appeared, had not Athena determined otherwise..."

At first I thought my memory and imagination had conjured Ion's voice, but there he sat, a wide, inviting smile spread across his face. I watched in astonishment as the simulacrum of a man suddenly bloomed with life. A solitary tear paused at the crest of his cheekbone before rolling down his left cheek.

Swift-footed Ion Theodore had returned from Illium's distant shores.

3 FROM COLDEST CAVERNS

"Pheidippides, come here," Callimachus gestured with his arm, "Look." The evening before, Callimachus, chief Archon of the ten generals who led the Athenian army, and General Militiades were studying a parchment that had been unrolled on a table.

"We stand here," he continued, pointing to a small peninsula on the map of Hellas, "alone...to stop the barbarian horde at the gateway to Greece. Everything we cherish will be crushed under the dust of these plains if we fail."

"His emissaries have already offered us their terms of surrender," said Militiades, whose ancestors had long defied tyrants. "Enslavement in return for our lives. The Eretrians have fallen. Their city lies in ruins, its temples desecrated—all because they joined the Ionians in a just revolt. Have we struggled across the centuries to become free men so that we may beg for a merciful bondage? Let the line be drawn here! At Marathonas!"

We sat together for almost an hour on that first visit. Though many words were spoken, my most vivid recollection was the look in his eyes as he watched me. He had the ease and warmth of someone who had last seen me only the day before, and the confidence that he would see me again the next.

"How was the funeral?" he asked. He spoke about Abraham as though he had just passed.

"Oh...you know, it was...sad." The thought of telling him the truth had sounded better in the abstract. Now, I didn't have faith that he would understand why I could not have been there.

"Thank God he had you," he said, then looked down into his hands for a few moments.

"Yes." Boy, how I wanted to change the subject.

"My dear, are you happy?"

"Of course I am." I wondered what made him ask.

"A teacher laid out ten bags of coins before his pupils. He told them that all but one contained counterfeit coins. The difference was imperceptible to the eye; however, each counterfeit coin weighed an ounce, the real ones, being of higher quality, weighed double. He then gave them a scale that yielded a precise weight and challenged them to make one, and only one, measurement. How could they tell which bag contained the real coins?"

"Can I take coins out of the bags?"

"As you wish."

"How many coins are in each bag?"

"As many as you like."

"I suppose you can't hold up the bags until you find one that seems heavier..."

"No. That's a form of measuring. The answer lies elsewhere," Ion was smiling. I wasn't sure if he had given me this question to prolong my visit, but my contemplation ended as my pager rang out from the inner pocket of my suit jacket. Its display told me it was a difficult-to-reach client. Ion understood that our time was drawing to a close.

"It was so wonderful to see you, Uncle Ion. You'll have to save the answer for next time."

"I can't believe how thoughtful you were to come find me. It is easy to be forgotten," he said with all the grace of a man who knew that he had been.

I felt an odd combination of energy and exhaustion. When I intimated that I might visit again, it didn't occur to me that it might hurt him more to see me once than never at all. Whereas I may have been content spending a few hours at the crossroads of our memories, his expression as I left revealed the enormity of his feelings. Ion's prediction of being forgotten was almost a self-fulfilling prophecy.

Almost a month would pass before I found myself once again sitting in Room 231. Ion said nothing about the gap between my visits.

He slowly moved towards the bed, retrieved something from under his pillow and then sat down next to me.

"Would you be my valentine this year," he asked as he handed me a pedestrian but cute Valentine's Day card.

"I'd be honored, Uncle Ion," I said, as a wonderful smile took over his face. "I'm sorry I didn't have a chance to get you a card."

"I didn't expect one, and you deserve a much more vibrant Valentine."

"Nonsense. Men my age are usually carrying way too much baggage."

"Perhaps I am just too old to carry it," he teased.

"I'll bet you're the most eligible bachelor here."

His laugh startled me. Not because it was an inappropriate response, but because it was so loud and genuine. "I am flattered you say so, but I have all too often chased the icon and forsaken love."

Ion reached out and took my hand. I felt his warmth as he curled my fingers around his. For a moment, I was again a young girl and Ion was in our backyard spinning tales of jealous Gods and eternal love.

"Why did you and my parents lose touch for so long?"

"It's a long story." He paused as if preparing to reveal a longer explanation and then exhaled slowly. "I was going through some difficult things back then. It was best that I kept to myself."

I asked him about the photographs on his wall. Most were fellow teachers or students at Horace Mann and he shared anecdotes about each as he went along. Most invariably ended with Ion saying—"I've lost touch with him."

But I noticed that Ion made no mention of one particular photo. It was in color, but its pigments had faded into muted orange and brown. It was taken at a beach, and in the shallows were two fishing boats. Ion, appearing to be in his early forties, was in the midst of several others. They were sitting near the dunes around a pit that had recently contained a fire. Lying in the sand nearest to Ion was a dark-skinned woman in a bathing suit.

Ion looked at it for a moment and then turned away as he noticed me watching him.

"What is her name?"

"Alexandra."

"Who was she?" I said, surprising myself with my directness.

"In another world…she was my muse," he uttered, blushing a little before looking away from me.

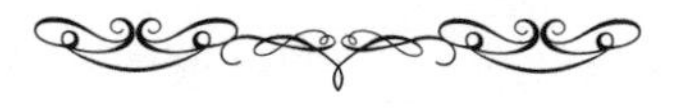

I propped Ion's card on my mantel and sat on my couch. I was sad, and I knew why. It was because of a Valentine's Day exactly thirty years earlier.

I had worked every job a nine year old could so that I could buy the mosaic. Hundreds of pieces of differently shaded red tiles had been arranged in the shape of a heart, set on a white-crackled tile background. I had seen it one afternoon at an arts and crafts store. It cost forty-two dollars plus tax, which was an ungodly sum of money for me then. But I managed to scrimp together two-thirds of it by running errands, pet-sitting and selling lemonade. I even secretly made my own peanut butter sandwiches each morning so I could contribute my lunch money to the kitty. Mom made up the difference when we purchased it the afternoon before the fourteenth. That night, she helped me wrap it and showed me how to tie the ribbons so that they'd twirl like spiraling confetti.

While the other girls in Ms. Straughan's fourth grade class addressed theirs to cute boys in our class, my card said, "to Dad."

At the appointed hour, after the dinner dishes were dried and put away, my mother said, "Abraham, why don't you sit down in the living room and I'll make you a cup of tea." That was my signal to retrieve the package from under my bed.

I watched with eagerness as he unwrapped the gift. He stared at it for a moment, and then said, "It's broken."

"It's made that way," my mother answered. "It's a *mosaic*."

He shook his head from side to side and laughed. "A mosaic, huh? Only a genius at retail could figure out how to sell broken pottery for a profit."

I ran from the room in tears.

Later that night, my mother came into my room and tried to comfort me.

"He read the card and he'd love to be your Valentine."

"Well I don't want him to be mine."

"How can you say that," she admonished. "He's your father."

"I wish I didn't have a father!" I blurted out. Looking up through my tears, I saw Abrahan turning away as he retreated from my room.

The time I spent with Ion was so different from my daily routine that I found myself visiting him more and more often. I could not manipulate him the way I did others in my professional life, nor did I care to try. When I set the agenda, he led me wherever he wanted to while allowing me the illusion of control. And no matter what I talked about, his eyes held me with fixed interest.

During one visit, I told Ion that I had been married, and that it hadn't worked out. I had purposely kept my story simple so as not to upset him—or me; but he looked so saddened. Still, Peter was not worth the trouble of talking about. He surely hadn't been worth the effort of marrying. He was a kind of human quicksand upon which I tried to build a family. Anyway, he turned out to be a real shit.

"Uncle Ion, I'm fine about it now, really I am." This was one of the few times I felt him become agitated. He stared at me with a kind of scowl, then pronounced his verdict. "This Peter fellow was unworthy, unworthy of you my dear and deserved to be banished from your life." I was glad I had not gone into the whole story.

"It's all right, Ion, I survived. I'm much stronger for it," I said, not sure if I were trying to convince him or myself of its truth.

"You have all of life ahead of you to discover true love."

"True love? No thanks. I'd prefer the Spanish Inquisition..."

"Even Professor Higgins became a believer."

"I don't plan on fetching any man's slippers..."

"What about having children?"

"Too late," I said.

"My dear, the Gods have ways of making even the most far-fetched ideas seem commonplace." I remembered that I was talking to a man. They all work under the assumption that everything is possible, and for them it often is.

"What about you?" I said, both out of curiosity and out of a desire to redirect the conversation. "There must have been great love in your life."

"I was a fool, and like most fools, I have loved strangers and chased them and wasted so much in chasing them."

"The woman in the photo?"

"The love that escaped me."

As I heard these answers, they only raised more questions. But it was obvious to me that Ion had no desire to speak of his past any longer. Though he could go on for hours about life in general, he rarely spoke of his own. I wondered whether this reticence was part of his self-effacing virtue or the result of deep pain.

One visit was different. I had come for what we liked to refer to as 'Sunday Brunch.' For some reason, the cafeteria food at his center was actually worse on the weekends than during the week, so I would sneak in fresh fruit, bread, and cheese and we would snack furtively in the farthest corner of the Recreation Room. With scattered vinyl lounge chairs, flimsy card tables, and a broken ping-pong table, nothing either of creation, nor recreation, could take place here. I heard the strains of classical music from a transistor radio held by a resident who sat off in another corner.

Something I said to Ion that morning opened a small crack in that door.

"Ion, I've never seen any photos of your parents."

"There are none."

"At least you have their images in your memory," I consoled.

"No. I never knew my father, and my mother... I was told she lingered for a few days after a painful labor. I was an orphan to the world." Right away, I understood that Ion was referring to a much greater estrangement than that of not knowing his parents. I sat almost speechless for the remainder of that afternoon as he shared with me the circumstances under which he came into the world.

Ion Theodore had been born a slave.

"I have no idea of my birth date," he began. "Not even the year. One day, my master decided I was twelve, so I was twelve. For the sake of celebrating a 'birthday,' I chose the day I first felt the freedom that most children breathe with their first gasps of air.

"I am from Limnos," he continued as I settled into the chair. "She is a sleepy island resting in the sea-lanes leading out of the Dardanelle Straits. Her volcanoes lie dormant; however, her wild red flowers and peaceful groves of Aleppo pines belie a volatile and violent history.

"I consider myself Limnian *and* Greek, for Limnos was once independent. Twenty-five hundred years ago, the Limnians kidnapped and raped a group of

Athenian women. They then killed the women and their offspring. The Gods punished them by making their women and livestock barren. The Oracle at Delphi gave them a chance to lift the curse. They agreed to concede independence to the Athenians if the latter ever sailed to Limnos in a single day. In 490 B.C. the Athenians conquered Mount Athos."

"A one day's sail from Limnos," I said.

"Yes, and we have been Greek ever since. At an early age, I was taken from Limnos to Turkey. I lived in Hamdibey, a village in the mountainous northwest. I have few earlier memories, but I recall feeling sad to leave Limnos."

"How did you learn Greek?"

"It was an old slave to whom I am indebted. He secretly taught me to read and write in the tongue of Homer. He was my first teacher. I learned much from him: how to run through rocks without injury, how to find water in the desert and how to wrestle. He showed me how an old man or a small boy could defeat a physically superior foe, using cunning instead of force.

"I saw him as a hero. So many nights I prayed for him to reveal himself—like Odysseus—and slay my cruel masters with the mighty bow that only he could string. He would not live to see my emancipation."

"I'm sorry, Uncle Ion."

"For what, my dear?"

"You were dealt a tough hand—not quite the ideal childhood..."

"My dear, *Time* is a delicately woven silk. At any given instant, each of us travels across it on a single strand. But when the Gods breathe softly on it, the subtle ripples cause one to traverse a different strand. Since none but the Gods see the whole fabric, none can know where the strands will lead—or with whom they may intersect. In another time and place, Paris may not have chosen Aphrodite and the Towers of Illium would still be standing."

It was amazing how he could dismiss such hardship by just broadening his perspective. That was part of why I felt safe with Ion. He was always showing me something where I saw nothing. We were two souls, adrift, each of us looking for any remnant of family and finding each other. But as I returned to my house after each such visit, its comforts made me increasingly troubled about Ion's half of a room in Queens.

Our strands of silk were about to interweave.

I visited Ion on my birthday. It was my fortieth and I swear I will maim the next person who congratulates me or even mentions the word *milestone*. We dined, as usual, in the facility's cafeteria. Somehow, Ion had arranged a candle to be placed in a brownie. It was stale, but I savored it.

I escorted him back to his room and was about to leave when he said, "Wait, I have something for you."

"For me?"

"Your birthday present."

"A present? You shouldn't have gone to the trouble."

"It was no trouble. But I must warn you that it's not new. I just didn't have a chance to make it to Bloomingdale's today," he joked. With that said, he reached under his pillow and handed me a parcel wrapped in pages of the New York Post. "Josie, the day nurse, helped me."

I slowly tore off the paper. I sensed it was a book from its size and weight, but I was stunned when I uncovered his copy of *The Odyssey*.

"I can't accept this, it's, it's too precious," I said.

"It has served me well and now it is time for me to pass it on."

"I don't know what to say. How can you part with this?"

"What is engrained in my mind can never be taken from me. I have traded a small pile of leather and paper for the joy that you may also know its beauty."

"But it must be worth a lot. It's obviously a rare edition."

"I had a rarer one once."

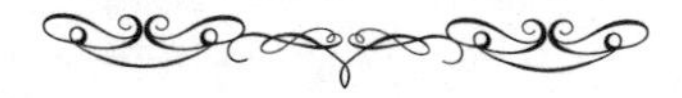

When I had first encountered the patients at the Queens Home, I had looked at them with detachment. It was how I looked at everyone. Still, I probably dismissed them out of hand, as most of us do, out of fear that I might end up trapped in a similar situation. Until I started visiting Ion, I had never considered that ending up in such a place could make the elderly so desperate. But in truth, we use our unprecedented affluence to delegate the care of our loved ones to strangers. Sequestered in sanitized homes, our job is done—with the help of a billion dollar industry devoted to relieving us of responsibility. It reads like a Madison Avenue ad for a cleanser—*no mess, no stain, no smell.*

I was glad to get home. Often, the solitude of evening made me feel lonely, but tonight I did not feel alone. Savoring the peace and quiet, I went around the house and turned off all the downstairs lights before retiring to my bedroom on the second floor. I slipped into bed and pulled my down comforter up to my neck. The sounds of the wind and sleet pounding against my windows made me imagine I was colder than I really was. In a few minutes, the heat from my body had made the bed nice and warm.

Opening Ion's gift to a random page, I gazed at the beautiful text. I imagined the contrast between my temporary sense of comfort and the cold uncertainty that Odysseus must have felt wandering the tumultuous seas. I was about to place it on my nightstand and turn off my lamp when I decided to look again at the inscription. There, below it, were two newly added paragraphs written in blue ink. Unmistakably painted with Ion's aging hand, though its imperfect lines revealed his subtle elegance.

Once, long ago, my soul was young and full of vigor
Now grown old and withered, resign'd to eternal hibernation
All hope lost of finding She with the spark that might trigger
That ray of womanly light—Athena's life-giving sensation.

My heart 'twas lock'd away for so long in coldest cavern,
Then, from Night's darkest slumber—She reach'd out,
Anointing my sleeping soul—and warmth didst return
Awakening to flourish, Love's seed anew didst sprout.

One night, a few weeks after my birthday, I had to return to Ion's nursing home to retrieve a file I had forgotten during my last visit. I needed it for a trial the next morning. The woman usually at the front desk had been replaced by her nighttime counterpart—a security guard who was less than eager to see me. He informed me that it was after visiting hours and that an orderly would have to get my file for me; but after fifteen minutes of waiting, the orderly hadn't shown up and my patience had worn out. I would have asked the guard to call again, but he had been on the phone since I arrived and, avoiding my gaze, didn't look like he'd be finished anytime soon. I doubt he even noticed when I walked past his desk and through the swinging doors that led to the residents.

What I saw when I got to Ion's room horrified me. Ion's roommate, Mr. Bruckheimer, was tied down to his bed; his mouth twisted open in pain. Nothing but a low rasp emitted from his lips. Ion was huddled on his bed in a fetal position. He didn't turn to see me when I entered the room, but curled up even tighter, pulling the thin blanket over his eyes. He cringed and gasped when I put my hand on his shoulder.

"Uncle Ion, it's me. What's going on here?"

It took him a few moments to regain his composure and tell me what was happening.

"He, he wouldn't take it."

"Wouldn't take what? Medication?"

"He wouldn't take it."

"Why not? He probably needed it..."

"No!" said Ion abruptly, sapping what little energy he seemed to have in him. "No," he repeated, a little softer this time. "He doesn't..."

"Doesn't it help?"

"Them. It helps them, not him."

I spotted a thin bruise on Ion's wrist.

"How did this happen?" He wouldn't tell me, choosing to roll his head to the side away from me. "Has someone been hurting you?"

Ion simply nodded.

"What? Why didn't you tell me?"

"If we complain, it gets worse."

The orderly on rounds appeared at the doorway. Startled at seeing me, he no doubt was about to deliver a sermon about how I wasn't supposed to be there. The look on my face changed his mind—feebly, he announced that visiting hours had ended.

Visiting hours had indeed ended.

So had Ion's residency.

4
BE ASHAMED TO DIE

"Pheidippides," continued Callimachus, "the Persians outnumber us by three to one. They possess cavalry, archers, and a fleet, which allows them mobility. They will surely attack when they learn how precarious our position is. Our only salvation is in the help of the Spartans. That is why you have been summoned."

Pheidippides face paled and his mouth dried as he stared at the map. One hundred fifty miles—each way.

"There will be no shame, nor shall any man question your courage or loyalty should you refuse this task," said Militiades.

The two generals waited respectfully until Pheidippides, a simple barefooted shepherd, was ready to speak.

"This was always my favorite room," I said to Ion, who was walking slowly beside me. "When I was a kid, these guys seemed much bigger. Now, they seem small, like children in metal suits."

Ion laughed at this remark. "I'm sure they looked quite large to stick-wielding peasants." We stood in the Hall of Armor at the Metropolitan Museum of Art. It was Friday, March fifteenth—the *Ides of March*. I vividly remember the date, not only because of Caesar's ominous warning, but because it was the night that Marty Schoenfeld died.

Ion was staying at my house for a few weeks while I tried to get him admitted to a home that offered a higher level of care. I went to law school with the intention of helping people like Ion's roommate, poor Mr. Bruckheimer, yet somehow the needs of the needy had become less important than the needs of the greedy. Ion had been lucky, but I thought about all the other people at the "elderly care" center who did not have anyone to come and rescue them. They would still have reason to be frightened at night, despite the harsh words I had with the staff. Who would speak out for them? The truth was, I could barely make time to help *one* person. The decision to take Ion out of there had been easily made in an instant, but I had no idea what I had gotten myself into. He needed three meals a day and doctor visits and companionship. I thought having a cat was too complicated. He would be better off in a community that really cared for its elders.

SWB was having a party to celebrate the firm's seventy-fifth anniversary. Since it was being held at the Stanhope Hotel, Ion had suggested that we arrive early and visit the Met. We walked through the Hall of European Paintings, pausing at the works of Tiepolo, Pannini and Rubens. Though I knew that Ion had seen these paintings dozens upon dozens of times, he looked at each as if it were the first time; savoring the ridges and valleys of their delicately crafted oils.

"You are incomprehensibly great," he said to one masterpiece by Pannini. "Look at the way he transforms light and draws your eye to his subject." There was a young art student who had set up her easel in front this magnum opus and was painting its scene onto her own canvas.

"Copying isn't quite art, is it?" I asked.

"All the masters began by copying masters."

"What do you think of Modern Art?" I asked, trying to anticipate what I imagined his sentiments to be.

"To me, anything after the Crusades is modern."

"It seems the first rule they teach today in art class is that there are no rules and that anything different from the way it was must be better."

"Art is governed by laws as inviolable as those of gravity," added Ion. "Just as our ears are soothed by harmony, eyes seek the aesthetic. These principles do not hinder the true artist—they liberate him."

We continued through the maze of rooms until we reached the Dutch Masters Exhibit. While he rested on a bench in the center, I walked the perimeter looking at the magnificent oils adorning the walls. I turned back at him. He sat transfixed, looking only at one painting. I observed Ion as he contemplated Rembrandt's *Aristotle Contemplating a Bust of Homer*. It reminded me of how he could sit in my garden for hours at a time without any obvious entertainment. I had lost my ability to do this, and I was envious of his gift of being able to shut out the world. While others passed by the Rembrandt and admired it for a moment or two, then moved on as if changing channels, Ion could create an entire universe from a single scene.

I wanted very much to see the world through his eyes. My brief time with him had taught me so much. But it had been unsystematic and indirect learning. I knew that he carried within him whole libraries, galleries, museums and concert halls. To learn about art or philosophy from Ion was a great adventure; to learn what they meant to him as a witness to history would be a much longer and harder journey. I was leading him back into life; he was awakening in me a life I never knew I had.

"Great to see you, Marianna," boomed a voice from down the lushly carpeted hallway.

"You too," I replied as an older gentleman, dressed in a classic gray flannel suit approached me. "Chris, I want you to meet my uncle, Ion Theodore."

"A pleasure. You have a brilliant niece, Mr. Theodore. The way she handled that Broadgate case, what a tigress. Keep up the great work," he said.

"Thanks. It didn't hurt that two of the arbiters played golf at the same club as George Wilkes. We were lucky to settle."

"Settle? I call what happened to Custer at Little Big Horn a settlement; what you did to the defendants, I call decimation."

I really didn't want to talk about this situation. My client's questionable actions had been rewarded and it had nothing to do with right or wrong. It was a competition to see whose attorneys could best choreograph the facts. It had all the trappings of a game without the fun. I was good at what I did, but I was never sure that what I did was good.

Ion and I checked our coats on the second floor and entered one of the five reserved banquet suites. Opulent chandeliers hung from intricate coffered ceilings; the mahogany paneled walls were adorned with original oils. There was a line three-deep at a bar that had been set up in one of the rooms, in another a large buffet table had been laid out with an assortment of delicacies. It is an art to be able to stand, eat, drink and converse while at the same time remaining poised and feminine. Armani helps.

I approached the buffet to get Ion a plate of food. As I walked past two associates, I heard one say to the other, "Hey, who's that old cranker over there?"

"I don't know, someone probably got stuck babysitting their grandfather," the other man laughed.

I didn't say anything, but my doubts about bringing Ion tonight returned; though he was also my handy excuse to escape early. I never looked forward to these affairs. They were little more than opportunities for associates to suck up to their bosses—or to get terrifically drunk, speak the truth and prepare their resumes in the morning. At every office party I've ever been to, there's at least one career kamikaze. On my way back to my table, I met Steve Payne, my boss.

"You made it. I thought you may have been under the weather."

"I took the day off to bring my uncle in to the City."

"Oh really, how nice," he said with utter indifference.

"Hey Steve, how are things?" asked a man of Steve's age whom I vaguely recognized.

"Great, Chuck. Oh, excuse me, Charlie Preston, meet Marianna Gardner." I still used Peter's last name. Habit and the fact that all my clients knew me as that made changing back to my maiden name seem more of an inconvenience than it was worth. There was also the fact that *Chaitowitz* was difficult for most to pronounce, let alone spell.

"I think we've crossed passed once or twice, but it's a pleasure to finally meet you," he said as he reached out and we shook hands. Steve had brought

Charlie's firm in as a client—it was what rainmaking partners were expected to do.

"By the way, Global Harvester just got served with a discrimination suit by some former employees in their Chicago office," Steve said to me.

"Did someone cross the line?" Charlie asked.

"Who knows," said Steve. "Sounds like another case of some women who just need a good..."

"Steve, you don't want to say that."

"You've got to lighten up a bit. I was just teasing."

"She has a point, Steve. Be careful or you'll be the next defendant." I'll give Charlie half credit for knowing I had a point, but he didn't get what it was either. Harassment isn't wrong because you can be sued—it's simply wrong.

"It's getting so you can't say anything these days without offending somebody," Steve said by way of defending the foot he had put into his mouth.

"Steve, there's a line between good fun and bad taste," I said.

"Fair enough. Anyway, I want you to handle it personally."

I knew he had asked me because I was a woman. It would be strategically unwise to have one of our male attorneys attacking a woman's credibility in a sex discrimination suit. I was competing in a male dominated game, one in which the rules were not only made by others, but were changed at their whim. If I'm compassionate, I'm the weaker sex. If I'm tough, I'm a bitch. If I'm moody, "it must be that time of the month again." Each day I have to avoid running aground on the jagged reefs of condescension or sexual innuendo. And how many times have I overheard the implication that a woman's achievement was won through seduction—not skill and sweat.

I'm expected to be "one of the guys," yet I am denied the camaraderie that men establish among themselves. I cannot even assume that another woman in the office will be my ally. Though she may share my situation, she wants that promotion as much as I do; one, which we both believe, carries a quota. If I fall, her chance to rise increases.

I excused myself from Charlie and Steve, knowing that there would be a joke made at my expense as soon as I was out of earshot. This is not paranoia—it is reality—I accept it like I accept air pollution. Some days my senses are so dulled that I don't notice, some days I can barely breathe.

As I made the rounds, the same attorneys who had scoffed at "the old cranker" were now asking me if he might write referral letters so that their children could attend Horace Mann. Their hypocrisy knew no boundaries. On the other hand, I wondered if they had any contacts at the Riverdale Home. One good recommendation deserves another.

I was ready to make one more round and exit quietly when I saw Tom walking toward me with a drink in each hand.

"You look like you might want one of these," he said.

"One?" I asked, "Or both?"

Tom was another lawyer at the firm, but not so much the rogue as his peers. He was professional and courteous, which counted for little at SWB. What did matter was that he was fastidious and talented.

"Let's toast," he said as he passed me one of the glasses. His nails were perfectly manicured and he had a nice tan for December. He wore a blue Egyptian woven shirt with white collar and French cuffs, the latter embroidered with his initials in dark navy and held together with lapis cuff links. Tom was always well dressed—elegant, not showy. He was in his mid-forties and exceedingly handsome with silver burnished hair.

"To Skull and Bones and the end of anything sacred," he offered. Earlier that year, Yale's murky secret society—a breeding ground for the good old boy network—had been forced to include women.

"First a few women, next thing they'll be admitting gays and lesbians. It's heresy," I whispered. Tom knew I was kidding, and he particularly got the sarcasm.

"Where is your escort?" he asked, chuckling at my last remark.

"My uncle. He's sitting over there," I said as I pointed towards Ion, resting quietly in a winged-back chair.

"How is he doing? I mean, how are things going at home?" he asked.

"It's not easy," I admitted. "I've actually been taking some of my long accrued vacation time and the powers that be, of course, have noticed. Steve said that he was surprised to see me tonight—thought I was sick." Aside from being a workhorse and a well-dressed man, Tom was my friend.

"They notice everything," Tom said and smiled. I felt a twinge of selfishness as I realized that Tom knew my frustrations far better than I ever would. We worked in a machismo business where gay jokes were passed around as nonchalantly as interoffice memos. Tom lived a whole other life that could not be reconciled with this one. He would never be able to bring his lover to an event like this. These people would be more accepting if he told them he had been a heroin addict. He never complained though; he had a quiet dignity about him. "You work long hours, doesn't he get lonely?" he asked.

"There is a woman down the street, Vivian, who used to be a nurse. She's retired now and lives alone. Ion doesn't mind her checking in and I feel better knowing that she's around in case anything happens while I'm at work."

"So the Riverdale Home is still the plan?"

"Just as soon as they have an opening," I said.

"Let's get going, Uncle Ion."

"Are you sure you don't want to stay longer?"

"Positive," I said with a grin.

As Ion and I made our way towards the elevator, I noticed that a crowd had gathered at the entrance to one of the other suites. There was a commotion that didn't speak of festivity; rather an air of apprehension gripped those who pressed together—eyes turned into the room. I saw Jeff Graham, one of the senior partners, tersely issuing instructions to two of the hotel staff who then scurried quickly through the hidden pantry doors. When the elevator opened, two EMTs bolted out; one was carrying a large silver metallic case and the other wheeled a stretcher.

I directed Ion to an armchair near the elevator and I moved towards Trent Lasky, one of my colleagues.

"Trent, what's happening?"

"It's Marty," he answered with an anxious look on his face.

"Marty? Marty Schoenfeld? What…"

"I don't know. One minute he was sipping a glass of wine, the next minute he's lying on the floor. Pale as a ghost. They called the paramedics right away. Thank God Sinai's just up the street."

There was nothing that I or anyone else from SWB could do but wait.

It was 8:32 P.M.

The party should have been in full swing, but the mood had quickly gone from jovial to grim. People mulled about, their conversations directed to the alarming situation unfolding before them.

"I'm sure he'll be all right, they got here pretty quick," I tried to spin some optimism into the dour mood that had descended on us. Eventually, the paramedics reappeared pushing the gurney that Marty was lying on. His body was covered in a white sheet from head to toe. His wife, Miriam, walked next to the gurney with her hand clutching his limp finger—the mascara around her eyes had turned into dark black circles. The elevator doors tightly shut behind them to the hushed silence of the banquet suites.

I was in complete shock. There had been talk of his being named to the

Management Committee, and even rumors about him being groomed as a possible named partner when Wilkes retired. Marty was one of those guys who absolutely never took vacation days—as a matter of fact, I don't think he even took one sick day. He had so much to live for and he had lost it all in a moment.

"I can see that you were quite shaken tonight," Ion said, breaking the silence as our car crossed the Triborough Bridge. We were in the back seat of a Lincoln sedan.

I managed a nod.

"What bothered you most?" I was taken aback by Ion's question, one he asked coolly and without much affect.

"It scares me to think that Marty could die so young; it seems so unfair."

"Unfair?"

"He couldn't have been much older than fifty. He's got a wife and kids."

"Yes, that is terrible; so swift and seemingly final. More painful to the ones left behind, I suspect. But is that the most awful thing about it?" Ion was looking straight ahead.

I pondered his question for a few minutes. Wasn't it obvious? I thought that any one of my reasons expressed a normal person's concern over seeing a colleague die. Although we were riding in a car, I suddenly felt as if we were walking and that only Ion knew where we were going. He sought a deeper answer from me, not an easy one. I had to remind myself that I was speaking to a man who lived with the awareness that any moment may be his last.

"One minute he's a major player with dozens of professionals answering to him and the next minute he's on his way to the morgue," I said still trying to see what he saw. I had the vague sense that we were approaching a door.

"This happens all the time."

"Of course, it does, but not this close to me."

The door was now right before me. I felt uneasy. Was this a door that Ion wanted me to walk through, or the one he faced every day?

"Perhaps it was just bad luck," he said.

Of course it was a bad break, but finally I could see where Ion was pointing me. Marty's success had come at a high price—he had chosen that path. All his money and power—what did that matter now that he wouldn't live to see his children grow up? And then there was Miriam who faithfully tolerated the absences while dreaming of their golden years together.

"Be ashamed to die until you have won some victory for humanity," Ion said. I had heard him quote these words of Horace Mann before. The door was wide open now and I sensed light flooding the abyss. I was quiet for a few minutes. Ion waited with the perfect patience of a maestro who knows exactly when to commence a new movement. "The things you have observed are true, but what *really* bothers you the most about the events of this evening?"

I stared out the window, looking into the dark clouds that had descended over Queens, searching for the courage to say what I felt.

"I feel like I've worked so hard and done so little."

"I see," said Ion. I knew that he did. He put his hand on my shoulder as tears welled in my eyes. I didn't turn to face him; I didn't want him to see me cry.

"So, what should you do?"

"I want to work the way I played as a child. I want to lose myself deeply in something I love."

"That is how I felt when I ran or when I sculpted. They were hard, very hard. Sometimes frustrating, but always fulfilling. The marathon is sacred, not the runner. Art is noble, not the sculptor. When I participate in these activities, it is not work, it is play, serious play."

"If I were to die tomorrow—what would the sum of my life be? What have I brought to the table? I've spent my life as a distant daughter and an ambitious attorney."

"You alone will know what you must do—what your higher purpose is. When you have found that truth, you will have won your marathon."

It was strange that he used that analogy because I often felt as if I had met Ion in the latter stages of a marathon, though he had commenced his running many miles earlier. Where he had come from, and where he was to lead me—I could but dream. Yet I knew I needed to learn the way quickly before he reached the end and left me to run alone.

"Have you?" I asked him.

"What?" He had been lost in his own thoughts.

"Have you won your marathon?"

"Many other wreaths, but not that one..."

We were soon home and as I crawled into bed I thought to myself how very frightened I had been by Marty's death. If I had died tonight, it would have been without making much of an impact on the world. It was a sobering thought, but I wasn't sure what to do about it. I wasn't ready to quit the firm and volunteer for the ACLU. I didn't yet know what to do, but I did believe that Ion was trying to show me a way out of the labyrinth.

I often couldn't tell if Ion was speaking with some great wisdom, or just with the hyperbole of age. I prayed it was the former.

5
ART OBTAINS THE PRIZE

"I am Pheidippides, son of Alkiviades from Nonakris. My ancestors dwelled in the land of Odysseus, sacker of cities. They braved the unknown seas to settle the shores of Achaea. I did not grow up to revere their courage so that I could dishonor them when my call to duty came. I am not born Athenian—but Athena has adopted and nurtured me as if I had sprang from her womb. What she now asks is indeed a great task. With your permission, I shall leave at the first light of dawn."

"Athena was wise to have adopted you, for I would have been proud to have called you my son," said Militiades. Moved by the young man's fearlessness in the face of death—he could not know that Pheidippides no longer cared about life.

That winter was particularly harsh. In all, I counted seventeen distinct snowstorms, several of which left me stranded in my home. When I was a little girl, snow seemed heaven-sent—a reason to stay home from school. The cream covered landscape was a playground as soon as my mom could outfit me in my hat, boots and mittens. Now, it was an annoyance to slosh through. The winters of my youth offered great snowmen and silhouette angels; now, the frozen crystals made my commute hell and ruined countless pairs of shoes.

The bitterness of winter preceded an unseasonably cold spring. Memorial Weekend finally brought some relief. In previous summers, I joined the herds of New Yorkers who scrambled each weekend to shared houses on Fire Island or in the Hamptons. But my unexpected housemate forced me to forgo my share this summer. Ion was on the waiting list at the Riverdale Home for the Aged, the one facility in the area that had passed my inspection. In the meantime, we were managing to take care of each other pretty well. Ion was looking better, but that wasn't saying much, considering his condition coming out of the care center in Queens. I didn't think he was fit to travel to the beaches of Eastern Long Island. Our getaways would be spent in the secluded garden behind our house.

It wasn't a particularly large area, but we made it a cozy sanctuary. Planters ringed the flagstone pathways and there was even a koi pond though I had never bothered to get the koi. It had a recycling pump and at the flick of a switch water flowed over a simulated waterfall.

In the midst of this enchantment, as trees and flowers reawakened from their winter hibernation, Ion grew listless. At first, I attributed his quietness to simple fatigue. However, as spring turned to summer, this condition persisted and I grew concerned.

Ion did not complain to me of any particular ailments, and only reluctantly allowed me to schedule some medical tests. It was a Saturday when I brought him into the city for his examination. Before I dropped Ion off at the doctor's office, we met one of his former students for lunch on the West Side. He introduced himself as Bill, but Ion affectionately referred to him as William. Bill was in town for a few days on business.

I planned to go to Horace Mann while Ion was being examined. I had received a call from a Mrs. Hart, one of the school administrators. Ion's mail was accumulating at the school, and it was his last known address for the old students and colleagues with whom he was not still in contact. But I also wanted to see the place that Ion spoke of so often and so vividly.

"Marianna, I'd love to join you," said Bill.

"Are you sure?" I replied. "It's out of your way."

"I'm sure. I don't get many opportunities to visit." He had a flight to catch the next morning back to his home in Los Angeles. He joked that until he was thirty, he thought the "West Coast" was Riverside Drive. I suppose the distance kept Bill from visiting Ion more often—but every month, Ion would get a letter from him, which he would quickly take to his room, never opening it in front of me.

One time I inadvertently opened one of the envelopes along with my own mail. The letter simply said "Love, Bill," with two quarters taped below.

"Ion, I opened this by mistake. What are the quarters for?" I had asked him.

He laughed and said "Ah, my dividends from Horace Mann."

"It's only fifty cents..."

"To me, it is all the riches of the world."

"I believe that you were Ion's favorite student," I said as we walked down Broadway from Eighty-first Street.

"I think we all felt that way, but that was Ion's gift. He treated each of us as though we were his one and only Plato."

The day was perfect, a quintessential bright summer day without haze or humidity. The maple, oak and elms of Central Park were alive with emerald foliage. As we approached the corner of Eightieth Street, I saw the distinctive orange sign of *Zabars*. Peering down that side street, I could see all the way across the Hudson River to New Jersey. It was indeed the kind of day that makes even jaded New Yorkers glad to be alive.

"It's wonderful that you've opened your home to him," he said. I didn't respond. A tinge of guilt swept over me. It was true that I had taken Ion in, but I knew it was only because there was still no opening at the Riverdale Home.

We got the subway at Seventy-ninth Street and in a few minutes we were on the Broadway Local on our way up to the Bronx. Bill was in his mid-thirties and stood about six feet tall with an athletic build. Traces of silver interrupted the dark hair near his temples. What little I knew about him came from the few anecdotes that Ion would tell me about his teaching life. Because Bill was still in touch with Ion, and because I knew that those two quarters each month must add up to more than fifty cents, I was predisposed to like him. At lunch, he proved to be a good storyteller as well as a generous listener. As we made our way uptown, I thought about how long it had been since I had made a friend. The train finally reached its last stop at 242nd Street. Across Broadway and as far as my eye could see lay the broad expanse of Van Cortlandt Park. To the west was a steep hill, densely covered with trees.

"Ion told me that he shared many important events with you, like your wedding and even Bar Mitzvah."

"Yes, he was at both. I will never forget the sight of him dancing with my mother at my wedding. He wore a light blue suit, white shoes and a navy ascot, she—a magnificent cream-colored gown. I have a beautiful photo of it. She passed away just one year later, so that photo is one of the last pictures ever taken of her."

"I am so sorry for your loss."

"Too young. Far too young," he said, shaking his head sullenly from side to side. "It meant the world to me that Mr. Theodore could be there for those events. Anyway, the marriage didn't last, but at least the Bar Mitzvah stuck," he laughed, snapping back to his light-hearted demeanor.

Rising from the top of the hill, on 246th Street, was the first building that made up the Horace Mann campus. A Gothic structure made of granite and covered with ivy, it was reminiscent of an English boarding school like Eton or Warwick.

"I would need a book to describe the eccentric teachers I had here. Glidden, Muscat, Allison and 'Inkee' Clark, our headmaster—he wore flamboyant chartreuse shirts tucked into red polyester slacks and drove an orange Cadillac convertible. They're just names to you, but to me and my classmates, they were the gatekeepers as we began our passage into manhood."

"You must have loved Ion from the start."

"I'm ashamed to admit that I used to think of him as a feeble old man, a chance for an easy grade without a lot of work."

"What changed?" I begged Bill to continue.

"Come on, I'll show you." We crossed the football field that formed the center of the campus and walked down a long series of stairs into a building that housed the school's gymnasium. We came to a dimly lit room, which had small grated windows. The floor was covered with black matting, with white circles and lines imprinted upon it.

"It happened right here," Bill said. "One day Mr. Quinn, our wrestling coach, was absent, so Mr. Theodore took over the practice. Mr. Quinn was a gruff Irishman who could bench twice his body weight. Mr. Theodore's build was the opposite and of course he was already nearing seventy. We were pretending to do the moves he showed us, but usually ended up in a twisted pile on the floor—laughing like idiots. Finally, Mr. Theodore asked us what we thought was the most important quality in a wrestler. We replied that strength was. 'It might appear that way,' he said, laughing at us. 'Wrestling, like life, rewards cunning and intelligence over brute strength. Remember, it is not strength but art that obtains the prize—and to be swift is less than to be wise.'"

"That's some lesson to learn at such a young age," I said.

"We hadn't learned it yet. Ion asked who was willing to step forward and challenge his theory. We all looked over at Ronald Hoffman. Ronald was the kind of kid who seemed to have gone through puberty before we could spell the word. He stood a head taller than Mr. Theodore and Ronald probably weighed in at a hundred-eighty pounds—it seemed an unfair contest."

"Ion wrestled a seventh grader?"

"No. Ronald wrestled—Mr. Theodore danced. At first, Mr. Theodore let Ronald believe he was getting the best of him. We were cheering for Ronald to pin Mr. Theodore and dispense with his silly theories about art and wrestling."

"I can barely believe this..."

"Believe me, the final move happened so fast that one moment Ronald seemed to be dominating Mr. Theodore and then the next he was flat on the mat. And just to show us that it was not a lucky move, Mr. Theodore pinned Ronald two more times. By then it was time to dismiss the class, and as he walked out, he said, 'Remember what you have learned today, my boys, it is not strength but art that obtains the prize.' I would never look at him the same way again."

Bill and I had left the gym and headed to Tillinghast Hall. I looked up and smiled as I noticed the engraving captured by Ion in the photo of my parents. I sought out Mrs. Hart. It was considerate of her to have saved Ion's mail; others would have returned it to the Post Office marked "undeliverable." Most of it was solicitations, but there was one item that caught my eye. It was that thin blue PAR AVION stationary that folds into its own envelope and on its face was affixed an international stamp.

Bill led us into the library to show me one of Ion's sculptures. I fingered the inscription Ion had etched on its base.

This visualized slag of captured time
Threadbare flesh of earthly harvests
Poured fiery from a crucible of molten bronze
Even as I have been poured from a crucible of flesh
By myriads of unknown progenitors.

Dearly beloved students of my happiest years,
This symbol fashioned from once cunning hands
Was made for you, my cherished friends,
A remembrance of days long, long ago
When we together, pursued a vision
The true, the good, the beautiful—the sacred trinity
Elusive quarry, precious reward
soldier on, be stalwart, heartened
May my blessing from shadow land bring fruition to your quest
And what is more—the trinity will lead you to Heaven's door.

"I knew your uncle for many, many years," said a tall, wiry professor named Lyall Dean. Prior to our introduction, Bill had whispered to me that besides being his seventh grade math teacher, Mr. Dean was infamously anal and perennially grouchy. Though he looked as if he could have easily embodied such character traits, he was anything but those things when Bill mentioned that Ion was my uncle. "Ion was the eternal optimist."

"Well, we have to be going, Mr. Dean," said Bill, a bit unsettled in his math teacher's presence.

Mr. Dean seemed to anticipate Bill's uneasiness, "I was tough on the kids when Billy was a student. I've mellowed a lot since then."

"I hope so, Mr. Dean. You once gave me a 'D' on a math test that was one-hundred percent correct. You didn't like the way I drew my brackets, you took off a point for each one—all thirty of them!" Mr. Dean had a soft smile on his face; he didn't look like a man capable of such harsh discipline. His eyes flitted about our surroundings, pausing, I presumed, upon Ion's sculpture. When he spoke, the details of math tests and poorly written brackets were overshadowed by a memory of Ion he wanted to share.

"I remember one hellish winter morning of freezing rain and an awful commute. I used to park behind Pforzheimer Hall—that's where Ion's studio used to be. In the short walk from my car to the door, I had already gotten soaked, and I didn't envy the first student who would cross my path. I saw Ion chipping away on a large bark with a hammer and chisel. I mumbled some half-hearted 'hello' when Ion said, 'The rain! Isn't it wonderful? How much the earth thirsts for its refreshing drink, and what beautiful flowers it will reward us with this spring.' By the time my foot hit the first step on the way to my classroom, I had smiled, and the demons of the morning commute had fled."

We left Tillinghast and walked down into the basement of the old headmaster's cottage, now used as the nurse's office. I observed the place where Ion had lived, worked and played for nearly thirty years. I learned that he slept on one of the cots used in the daytime by sick students. His bathroom was the public one in the corridor.

"You should have seen this when it was Mr. Theodore's studio," Bill said, as he pointed out the room next door to the infirmary. "It was like an underground annex of the British Museum, filled with paintings, sculptures, works in progress and wood ready for carving. After graduating, when I would visit, I loved to see eager new faces working away before the Master—the continuum of life and creation in which I had played my small but necessary role. Along that wall was a makeshift kitchen—a small hotplate with a half-sized refrigerator below it. He had a little Victrola on which he played old vinyl recordings."

"He still has it. And I believe that I've heard every single one of those records!" I smiled.

"Have you ever had the pleasure of having Mr. Theodore cook for you?"

"Ion cooks? He doesn't cook at my home."

"Well, you're missing out. He used to whip up dishes with tomatoes, chickpeas and potatoes. Olives and feta cheese were always in abundance—and of course, a special wine."

"How old were you?"

"Twelve, maybe thirteen."

"Ion gave you alcohol?"

"He taught me two things by treating me more as an adult. First, with privilege comes responsibility."

"And, the second thing?"

"A little Greek firewater never killed anyone."

"Two tokens please," Bill asked the clerk as we re-entered the 242nd Street Station.

"Bill, why do you send Ion money every month?"

"I once sat for Mr. Theodore while he crafted a bust of me. When he presented it to me as a Bar Mitzvah gift, my mother insisted I pay for it so I would appreciate its value. Mr. Theodore devised an installment plan. I was to pay him one dollar every month for the remainder of his life or mine, whichever was shorter."

"You said a dollar a month, didn't you?"

"Yes, that's right..."

"But I opened one of your cards once and only found two quarters..."

"Are you speaking as his attorney?" Bill laughed.

"Don't be silly. I'm speaking as his financial advisor."

"I almost died. We renegotiated."

"You almost died?"

"I had *viral encephalitis* the summer after my H.M. graduation. I was in a coma."

"You're kidding?" I said, immediately realizing that it wasn't the sort of subject one kidded about. I quickly added, "You're lucky to be alive."

"Yes, lucky, I suppose. Mr. Theodore came to the hospital every day and as he sat by my bedside, he'd read aloud my favorite passages from *The Iliad*."

"That's unbelievable devotion."

"Ion was so concerned that I was trying to get out of my debt that he suggested we cut the monthly payment in half. With all the red meat I eat, I'll probably have that payment down to a quarter within a few years," he laughed.

"Maybe he'll even owe you money soon."

"The man who saved my life could never owe me anything..."

6
THUS WHISPERED XANTHOS

Pheidippides reached the peak of Mount Pentelicus. In the valley near the Sanctuary of Herakles, the Athenians had encamped in hastily built stockades of earth and wood. Pheidippides gazed across the Attican plain at the Persian host. Six Hundred ships of Darius' navy lay anchored in the Bay of Marathonas. Men, horses and supplies were being unloaded onto this once deserted shoreline.

"It is good, my comrades, that the Gods have spared you this view," thought Pheidippides. "You will have to engage the barbarian host soon enough, let not their numbers put fear into your hearts."

From Carthage to India they had been summoned. Pheidippides saw Medean archers, Lydian cavalry, Egyptian charioteers, and high-booted Phyrgians. There were Mysians with sharpened stakes; pointed capped Scythians; Arabians mounted upon beasts they called camels; and Ethiopians in lion skins who, brandished stone-headed clubs and spears crowned with gazelle horns.

And finally, there were the dreaded 10,000 Immortals.

Ion's exuberance at hearing about my afternoon at Horace Mann disappeared faster than white snow on a New York City street. For days, and without any apparent reason, he grew more melancholy. Eventually, my quiet concern had turned to bald-faced worry.

Very late one night, long after Ion had gone to bed, I noticed a light still on in his room. I opened the door to see Ion sitting upright on the edge of his bed. Facing away from me, I heard him speaking in his mother tongue. His voice had the distinct rhythm of a dialogue—he would say something and then pause as if waiting for a response. He appeared like a crazy man whose latest neurotic manifestation was ranting to an imaginary listener—in Greek.

Not knowing what to do, I withdrew and closed the door gently behind me, then stood in the recesses of the hallway. I hardly believed what I had seen, but I could still hear his soft utterances. A few moments later, the light under his door was extinguished, and all was dark and silent again.

I felt like the rug had been pulled out from under me. I was happy to take Ion in temporarily and I wanted to make sure he received proper care for as long as he lived. But I did not understand what I had just seen. Whatever it was, I felt powerless to help him.

The next day at work I tried to keep my mind off of the events of the evening before, but the memory of Ion speaking to an empty room saddened me. When I arrived home that night I waited to see if Ion would broach the subject.

At dinner, I studied Ion closely, trying to detect what he was thinking. "You've had me worried, Ion."

"I know that I have seemed pensive lately. There has been much on my mind."

"What's troubling you?"

"My dear, do you know the story of Xanthos?"

"No, I can't seem to recall that one." I loved the way Ion would ask me whether I knew the obscure mythological references he made, as if he really believed I might.

"He was a talking steed that pulled the chariot of Achilles."

"Oh, the talking steed, of course," I said, taking the dull approach, but Ion didn't seem to be listening to me.

"Xanthos warned Achilles that soon he would not be able to bring his master home safely from the field."

"It's an interesting story, Ion, but what does it have to do with you? Is everything okay? Didn't Dr. Riggs give you a clean bill of health?"

"Ah, yes, indeed he did," laughed Ion, "and we would not want to accuse Dr. Riggs of questionable optimism. But I too have recently had a vision, and in this dream, my steed also whispered to me."

"But it was just a dream," I said.

"Perhaps I choose to heed them for are not dreams the things that change worlds? I must go to Greece. As soon as possible."

I thought, no, I hoped that I had misheard him—but I knew I hadn't.

"Why?"

"An old friend, a priest, needs me."

"I can appreciate your desire to return to your homeland and help a...."

"What would I do if something happened?"

"There is no danger there that cannot find me here."

"Ion, this is not like deciding to take a drive to Montauk over the weekend. You're talking about traveling halfway around the world."

"Only a quarter, my dear," he said, as if this distinction would shift the balance in his favor.

"I cannot go alone," he added.

"There are so many reasons why we can't go to Greece right now."

Oh, you have a partner in this scheme. Who could be that irresponsible? Ion merely looked at me with eyebrows raised.

"I can understand your concerns, but remember, achievement often comes in the face of adversity."

"Yes, as does failure."

"True—failure as well. But the value of anything is commensurate with the risk and effort of obtaining it. Or perhaps one should always choose the safer road—the one that leads nowhere."

"How do you know which one is the right road?" I asked.

"That's the point. If you could know, then there is no risk, and nothing achieved."

"Your position is admirable, Ion, but I must make the rational decision. For the moment, I'm responsible for your care and there are so many factors to consider," I said, sounding like a third year law student preparing for the bar exam. "You have doubts."

"Don't you think any objective person would?"

"Who is objective?"

"How about Dr. Riggs?"

"He was still learning to walk while I was climbing Mount Olympus."

"Nevertheless, I'm going to call him tomorrow. If he gives his blessing, then I will consider it. And I'm only promising that I'll *consider it*. No guarantees!" I never thought that I would consider it, but I'd have said anything to get myself out of an impossible argument with the master debater. In an hour, we were in his room as he reclined in bed. I put one of his favorite albums on his Victrola. Turning off his light I moved away from the bed.

"I must find my love," I thought I heard him whisper.

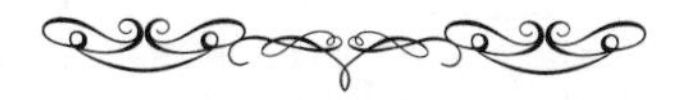

The next morning a neighbor whose elderly father was visiting took Ion to the Jewish Community Center in Great Neck. They had an extra ticket to one of a series of six musical performances, each week focusing on a different composer. Today's program featured Edvard Grieg and the *Peer Gynt Suite*. Ion was feeling well enough to join them, but he was disappointed that I couldn't come. I needed to get some things done around the house, but really I was happy to have a few hours to myself. I needed to think about what was really best for Ion—and for me. First, I telephoned Dr. Riggs.

"Hello, Marianna. I have several patients waiting for me; what do you need?" he said with the aura of self-importance that doctors love to use. "Is Ion feeling all right?"

"Oh yes. Perhaps too fine—he broached the subject of traveling; I'm concerned that it might be too much for him."

"A little traveling might not be so bad. A change of scenery often does wonders for the elderly. Where does he want to go?"

"Greece."

"To Greece?" I could clearly hear a distinctive pause as he cleared his throat and repeated. "He wants to travel all the way to Greece? Haven't you told him how difficult that would be?"

"Of course, but he is determined, and he has no fear of what might happen."

"You know that I hold your uncle in very high regard, and like you, I want his happiness as well as his health. But I think that my opinion as his physician is much more relevant."

"Of course."

"I can't recommend such a trip in good conscience."

"He takes walks around my neighborhood every morning," I said.

"His body is amazing, there's no doubt. I've rarely seen patients of his age in such phenomenal physical condition, but there are still risks. I'm sorry, I strongly advise against it," he said as he finished enumerating the obvious arguments. I knew what Dr. Riggs was going to say long before we had spoken—I just needed someone else to be the bad guy.

I went upstairs to open Ion's windows and strip his bedding. As I tossed the pillows aside I uncovered a letter. It was the foreign letter that had been in the stack I had brought him from Horace Mann. I paused for a moment, wondering whether or not to read it. I felt that I had the right, strongly suspecting the missive had been the cause of Ion's emotional and physical depression and his urgent desire to return to Greece. And, as an attorney, I was privy to all manner of details about my clients and their dealings. I was sworn to keep all such knowledge confidential; it is the inviolable rule. Feeling justified that I was acting in my uncle's best interests, I opened the singly folded page.

It was, as I should have anticipated, written in Greek.

Taverna Tony's was the only Greek restaurant in Old Westbury. It was fine dining, not the typical New York diner serving souvlaki and gyros. I ate here once or twice a month—mostly for a change of pace from the Italian and French eateries that were my more frequented haunts.

Tony, the proprietor, had created a beautiful setting in an old adobe style building. Wisteria wove through pergolas and high ceilings echoed the nightly live music he provided. I'd never been to Greece, but I imagined this place was authentic—not counting the view of the parking lot and Long Island Expressway. Still, I almost forgot that I was in Long Island as I stood on its shaded terrace.

Tony was expected back in about fifteen minutes. I went to lean against the hostess' podium when Zeno, the headwaiter, suggested I'd be more comfortable at a table right behind it.

"It's taken," I observed. I vaguely recalled having seen the man sitting at that same table before.

"It's all right, that's Tony's father. He visits every month. I'm sure he won't mind if you join him."

"Zeno! Why are you keeping such a beautiful woman all to yourself?" the older man said as we approached. Zeno gave me a reassuring smile and returned to his customers.

"Pleased to meet you, I'm Marianna Gardner."

He leaned forward to kiss my hand.

"Marianna, what a musical name. Mine is Tasos. To what does this simple farmer owe the honor of your company?" He looked nothing like a farmer, nor did he appear simple. When he stood to greet me, I got the full impact of how imposing he was. Wearing a grey suit over a black shirt, he was tall and barrel-chested, and tanned skin wrapped around his clean-shaven chin until folding into a round cleft. His long, silver hair was slicked back and similarly colored strands appeared on his knuckles and chest—a tuft of which protruded above his V-neck collar.

"I hope you don't mind my joining you. It shouldn't be long."

"It cannot be long enough." I wasn't sure if he was flirting, but he certainly wasn't lacking in charm. Though in his mid to late sixties, I could tell from the way the hostess and female servers gazed at him that he had a hypnotic effect on younger women. "Please, take some refreshment," he said while holding up a dusty bottle that looked like it had been buried in the cellar.

"No thank you, it's too early."

He poured himself a glass.

"It is only too early when the grapes have not yet fermented. This bottle was made from the vines of my island."

"Your island?"

"Ithaca. The place of my birth. I have a hundred hectares of fig and olive groves that flow from my house down to the sea. From there I can see across the sparkling blue waters to the island of Cephallonia. Nothing made by the hand of man compares to the view that graces my veranda."

"Your home sounds beautiful."

"I have brought a piece of her with me." Tasos reached into his breast pocket and withdrew a vial of green olive oil. "Would you care for a taste?"

"Plain?"

"It is the best way to taste the virgin." He poured a drop onto his index finger and brought it to his lips. I watched his head sway as if he were intoxicated, which I suppose he was.

"I've never seen someone so smitten with food," I said.

"All of our senses need to love—without desire we are nothing. But this talk makes me homesick. To be *orphaned*; to be *abandoned*; to be *in love*; and to be *far from Greece*—the last is the most painful of all." Tasos laughed. In the background, waiters yelled *"Opa! Opa!"* and two musicians began to play traditional folk songs.

Zeno returned to our table to say that Tony had telephoned. Something had come up and he wouldn't return for at least an hour. He suggested I leave the letter for him to translate at home.

"It is a pity you are not speaking Greek," Tasos said as if that inability were some rare disease. "No matter, it brought you here, to my table. Would you allow me to see this letter?"

I handed it to him and he unfolded it slowly. Blinking a few times, he reached into his other breast pocket for a pair of spectacles.

"This is from a Holy man," he said, as if pondering whether it was sacrosanct to read the words meant for another. "Ion, he is..."

"My uncle."

"I see. Your uncle must go to him—to this Priest—right away. There is no doubt."

Before I left, Tasos had written down the full translation. I will not forget his parting words.

"A Greek priest does not take his vows lightly. Ion must go. Ion must go to Greece," repeated Tasos, bowing his head slightly.

ΑΓΙΟΣ ΠΑΝΤΕΛΕΙΜΩΝ

Dearest Ion:

Forgive the years of silence my old friend. It has been too long and I must now do the unthinkable and break my vows. You must come as soon as possible. There is not much time.

I know how much you loved her. Forgive me.

Panayiotas Kyriazis
Episkopos tis Marathonas

There had also been a photograph in the envelope. Its sepia image added color to a past that I never could have imagined. As I stared at the image's solitary figure, She was the same woman from the photo I had first seen in Ion's nursing home. I realized that I knew nothing about her, except her name. What torments had loving her brought to Ion, or to Panayiotas? Alexandra was pale skinned, dark eyed and alluring—enough to seduce the heart of an older man, even of a priest. On a hilltop behind her was the crumbling ruin of a marble temple.

Ion would be home in about an hour. I replaced the letter and its contents under the pillow, but not before scanning the photo onto my computer. There was someone else I wanted to show it to, a classmate of mine, Warren Giles. He had become the head of the Antiquities Department at NYU. I sent him an email with the image attached, asking him whether he recognized the ancient temple.

"Did you give any more thought to our trip?" he asked.

"I couldn't reach Dr. Riggs yet; I promise I'll try again first thing tomorrow. I'm exhausted, Ion. Do you mind if I call it an early night?" I said, hoping to avoid any further conversation. I wanted to buy myself some time until I could find a compromise that would ease Ion's depression and my conscience.

"Is not the doctor an excuse?" He uttered it calmly, turning his head only slightly from me. He had stunned me but I pretended only to be slightly confused.

"An excuse for what?"

"An excuse for *you*."

"Because I don't understand why you would risk your life to go on this trip?"

"No, I think it is because you do understand. It is an excuse for you."

"Okay, there is another issue," I said, hating to bring it up, but I felt that Ion was being unfair. "You have no idea how many client matters I have coming to a head. I can't imagine how I would justify taking the time off so suddenly."

"Justify. Justification. Is life but an economic balance sheet—how many hours we can bill, how many dollars we can squeeze out of our lives?" To his mind, Ion was making a rational argument, but he was beginning to push my buttons.

"Now you're starting to sound like my father."

"Ah, you invoke the father, but is it as Cordelia—or Goneril?" I was irritated and then embarrassed. Did I fear what I might lose if I took the risk, left everything behind, and followed him? Or was I afraid of abandoning another father? "It's hard not to look away from the end. One's own demise and the dying we see all around us?"

"I wish I could have seen him one last time before he died."

"I know, Ion said, "I did. I was there at the funeral. It was, as you said, simple and dignified."

I was dumbstruck—caught in a lie. A really awful lie.

"Ion, I don't know what to say, I..." I began to say and then swallowed my sentence.

"Several of his friends were there to comfort him at the end."

"How? There was no forewarning—he died of a sudden stroke."

"That is true, of the stroke—but not of his dying. The year before he died we talked about many things—his life, his health, you. You were so busy all the time, he worried about you. But his heart had been failing."

"Why didn't he tell me?"

"Did you expect he would burden you with such news over the telephone?"

"I had wanted to visit him, many times, really. It was an incredibly hectic year for me."

"Yes, of course it was."

"I was vying for a partnership."

"He was vying for his life."

All of the excuses I could muster for the sin of missing his funeral made it appear venal in the light of this new and even more unforgivable one. My father had been sick and he had not, could not, tell me anything about it. The terror I felt now was not the guilt of not having known but the guilt that I was the real failure of his heart. He knew what I had become—a self-centered monster. I had vengefully fallen in love with ambition. What I had hated in my husband and in my work and in myself, I tried to avoid by hurling myself into work and into beating my way through corporate doors and corporate glass ceilings. My father knew it from the times I called, making full use of a daughter's rights and regaling him with my troubles, yet I could not bring myself to ask what he needed or what I owed him.

"My dear, we busy ourselves year to year, day to day, minute to minute with errands and meetings and crises. And, of course, they are all crises except at rare moments and only from a certain perspective. It is from the perspective that everything we cherish, our food, our clothes, our homes, our flesh and blood—will disappear, will perish. This is why each choice we make is so important."

"It's too late," I said.

"For him, perhaps, but not for you."

"What can I do?" I asked, my defenses broken down at last.

"Come with me to Greece."

"Helping you is important to me..."

"It's not for my sake."

"Then whose?"

"Yours."

"What could there be for me in Greece?"

"It's not the destination, it's the journey. It will give you a chance to pause, to reflect at some distance upon the illusion of life you have created."

"What's wrong with the life I've worked so hard to create?" I said before I could stop myself, the lawyer in me never quite taking a back seat.

"*That* is wrong. That you still need to ask such a question. It's why you cannot find love. Shh, do not feel the need to defend, I have known you too long. Your life has become all about you and it is a lonely perspective. It is time to make room for other people, new experiences. Do not wait until it is too late—come to Greece and unburden your heart."

Fortunately, Ion did not pin me down any further that evening before I turned off his lights and bid him a goodnight. I felt that he was offering me an opportunity—that loathsome word—for redemption as if this single act would atone for all past sins. Whatever the motives, I knew that this brief time with Ion had brought me to a crossroads. One path could lead me into the safe, comfortable twilight. The other road, the one fraught with uncertainty, held the possibilities of worlds I couldn't yet imagine—if I dared to pursue it.

7
THE ROAD LESS TRAVELED

Reveling in the rush of his blood—Pheidippides' senses were alive with clarity and power. In the distance rose Greece's soaring peaks, the stepping-stones upon which the Gods ascended to Mount Olympus. He was a warrior, but when he ran, he needed no armor, no heavy shield, no iron sword or long ashen spear. He wore only the thinnest wisp of cloth around his torso to give protection from the sun by day, and from its absence at night.

Fear and doubt circled in the distance like a pair of vultures waiting for him to stumble. Three hundred miles to the gates of Sparta and back. Three hundred miles without rest or delay—tempting his will to the very precipice of death.

By the time I got to my office Monday morning there was already a response from Warren.

From: wgiles@nyu.edu
To: jumpingdolphin@aol.com
Subject: Re: Photo

Marianna, please call. Found photo fascinating, took the liberty of contacting a colleague who is an expert in the field. I suggest we meet as soon as possible. I will come to you if more convenient.

Regards, Warren.

I called him, but he wouldn't tell me why he needed to meet in person, or why so soon. My noon appointment had cancelled, so I suggested that he come to my office. I'd take lunch at my desk. It would be more important than ever for me to be seen working around the clock if I was going to disappear for a few weeks.

"I know you've got the days coming, but you couldn't have picked a worse time to ask for it," stated Steve. "I've got Jim and Mike out the last two weeks of August; and I'll be in D.C. for the Capstone anti-trust hearings."

Even though I was a partner, and the term "boss" is euphemistically avoided, I still had one and Steve Payne was it. He kicked his chair back and placed one of his fine English wing tips on the lower right drawer, which he had opened for this purpose. Though expensively dressed, Steve always tried to seem casual, even sporting. It was part of his strategy of putting people slightly off balance. I sat across from his desk, on which were several neatly arranged piles, calculated to impress any viewer. Steve's briefcase sat open on a credenza to his left. I recall he used to keep a Metro North train schedule in it. It had vanished along with his marriage and home in Westchester County.

"Steve, I know it's not ideal, but I didn't exactly plan it this way. I've told you about the gentleman who lives in my home; I pointed him out to you at the firm's anniversary party."

"Oh yes, yes, I remember him. You haven't been able to find a situation for him yet I guess." Steve was a prick. I bit my lip to repel the urge to comment.

"It's important for him to return to Greece—it's to visit a friend who may be quite ill. Believe me, Steve, this is not my idea of a vacation." Now, nothing Steve could say was going to dissuade me from making this voyage if for no other reason than to assert that I could.

"I appreciate your concern for family—we all share that. But there are other virtues..." he began. I knew that Steve shared nothing of the sort. "Look, Marianna, I know you appreciate the upcoming calendar. We've got a dozen 10Qs to prepare, a major proxy going out for Citibank, and Merrill's got pressing SEC compliance issues."

"Nothing due before I return."

"What if something unexpected pops up?"

"Then it does. There are other people here qualified to handle emergencies."

"I'm really disappointed in your selfish attitude," he said under the pretense of moral rectitude. Attitude, was it? A character defect I was meant to feel by insinuation. It was the kind of thing this lanky ex-crew jock from Yale learned in a secret society. I was infuriated by his condescension but allowing for such an emotion only opens the door to rage—a trap that played into his accusation.

"Selfish?" I was seething, but managed to regain my composure. "Who's selfish, Steve? Who can't have everything he wants?"

Steve shot forward in his chair and stood up, coming around his desk to stand behind me. I felt momentarily trapped as he stood between me and the door—my only escape route. Here was another boys' club parlor trick—intimate sexual threats while "asserting authority." Complain and you're crying wolf in a sexual harassment suit. Say nothing, and you're encouraging advances.

"Let's not go there," I heard him say, almost feeling his breath upon me as he moved close.

"I won't if you won't," I said as I turned and looked him right in the eye.

"All right, I get the idea."

I doubted if he did, but I felt better when he moved back behind his desk.

I had prevailed, but Steve had succeeded in making sure that I didn't enjoy it. I knew that my defiance was going to cost me.

Warren Giles arrived with another, quite older gentleman, named Dr. Manfred Schaffhausen. His emphasis of the title "Dr." told me that he had little desire to be called "Manfred," and "Manny" was certainly going to be out of the question. There was not enough room for us to sit comfortably in my office, so I ushered them and my sandwich into a small conference room down the hall.

"Forgive me for eating while we talk, I just don't have a lot of spare time today. Do either of you want anything?"

"Nothing for me," said my old classmate.

"For you, Dr. Schaffhausen?"

"No, thank you very much. I have an engagement at one o'clock," he said as if to let me know that his time was even more precious than mine. Warren mentioned that he did freelance work for Sotheby's, but why he was here was still a mystery.

"So, Warren, I didn't expect you to respond so soon," I said after we dispensed with a who's who and who's where from our graduating class.

"After seeing the photo, I took the liberty of contacting Dr. Schaffhausen. He's one of the world's leading experts on ancient artifacts. He's written a couple of books on the subject..."

"Three, to be precise," interrupted the good doctor, a humorless and portly man. Schaffhausen still had a thick Germanic accent and his eyebrows were thick and white, with wild hairs sprouting from them as well as from his ears.

"I don't get it, Warren. I was just wondering whether you could identify anything from the photo."

"That was easy. It's the remains of the Temple of Aphrodite on Limnos. It dates back to the Sixth Century before Christ."

"Okay, and its significance?"

"Very little. Strictly a class B ruin. Nice for archaeologists and the Limnian tourist industry. Dozens of ruins like it all over the Mediterranean."

"So why the house call?"

"Where did you get this photograph?" Schaffhausen asked.

"From my uncle. I came across it in his room."

"And where, precisely, did he acquire it?" he continued sharply.

"Excuse me, am I being cross-examined here?

"Please forgive Dr. Schaffhausen. He's the best in the business when it comes to this sort of thing."

"What sort of thing?"

"Have you heard of Pheidippides?" Asked Warren.

"He's the runner who delivered the news after the Battle of Marathon?"

"Then perhaps you are also familiar with the *Obol of Pheidippides*?"

"An *obol*?"

"The ancient Greeks placed a coin on the tongue of the dead to tip Charon—the boatman who ferried souls across the River Acheron. No tip, no voyage, no Elysium. As was customary for all Greek warriors, Pheidippides carried his into battle, but he was buried without it. Experts believe it had been lost during the battle, and in their hurry to ward off the Persians, his comrades had simply forgotten it." The story sounded vaguely familiar, but like so many ancient fairy tales I gave it little credence.

"How do you know he wasn't buried with it?" I asked.

"Good question. Ten years later, in 480 B.C., the Persians again invaded Greece to avenge the humiliation at Marathon. Before they were defeated, the grave of Pheidippides—symbol of the earlier Greek victory—was desecrated. When his remains were unearthed, no obol was found. It is said that Pheidippides could not cross into the underworld, and that his soul wanders the earth until he can win his final victory and be reunited with his obol."

"Gentlemen, I love mythology as much as the next person, but what does this have to do with the email I sent you?"

"Here, take a closer look," said Warren as he extracted a loupe from his inner pocket. "Look at what the woman is wearing about her neck."

"It's a pendant." No more than an inch and a half across, the actual coin part of it was soldered in four joints to a larger circumference of metal, which framed the inner work. Along the top of this outer ring was welded a decorative wave-like piece through which the necklace was looped.

On its circular face was a raised relief of a man running. Wings spread out behind his helmeted head, and smaller wings fanned from his heels. His perfectly sculpted chest and abdomen still had the precision cuts of the artisan. Wreaths were clutched in each hand of his outstretched arms. The moment was a marriage of matter and motion—the wind itself given human form.

"Now look at this," Schaffhausen said as he opened a leather-bound album. Behind a protective plastic covering was a drawing of an icon on old parchment—it was similar to the one that the mysterious woman wore. When I looked closer, I could see that it wasn't a drawing, but rather a charcoal rubbing. Schaffhausen became animated; he sat upright and moved to the edge of the chair.

"All my life I have searched for this obol. Until now, I have seen only drawings and read descriptions of this magnificent artifact. I have fended off countless skeptics who have questioned its existence, my scholarship and even my sanity. They were fools. And finally I see it in this photo."

"Okay, assuming that it exists, does either of you really believe that this is the same thing? There have to be a lot of coins that were minted just like this one."

"See the markings, there," Schaffhausen could barely mask his irritation with me as he pointed to the space below the runner's legs. "The two grooves running parallel to his legs, meeting at that vertex there."

"It's a Greek lambda," added Warren.

"And?"

"Herodotus' history of the Battle of Marathon is scant. Fortunately, excavations in Attica turned up writings by a soldier named Lavetos who had fought at Marathon. He wrote of the 'fleet-footed runner' who brought the news to Athens and identified the pendant he wore—the one with the lambda."

"Why was there a lambda inscribed?"

"We believe that it was engraved by the Spartans—the Lacadaemons—when Pheidippides made his visit. The lambda was the symbol they wore on their shields."

"Can't someone just make a replica and stamp that marking on it?"

"Any good metallurgist could detect a fraud."

"I still say that the resolution is hardly conclusive—it could be anything, a shadow, a dent, a smudge on the lens," I said taking another look at the photo through the loupe.

"Maybe it's the man-on-the-moon. But when you have spent almost half a century seeking something as coveted as this, you do not take any possibility for granted. And I can assure you that it is not a fantasy but quite real. It once belonged to the Emperor Trajan. Rome fell and it was lost, ultimately making its way to Istanbul, then to the Holy Land with the crusaders."

"That's a long time ago. When was it last seen?"

"In the heart of the Third Reich."

"How could the woman in the photo have it? She didn't look like a Nazi."

"It was once in the private collection of Count Von Wildenstein. During the rise of the fascists, there was an unlikely romance between the Nazi elite and the German aristocracy. Eventually Hitler's paranoia prevailed and he ordered most of them imprisoned and tortured. Wildenstein was no exception—he and his family were executed in 1939."

"I still don't see the connection," I said, getting a little frustrated at his lengthy narration.

"His mistress vanished before the SS arrested him and plundered his estate. A massive search for her ensued—there was quite a price on her head."

"What was her name?"

"For obvious reasons, the identities of mistresses were closely guarded. Perhaps the woman in the photo is her."

"I see. So what can I do for you?"

"Is it possible for you to ask your uncle about it," asked Warren, who was almost immediately interrupted by Schaffhausen.

"You must question him. Maybe he can recall something of the woman who wore this pendant, possibly her whereabouts today."

"Slow down doctor. The obol looks like an old etching and the woman might have been sleeping with a Nazi—I think you're on a wild goose chase."

"Can you imagine the value of such a thing?" said Warren with a slightly anxious grin across his face.

"Collectors speak of it as the holy grail of the pre-Christian world. Its value is, in a word, inestimable. Ten Million? Twenty Million? What collector wouldn't ante up twice those sums for such a relic?" said Schaffhausen.

"And imagine its import to history—it is a testament to the continuity of Western civilization," added Warren.

"Here is my card," said Schaffhausen. "Please contact me if you learn anything."

"Why should I help you locate it? It doesn't belong to you."

"To whom does it belong? I suppose Pheidippides had a legitimate claim; for the rest of us it's a matter of possession."

"Who were those guys?" Tom asked me. He had been coming out of the elevator bank as I was walking out Warren and Herr Doktor. "They didn't look like our kind of clients."

"They're not. The tall guy was an old college friend. I'd never met the older one before."

"What's the story?" he asked.

I gave him a look that said the rest of the office didn't need to hear it.

"So, what's going on? Who was that older guy? He gave me the chills," Tom said once we were behind closed doors.

"Nothing. A wild goose chase. The younger one's into antiquities at NYU and the old creepy one, well, he's like someone out of *Raiders of the Lost Ark*. They think an old acquaintance of my uncle had an ancient Greek relic. It was in some photo he had and they want me to ask him where it is now. But that's not what I wanted to talk to you about," I said. Tom nodded expectantly. "I'm leaving the office for a few weeks to take Ion to Greece."

I waited for a hysterical response, but I should have known better. All Tom said was, "What about the home in Riverdale?"

"There's a priest dying and he's called Ion to his bedside. Ion can't make this kind of trip alone; the Riverdale Home will be there when we get back."

"And Steve was fine with this?" he asked, somewhat confounded.

"I didn't give him much choice." Tom looked at me for what seemed like a long time. I couldn't tell if he was lamenting his own inability to play such a strategy.

"A Holy Man waiting to whisper his last words, huh? Well, maybe he knows where that relic obol is," said Tom, a wry smile on his face.

"I'll be sure to ask him. Maybe he can tell me where to find Merlin's Wand while he's at it," I said as Tom and I shared a laugh. I didn't believe the story of the obol for a moment; I've seen too many get-rich-quick schemes. And when I get involved, it's usually suing someone for fraud.

I folded the photocopy they had left of the etching into quarters and slipped it into my briefcase.

At home, Ion and I sat in my kitchen having dinner.

"We're going?" Ion said, almost in disbelief. "What about Dr. Riggs?"

"I spoke to him this afternoon," I smiled nervously, hoping that Ion would not suspect my ruse.

"I didn't expect him to give his blessing," Ion said with an amused look.

"Neither did I, Ion. Neither did I."

"It's a miracle that he had such a change of heart," he said.

"What do you mean?"

"When he called, early this morning, he was adamantly against any traveling. The Gods have ways of making the impossible commonplace." I wondered whether Ion was a saint or a devil—or a little of both.

"Yes, commonplace," I whispered.

I had gotten my hair done yesterday on the way home from work, and this morning I stopped by a little Korean run salon for a manicure and pedicure. Lucy, the proprietor, had just put in a new special chair that massaged my back while my feet soaked in warm, swirling water. It's possible these amenities would be available in Athens, but any girl can tell you, when you find someone who does your hair or nails right—you don't experiment. And despite the cute packaging, you only use the soaps or shampoos found in hotel bathrooms as a last resort.

I checked the weather in Greece—it would be hot and sunny, and consistency is good when packing. I picked two very nice outfits by Donna Karan and hung them in the garment bag; I didn't know quite what to expect of the fashion in Athens or who we might meet. I then chose mostly casual clothes, jeans, skirts, tank tops and shorts. I didn't think the hotel in Athens had a pool, but I made sure to include a bathing suit. Next came shoes and accessories. In went my favorite pairs of Manolos and Pradas, and then comfortable flats and sneakers in anticipation of a fair amount of walking. The latter would also serve me if I got the urge and opportunity to jog. Handbags were always more difficult choices, but I picked two: a Fendi for the evening and a leather Birkin by *Hermes*. The latter would easily fit all of my necessities as well as a Michelin guidebook I had purchased for our trip. At the last minute before zipping the suitcase, I tucked in a pair of hiking boots, just in case.

Later that evening, we retired to Ion's room and I sat with him on his bed. He had pulled his comforter up to his chin, as if it were a shield. As he laid his head back into his pillow, I combed away a few locks that had fallen over his eyes.

"Well, my marathoner, rest your limbs tonight; we can plan our trip over breakfast," I said. His eyes fixed upon mine in the soft glow of the room. In them, I could almost see a different person; an ageless soul looking out from the imprisoning mask of an old man. I had never seen such serenity before, not even in Ion. He closed his eyes, but I could tell that he was still awake because a wide smile came across his face like a gentle wave. In its wrinkles I saw the years of agonies and glories that most can only read about. Now a new chapter was about to be written in the land of his ancestors, an epilogue to an already voluminous life.

I closed his door, sure that he had finally fallen asleep, though the smile had not completely faded.

8 HOMEWARD BOUND

Pheidippides took the old mountain road above the village of Elevsis. He had already run more than thirty miles. The late summer days were beginning to shorten, and as twilight approached, he knew he'd soon miss the comforts of the Sun's warmth and the safety of its light. When it had receded, he would navigate by the stars—a skill he had learned from his father—who learned it from his. The ground varied with each step, from soft, dusty earth, to hard, compacted soil, to jagged, buried rock, to loose stones and boulders—all of it serving to jar his pace and rhythm. In some places, short vegetation, grown thick with brambles and sharp thrushes, scraped his legs and bare feet until they bled.

Darkness shrouded him in its black cloak, and the moon was waxing though it had not yet risen over Hellas. He crossed the Korinthian land bridge—the thread onto which the Peloponnese hangs. Here, sailors hauled their ships overland rather than sail around the dreaded Cape Malea.

Manmade fires twinkled against the velvet earth as if it were an enormous black pool reflecting the stars above. He would make his way southwest towards the lion-adorned gates of Mycenae—the city of Agamemnon. Then along the coast until he reached the Plaka River, where a lighthouse atop the rocky outcroppings marked the village of Leonidion. Turning into the heart of Lakonia, he would cross the Parnon Mountains. Should the mountains spare him, he would descend into the valley of the River Eurotas where lived the fiercest warriors of the ancient world.

The day had finally arrived—we were going to Greece.

I would let Ion sleep for another hour. Pouring myself a cup of coffee, I walked out to the backyard and sat down at my garden table. Soon I was daydreaming of the adventure we were about to undertake. Two weeks earlier, I sent Panayiotas a letter letting him know we were coming. I tried to call but had no way of obtaining a telephone number for the monastery. I trusted that he would be heartened by the news of his old friend's return.

The garden was Ion's sanctuary, a place where he could retreat and contemplate the world around him. My workweek is nothing but rushing from place to place, and I cherished spending a few idle moments in peace. I imagined all the new places I was going to with Ion in Greece, and all the time I would have for this kind of contemplation. By the time I looked at the clock again, it was a quarter to eight. I quietly walked upstairs to Ion's bedroom.

The first thing I noticed every time I saw him was how handsome he was; not just for a man of his years, but for a man of any age. He reminded me of Abraham, though I wondered if my father would have aged as well had fate allowed him the years. And though time had humbled Ion's proud posture, his athletic endurance was still obvious in his strength and grace. There seemed no rift between his body and spirit, each forming and informing the other.

Ion's skin had the glorious olive complexion formed by generations of natural selection under the warm Mediterranean sun. His chiseled, angular jaw and aquiline nose completed the picture of his exotic countenance. Framing his weathered face were long flowing curls of hair, turned a majestic shade of white over the decades. These glorious locks rested on his pillow in wild disarray about his head like a halo or like the wind-blown hair of a long-marooned sailor.

"Good morning, Ion, I'm sorry if I woke you." Long ago I had painted the room a light shade of periwinkle with navy blue wallpaper below the chair rail. Prints of suns and moons replete with faces floated below the crown and ceiling of trompe l'oeil clouds. I had special plantation shutters put on the inside of his windows, so the room was still dim, even though the sun had now flooded the rest of the house with light.

"My dear, I would curse my waking if not for the fortune of opening my eyes to see you standing here." It made be blush. I believed he actually meant it and that he saw beauty in me that I had ceased to see in myself. Though I was less than half his age, he made me feel half mine.

In his own way, Ion Theodore was very elegant. He never had much money to treat himself to expensive clothes. but the limitations of his means never prevented him from dressing with style. Today, he picked out a tan button-down shirt with dark brown slacks and a beige glen-plaid sports coat. I helped him put on a dark pair of woolen socks, over which I slid his leather sandals. I wondered if I had ever seen Ion in anything but bare feet or sandals. Somehow, these just seemed to suit him perfectly. One last touch—he went over to his dresser and pulled out a silken ascot from the top drawer. Ion loved ascots, and he looked, as the English might say, "absolutely smashing" in one.

Everything about him was attractive, though our relationship was and only could be Platonic. It's not that I ever considered him for a lover—I was seduced by something more transcendent. But such labels are only for the sake of outsiders looking in; they are worthless to those who actually experience.

I telephoned Vivian, the woman in the neighborhood who would pick up my mail and generally keep an eye on my house. I lived closer to a dozen other families but I rarely saw them, except when they pulled in and out of their garages in expensive automobiles or came out to yell at their gardeners. My immediate neighbor's first words to me after I moved in concerned an old garden wall protruding fourteen inches over their property line—painfully reducing their ability to enjoy their two-acre property. So much for welcome-baskets.

The taxi picked us up at four o'clock. I left plenty of time, anticipating traffic on the Van Wyck Expressway. Having been on that roadway at every conceivable time of day or year, I can authoritatively tell you that *Van Wyck* is Dutch for *parking lot*. Ion and I made our way to our gate in Terminal One. A few minutes after we had arrived, a noisy group of young teenagers appeared. They were accompanied by three adults, one of whom sat next to me. His lengthy sigh of relief told me that he was having a long day.

"Excuse me, I was wondering if these kids are part of a school trip?" I asked him. He appeared to be in his mid-forties and was dressed in jeans with a button-down shirt and tweed sports jacket.

"Yes we are. These students were in my Ancient History class last semester."

"Is this part of the curriculum, or just vacation?"

"A little of both," he smiled. "The 'cover story' that we tell the parents is that it's a chance for the kids to visit some of the places we studied, but everyone knows it's a little adventure in freedom. By the way, I'm Adam, Adam Gittleman," he said as he reached out his hand.

"I'm Marianna Gardner, and this is my uncle, Ion Theodore," I said as I shook his hand. He let his palm linger in my grasp for an extra moment or two as his rich, brown eyes caught mine.

"Mr. Theodore, it's a pleasure to meet you sir," he said as he got up to stand in front of Ion who returned his smile and a shake of his hand.

"I overheard that you are a teacher."

"I am."

"And your colleagues?"

"We're all from the Dalton School. That's Sue Walker," Adam pointed to a woman who was still at the counter talking to one of the agents, "She's our Art History teacher. We're also traveling with Robert Shaw, the head of our History Department."

"Are they on our trip, too?" asked one of the students near Adam.

"No, I just met Mr. Theodore and Mrs. Gardner."

"It's 'Miss,' but please call me Marianna." I hate that awkward moment, whether or not it comes from someone with an agenda to ascertain if I'm *available*. There was a brief period when I used the prefix "Ms.," but all that did was confirm that I was single *and* harbored an attitude.

"I'd love to get a few things from sundries shop I saw on the way to our gate," I said to Ion as I stood up and slung my handbag over my shoulder. "Will you be all right if I leave you here alone for a few minutes?"

"Of course, my dear, not to worry," Ion replied.

"I'll keep your uncle company," Adam interjected. "Mr. Theodore, your name sounds Greek. Were you born there, or perhaps you're of Greek ancestry?"

"Both. But I have spent the majority of my life here in New York."

"Leave him with me, Marianna. A native Greek and an aficionado of Hellenic culture—I'm sure we'll be just fine."

When I strolled back about fifteen minutes later, I could see that the scene had changed. Sitting in a semi-circle at Ion's feet were six or seven of the students.

"True, they produced some of the greatest math and science ever imagined, but they did so with the keenest sense of aesthetics." I heard Ion saying, immediately realizing that he was speaking of his ancestors. "They were obsessed with the notion of golden ratios, proportions of geometric shapes which projected the ideal harmony to the human eye," he continued, with an unmistakable sound of pride in his voice, "Children, *the stamp of Greece is on all the art and all the thought of the Western World*. Nowhere else was there ever a more perfect union between art and science—neither of which can be created in the absence of the other. Their temples defy an engineer's logic while tempting the eye's desire. The Gods may have formed the Earth but the Greeks made it beautiful."

I smiled and said to Ion, "I can see it's not safe to leave you alone for just a few minutes. What are you doing to these poor kids? It's their summer vacation."

"Speaking of schools, thanks for not mentioning that your uncle taught at Horace Mann. I had a chance to impress him with how much less I know about my subject than he does," Adam laughed.

"Sorry. I thought you'd get a kick out of finding out for yourself."

"Ladies and gentlemen, in a few minutes we will begin general boarding for Olympic Airlines flight number 701 bound for Athens, Greece," came the announcement. "At this time, we'd like to board only those passengers traveling with infants or those needing special assistance..."

I wasn't going to say anything about Ion needing special assistance, but he said to me, "Let us show our enthusiasm by being the first to board tonight."

I helped Ion to his feet and we walked slowly towards the gate. I could see him acknowledge with a smile and slight bow of his head the two women who checked our boarding passes. His gaze soon focused beyond them and down the blue-carpeted tunnel. It bent to the left as if to suggest another road or another possibility but there was only one path here. He broke free of my grasp. It was not with any sudden or violent gesture but with the sure and powerful acceleration of a man focused on his goal. He walked ahead of me, revitalized like a long-distance runner on his final lap—already smelling the pungent leaves of the olive wreath.

I resisted my impulse to catch up to him. He seemed to stand taller and move with more swiftness and grace than I had seen in our time together.

I watched as his solitary figure approached the portal ahead. Before passing into the plane, he glanced back. I assumed that it was at me, but he looked as if he were gesturing farewell to someone behind me. I looked but saw no one.

He turned and in a few swift steps had disappeared.

Ion Theodore had left the New World behind.

9
THE ODYSSEY

Pheidippides would set his eyes upon some sight a half-mile away. To reach that spot—that was all he had to do. Nothing else mattered, no other destination existed. Once attained, he would identify the next spot and the next. He imagined himself running, not over rock-strewn mountains, but across the endless golden wheat fields and fragrant eucalyptus groves of Elysium.

"Where is Elysium?" the Young Pupil asked the Ancient Narrator. "Is it the next village Pheidippides will reach?"

"My child, Elysium is a land that exists at the farthest edge of the world at the limit of the deep-running ocean—well beyond the great Pillars of Herakles. No one can travel there by foot or by ship. Only the Gods can lift a spirit there after breath has left the body—and only if that person is worthy."

"To go there you must die?" The Young Pupil asked.

"We must all cross over from this life someday. The only one who must fear death is the man who has not lived."

As Pheidippides left sight of his compatriots in the Plains of Marathonas, he thought of her—of Leontia. He knew that he was not yet worthy of Elysium.

The Olympic Airlines 747 roared down the runway and leapt into the sky like a magnificent blue and white bird of prey, her talon-like landing gear retracting below outstretched wings as she soared upwards. The Captain banked sharply to the left and steered out over the choppy waves of the steel-gray Atlantic. I felt both the constraint of being pressed back into my seat and the exhilaration of release as the plane continued its steep ascent.

Soon, beneath us, lay the rocky coast of Newfoundland and the cold, dark waters of the North Atlantic. I imagined the breakers crashing ceaselessly against the shore as we floated safely above the warring elements. The rugged cliffs receded beyond my line of sight, leaving nothing but boundless water—broken only by cresting white caps, which danced across its surface.

As the plane soared and the cabin filled with the hum of the engines, I could hear the ever so slight click-clack of the ebony beads. My eyes drifted down to Ion's hands. They were spotted and gnarled from age and arthritis, but still strong and supple, as though ready in a moment to wield a chisel against recalcitrant marble or to caress soft clay into form. The worry beads—or *komboloi* as they are known to centuries of Greeks—were strung together on a loop of silk thread. Resting between the thumb and index finger of his right hand, a barely perceptible motion made them break into rhythm. It was a rhythm that measured the slightest tolling of fear under the self-assured drone of the great engines.

"It's hard to believe that something so heavy floats above the clouds," he whispered.

"I know what you mean," I nodded and left it at that. Ion looked anxious and I didn't want to make light of it. I was amused though, that such a rational man—a man who understood the scientific principles behind our flight—would be so unnerved. I suppose once you internalize the fate of Daedalus, flying can never be a simple matter.

"Whatever our mode of transportation, are we ever satisfied with where we are? I have discovered that no matter how far we wander, or how fast we get there, we long for home," he finished his train of thought.

"Ladies and Gentlemen, this is Captain Jiavaris speaking. I'd like to welcome you aboard Olympic Airlines this evening for our non-stop flight to

Athens. Our flight path this evening will take us out over across the Arctic Circle passing over Greenland. We will then head southeast over the British Isles and continental Europe, entering Greek airspace near the Island of Corfu."

"Corfu is beautiful," Ion said. "She rises out of the Ionian Sea like a shield lying on the misty face of the water—dutifully guarding the northwestern gateway to Greece and the cradle of Western Civilization."

Soon enough I felt the plane leveling at its cruising altitude in perfect equilibrium between heaven and earth. I was indulging myself in the perfumed pages of *Cosmopolitan* and its media driven images of youth and beauty. I had picked up this magazine because I wanted something easy to look at without the intensity of *Barrons* or the politics of *Time* or *Newsweek.*

I couldn't help being made self-conscious by Ion's gaze. I tried to hide the cover and its announcement of yet another discovery about female orgasms. What would he think of me, this man of grace and learning, indulging my vanities and neuroses in the gloss of mass therapy? Was it condescending of me to think that because he was now so old that he knew little of women or of vanity?

"These models are so young—and thin!" I said with a little disdain, attempting to distance myself from the magazine. "I can remember as a young girl seeing them as sophisticated women. Now, I'm old enough to be their mother."

"They do not compare to you, my dear. And in my years I have seen enough of beauty and its mimics for you to trust my judgment."

"My dear," Ion turned to me, "I hate to trouble you so soon after take-off, but…"

"That's fine," I interrupted him. After living under the same roof for some time now, I could anticipate his needs.

We sat in the window and middle seats in a row of three. I turned to the passenger on my left who occupied the aisle seat. When we boarded, I had hoped that we would have the row to ourselves. Right before the attendant had closed the door I saw a stately, elegant woman enter the plane and head for our row. Despite almost having missed the flight, she was the epitome of calm, virtually floating into her seat as though she knew it was meant for her.

I guessed her to be in her late fifties; she had the definite appearance of a woman of means. She wore a camel-colored hand-stitched suit over a cashmere sweater and a pair of golden brown snake-skinned pumps. Around her neck was tied a blue and gold *Hermes* scarf. She was so impeccably dressed for our midnight passage that I wondered if she had come from a formal dinner party or was on her way to an important business meeting in Athens. On her right hand, which rested on our shared armrest, she wore two rings. One bore some sort of insignia, the other was an antique wedding ring set in gold. A wall of silence had remained between us for the first half hour of the flight, but now I needed to break that silence.

"Excuse me," I said, "We need to..."

"Adonia," I heard her say as I felt the simultaneous presence of her right hand on top of my wrist. "Adonia Stavropoulos. I insist that you call me Adonia," she smiled, and quickly got to her feet.

"Beautiful Lady," I heard Ion from my right, astonished at his sudden interest in this woman and the apparent forwardness of his statement. I turned to him and must have looked perplexed.

"*Adonia*—it means *beautiful lady*," he said to me, and then, looking across me at Adonia. "Your parents showed great foresight."

"Kind of you to say, but it was more hope than foresight."

"Their hopes had the ears of the Gods."

She turned to me and whispered but not too softly, "By any chance does he have a brother?"

"Regrettably he's an only child," I told her, cracking a smile.

I went to retrieve a few extra blankets. When I returned, Adonia and Ion were conversing in Greek. After removing his sandals and taking a few minutes to carefully wrap his legs and feet, I also draped a blanket around his shoulders, while making sure his air-conditioning vent was off.

"Are you sure you're comfortable?"

"My dear, what is the minor discomfort of one night's travel when compared to the ecstasy of returning home? A thousand such nights could not deter me from this journey."

I knew there was more to it than the simple sounds of a homecoming that Ion had chosen to categorize it with. There was something. Something there in the hamlet of Marathon. Something buried in the heart of a dying priest that still denied him the peace he sought.

Just when Ion seemed as if he might drift off to sleep, we were confronted with the confusion of in-flight dinner service.

"Chicken or lamb?" came the inevitable question. At 32,000 feet over the Polar Ice, one's epicurean choices are quite limited. We both chose the chicken. I watched Ion gracefully tuck his napkin into his shirt, and set himself to organizing his platter. Ion always observed the most impeccable manners even under the most casual of circumstances. He was fumbling, trying to get the silverware out of its plastic bag and my attention drifted again to his hands. I watched them trembling slightly as he struggled. It saddened me to watch him exert such effort over such a once simple task. The thought of his hands and the beauty of what they had created highlighted the injustice of ageing. He had the hands of an artist, a sculptor. From mere lumps of clay, they had crafted whole worlds and had animated countenances, and breathed souls into lifeless matter.

I waited as long as I could before I finally reached over and said, "Let me help you with that. They make these things so hard to open."

"My dear, just when my mind has matured enough to be able to do something useful with my life, my body has decided to drift into early retirement," he said with a mildly sardonic grin.

Ion touched my hand. "I am so very excited," he said.

"So am I, so am I."

"Was it difficult for you to get the time off on such short notice?"

"Not at all," I lied. Ion already thought that my working at SWB was an affront to my dignity, so I didn't want to tell him of my altercation with Steve.

"I'm glad."

"Glad about what?" I replied.

"Glad that it was no problem getting the time off," he said and I wondered for a moment whether I had been talking out loud.

"You're lucky you don't have to answer to anyone."

"My dear, we all have a boss. Mine counts the days until my final resignation," he said with a smile.

I did not like to think about Ion's death. Though it was as inevitable as the trees shedding their autumn leaves, I wanted our summer to last forever.

"Ion, my guess is that you have cheated Death so many times, he is weary of you," I said, trying to keep these thoughts light-hearted.

"Yes, indeed I have, haven't I?" he laughed. "But I can't indefinitely postpone my appointment in *Samarra*."

"What appointment?"

"It's an ancient tale of a potter who lived in Baghdad. One day, as he was selling his wares in the marketplace, he spotted Death. Not knowing for whom

Death searched, but wishing to avoid any contact with him, the potter quickly packed up his goods, mounted his horse and rode north as fast as he could toward the village of Samarra. When Death asked a nearby merchant what had caused the potter to flee in such haste, the bystander nervously replied, 'Great Prince of Darkness, your presence instills dread in the hearts of men. Perhaps he thought it safer to be far from you.' To that, Death responded, 'How unnecessary, he had nothing to fear here in Baghdad. I do have a rendezvous, but my appointment is later this evening—in Samarra.'"

I realized that my anxiety over Ion's parting was also a mask for my own fear of mortality.

"I guess we're afraid of death because it is unknown," I said.

"Ah, yes, the irrefutable paradox: death is certain and it is certainly unknown," Ion was at play in the field of our greatest fear. "I see Death as the threshold of another adventure in a longer journey—all the more exciting for being unknown."

"May I take those?" came the welcomed voice of the flight attendant as she finally had come to collect our trays.

"I don't know about you, but I thought that food left plenty to be desired," I said to Ion, who was carefully folding the napkin that had rested on his lap.

"My dear, it is better than the food of a slave," he said. It sounded somewhat humorous, but I knew his words shielded an experience that was anything but funny. It was difficult for me to confront the evil, which had once imprisoned him, and I felt compelled from time to time to tell Ion how sorry I was for what had happened.

"Sorry? Why? Remembering is one thing. But self-pity, any pity revivifies the work of the cruel."

Had I taken my freedom for granted? Had I vigorously defended it against all forms of erosion, or had I allowed my own life to slip into a form of bondage. Ion always told me that not only did one need to be free *from* bondage but that in order to remain free, we had to be free *for* something.

I was deeply touched by the pain Ion must have endured but I was yet more humbled by the fact that he never diminished the importance of my own anxieties. And what was even more moving was the fact that he never invoked the enormity of his personal struggle as the measure of any human suffering. What were my stresses but the results of a life lived too easily, an abundance of luxury and freedoms without responsibility—or the true knowledge of how these things had been earned?

"It pains me so to think of that time," I said, knowing that my response tonight would be no more adequate than it was on every other occasion.

"My dear, who knows what path I may have chosen had I been born in comfort or affluence? Perhaps I would have lived an empty existence; maybe I never would have become a teacher, or met you."

I felt myself blush at the power of fine-hammered thought, but also I shuddered at the fact that he was not being merely charming in underscoring the possibility that we may never have met. I caressed his hand, and felt the warmth of his statement. I wasn't really sure what to say, but the only thought that came out was, "But what a great price to pay."

"Yes, it once seemed great. But one moment with you makes it fade into the twilight of distant memory."

"Have you ever written these stories?" I asked him.

"No," he said almost emphatically.

"Never? Not even for yourself?"

"I once kept journals. It was nothing really—foolish scribblings."

"They're probably fascinating. I'd love to read them."

"I lost them a long time ago."

"Lost them? You must have been devastated."

"What is most precious is often lost." It troubled me that such a credo had become part of his expectation.

I could see that Ion's eyes had grown heavy. I propped a few pillows on the side of his head after pulling down the shade so that he could lean comfortably against the window. He spoke in a barely audible whisper as he seemed to float back to our earlier conversation.

"Remember, though men can subjugate other men by force—no man can ever own the soul of another..." Ion said as I watched his eyes close. At that moment, I knew that the Gods had special plans for Ion.

Though born a slave, he was not destined to die one.

10 THROUGH THE EYES OF A STRANGER

"I never was, am always to be. No one ever saw me, nor ever will. And yet I am the confidence of all who live and breathe on this terrestrial ball. Who am I?" asked the Ancient Narrator.

"I do not know the answer," responded the Young Pupil, "who are you?"

"I am tomorrow."

Pheidippides thought about tomorrow and the audience he would seek with Kings Leonidas and Cleomenes. He had passed the great Argive Plain, and was far down the coast. The pain had become so intense and so unrelenting that it numbed his ability to sense it. He pondered how he had taken such a simple thing like the rising sun for granted. Now, it meant everything in the world to him.

"What other great gifts have I treated with such apathy? A soft place to sleep? A long, unhurried drink of water? What treasures I would trade for just these few things." But he knew that there was someone else that had prompted such reflection. One whose love he had taken and not returned.

"Alas, Pheidippides, now is the time to think only of the next footstep, the next sunrise, and tomorrow in Sparta."

I watched Ion drift deeper into sleep. My eyes caught the slow rise and fall of his chest. I stared at him like an anxious mother watches each breath of her newborn; terrified of the fine line between sleep and death. Each breath meant more time with this extraordinary man, yet each was also slowly dissipating his life. As the mists of old age settle, we inevitably return to a state of need. The metamorphosis back to the cocoon is made more bitter by the knowledge of this diminishing independence. After a life devoted to enabling and ennobling freedom, it is worrisome that we should end up bound to others for the simplest mobility and facility of bodily functions.

I was so consumed with my thoughts that I hadn't noticed Adonia getting up to leave her seat, but my attention was drawn to her as she returned. She walked with the air of a woman who was accustomed to having attention lavished upon her precisely because she seemed indifferent to it. Her pronounced features exuded strength without overpowering her delicateness, and the wrinkles etched around her eyes highlighted their warm confidence. Her deep brunette hair unabashedly displayed a solitary streak of silver. It appeared less a sign of surrender to the changes of time than a banner of triumph for a life well lived. I was to be drawn to her. She embodied a spirit of possibility that I admired and on some level, envied.

"Are you and your husband on vacation?" she broke our silence.

"Husband?"

"Oh, I'm sorry, you two seem so much in love."

"He's old enough to be my father with an extra score thrown in," I responded, surprised that she could think that and perplexed at the way it made me feel.

"And that should preclude love?"

"But, I hardly think it's likely given..."

"Husband, soul mate, lover—words, words, words. What is likely and what is true are not always the same. And your passion is true and unmistakable."

Was she a loon or a sage? Clearly, this woman had no patience for society's repressions. She not only ignored the rules of the game—she had the audacity to create new rules and new games. That made her seductive but also dangerous. I decided to follow her alluring voice whether it lead to enlightened discourse or the boredom of interminable conversation. But I couldn't shake the curiosity of why she had thought that? But then again why should I care? She knew nothing about me, or so I presumed.

"He's a dear friend of my family," I answered in an attempt to acknowledge her while deflecting my own diffidence.

"Why do you travel to Greece together?"

"It's a long story," I said.

"It's a long flight," was her answer.

I was flustered by what the eyes of this stranger had seen.

"My ex-husband seemed to live on a plane," I said in another attempted diversion, and then was surprised that I had revealed more about myself than I had intended.

"Well, you seem to have made quite an improvement."

"Improvement? In what?"

"In travel companions."

"I'm still surprised that you thought he was my...husband," I said, immediately unsure of what my question might reveal.

"Are you embarrassed at the thought of loving someone twice your age? I suppose I too would have been once. But the love of my life flew in the face of all expectations and all odds."

"Well, you know the way society is."

"Didn't the great American Thoreau say, 'follow the beat of a different drummer, no matter how measured or far away'? I can sense his sweetness and power," Adonia said about Ion with unexpected candor. I sensed her unmistakable attraction for Ion. And though she was off base, I felt an inexplicable jealousy at her unabashed ability to express her feelings.

"I noticed earlier that you two conversed in your native tongue."

"I had asked him where he was from. When I said that Limnos was terrifically hot this time of year, he said that the memory of his island still burned in his soul."

"Did he say why?"

"He wouldn't elaborate."

"That's odd. I wonder why?"

"Imprisoned in each of our hearts is one story too awful to tell but too painful to keep shackled in silence."

"I'm afraid I've written a few chapters of that book," I said.

"I see. I think then we have much to say to each other."

At that moment I was thankful I had been deprived of the luxury of an empty aisle seat.

"Adonia, I would love to stretch my legs for a few minutes. Would you join me for some conversation and coffee?"

"Make it tea and you're on," she answered cheerfully. We slipped inside the galley—its closed curtains created a cozy little oasis to carry on our conversation. Standing was already easing the stress in my neck and shoulders.

"To what does Ion owe such a blessing?" She asked as we stood face to face for the first time.

"In what way?"

"To command your solitary devotion. One could easily imagine that a woman as beautiful as you would have…"

"Let me guess, a husband?"

"Well, yes. It does strike me as…"

"Odd that I am not married? It's not all it's cracked up to be," I said, and then regretted.

"I'm sure you must have some Greek in you," she said, navigating around what was still a sensitive subject.

"Not really, but I'm flattered that you'd think that."

"It's just something in your eyes, and the fact that you are very beautiful—but I am biased. You have not told me why you have embarked on such a trip. A vacation?" she said with the hesitation that let me know she doubted it was.

"Hardly. Though I'm hoping to sightsee a bit. I've never been to Greece."

"It is said that to know Greece takes a lifetime—to fall in love with her takes but an instant."

"I can't believe I waited so long."

"And why now?"

"It's Ion. We're going to visit an infirmed friend, a priest."

"Lost touch?"

"I don't believe they've spoken for years. There was some sort of falling out, probably over a woman. And now the priest has decided to come clean before he dies."

"The intrigue of it!"

"Yes, it's shaping up to be an epic tale. A couple of guys showed up in my office last month and told me about some ancient guy who was buried without his obol. Seems he's still wandering the earth searching for it."

"I hope he finds it."

"Don't tell me you..."

"What? Believe that spirits survive the flesh? Perhaps."

"I know the Greeks take great pride in their history but those old stories are just stories."

"It's not just a matter of story versus history. It's a vision that informs how you see and, most of all, how you act."

"So you believe some of those ancient myths?"

"What do you mean by myth?" she asked me with a smile.

"A story that isn't true."

"What's true? Science can go very far, it can pile up a multitude of 'what,' 'when' and 'hows' but never, ever a 'why.' And when knowing that one 'why' becomes more important than all the rest, then you may find that these myths hold great truths."

"The more I try, the farther I seem from discovery. Frankly, I'm not even sure what I'm searching for."

"It is not just *where* we look, but *how*. You must not be afraid to try new ways to discover what may lie right before your eyes."

"You are very wise," I said.

She laughed at my words and then added, with self-effacing levity, "Time has helped me accumulate a little wisdom but it hasn't eclipsed my vanity. I wouldn't mind being less wise in a younger body."

Returning to my seat, I gazed over Ion and out the window. Moonlight illuminated the wing of our craft. I could see the moon and only one star, or perhaps it was a planet. The hard metallic edge of our wing was the only other object visible in the night sky.

I imagined the plane almost still, floating in this envelope between earth and space. So many times in my life I had wanted to make time stand still, to stop the world around me, to take a deep breath and sort things out.

Soon the gentle vibration of the engines was slowly having its hypnotic effect on me. All was silent except for the rush of air coursing through the plane's turbines, tirelessly working to help keep the plane aloft and flying towards Greece.

11
A PRICE TOO STEEP

When Pheidippides was a boy, an approaching army of Spartans threatened Nonakris. He was not sure what caused the dispute, but he knew the consequences should his village surrender or be defeated. He begged his father not to go as the older man put on his bronze armor.

"If ever you must face a Spartan—never show your fear. Show courage and you will earn their respect," his father admonished.

"What if you are wounded... Or killed?"

"Remember my son: pain is brief—glory eternal." Pheidippides could still imagine his father carrying his magnificent wood and bronze shield as he left their home.

Spartans were rarely bested, but that day they were forced to withdraw. Pheidippides watched the triumphant warriors of Nonakris return. His chest burned when he could not make out his father amongst them.

Idomeneus had brought back his father's shield. He told Pheidippides that his father's dying words were of him, calling Pheidippides—DORO TON THEON—a gift of the Gods.

Pheidippides knew that his anger must remain buried on the field where his father fell, but as he approached the den of the Lacedaemons, old wounds felt newly opened.

Several jolts of turbulence brought me back from my much-needed nap. The jarring of the plane made me instinctively look to make sure Ion was all right, but it seemed to have no effect on him. Perhaps it was a gift of old age, to be able to filter out extraneous sound and motion.

For me, however, the next few minutes were nerve-racking. I was far from a seasoned traveler, and I abhorred the feeling of free-fall as if we were a snow flake tossed about in a winter squall. Fortunately, it abated quickly, and we settled back into our harmonious flight, though my hopes for some restful sleep had been dashed.

I felt as if I had been on the plane longer than I actually had. I'd like to add a corollary to Einstein's Theory of Relativity. I'll humbly call it *Marianna's Law*: Time slows proportionately to the square of the number of times you look at your watch.

Unbuckling, I carefully climbed over Adonia's legs while she slept soundly. Before we had left the galley, she had given me her address and phone number. I hoped that the possibility of seeing her again was more than just polite chatter. I had thrown out so many similar pieces of paper over the years.

I made my way slowly aft. In the dim light of the cabin, I could make out the face of a man looking at me. It was Adam. I looked around and saw his students lying in the most awkward positions imaginable in vain attempts to get comfortable. He offered me his seat, but I told him I'd rather stand.

"I'd love to stretch for a bit too. Mind some company?" he asked politely.

"Not at all," I said, but I was just being polite. I wasn't in the mood for conversation at this ungodly hour.

"Ion told me that you were an attorney."

"Yes, I'm a partner at Schroeder, Wilkes & Barron."

"In a Jewish family, do you know what they call the son who becomes a lawyer?" he asked.

"No, what?"

"The kid who can't stand the sight of blood." I laughed. "Do you know what they call the son who becomes a teacher?" he continued.

"Okay, I give. What?"

"Adopted."

We stood in a vestibule at the rear of the plane. There was no one else stirring.

"That turbulence woke me up," I offered.

"Sailors hate it. I was reading about it in my *Fodor's Guide*. It's the *bora*—a north wind that whips up the Ionian into a mean and battered sea as a reminder of Poseidon's wrath. Seamen still pay homage to him for a safe journey across these waters."

"He's still pissed over Odysseus killing his son, the Cyclops."

"Could I be dreaming? Can it be that I have met a woman who is not only stunning, but has such knowledge on the tip of her tongue," he said to me with a genuine look of amazement in his eyes.

"You would be overestimating me, in both categories. You just happened to choose a story that Ion's told me many times."

"I'm still astounded, but I thought that he taught art."

I laughed. "My uncle teaches life, he just happened to be in the Art Department. He's done so many things. Poet, choreographer, artist, teacher, champion marathoner."

"Great, I finally meet a nice girl and she lives with a man who is a combination of Achilles, Aristotle and Aeschylus."

"I have no doubt that you do all right with the ladies." I was quite taken aback that I had said that.

"Well, my ex-wife didn't think so."

"How long were you married?"

"Almost fifteen years."

"Whew," I said with a little whistle, "that's a long time. What happened?"

"Irreconcilable differences."

"That's quite a diplomatic answer."

"I'm over the anger, dammit," he said with a wink. "It was really over years earlier, but for the sake of our daughter, we stayed together. Here, let me show you a picture of her," Adam said, as he reached into his wallet for a small photo. It looked like a high school graduation picture. "She's a senior at Columbia University. She made the Dean's List last semester."

"She's beautiful, Adam. You must have married very young."

"We were just kids. She was working in Boston while I was in graduate school at M.I.T."

"M.I.T? Is that where you studied ancient history?"

"No," he chuckled, "I would have been stoned to death had I majored in history there. I was at the Sloan School of Business."

"I'm a little confused..."

"Before teaching, I was an investment banker with Morgan Stanley—M & A."

"It doesn't get any better than Morgan Stanley."

"So I've heard. But I grew to hate it. The problem wasn't the firm or the money—both were great."

"Then what was it?"

"The pain in my chest as I lay in bed. My ex thought it was in my mind—it probably was. Perhaps if I had a real heart attack, it would have been easier for her to understand. But I felt trapped. First there was the mortgage, and then the private school, then the Olds and the Chevy became a Jaguar and a Lexus SUV. I made just enough money to fear losing my job, but never enough to be free of it. They don't teach you that in B-school. It's a vicious cycle for which there is no endgame, or as we say in investment banking—no *exit strategy*."

"You walked away from Morgan Stanley to become a teacher?" I was starting to think that either Ion had slipped Adam a fifty to tell me this story or I was far from alone in having doubts about my corporate slice of the American Dream. Still, Morgan Stanley!

"My wife was just as astonished as you, but her astonishment turned to bitterness."

"But you were so successful..."

"At what? Did I cure cancer? Did I write a book that changed people's lives? Did I give an elderly man a loving home? Try none of the above. All I did was make more money than most people. I know that I touch my student's lives—I know that I make a difference. I want that to be my legacy."

"Still, it seems a steep price to pursue a dream."

"What is a dream worth?" he asked. "So many late nights at Morgan, I dined with strangers talking about mergers instead of helping my daughter with her homework or going to her recitals. That price was too steep."

"No regrets?" I asked.

"Just one—that I didn't see my true path sooner."

We took turns looking out through the small circular window in the rear emergency exit door. The entire horizon, from the sky above, to the edge of the distant clouds, glowed with blue light—from darkest cobalt to brilliant indigo to a thin cusp of almost white cerulean. The sun rises earlier from 39,000 feet above the earth so I was treated to a dawn that no one below me could yet see. As the first rays of yellow chased away the blues of night, I could make out traces of a jet stream. It must have passed us in the dark going to where we had been. There were no other signs of human life here. All was sea and sky. To the east lay a thick blanket of clouds, which pulled up across the horizon like a down comforter.

Soon, immense rocky outcroppings pierced the glittering surface of the deep blue waters below, breaking its smooth plane, as the Ionian Islands came into view. The shores seemed to rise vertically out of the sea, broken in some places by coves and stretches of beaches. I imagined the days when seamen navigated by the stars and kept constant vigil for squalls and rugged coastlines. I wondered how many of them lay entombed in watery graves below, their bones warped black by the sea.

As the sun slowly rose, its light danced on the water's surface—shimmering and glittering as if it were being sprinkled with embers from a burning fire. The wakes of boats cut white streaks across the textured water like frozen images of shooting stars.

When I got back to my seat Ion was still sleeping. We raced east across the vast Peloponnese. So often he spoke of the fragrant olive and eucalyptus groves, bright turquoise waters, sun swept beaches and majestic mountains of his native land. He left Greece, but Greece never left him.

There was something else quite extraordinary in his heritage. His life had a depth beyond that which could be explained by his age and the breadth of his experience. Echoing from the distant past, his ancestors seemed to come to him when he needed inspiration the most. I envied his lineage, his ability to be connected with something so steeped in tradition and so lasting—especially in a world where everything was increasingly fleeting.

The darkened recesses of row 32 had become a little cocoon in which we huddled together, safe from the winds that howled around us. And though our cocoon was surrounded by several hundred other passengers, when I was with Ion, it was easy to feel oblivious to all others.

I watched him closely. I could see the faintest traces of his legs twitching, as if in motion, and I was sure that he was running in a landscape of his mind's creation. Did he see himself once again as a young man in these nocturnal visions? I could imagine his body glistening beneath the blazing sun, hair flowing behind him like plumes of black fire as his resplendent muscles carried him aloft but for the fleeting touches of sole to ground—in defiance of gravity itself.

And was I there, with him, in his dreams?
I knew he was often in mine.

12
THE GATES OF SPARTA

During the night, Arcadia's dry, rocky terrain became a cold and barren wilderness. For nearly thirty hours, Pheidippides had no rest and no shelter. At the mercy of the elements, he was absolutely alone. He knew that to give in now to the temptation to stop, even for a moment, was to concede that he was finished.

The ground beneath his feet gradually steepened as the crest of Parnon reflected the rays of the impending dawn. Whatever fear he felt about its painful slope was mitigated by the joy that the sun was approaching.

He finally reached the base of Parnon at the first golden light of dawn. A steep spinal ridge running from the Alps to the very tip of Lakonia, it is the southernmost protrusion of the Balkan Massif. Just over that ridge, a formidable limestone formation rising 6,300 feet above sea level, lay the green valley of the Eurotas River. Beyond that—the Gates of Sparta.

"Ladies and Gentlemen, this is your Captain speaking. We've begun our initial descent. Air traffic over Hellenikon Airport is light this morning. We should have you on the ground in about twenty minutes."

When I turned to wake Ion, I was pleasantly surprised to find that he was already awake, and was looking at me. No matter how much I tried to care for him, somehow I always had this feeling that it was I who was being looked after. His first words were the compassionate, "I hope he is not suffering."

Olympic Airlines Flight 701 roared out of the heavens towards the fast-approaching tarmac. Plumes of smoke disbursed wildly as her sixteen enormous tires met the ground. Her wings flapped open to slow us down. I loosened my grip on the arms of my seat only when I felt the plane's motion reduced to a nice comfortable speed.

Ion and I waited for the other passengers to retrieve their carry-on luggage and make their way slowly down the packed aisles. I struggled with my shoes. My feet seemed to have expanded by two sizes during the flight. I could see Ion laugh at me in his good-natured way as he summed up my predicament, one that would never befall a sandal-wearer.

"Let us rejoice in our homecoming," said Ion as he stretched in the aisle and made his way forward.

"You mean 'your' homecoming, Ion. I'm a tourist here. I'm glad you slept. You managed to miss a very bad movie and several patches of turbulence."

"At my age, child, the difference between wake and sleep begins to blur."

"I'm looking forward to meeting Father Kyriazis."

"I do not know anyone more faithful to God and more favored in return."

"How did you meet him?"

"It was a few years after World War II, but war did not end for the Greeks on V-E Day as it did for the Americans. There were bitter enmities formed during the years of conflict. Factions of collaborators, freedom fighters and communists wreaked vengeance on each other and on the innocent during a period of violent anarchy. There was famine, disease and misery. I was in Athens with a group of Greco-American volunteers. Panayiotas was finishing his Theological studies. We met during a Red Cross blood drive. It was a time of overwhelming suffering and sacrifice in which I saw the best and the worst of what man can be."

"What brought you two to Marathon?"

"Panayiotas had just had been assigned to the Church of Panteleimon and he invited me to come for a very special baptism."

"Really? Whose?"

"Mine."

"Passports and immigration cards please," requested the young officer with professional efficiency. He seemed to be in his early thirties and obviously took his job seriously.

"Where are you traveling from?" he continued, in decent English.

"From New York," I replied.

The officer loosened up as he looked at Ion. "Ah, America! I have unfortunately not been there yet, but I have sister who is going to university in Boston. Is not far from New York, I think? Are you travel in Greece for business or pleasure?"

"Pleasure." He opened my passport. All was in order, and he stamped it on its very first page.

"Excellent, I am sure you will find Greece a rewarding place to visit. It is extremely rich in history and culture," he continued. "And where will you be staying?"

"At the Hotel Plaka in Athens."

"Mmm, this is very interesting." At first I thought he was referring to my choice of hotel, but then I noticed he was studying Ion's passport intently, flipping back and forth through its pages.

"Is there some problem officer?" I asked politely.

"I'm afraid so," the officer replied, with the uneasiness of a man who did not want to be the bearer of bad tidings. "Would you both please to come with me?" I anxiously followed him into a small office used by Immigration Control.

The officer sat on the edge of a large metal desk and continued, "Sir, I am noticing many immigration stamps—you are traveling to Greece much over the years. A problem is I am seeing some from 1950's. It seems that your passport has expired for long time. I am surprised they did not stop you in New York."

"Expired? What does this mean to us?"

"I must to inform you that you will not enter Greece."

I had been so busy getting everything ready for our trip that I had overlooked the most obvious item of preparation.

"We'll go to the U.S. Consulate," I said with a distinct note of desperation in my voice.

"It is not so simple. To get to embassy, he must first enter sovereign Greek territory. Without valid passport, this is not possible."

"But what if a tourist had lost their passport; hasn't that happened before?" My stress level was rising. To be this close and fail was a frustration of indescribable proportions.

"Madam, this happen many time," the officer replied, being even more courteous than before—I could tell that he was deriving no pleasure from what he was telling me. "But is not same. When happen, visitors are already legally in Greece. Must go to consulate before departure."

"There must be something we can do. We can't just stay here in the airport." I was on the verge of tears.

"I am very, very sorry, but our immigration laws give me just one procedure. Your uncle must return to United States on next available flight. Then, he can go to get new passport issued. I believe there is Delta flight for JFK in maybe two hours. We can check to find seats. I think you will want two seats, no?"

"This is insane," I cried. "My uncle just flew over ten hours." I was beginning to beg. "Please, you don't understand how important it is that we are allowed to enter Greece. You just can't send us back now." I felt like Dorothy being shunned from the Emerald City—only this was no fairy tale.

"Believe me, madam, if is anything I could do, I would. I do not like to cause you aggravation, but this is simple rules." I realized that he was not the problem, it was my carelessness that was to blame.

"You've got to be fucking kidding me. Let me speak to your supervisor," I barked, changing tack and losing my cool.

"Madam, I am supervisor. And this language is not getting you in my country either."

"Damn it, I demand to..."

"Dorando Pietri," Ion Theodore laughed, as he spoke for the first time during this entire exchange. He was smiling broadly, as if amused by the spectacle unfolding in front of him. He appeared more like an innocent bystander than the subject of the current crisis. In fact he looked quite entertained.

"I am sorry, sir. What do you say?" asked the officer.

"Not *what*, but *who*, my good man," he laughed softly as he repeated,

"Dorando Pietri. Dorie, as we used to call him," Ion continued. "Nice Italian fellow, very humble and unusually quiet. A great marathoner, perhaps the best in the world. It was 1908, the Games were held in London. They were originally supposed to be in Rome, but Vesuvius erupted and they moved them to London. Did you know that?" he asked the young officer, who drew closer to hear Ion's soft voice.

"No sir, I am not," he replied.

"Dorie led for the entire course of the marathon. A record pace, a flawless run. He entered the stadium for his final lap. So far ahead, he could have walked to the finish line and still never seen his nearest competitor. But do you know what happened to poor Dorie? He just stopped. He had run over 26 miles and could not muster the strength to go the last 200 yards! Glory was so close he could have crawled and still won, but he had nothing left."

"My father was runner—5,000 and 10,000 meters," said the officer in a softer voice. "He was captain of track and field unit of Royal Hellenic Army. He was going to run in Pan-Hellenic Games in 1958, I know he dream of Rome in 1960."

"What happened to his dream?"

"He hurt his leg very bad on a training maneuver. It is heal, but he never run again. He live a good life, but I could feel his loss whenever he watch others run—always dream what might have been. He pass away two years ago." The officer had a far away look in his eyes, as he reminisced about a man who was so obviously his hero.

"What inspired your father to start running?" Ion asked the young man.

"Spyridon. My father always talk about his feats, though he never see the great man run. My dad pretend that he is Louis when he ran as a boy."

"Ah, yes. *Egine Louis*—to run like Louis," Ion smiled. "In the Pan-Hellenic games of 1928, he was the first man to greet me at the finish line, as befitting a coach." All of a sudden, I felt the officer's demeanor shift, as if he felt a whisper in his heart. A look of great relief came over his face. I knew at that moment, before he even spoke, that he would not let Ion fall short just meters from the arrivals terminal.

"You did know the great man? He is your teacher?" he asked Ion, who merely nodded. "Listen to me," the officer was now addressing me, "You are going to make very big promise. Monday morning, you will be at Consulate to tell your uncle's passport is lost. You will get new one and be sure this one is very 'lost.' If he will leave Greece with this passport, I will look for new job by same afternoon. I pray what I do now is secret forever."

"I promise I'll do as you say. First thing Monday morning—9:00 A.M. sharp. You have my word. I don't know how to thank you." I reached out to take the officer's hand, when something made me lean forward and kiss his cheek.

"Do not thank me, thank your uncle. I only wish my father could be live to meet a man who is know Spyridon and who win glory in Pan-Hellenic Games." The officer smiled for the first time since we had walked up to his station.

"I can take no responsibility for your kind deed," said Ion. "The Gods have ordained it, and you have been chosen to be their noble messenger. You are indeed a fine young man." The officer just looked knowingly at Ion. I doubt that he really believed that "the Gods" had anything to do with his decision, but as I looked down upon my fragile uncle in the midst of the stern formality of Immigration Control, I was not so sure.

"May they bless you and guide you on your journey," the officer said as he led us to the doors marked "NOTHING TO DECLARE." It was official, Ion was in Greece. He had arrived.

My heart took a few minutes to settle down after our narrow escape. While we waited for our baggage, I turned and asked Ion "Weren't you a little worried there? He was ready to put us on the next flight home."

"Not at all, my dear, not at all." Ion held my hand to his face. "Ion Theodore has not lived this long and traveled this far to be turned away at the Gates of Sparta."

I thought of coincidences. What made us choose that officer's line? Would any of the others have cared about Dorando Pietri? Did any of their fathers want to *run like Louis*? Would it have mattered? I knew that it didn't. Ion would have found the magical link to any one of their hearts and forded his way through the gauntlet.

We made our way outside where there was a long line of waiting taxis. Ion exchanged a few words with a tall dark-haired man in the first one. What was odd was that I was used to taking the lead, and used to negotiating. But here, I felt vulnerable, like a stranger—a non-Greek-speaking stranger—coming to town. The driver smiled and introduced himself as Yannis as he stowed our luggage in the trunk. In another minute, we were heading out the airport's exit.

I gazed up into the cloudless Aegean sky and wondered what lay at the end of our travels today. I heard the engines of another 747 as it roared down the runway and lifted into a steep climb—heading for ports unknown. I was thousands of miles away from my life in New York, but it may as well have been thousands of years, so immense was the distance I felt to my existence of yesterday.

Perceiving a freedom unburdened by identity and unfettered by fear, I wanted to savor this new world that beckoned me from the old.

PART TWO

THE WALL

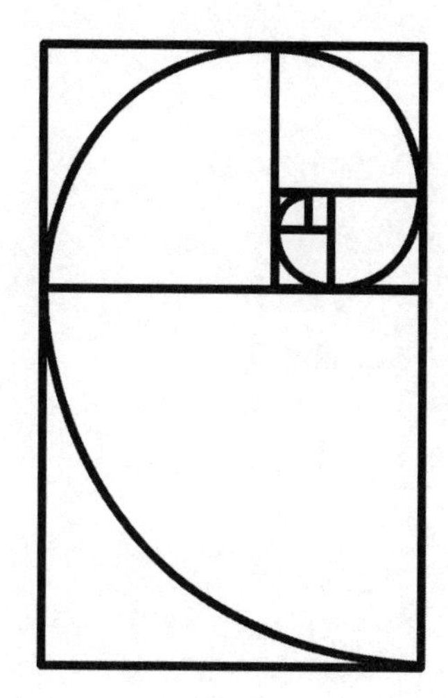

13 THE EYE OF GREECE

Sparta, bounded on the west by the Taygetus Mountains, sprawled out across the great Lakonian plain. The most impressive thing about the 'Gates of Sparta' is that they do not exist. It was said her protection was cast of something mightier than stone—it was made of Spartans.

Pheidippides approached the city from the east on one of the four main roads that led towards its center. Two warriors stood watch near the eastern gates. Long flowing hair, perfectly groomed and tied in back, protruded from red-crested helmets. Their bronze armor glinted in the sunlight; and the smooth surface of each shield was emblazoned with a stark "Λ".

"What's this?" I asked Ion, running my hand across a large padded bar that ran the width of the taxi's back seat. It reminded me of the tractable metal bars on roller coasters.

"Some tourists feel more comfortable holding on," he said with an indifferent smile.

"I doubt it could be any scarier than a taxi ride in Manhattan," I said with the typical arrogance that nothing compares to the life experience of a seasoned New Yorker. Ion had settled back comfortably. One of the advantages of his smaller frame was his ability to fit into spaces not designed for human comfort. I laughed at the thought of naïve tourists clutching this waist-high roll bar.

Yannis was twirling a large set of *komboloi*. When he noticed me looking at them, he said, "You want?" Looking back over his shoulder, he handed me a smaller set of beads that had been dangling from his rear view mirror—whose only use seemed to be as a place to hang *komboloi* and a Jesus Christ figurine. I took them out of politeness.

"Many peoples use when stop smoking."

"That's great. Did you just quit?"

Yannis let out a loud laugh and shook his head at me, almost in disbelief. "Smoke with left, make beads with right," he proudly proclaimed while pulling a pack of cigarettes from his breast pocket and lighting one. It didn't take a math degree to figure out that this equation left the steering wheel and gearshift shorthanded.

I was quickly indoctrinated into the three laws of Greek driving. Law Number One: There are no traffic laws. Law Number Two: Get from point A to point B in the least amount of time with the least regard for life and limb. Law Number Three: Do not be discouraged by the number of lanes, there is always room to squeeze in another one. Apparently "passing," no matter the impracticality or danger of the maneuver is a Greek driver's rite of passage. Pun intended.

"Are you from Athens?" I said, attempting small talk as we headed north on *Leoforos Posidonos*.

"No. Peloponnese. Yithion, near Sparti. Where comes real Greek mans. No Turks, no Germans. Never in Lakonia. Real Greek mans no conquered." I found his unabashed machismo refreshingly amusing. I watched the speedometer exceed a hundred-forty kilometers per hour even though we were weaving in and out of moderate traffic. What made our speed all the more extraordinary was the fact that Yannis did not seem the least bit concerned while tailgating other vehicles so closely that you could no longer read their bumper stickers, especially the ones which probably said 'If You Can Read This—You're About To Crash!'

What is a nanosecond? If you said it's a billionth of a second, you'll make a good scientist. But it's really the length of time a New Yorker waits after a traffic light turns green before honking his horn at the car in front of him. The Greeks have taken horn blowing to a new dimension—here it is a romance. And I've seen insane drivers trying to pass on narrow country roads, but until now, I have never seen anyone try it in the same lane. Yannis would pull up behind the car in front of him and flash his headlights. If the other driver didn't get out of his way fast enough, which was never, he would pull even closer and exclaim, "bad driving always womans or old mans." Upon passing the offender he'd say, "See. Womans driver!" Then, as if correcting himself for my sake, he'd sheepishly add "*Greek* womans!" and then laugh at his own cleverness and masculine prowess.

It was all the more exciting to him when another driver simultaneously attempted the same maneuver in the opposite direction. I was scared shitless. Every few moments I thought for sure we were going to have the kind of accident that requires dental records to identify the bodies. I knew he was enjoying watching this American "womans" squirm nervously in her seat.

"Hey, watch it there Yannis, I'm a woman and I'm a damned good driver."

"Yes, very, very good driver I am sure," he said while rolling his eyes and smiling. I knew that he rolled his eyes because he had no qualms about turning his head one hundred eighty degrees when he addressed me, causing me to tighten my grip on the roll bar that I was now thankful had been installed.

To our left, ferries and tankers made their way slowly across the turquoise sea. The Romans built roads to the far reaches of the civilized world. The Greeks sailed upon their roads—anywhere the sea could go, there went the Athenians.

I cracked my window to let in the soft Aegean breeze. I smelled the sea between gusts of diesel. Perhaps I expected magic and that made what I saw all the more troubling. First, there was the pollution enveloping everything in a halo of brownish-yellow. No sense of space or order governed the traffic and there was the dissonance of so many rude horns. If this was the birth place of democracy, here it had become the demos demon of the mob pushing and shoving its way in loops and circles on the way to getting the day done.

"Want to know how Athens get name?" said Yannis.

He didn't wait for my answer.

"Athena and Poseidon very much love this village. Make contest to citizens. Best gift—win city. Poseidon strike ground. Water come up but very, very salty—no good drink. Very bad. Athena strike ground and there is growing olive tree. Greeks like very, very much. Use for cook, for the light, for eat, for clean the bodies. For this miracle, peoples are choose Athena to take name for city. Now very, very dirty—I thinks Athena wishing Poseidon win," he laughed.

Ion stared blankly out the window smiling as though in recognition.

"How much has it changed Uncle Ion?" I asked, projecting my disappointment onto him.

"Not much at all, really. It's still a palimpsest."

"Palimpsest?"

"Layers, layers of history."

In one word, he had it. There was a great city and a great civilization before us sticking out in fragments and ruins among an entirely new storied city that whirled about indifferent to the fantastic legacy that lay beneath and still within it.

We turned right onto *Leoforos Singrou*, heading northeast towards Athens proper where a third of all Greeks live. Rising above Piraeus and the wide Saronic Gulf like a sprawling marble and concrete fortress, she presides over the rugged Attican peninsula. Ion told me that only a century earlier, the region was covered with olive groves, the hills gleamed white with Pentelic marble quarries and sheepherders still grazed their flocks on the slopes of the Acropolis.

Athens looks nothing like Paris, or London or Prague. Though she is far older than any of them, she appears to have been built in the 1950's. Her ancient structures stuck out here and there like giants trodden over by Lilliputians, ignorant of her sleeping history. The boulevard was lined with façades of lifeless stone and glass, devoid of architectural character. Yet despite the newness of her face, I could feel her oldness everywhere. But there was a life in the air, and I began to feel that here, anything was possible.

The harbor held all manner of vessels. Among them was a phantom, a great whale of a ship, the Dutch cruise liner *Rotterdam*. It dwarfed almost all of the ships around it, including some of the tankers and of course many of the magnificent yachts, which, in turn, dwarfed the smaller barges and the tiny fishing boats. There is something godlike about the ability to master scale. According to the signage, at the bottom of the harbor and under the keel of that great ocean liner, lay the scattered remains of Themistocles' triremes—the swift ships of war that saved a nation.

Unlike a *Leoforos*, which is a grand boulevard, or an *Odos*, which is a normal street, a *Steno* is a *really* tiny street. The extra narrowness provided more exciting challenges to Yannis, who was constantly driving the van on the curb to avoid hitting the cars parked on the opposite side.

Ion gazed out the window calmly, seemingly oblivious to the wild ride we were taking with the smoking, chatting, laughing, bead-twirling taxi driver from Yithion. As we passed through the heart of Athens, Yannis pointed out several sights. But he drove by them so quickly, that by the time I could veer my head, they were too distant to see.

There was one exception.

I believe that I have seen no fewer than ten thousand pictures of the Parthenon. It is perhaps one of the most photographed architectural sights in the world. Descriptions of it figure prominently in every Greek guidebook. Postcards flaunting its profile, in every season and at every time of the day or night, could be seen every few feet since we landed at Hellenikon Airport. It adorns t-shirts, posters, postage stamps and its form has been replicated all over the neo-classical world, like the Eiffel Tower, the Empire State Building, the Pyramids of Giza—every bit the international celebrity.

I thought that this saturation of Parthenonian images entitled me to believe that I actually knew it. Perhaps, I even felt jaded, and assumed that the reality could not possibly exceed the hype. But nothing could have prepared me for the sight of it looming atop the Acropolis as we approached from the southeast. Faded to a skeleton from it's once gleaming and robust form, it still presides over the city and a nation, rising boldly in defiance of millennia of fires, earthquakes, wars, urbanization and the erosion of man's pollution.

"I can't wait to climb those steps and see the summit."

"And I shall accompany you," said Ion.

I wanted to see this with him, but even from this distance, I knew that Ion could not ascend its many steps. It was ironic to think of Athens' oldest legacy being off-limits to the old.

We had arrived at the Hotel Plaka. Yannis broke out into laughter as I paid him. I gave him a quizzical look, then realized that he was amused at watching my left hand involuntarily twirling the *komboloi* he had given me. After that ride I could have used general anesthesia.

I wanted to go to my room and freshen up, but Ion was anxious to see Panayiotas without any more delays. I didn't blame him, so we stopped just long enough to check-in and drop off our bags. Yannis was happy to wait. A few hours riding with some well-to-do Americans beat hustling the streets for local fares.

We turned onto *Leoforos Mesogeion*. I saw the first road sign with its unmistakable distance.

Marathonas 42—in miles, 26.

"Why you go Marathonas?" Yannis asked Ion.

"An old friend. He's ill and I must see him," said Ion. It was true, but I am sorry Ion told him this bit of information. Yannis, the Good Samaritan, only used this as a justification to shed any last pretense of driving safely.

"Twenty years. So much locked away in silence's tomb," Ion said to me, drifting off in his thoughts.

Marathonas 28.

The air was filled with the fragrance of conifers and the salty smell of the Mediterranean breeze telling me that the sea was once again not far away. I gazed out across *Pediada Marathonas*—the Plains of Marathon. They stretched from the mountains on our left all the way to the distant shore. All around were forests, broken by the clearings notched into them by farmers. I could see their orderly fields of olives and domesticated flowers.

"They came ashore there," said Ion, pointing across me to the northwest.

"Who?"

"The Persians. Guided to *that* spot by Hippias—a Greek tyrant turned traitor."

"He was the one who coughed up a tooth, wasn't he?" I said, proud that I had remembered one of Ion's many stories.

"Yes, it was an omen of doom for the barbarians. But I suppose victors write not only the history, but also the meanings of omens."

"Any good attorney can do that for the right retainer," I added, eliciting a laugh from him.

Marathonas 7.

"Drive to Marathon start?" asked Yannis.

"What's he talking about, Uncle Ion?"

"There's a plaque where the marathon commences."

"Was that where Pheidippides started?"

"Nai, yes it—" started Yannis, but before he could finish, Ion interrupted him with a simple but authoritative 'No.'

"Oxi?"

"It is the route of the modern marathon. Pheidippides began over there, between Kotroni and Agriliki. The route to Athens lay over the mountains, not along the sea. Believe me, the road to Athens lay that way, over those mountains," said Ion with an aura of knowledge that no one was going to question.

"He maybe is right," said Yannis with his eyebrows slightly raised. "No one knows way Pheidippides runs. Why not over mountains?"

"It was over there that he began. There is no doubt," Ion repeated.

I was anxious to meet Panayiotas and to discover the secrets that this monastery in Marathon shielded in its bosom for so many years. It wouldn't be long now—assuming Yannis didn't find some way of sandwiching us in a vehicular pile-up.

We drove for approximately a mile or two south of the town center before making a right onto *Odos Plataion*, then after another mile, we forked left. Quickly losing the pavement, the road became dry compacted dirt. Panteleimon's ancient copper dome was the first thing that I saw. Its once shining metal had tarnished into hues of blue and green. Like the silver streak in Adonia's hair, its telltale sign of age only enhanced its beauty and dignity. The old masonry of the church impressed me with stark whiteness, brazenly declaring its purity.

The structure looked like it was built in the shape of square cross with several rounded corners on each side, dominated by that large dome rising from its center. It was very compact and efficient-looking. Its exterior was stuccoed, and its roof, except the central dome, was made of layers of clay tiles whose mortar was cracked and disintegrating.

We were finally here. Fourteen hours and forty minutes after leaving my home in Long Island—we had arrived in Marathon.

14
THE ORPHAN

The two sentinels stared into the mist as the ghostly figure approached.

"Halt stranger! Who dares approach the city of the Lacedaemonians? Prove whether thou be friend or foe, or prepare to join thy ancestors in the underworld." For an instant, Pheidippides considered running from them to avoid their quick-tempered blades, but he recalled his father's advice of how to face the Spartans.

"Stand aside, for you address a free man from the noble city of Athens," Pheidippides replied. "I am surprised. I had heard tall tales of Spartan courage. Yet, now I only see two boys who must bare their swords against an unarmed man. Nevertheless, I shall gladly throttle both of you if you raise them in anger. After my run of a hundred-fifty miles, it should be a fair fight."

"He's gone," said Ion, so nonchalantly that I was unable to grasp the significance of his simple phrase. We had just pulled onto the dirt driveway that led to Panteleimon.

"How can you tell?"

"I know. It is in the air," Ion said as he dropped his head into his hands.

"Ion, think positively. There's a man coming out of the church now. Yannis, pull over there, please." He did as I asked. "It won't be long now and you'll be reunited—you'll see."

"I'm very, very sorry to be telling you this sad news," said the black-robed man.

Yannis looked disappointed as if had he only driven faster, we may have made it in time. There was nothing any of us could have done. His life had ebbed away before Ion had even received his letter.

"Family not here now, coming soon," the priest added with a bow as he retired back into the dark recess of the church. "Many pardons, many pardons, many pardons..." His voice faded as he withdrew. Had we been like Dorando Pietri after all?

Friday night, my first evening in Athens, offered two lingering memories. One was of the Acropolis. My room on the fifth floor had an unobstructed view. It was fully illuminated and the reflection from it façade made it appear golden against the dark skies above and behind it. The second was the howling from packs of dogs. I had noticed that homeless dogs freely roamed the streets by day, at night, they sang to each other from Plaka's deserted alleyways.

It would be the only night we would spend in Athens. When Panayiotas' nephew, Yiannis Diogenes, learned we had headed back to our hotel, he telephoned and insisted that we come to stay with his family at Panteleimon. I had mixed feelings. I'm a city girl, and at least Athens had amenities of a metropolitan center. But Ion felt it was best, and after what he had suffered today,

I didn't want to argue with him. Perhaps we could spend a day or two there to be polite.

By the time Ion and I had finished the hotel's breakfast, Father Diogenes' two sons were waiting for us in the lobby.

"Welcome in Athens, Mr. Theodore. And you must to be the beautiful Marianna. I am call myself Milos." The younger one of the two clasped my hand.

The older one added, "Mr. Theodore, when father is telling us you traveling with niece he is not saying she is Aphrodite. I am Dimitris, first born of my father," he said with a slight bow as he too reached for and then kissed my hand.

Milos immediately took my bag and said, "Please, for allow me help you. Shame Dimitris, are you not see her hands very, very soft to carry heavy bag?"

"I am teach you well, brother," he said, then under his breath added with a knowing smile, "perhaps is too well."

"Since your hands are being free, Dimitris, why not you getting van. We are wait here for you." Milos added, "Here brother, you are maybe need these," he said as he tossed Dimitris the car keys.

"It is being my pleasure. Oh, one minute please. I am no remember where you are park car, brother. Much easier if you are bring to us. Bad to make guest wait while I no find." With that, Dimitris tossed the keys back to Milos.

"Not remember where is van? You make joke, no?"

"Now, now Milos, very bad argue this things, very silly. So now you go." Milos turned to me and said quietly, "You must to forgive my brother's mind, have good intention but God not bless him here," using his finger, he tapped the side of his head. I heard Milos mutter something in Greek to Dimitris, which didn't sound flattering by its tone. He then turned and took off in a brisk-paced walk to retrieve their parked van.

Dimitris waved to Milos, then turned to me and said quietly, "You must to forgive my brother. He mean well, but still act like boy." I laughed. Being an only child, I was spared the pleasures of sibling rivalry.

In a few minutes, Milos pulled a white van up to the curb where we waited. It was an old 1970's Toyota, white but covered in dust. He jumped out and ran around to grab our luggage. It was amusing to watch the two boys fighting over our bags, each trying to outdo the other. They both carefully helped Ion into the back of their van.

As I was about to enter and sit next to Ion, Milos said, "Marianna, make much better seat in front, much better for you."

"Thank you Milos, but I don't mind sitting in the back," I politely replied. But Milos was insistent.

"All Athens is waiting you see her—please not say no to her!"

I glanced at Ion, but before I could say a word he said, "He is right, my dear. Feast your attention on Athens and what lays ahead."

Milos opened the front passenger door and as he helped me into the van, Dimitris walked around the car and jumped into the driver's seat.

"Dimitris, what you are do? I am drive."

"Milos, you are work very, very hard all the day and you are drive very far to here. I am remember say I will drive home."

"I am not remember such things," said Milos.

"Ah, now who is have weak mind?" Dimitris said, as he tapped his forefinger to his head, mocking Milos' earlier gesture to me.

"Oh, what a sweet and thoughtful brother you have Milos, you must be so proud of him," I said, innocently throwing a little more fuel on their fire.

"Yes, his kindness is not know limits," Milos mumbled as he climbed into the back.

"Remember, my brother, age and experience is win over youth and eagerness," Dimitris said as he shot a smug glance towards the back seat.

"Indeed, my brother, I am remind you of this things when you are old and gray," replied Milos.

"Are you and Milos on summer vacation from school now?" I asked.

"I finish school. Dimitris is return now in fall," said Milos.

"So you work the farm?"

"For this time," Milos replied.

"My brother always is dream of better life," said Dimitris.

"It is good to dream," said Ion.

"But is not grass more green in other valley?" said Dimitris.

"Sometimes it is," Ion laughed.

"You see, Dimitris, there is more to the world than village of Marathonas."

"And I seek to find it through God," his older brother replied.

"I wish to travel and see *His* creation with my own eyes. What are you think about this, Mr. Theodore?" asked Milos.

"I think you both must travel the paths that are true to yourselves—they will probably not be the same or right for the other."

"When our father and mother move here, it is no electricity or inside toilet. How you and Panayiotas live this way?"

Ion laughed. "We rose with the sun and when it set, we breached the dark by candlelight or oil-burning lamps—as our ancestors did—in harmony with the world around us."

"I love harmony too, Dimitris, but there is running water now, isn't there?" I asked him, not as excited about the way ancestors lived as Ion was.

"Have municipal water. Very good pressure—very good so close to reservoir."

"I remember an old well that we would pump for our water in those days," said Ion.

"Nai, well is okay Mr. Theodore. Is same like you and Panayiotas remember it."

"I recall your father visiting Panteleimon as a young boy, but I have never had the pleasure to meet your mother."

"Our mother was leave two days now to see her *Mana* on Skyros. Grandma is have no brothers or sisters and husband is dead for many year." I learned that *Mana*, like our version of mama, is an affectionate Greek term for mother.

"I'm sure your father misses her a lot already," I said.

"He does, even it's only few days. We are thank God other grandma is stay with us, now that Evangelis is for now in house."

"Evangelis?" I asked.

"Nai, orphan boy. He is with us until bed can be open in orphanage, but wars in Balkans make very many refugees—is very, very bad—many child suffer."

"Great beauty often awaits those who suffer ignoble births," Ion said as he gazed down at his hands from which the *komboloi* began to clatter softly.

"What happened to his parents," I asked, not sure if I wanted to know.

"He is say that mother and father dead. We have search in papers and find no one is claim him. All we knowing he is Greek or Macedonian."

"How did you find him?"

"He is find us. He say he follow blue and orange lights. Father think he means stars of Gemini—Castor and Pollux. It mean he is come from north. Many wars, many orphans. We are seeing scars across his back and sides. Looking like burns from rope."

"Scars, that's awful. What a deliverance for him to have found your family."

The boys shot nervous glances at each other, but neither spoke.

"Yes, it is like he fall out of sky, but father believe deliverance is ours. It is because the *musterion*," said Milos.

"Moo-stay-ree-on?" I repeated.

"Yes, it is like *ainigma*."

"Ah, enigma. A mystery…"

"*Nai*, there is a… mystery and only orphan is hold the key. It is last words of Panayiotas," added his brother.

"Really? How exciting," I said, but the long stares coming from them let me know that this wasn't a subject they took as amusement. I wanted to delve deeper into the origins of the orphan-child and this strange tale, but two near-death driving experiences, and the boys blaming each other, caused the subject to be lost.

Their revelation aside, another strange thing happened as we looped back through Syntagma to pick up the road to Marathon. Ion had become very quiet. Perhaps he was still tired from our trip, or perhaps he was lamenting the loss of his friend—or both.

The boys were taking turns bringing my attention to places of interest when Ion suddenly bolted forward and said. "Stop! Stop the car, please."

"Mr. Theodore, are you okay?" Dimitris asked as he pulled the car to the curb.

"Are you all right, Ion?" I added hastily my heart palpitating and expecting the worst.

"I'm sorry if I startled you. I just want to get out and stretch my legs."

"Stretch your legs? Are you sure you're feeling all right?"

"I am fine, my dear."

Dimitris had already come around to open the van's sliding door.

"Ion, let me help..."

"No," Ion said to me, politely, but with a firmness that let me know that he wanted to be alone. The three of us sat in the van as Ion slowly walked under a large archway of carved stone and marble. Ion stood underneath it for a few minutes, but he didn't look at it. Instead, his eyes surveyed the surroundings. Then, without a word or gesture, he walked into the gardens that stretched beyond Hadrian's Arch.

"Dimitris, I'm a little worried, is it possible you..."

"For me, is no problem. I am follow him," he said as he walked in the direction Ion had disappeared.

Milos and I made a little small talk, but I had my attention on Ion and what he sought. There was something else that I had observed, and that was how invigorated Ion had seemingly become. He was as a different man from the one I had found in Queens. I ascribed his withered state then as more of an emotional resignation than physiological debility. Something here, perhaps in the smell of the air or sea, had given him a boost of strength.

In about fifteen minutes, Dimitris came running back towards the van.

A little out of breath, he said, "I am not want he see me follow."

"Is he..."

"He is okay."

"What in the world did he do in there?"

"First he is walk then he is sit on bench to watch pigeons."

"He sat on a park bench and watched birds? Why would..." but my words were cut short as Ion appeared once again under the arch and made his way back into the van with Dimitris' help. As he stared blankly out the window, I think he sensed that I wanted to say something.

"I was just remembering an old friend," he said with a long deep sigh.

15 THE FAMILY BUSINESS

Pheidippides rested in the barracks of Agapenor, the Spartan commander of the guards, and could not help but notice the deep red welts which criss-crossed his muscular back.

"Whippings at the Altar of Artemis Ortheia are part of the training rituals laid down three hundred years ago for one purpose—to forge warriors of unrivaled toughness," spoke Agapenor. "When I was born, elders came to inspect me, as they do every newborn. Had I been deemed feeble—I would have been left to die on the slopes of Mount Taygetus. Fortunately I was robust and healthy, but I had a brother whose fate was that which I have described."

"I am sorry for your loss," said Pheidippides compassionately.

"My brother was weak, and I was strong. Had it been reversed, he would have shed no tears over my death."

An elderly woman appeared on the portico as we drove up. She was dressed in three shades of black, perhaps still in mourning over the death of her brother. Milos kissed her as Dimitris assisted Ion out of the van.

The old woman looked over at me dragging my suitcase, reached up and twisted Milos' right ear, causing him to wince in pain.

"Piyaine na tous voitheisis," she snapped.

"Nai Mana, Nai, I am help them," he replied as she let go. He quickly sprang over to me to relieve me of my bag.

"Milos, that's not necessary. I'm used to carrying my own bags," I told him as he reached for the handle of my suitcase.

I noticed his face turn paler as he pleaded, "Grandma is no happy when woman is do what she is call a man's 'privilege.'"

I laughed and let him take my suitcase. The women here had not burned their bras anytime recently. Milos took all of our bags out and one by one walked them into the farmhouse. As Ion approached this brooding figure of a woman, I noticed her brushing back the gray hairs, which had fallen over one eye. Her looks were a paradox—some features suggested youth, others an ancient demeanor. Everything about her seemed to have evolved for efficiency and strength of purpose. Though plain in appearance, I felt there was something extraordinary about this woman.

"Then exete alaxei katholou," Ion said to her, as he took her hand and laid a kiss on its upper surface. A broad smile formed across her weather worn cheeks.

"What did you tell her?" I asked Ion.

"That time hasn't changed her. Let me introduce you to Eftehea, Panayiotas' sister," he started to say, but she interrupted him.

"Kai pia einai afti?"

"Eftehea, afti einai I kori tou kalou mou filou apo tin Ameriki. I am telling her that you are the daughter of my dear American friends."

"I am so happy to meet you Eftehea," I said as I extended my hand. She looked down at it, and shook it, but there was an aloofness in her grasp as if she took my hand only out of politeness—then withdrew it as quickly once the obligatory greeting was over.

"Does she speak English, Dimitris?" Her blank stare gave me my answer.

"Do not be worry. Grandma is warm slow to new peoples."

I followed Ion inside the farmhouse—he walked with the ease and certainty of a man who was right at home.

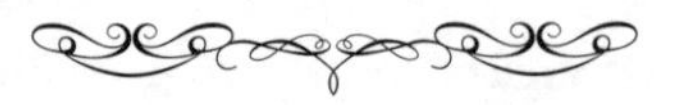

Milos dropped my bags in a room which was located at the end of a long corridor on the southwest corner of the house, and then lead the two of us into another room, which was a few meters back up the hall.

"This my room," said Milos as he placed Ion's luggage down upon an old wooden table. "For you now Mr. Theodore. I am sleep in room with Dimitris."

"And Evangelis?"

"He is sleep with grandma."

I looked about the room. There were none of the trappings I had come to assume were the necessities of life to any young boy—stereo, telephone, sports equipment, though on the wall above his bed was a poster of New York. It was a well-known shot of lower Manhattan, looking north from the mouth of the Hudson. It was the last picture I would have expected to see here, 6,000 miles from Battery Park.

I easily unpacked Ion's suitcase—he traveled very lightly. The exception was a few books that he brought. I suppose that some people travel with a Bible. For Ion, it was Homer's *Illiad*, Milton's *Paradise Lost* and a book of sonnets by Michelangelo. He had read them all numerous times, so they seemed to have made the journey more to provide comfort than as current reading material.

Ion was content to relax alone, so I returned to my room. In it was a single bed and a small dresser opposite it. I tested the mattress. It was soft, stuffed with an abundance of sheep's wool, and the bedding consisted of just two clean white sheets. I doubted I would need a blanket. On top of the dresser was a small lamp, the only one in the room. The walls were barren, except for the cracks and discoloration hewn by centuries of time. There was a large window on the south wall, which looked out over the farmhouse's acreage and then out to the sea and the endless horizon. Even though it was daytime, it wasn't that hard to darken the room. The windows had large wooden shutters on the outside which, when closed, shielded the room from the sun's light.

Milos had come down the hall and knocked on the door, though it was open.

"Come on in, Milos."

"Grandma is want to know everything is okay."

"It's perfect. Tell her I will be just fine. Milos, I don't think she likes me," I said, partially teasing, but partially not.

"She good womans—like Greek from old times. Is never good cross such womans, but she very, very good. Wrath of Achilles is nothings like fury of Greek womans," he said while laughing. "Maybe she mad from words of he is say she have, how you are say—a *crush* of Ion?"

"A crush?" I said, unable to contain my smile.

"She is say 'Oxi, Oxi,' but even for her the no is very, very strong," his lips formed a thin smile. "And her blush is no hide anythings."

I thought about how a half-century of time, in reverse, would transform each of them. She would have been in her twenties, and he would have been a maturely handsome man in his mid-thirties—every bit the Greek hero.

"Well, we'll have to keep our eyes on them, won't we?" I said.

"Tell me about New York," he said excitedly.

"Would you like to go there someday?"

"For me it is big dream. But it is not please father when I am speak of this."

"Why? It's a pretty safe place to visit."

"No worry about that—I am strong, can take care of any problems," he said as if I had affronted his masculinity, then just as quickly slumping his shoulders he added, "Him is fear that to see is not enough for me."

"I understand. He wants you to study Theology, doesn't he?"

"Yes. But for me, is not my dream. I am respect him but am not feel same devotion to church. I cannot share this feelings to him, his life is church."

"Many parents want their children to follow in their footsteps; it's normal. He'll respect whatever path you choose, I'm sure of it."

"I am think things very, very different for the Greek families. At least he can be hope one son is no disappointments. Dimitris is finished Theological academica in one years."

"Why are you unsure?"

"I am think someday to make family."

"I thought Greek Orthodox priests can marry. Your father did."

"Panayiotas was the *Episkopos Metropitis*. This is very, very high position in church. Mans devoted only to church is achieving this. Mans with family never is rise above a Papas, a simple priest. For father, it is dream that we rise to where he cannot. I am want very much please him, but I am not find strength to choose..." his words trailed off, and I paused, waiting for what followed, but

I could tell he felt too awkward to complete his sentence.

"I don't see how the women would allow you," I said with a wink, but I think I had embarrassed him further.

"What about you. Do you study in family business?" he asked, changing the subject.

"Oh no," I laughed. "My father worked in the garment center in Manhattan. There was no family business to inherit. He never made much money at all."

Milos looked surprised. "I am assume that you are grow up with..."

"Money? Very little to speak of."

"I am believe all Americans drive Cadillacs and make steaks in backyards of big houses."

"Sorry to disillusion you. Long before I was born, my mother used to sew garments in the basement from the scraps of fabric my father brought home from his job. He walked both ways, four miles every day, to save the nickel bus fare."

"What is this 'nickel' buying?"

"Eventually, an education for his daughter, so that she wouldn't have to walk to work." I felt a lump in my throat while telling this stranger about the sacrifice of my father. "Anyway, Milos, when you're ready to go to New York, you'll have a great time..." Our conversation was interrupted by the sounds of a child's voice.

I heard no footsteps, but something made me shoot my gaze over towards the doorway. There at the threshold floated the sweetest pair of brown eyes peeking hesitantly around the corner. As soon as my eyes found them, those beautiful globes disappeared.

Milos called out into the hallway and then said to Evangelis, "Ela mesa yia miso leptaki," and then to me, "I am say for him come to greet you and you are no bite."

I watched as those eyes appeared once again, tentatively peering into my room. But that was as far as Milos could coax him. He just stared at me for a few moments.

"Say, *mai lene* Marianna," Milos coached me.

I repeated the words. Evangelis blinked a few times, and then ran back down the hallway.

I laughed. "I have that effect on some men. Perhaps later he'll be more comfortable."

"Him very, very shy. I must now to help brother in field before father is come. I see you later."

I pulled open a suitcase. I liked to get this ritual over with as soon as possible whenever I traveled. It made me feel more organized and grounded in my new environment. I laid my shoes out under the old wooden bed, pausing for a moment as I held my running sneakers. I wondered whether packing this item had been a result of wishful thinking, or the start of my honoring my New Year's Resolution—the one I just made a mere eight months earlier.

I wanted to take a quick shower. As I moved down the short corridor, I saw those sensitive and vulnerable eyes again, and like before, they vanished almost as soon as I had seen them.

The tub had a hand-held extension, which I could hook onto an attachment fixed at the height of my neck. Europe might have a monopoly on culture but they sure as hell haven't mastered the simple shower. I adjusted the temperature and stepped in; the warm water began to cleanse me of the vestiges I had brought with me from my old life. And as this veneer slowly washed away under the soft waters flowing from Lake Marathon, I thought of those eyes, the pain they masked, and the love they held captive.

16 THE FIRST SUPPER

"When we are infants, we are bathed in wine, for the bite of the alcohol tests our strength." Agapenor continued. "Weaker babies seize and die; the strong become stronger, with skin toughening like leather. Childish habits like crying or fear of the dark were sternly rebuked, and I was constantly exposed to searing heat and frigid cold to make me impervious to the elements. This was my life until I was seven years of age, when the city took over my training. Taken from my parents, I lived in barracks with other youths. There, a paidonomos would direct my education for the next thirteen years."

"This sounds so brutal. So much in the pursuit of war," was all Pheidippides could utter.

"Compared to our training, we come to learn that war is pleasurable."

I overheard them before I saw them. They seemed hidden in one of the dense groves of trees that populated the otherwise expansive, golden fields. Though I wore hiking boots, my legs were bare to the bottom of my shorts and well exposed to the sharp burs and occasional thorns on the low-lying scrub and occasional rose bush. Suddenly I was upon them, yet still hidden from view as they repaired a fallen fence.

Their smooth and bronzed backs arched in the sun as they took turns holding and hammering a support post. Milos swung a large sledgehammer, almost like an ax, lifting it above his head and bringing it down precisely on top of the post that Dimitris held steady. Each swing had a rhythm to it, and as his body swayed in the vernal heat, the sinews of his lean muscles expanded and contracted.

"Hit it hard," I shouted, surprising them and stopping their work. Dimitris turned suddenly, pulled his tee shirt from the ground and in a gesture of modesty, clutched it and pulled it over his head. Milos dropped the sledgehammer, smiled, and drew a deep breath at the end of which he yelled, "Hello, Marianna. You are come to help?" Dimitris reached down and grabbed his brother's shirt and slapped it lightly in his face.

"Milos, please, she is guest."

"Oh, don't mind me. You looked just fine the way you were," I said. "It's so hot, I wish I could shed mine," I added and there was a sudden silence filled with slight embarrassment.

"And why not—this is Greece," Milos shouted with a smile. Dimitris hit him again with his shirt, this time slightly harder. Milos lunged at Dimitris and I watched as sweat covered arms and torsos interlocked and various holds were applied, and counter-applied, until laughter broke their violent play.

"I am forget, you are young and still learn the manners," Dimitris said matter-of-factly.

"At least I am still young enough not to forget." Milos shot back while putting on his shirt.

I looked at the two of them, both indistinguishably young and strikingly handsome, defining themselves against each other. Both wanted to be men but I could still see them as boys.

"It is lucky for you papa is need fence fixed—if no, I am finish your lesson," Dimitris added, puffing a bit.

I offered to help Eftehea with the evening meal—but I sensed she considered me more of a hindrance in her kitchen. I am not what you would call the epitome of a homemaker. I watched Eftehea preparing the lamb. It's strange how we have disinfected ourselves from the basic necessities of killing and preparing the foods for our feasts, preferring the sanitized illusion that meats come in nicely wrapped cellophane packages. After she had seasoned it, she ran a long skewer through its center, and set it on a large platter.

She motioned for me to follow her outside to a large masonry fireplace used for cooking. The opening was at waist height, and there were large metal frames on each side. These had slots into which skewers could be placed. I helped her gather some wood that was stacked in an alcove on the fire pit's side. After she had the fire going, she hefted the lamb above the hot embers.

I thought about how many hours she must spend every day at the task of preparing food for the family. Meals have been made so convenient for me—vast supermarkets, or gourmet take-out foods that one microwaves to create the illusion of having made something. And when even that is too complicated or time-consuming, I am one phone call away from having any kind of food imaginable delivered to my doorstep. She moved about the kitchen with the steady purpose of a woman who saw being a woman as a privilege.

I helped her to set the table, and by the time we had finished, Ion had woken from a nap he had taken during the height of the afternoon sun.

"Did you rest well?"

"Like a child. And you?"

"I've had a busy afternoon. I got a lesson in the kitchen from Eftehea."

Ion broke out into his high-pitched laugh. "Really, I would have loved to have seen that. Would you join me on the portico for some *ouzo* and *meze*?"

"I'd love to," I replied. Ion and I found two chairs outside the house near the roasting pit. It wasn't too hot, the sun having already begun its retreat across the mountains behind Pentelicus. A sweet-smelling breeze enveloped us, and rustled through some jasmine trees, in whose shade we sat together. The dancing wind alternatively brought to my nostrils the scent of the sea and the savory smell of roasting meat.

Ion smiled as I watered down my glass of *ouzo*—turning my libation milky white despite the fact that its two ingredients were both clear liquids. On a blue and white platter was an assortment of *meze*, or appetizers: *elyes*—olives from Kalamata, *feta* cheese, *dolmathes*—stuffed grape leaves and *aftherina*—a kind of fried fish. The latter was very salty, but when washed down with the licorice-flavored *ouzo*, it left no fishy aftertaste. I have learned that *ouzo*—even diluted—leaves little room for any aftertaste other than its own.

"I can't believe we finally made it to Greece!" I broke the silence of our contemplative state.

"I waited too long."

"I'm sorry, Ion."

"For what, my dear?"

"About your friend..."

"I have learned to accept life's unexpected turns. There is usually a reason." Ion stared out towards the sea and then said to no one in particular, "*The mountains look on, Marathon, and Marathon looks on the sea; And musing there an hour alone, I dreamed that Greece might still be free; for standing on the Persians' grave, I could not deem myself a slave.* I wander. It is this place; it makes me dream."

I thought of the life I had built in New York. A city that in its complexity and constant motion makes one feel the possibilities of change and in that change a certain homelessness. As much as I loved it, its thin topsoil did not seem suitable for the ancient idea of roots.

I didn't immediately see Father Diogenes when he walked into the kitchen, but I felt him. I turned before he had a chance to speak.

"Welcome, welcome to you both," he said with his arms outstretched, his floor length black robes making him appear to glide across the floor. "Ion, it is so good to see you again, you are just as I remember you."

"Then you must have remembered me as very, very old," laughed Ion as he and Father Diogenes embraced and kissed each other on both cheeks.

"I am so relieved to embrace you, to know that you are well. Let me kiss you again for Uncle Panayiotas, he wanted this moment so much," he said as he kissed Ion again on both cheeks.

"I see that time has been quite generous with you too; and your sons are as handsome as a father could ever hope his sons to be. You have made my old friend proud."

"He loved you very much, Ion..."

"Not nearly as much as he was loved."

"Bless you. And you are obviously Marianna," he said as he came over to me. He clasped my hand warmly in both of his.

Father Diogenes stood at about five foot seven inches tall. His jet-black hair didn't seem to end at his sideburns, but continued downwards, circumnavigating his head with a long thick beard. He was quite pale, in contrast to his sons. I learned that a few years earlier, Father Diogenes had taken an ecclesiastical tour of the States. As a result, his English was excellent.

"I can't express how thankful I am that you have allowed us to come and stay here. You have a wonderful family," I said, completely forgetting the special greeting in Greek that I had practiced at home for the last few days.

"To spiti mou einai to thiko sou, I think you say 'my house is your house,'" he said, then turned to Dimitris. "Have you seen that our guests have everything they need?"

"I am think so, father..."

"He, and Milos, could not have possibly been more helpful," I said, eliciting a smile from Dimitris.

"And Milos?"

"He is out back helping Evangelis with his game of make-believe gardening."

"That boy loves to garden. It's one of the few times he seems to be lost in play, forgetful of his past."

"He seems very quiet," I said.

"We can only imagine what he has lived through."

"Why did he talk about orange and white lights?"

"The two brightest stars of Gemini are unmistakable—Pollux is an orange giant while his brother Castor burns white. Perhaps someone taught him to follow this constellation."

"It is hard to know what he remembers and what he has chosen to forget—what is real and what is imagined."

"Ti oraia einai afti," said Eftehea to Father Diogenes.

"Yia sou Mana, signomi pou aryisa," he replied as he moved closer to her. They also kissed, but then she spoke to him with a stern maternal voice.

"Mana says she is worried that Ion must be starving, and that I should save the chatter for later. Dimitris..."

"Yes, father."

"Before supper, please go to the cellar and retrieve a bottle of our most special wine."

Eftehea had set a beautiful table, complete with candles and flowers—picked an hour earlier from the garden. On a large platter in the center was the lamb, carved into smaller, and happily for me, unrecognizable pieces. Salads of dandelion greens and *melitzano*—marinated eggplant—sat on opposite ends of the table. There was also a smaller bowl of olives, and a plate of feta cheese. There was a spouted tin of the first pressings of olives—the omnipresent fruit.

Father Diogenes sat at the head of the table, and Ion sat at the other end. I was immediately to Ion's right, and Eftehea sat on his left. The boys flanked Father Diogenes, sitting across from each other, with Milos being to my immediate right. Evangelis had already eaten and had been put to bed.

At most American tables, at least three people would already be eating before the remaining guests would have sat down. Here, the movements were far more graceful, as if choreographed to an ancient rhythm, which honored the tradition of mealtime. It's possible that I was observing something unique to the Diogenes' home, or to that of a priest's family, but whatever the cause, I enjoyed the reverence that preceded our consumption.

When everyone was settled, Father Diogenes commenced grace. The words were Greek, but I felt their intention. After this formality, all raised their glasses in toast. A chorus of *Yasou* and *Yamas* rang out as glasses were clinked. The boys looked at me, and I chimed in with my own "Yamas!"

"Whew! This is incredibly strong!" I rasped after taking a sip of the pungent *retsina*.

Father Diogenes smiled. "During the Ottoman occupation they tried to forbid the Greeks from making wine. They put resin in the barrels so it would be too bitter to drink. We drank it anyway, now it is our custom. To our patron saint, Panteleimon," he offered another toast. "*Yamas*!"

"What was he canonized for? You'll have to forgive my scant knowledge of saints," I said.

"He was a doctor, martyred after refusing to yield his beliefs in the face of Roman vengeance. His name literally means *one who forgives all*. Would anyone else like to propose a toast this evening?"

"To Ion and his lovely niece," declared Dimitris without missing a beat.

"Well chosen," said Ion, looking straight at me. "Without her this could not be—and I would no longer be."

"I'd like to toast *to ya ya*," chimed in Milos using the affectionate term for grandmother, "for her prepare a meal fit for a king..."

"...and a long lost shepherd," whispered Ion as our glasses were clinked again.

"Marianna?" said Father Diogenes, looking towards me with a raised eyebrow.

"I'd like to honor you and your family. I am so touched that you have opened your home to Ion and me, and I am a stranger to you."

"It is a Greek custom, we call it *philoxenia*—a love of strangers," said Father Diogenes as glasses were raised and contents reduced.

"What about you, Mr. Theodore? Will you honor us with a salutation?"

"To my old friend, the patriarch of the only family I ever considered mine."

There was a soft murmuring of acknowledgement at this last toast for the man who was absent yet had brought us together. With grace and salutations declared, all formality was dropped. Good, hearty eating and enjoyment of the feast commenced in earnest. Platters were being passed around the table, and I helped myself to a sampling of all of the delicacies which comprised our bountiful table.

"You see that our village is very small," Father Diogenes said to me.

"Small indeed, yet great in its glory," interjected Ion.

"Ion's right," I said. "Even 'marathon' has become a word in our language—it's synonymous with any great undertaking."

"Here, it comes from the word *marathos*—meaning fennel—which grows wild here. It is an ancient custom that in remembrance of the Battle at Marathon, we will put fennel in our olives." I had noticed them in the dish of olives without realizing their significance.

"How was your flight?" Father Diogenes asked Ion a few minutes later, as we continued to dine.

"It amazes me that in one night, we traveled a distance that ancient mariners took months to navigate—if they survived," he mused.

"When you first made the trip, planes had propellers," I said.

"Propellers yes, but wings, no. My first trip was by steamship," laughed Ion.

"What do you do for a living, back in New York?" Father Diogenes asked me.

"She is lawyer in very, very big company," said Milos.

"Really, how exciting," said his father. "Is that a common profession for a woman to go into?"

"There are women in every field, but few female partners in my firm."

"That's quite an impressive accomplishment," Father Diogenes added.

I then proceeded to speak of how intense my career was and then rambled on about big clients, big cases and big verdicts. Noticing that I had monopolized the dialogue, I asked him "Father Diogenes, I don't know much about what a priest does when not leading a service. Was it church business that called you away from Marathon today?"

"I had to give a gentleman his last rites."

"Oh my! Did he pass peacefully?"

"Only he knows that. But he lived a long and wonderful life, there should be no regrets. Tonight, he sleeps in the Kingdom of Heaven." In one sentence, spoken without melodrama, Father Diogenes had underscored how much I inflate the significance of my work and its pressures—as if the world couldn't survive without SWB and it, in turn, couldn't survive without me. The way my colleagues and I boasted about our profession, one would think we dealt in matters of Life and Death. I was humbled in the presence of one who really did.

"I don't know how I could handle a job in which I would to confront such painful reality."

"Which reality is that, that we all must pass on one day?"

"It's one thing to philosophize about it, another to hold its hand as life slips away, I think."

"It is not the highlight of my 'job' as you call it, but remember, I helped prepare his soul for an even more important journey. Besides, last rites are necessary to make way for moments like tomorrow."

"Tomorrow?" I asked.

"Yes, I have the pleasure of administering first rights. *Ta Vaftisi*—a baptism—we shall introduce a child to the word of our Lord. From last rites to baptisms to last rites—the regeneration of life must continue. It is the balance between life's joys and sorrows that makes my path navigable."

"For me it is only path," interjected Dimitris. "As my father choose and Panayiotas before him," he continued with an air of pride. The implication was obvious, though Milos remained silent.

"That is indeed a wise and noble path, Dimitris, but fortunately, not everyone chooses it," said Ion.

"Why is fortunate?" Dimitris asked, shooting a glance across the table towards his brother.

"If every one were a shepherd, whom would they lead?" he said, as I noticed him place his hand on Milos' forearm.

"Do you think the family would mind if Ion and I came to see their son christened?" I asked.

Father Diogenes laughed. "There are no church memberships or invitations needed here. All who wish to partake of the services, even if just passively, are welcome. I am certain that the family will be much honored to have you witness such a sacred event in their lives."

"Speaking of baptisms, Ion, you never told me the rest of your story."

"What story, my dear?"

"You know the one I mean. Don't think you can mention that you were baptized here and leave it at that."

"Ion, you were baptized, here at Panteleimon?" asked Father Diogenes with some understandable surprise.

"Almost forty years ago. Panayiotas, was the new *Diakonos* here at Panteleimon."

"How is this possible?" asked Milos. "Why no when you are baby?"

"I was a slave to the Ottoman—they were not Christian."

"So what happened, Uncle Ion?" I asked.

"A simple baptism, that's all. Oil, water, praying, crying, crawling to church on our knees. Pretty straightforward."

"You crawled here on your knees? No offense to the holy, but why on Earth did you do that?"

"We were younger and far more impetuous back then. But I did learn two great lessons that day. The first was that through sacrifice lays salvation."

"And the other lesson?"

"Crawling hurts." Ion smiled, but it was a painful smile, as he seemed to momentarily relive the feeling of the sharp rocks beneath his soft flesh. "Speaking of walking, I am looking forward to taking some long ones around here with you, my dear," he said to me, deflecting interest from what I thought was the most fascinating topic of the evening's conversation.

"Wait a minute. Is that all?" I asked, expecting a much more elaborate story. "The Baptism? What happened, Uncle Ion?"

"There is nothing more to tell, it is just a tale of a lost sheep..."

"Lost, but apparently found," said Father Diogenes.

"Yes, found… Here at Panteleimon."

The sun sets late in the Greek summer. After our meal, I was fatigued, but instead of lying down, I went to the sea. Finding a vantage point high above the waters below, I just sat and watched.

As a student reading Homer, I always believed expressions like a *rosy-fingered dawn* or a *wine-dark sea* to be the hyperboles of poetry. That was until this evening as I watched a Greek sunset.

The waters were an unimaginable shade of fluorescent azure—exaggerated by the limestone formations that dropped off steeply and reflected the sun from beneath the surface. Rays of sunlight fractured into millions of sparks snapping silently on each ripple, glittering like a field of bobbing diamonds, before slowly turning a mix of indigos and violets. Layers of striated clouds appeared like vaporous layers of sedimentary rock—or the twisted fibers of cotton candy at a county fair. As the night sky deepened into cobalt, the sea below swelled like a chalice of burgundy wine. On its eddies danced millions of tiny fires which only extinguished as the sun passed the horizon. Only the crescent moon gave the scene anything resembling familiarity. The Gods had spoken, and all of man's wonders paled in comparison to this Olympian display of true power.

As I lay down to sleep that evening, I thought about the *retsina* and the salty olives bathed in fennel. There was no escaping the deep tradition of this land and its saturated antiquity. It permeated the air that I now breathed, it flowed in the holy waters of the baptism, it even flavored the very food I consumed. I was a stranger, yet I was beginning to feel the rhythms of this place.

Drifting into deep slumber, the last thought on my mind was an artist and a priest crawling on their hands and knees to the altar.

17
VAFTISI

"I have heard that Spartans preen themselves before battle," Pheidippides said *to Agapenor. "Surely at a time like that, men have far more important things to consider than vanity?"*

Agapenor laughed before he answered. "Lykurgus said 'well groomed hair makes the handsome more beautiful and the ugly more frightening.' When we beautify ourselves before battle, we concede not to vanity—we prepare to die. Every Spartan warrior marches with the admonition of his mother—H TAN H EPI TAS—return wearing your shield or lying on top of it. For when the shields of two great armies clash, and the Spartan warrior surges forward despite pain, hunger and bloody wounds—that is the moment that defines the greatness of our people."

I was disoriented. Lying somewhere between night and day—sure of where I wasn't but not of where I was. I didn't get up right away, taking a few minutes to reassemble the pieces of how I had come to be in this bed and in this state of serene wakefulness. I had no idea of what time it was, and I was pleased. So much of my life back in New York was spent caring about the time, accounting for hours, minutes and seconds. And the more events I crammed into these moments, the more they passed with meaningless brevity.

I went to the window. Its panes were obscured by heavy wooden shutters. I marveled at the confluence of the old and the new—then it struck me that the new was decaying faster than the old. The windows were crying out for a fresh coat of paint, while the ancient walls stood defiant in the face of time.

I pulled the shutters inward and drew a deep breath. A mist of pastoral warmth brushed my face as I detected traces of moisture from the sea. There was the aroma of evergreen from Aleppo pines and strains of jasmine danced on the breeze whistling through the louvers. Bleating sheep sounded in the distance. But the most remarkable sounds were the ones I could not hear—absent were the engines, horns, airplanes and the urban buzz that form the ambient noise of my life back home.

I was eager to explore.

I picked up my watch from the dresser, and then decided against putting it on. Tiptoeing down the corridor towards Ion's room, I discovered that I was the last to rise. Eftehea poured me a cup of coffee that I carried out to the portico. Evangelis was playing in the little area on the side of the house. I wouldn't have called it a yard, at least not the trimmed grass variety I was accustomed to. I always associated lawns with escaping the steel and cement city to Nature, though they are anything but natural. They are temporal testaments to our desire to domesticate and control our environment. When we move on or simply stop mowing them—they revert to their wild state—reminding us of how illusory that control is.

"Excuse me Father, I didn't see you there." He was sitting in a solid wooden chair to the left of me as I came outside.

"Good morning, Marianna. I was watching Evangelis."

I almost gasped as I took my first sip of coffee. Father Diogenes laughed.

"Strong, no?"

"That's an understatement, Father." As I stared at the bottom of the cup, I saw what appeared to be a deposit of thick brown sludge. It had the consistency of honey and the color of a spittoon of chewing tobacco.

"There are those who can read a person's fortune from the coffee's residue."

"I'm not sure I'd want my fortune told."

"The age old dilemma of when to know and when to learn."

"Did you see my uncle this morning?"

"He's with my sons. They're repairing our tractor. I need it later, after the services."

"It's hard for me to imagine your eminence on a tractor."

"Wasn't our greatest teacher born in a manger?"

"Yes, I suppose you're right, Father Diogenes."

"Please, do not call me Father Diogenes. I am Yiannis."

"I'm not used to calling a priest by his given name."

"If the Lord lets us call his son by his first name, who am I to stand on formality?" We both laughed.

"Thank you, Yiannis. How is he doing?" I said gesturing towards Evangelis.

"He seems a little happier, but it is not so good for him to adjust too much, he'll only have to move on soon."

"Dimitris told me how overcrowded the orphanages are."

"I am never happy when their businesses are booming, but I received news yesterday of a possible space at *Orfanotrofio ta Angelouthia*, the main orphanage in Athens. I will go there this week to begin the process." I wasn't raised believing that anyone had died for my sins, but while I slept in comfort, men like Father Diogenes stood guard—bearing humanity's ills on their shoulders.

"May I accompany you, if you think it would be all right?"

"For them, it will be no problem. I'm more concerned if you will be all right." It took me a moment to understand the implication of what he had just said.

I looked back at Evangelis and said, "He seems so innocent, like an angel," I said. I noticed that Father Diogenes was laughing. "What's so funny?"

"That's his name."

"What?"

"Evangelis—it means *innocent angel*." I heard Eftehea call out to Father Diogenes. "Will you excuse me, that was Mana letting me know I need to prepare for church. I'll send her out to watch Evangelis."

"I'll watch him," I offered.

"Are you sure?"

"I'd love to, really. If he'll let me, that is."

"Wonderful." He turned to Evangelis who was busying himself with a small trowel he had found. "Prepi nap au pau na estimaso ti litourgia. I Mariana tha mini kondasou, then milai Elinika."

"What did you tell him?"

"To go easy on you, since you can't speak Greek," he laughed softly to himself as he walked away.

I sat and watched Evangelis. Black velvet. That's the best way to describe his close-cropped hair. Dimitris had guessed he was around six or seven years old, judging more from his speech than his malnourished physique. He was small and gaunt with the cavity of his upper abdomen accentuated by protruding ribs. The only things that appeared above average in size were his ears, which tilted slightly outwards. But for some dirt on his hands, knees and face—he appeared the essence of piety. He neither smiled nor frowned. He played in the soil not as a child making a mess, but above it, honoring it, molding it.

He was deep in concentration, digging small holes. He would first dig out some dirt, and then methodically pile it next to the trench. He placed small leaves and pebbles in the hole, then scraped the loose dirt back into it, patting it down. He was trying to plant something, perhaps he had once seen Yiannis, or some other adults, tilling and planting the fields. Too bad he had planted rocks and dead leaves. It looked as if he wanted to create life, to see something, anything grow. So much around him had died or disintegrated, maybe he had decided to take matters into his own hands. A plan came into my mind—but it would have to wait for later that night, and I would need to procure something from town.

Evangelis didn't look at me, at least not when my eyes were on his, though there were moments when my eyes drifted away that I felt his gaze. I decided to move closer to him. I stood up and took a step forward, but with each foot forward, he slowly moved away. It wasn't an obvious evasion, but sure enough, I couldn't get closer to him, not without breaking at him quickly. When I retreated back to the portico, he moved closer again, without any indication of purpose or premeditation. It was as if there were an invisible string attaching us, and it would not allow anything greater or less than its length between us. I could not get closer to him, and he could not get farther from me.

Innocent angel—what key do you hold? Patience had never been one of my virtues. Luckily, one is never too old to learn.

Ion and I slowly made our way towards the church.

"Ion, you never speak of God. I'm not sure what you believe."

"I had no exposure to the faith of my parents, if they had faith at all. But all men have God, whether they see him or not."

"I'm surprised. Whenever you speak of religion, it's usually with frivolity not reverence."

"It is the rigid ritual without substance that I find frivolous. Formal mechanics of faith without spirit means nothing to me. But I have *seen* God."

"You've actually seen God?"

"Once, when I stood in the Sistine Chapel. Not at the altar or in the scriptures, but on the ceiling. And the divine hand was that of a flesh and blood man, the stroke of creation came from his brush and from the palette of his own mind. Who today remembers Pope Julius II—yet who can forget Michelangelo? I do not believe in the untouchable—I am touched by the unbelievable."

"Last evening you said you were a lost sheep who was found."

"I did not speak of me."

"It wasn't you? But you acknowledged Father Diogenes..."

"I told him the only thing that I could say—what he needed to hear."

"I don't understand, Ion."

"I was lost, but I was not the sheep."

"Who then...?"

"Panayiotas."

We had just reached the front steps of Panteleimon. The depth of what I still didn't know about Ion's life, about my own feelings and my faith, was unfolding before me. I entered through the large brass doors, gripped by a feeling that I was traveling in a direction from which there was no way back.

I had never been inside an orthodox church. As I entered, its exterior veil of simplicity quickly evaporated. It was lavishly decorated, with ornate gilded columns and intricate murals painted upon the domed ceiling and along every wall. Dozens of scenes depicted Christ in different stories from the Bible. In the central dome, he was surrounded by his disciples and Saints appeared in growing circles around them. What made the scenes so brilliant were the colors.

Absent were the muted hues of the pre-renaissance. These were alive with bold pigments, which ran across the spectrum of color. The floor was laid in large marble tiles, and my eye was drawn to the center of the floor, directly beneath the great dome. Inlaid in black and sienna marble was a mosaic of *Dikefalos Aetos*, the two-headed eagle, symbol of Constantinople and Greek Orthodoxy.

Everything was already in place for the baptism. The altar had several prayer books, wrapped in cloth, and there was a small bottle of olive oil. In front of this table was a large brass urn, filled with the waters that had been blessed by Father Diogenes in preparation of the child's purification.

Ion placed a few drachmas in a collection box and then chose two candles from a tray next to it. We lit them and placed them in a large, wrought iron candelabra. Ours were the first, but soon, it would be ablaze with those of Panteleimon's parishioners.. Ion and I took seats to the far left of the main pews.

The family of the child had arrived, and guests were streaming into the church. The boy, I guessed him to be about six months old, was clad in a one-piece blue jumper. It was a big day for him, but I suspect an even more important day in the eyes of his parents. Today, they would send their child through the same rite of passage that they and their ancestors had traversed.

Fathers Diogenes and Xenopoulos had come out. Each had on his traditional long black *Raso*, but over the top, each wore a unique and special floor length vest, which was woven from a light material like linen. Dozens of red crosses and eagles were embroidered on the white backgrounds.

The congregation had now gathered forming a semi-circle around the priests, the boy, his parents and the couple chosen to be godparents. Father Diogenes began to recite prayers in an archaic form of Pontic Greek used now only in Eastern Orthodox churches. He spoke into a microphone that he held in his right hand. Dimitris and an elderly man stood behind pulpits. They read from the *Evangelio*, the Greek Orthodox Bible, and the *Palia Diathiki*—a Byzantine translation of the Hebraic Torah, the original Five Books of Moses.

Father Diogenes asked the child's father whether his son was ready to repel Satan and to accept God and Jesus Christ. The father answered affirmatively, but I could see that the child was more interested in playing with the microphone than repelling Satan. As Father Diogenes held it near to the father's lips, the boy would make a grab for it, successfully on a couple of occasions. The Papas didn't flinch as he wrestled the microphone back, apparently not the first time he had to participate in this cat and mouse activity.

The *Ieria Amfias*, the white overvests, were pulled back and tied. While the prayers continued, I watched each priest slowly and methodically unbuttoning his shirt cuffs and folding them back over the *Rasos* until arms were bare. Next, the olive oil was poured into the urn while Father Diogenes recited the holy vows.

The parents then removed the boy's clothes. Naked, he was brought before God and the assembled congregation. Father Diogenes raised the child in both arms as Father Xenopoulos anointed him with the Holy Water.

Ion was perfectly silent and reverently took in the pungent air redolent with the flowers in the rosary garden. I watched him observing the censer's smoke dissipating into the air and with it the incantations invoking Life and God and renouncing Death and Evil. Above the altar hovered the dark wooden image of Christ—mortally wounded—yet strong and triumphant. The Savior was severe and sinewy, muscular, and almost naked in his suffering, a man and yet a boy, a God and a waif.

I had always thought of Christianity as a religion of the desert, one cooled and healed by the cleansing presence of water. It began with Jesus' trial in the Galilee wilderness, forty days and forty nights of temptation. This was followed by his baptism at the Jordan and his ministry as a fisher of men's souls. It was easy for me to see Jesus in the beautifully painted basin of water that now cleansed the child of the dust and sweat of this summer morning. The freshness of the Holy waters seemed at odds with the solemnity of the ritual—that of a child washed of sins he did not yet commit.

My eyes had wandered to one of the frescoes, a scene of a handsome man with a lyre being sent down what looked like an abyss or a river—I could not tell which—while a figure who looked like his mother mourned his loss from above.

"Who is that?" I whispered to Ion, who seemed to be staring intensely at the same scene.

"Orpheus," he said softly, without turning his head. I looked at Ion's curls and the curls of the figure.

"But he's a..."

"My dear, the pagan gods were the precursors to the God of Abraham. Orpheus was an enchanted son who suffered in love and suffered in death at the hands of the furies. His head flowed *down the swift Hebrus* as the poet said."

"Ion, I'd swear you could have sat as the model for that Orpheus."

"I did. I sat a long time before a mirror—on a scaffold next to my brushes and paints."

"So you helped to paint this church?"

Ion nodded.

"*Vaftisizetai doylos Andreas eis to onoma toy Patros, to Yios, kai toy Agioys Pneymatos*," said Father Diogenes with the solemn intonation of the heavens. I felt the words—'I baptize you, Andreas, servant of God, in the name of the Father, the Son and the Holy Spirit'—as into the waters the child was submerged.

"So, how on earth did Panayiotas get you to come here and be christened?" Ion and I continued our dialogue.

Ion laughed. "We both had consumed a lot of *firewater*, and he made me an offer I couldn't refuse."

"Wait a minute, Ion. You and he were drinking..."

"We were beyond drinking," he said. "We were drunk."

"Drunk? A Greek Orthodox Priest?"

"He came to me one night, after a particularly strained day of relief work. Under his garments, he was carrying a bottle of *Tsiporo*, a very strong grappa indeed."

"I can't believe it."

"Yes, he must have been quite resourceful to commandeer such a hard to get commodity."

"That wasn't what I meant..."

"We were both working in Athens during the famines and there were outbreaks of every disease short of the plague. Panayiotas was assigned to the Church of Saint Sabbos near Ampelokipi, and I was a volunteer with the Greco-American chapter of the Red Cross. There was scant medical relief, and people languished without food and water. We tried to save them, to provide some sustenance for the suffering, but many we could only make comfortable in their last days. When Panayiotas entered my room that night, he had a look on his face of utter despair. He sat down next to me and dropped his head into his hands and groaned. When he looked up, the rims of his eyes were red."

"'Ion,' he began. 'I don't know what kind of God would do this.' It was what we both had been thinking. I had long had this thought but felt I had no right to utter it to someone as devoted as Panayiotas.

"'Perhaps, Panayiotas, it is too much for us to think about what kind of God oversees this world.'

"'I can't help thinking of it. I have devoted all that I am to God.' He had just gotten word that he was to become the O Papas tis enorias tis Marathonas—the priest of the community of Marathon. 'But when I think of all of this suffering, I wonder. Can God be good and omnipotent? If He is omnipotent and people suffer, then He cannot also be...' Panayiotas stopped, and gulped his words then continued his train of thought. 'If He is good, then He cannot be omnipotent.'

"'Does God command the impossible?' I asked him.

"'Didn't He ask Abraham to sacrifice his son—how could any man believe that could emanate from a God who is just?'

"'Didn't He sacrifice his own?'

"'Yes, but when I look around me I see death everywhere, nothing but the face of death, and I am terrified...'

"'Of dying?'

"'No...of doubting.' It seemed to me that Panayiotas reasoned because he suffered.

"How did you respond to him?" I asked.

"I suggested that perhaps he should not reason. I watched as Panayiotas' face grew longer as he said to me, 'Maybe you are right. It is not for man to reason about God—that is faith. But my faith is waning. Why do you work with me—you are not a believer?'

"'Panayiotas, if you want to know what a man believes, don't ask about his theology, watch him in his deeds, what he does, how he conducts his life. Then you will know if he believes.'

"'And what of your soul, my dear Ion?'"

"*Vaftisizetai doylos Andreas eis to onoma toy Patros, to Yios, kai toy Agioys Pneymatos,*" rose above the din of the church and our whispering as the child was lowered into the cleansing waters again.

"'We are both Greek, Panayiotas, and we both know that before Christ there was no separation of spirit and flesh, form and content. They were all one, each sanctifying the other. That was an assumption that helped the ancient Athenians make great art.'

"'But, Ion, it was pagan art.'

"'Perhaps, but it was of the spirit, don't you believe that?'

"'It is hard not to.'

"'Art has made a convert of me, Panayiotas.'

"'To Christianity?'

"'Its essence, the promise of the spirit suffering with the flesh.'

"'Can you prove this?'

"'Prove? Now, there you are again, Panayiotas, unable to accept matters on faith.'"

"And then he outmaneuvered me at my own philosophizing. Panayiotas turned to me and said, 'Perhaps my friend, it would restore my faith if I could complete your conversion in the Holy Waters of Panteleimon.' I told him to ask me again in the morning when I could tell if it was my soul and not the spirits talking."

"He remembered to ask?" I said.

"He had a memory that could pierce the strongest *ouzo*."

"So, you restored his faith, and he saved your soul. A good bargain?" I quipped.

"In the end. But I wandered, first, for a long time. Searching for some divine sign, before I could return to my appointment at the altar."

"Did you find one?"

"I returned."

"*Vaftisizetai doylos Andreas eis to onoma toy Patros, to Yios, kai toy Agioys Pneymatos*," said Father Diogenes in the background for the third and final time.

The young boy, crying at the top of his lungs, was now wrapped in cloth and held in his mother's arms. He would soon be dressed in a new outfit chosen for this occasion. "And I was baptized," said Ion. "But that was nothing more than ritual, the form over the substance. Evidence of my rebirth can be seen elsewhere," Ion said, as he glanced again at animated forms that graced the church's walls. "I was baptized all right, but not by the cross—by the scaffold."

"I still can't get over thinking about you and Panayiotas crawling here."

"Penance, my dear. Penance and joy. It hurt, but I was thankful that I could feel. When I returned here to Marathon, I was dead. Here, discovering my art, I felt reborn. I could create—I could express passion without purgatory—I could be free. I lived here for nearly two years, painting and restoring many of these frescoes in return for food, board and salvation," he laughed. "Given the constant misery and suffering of that time, only a man of God or an insane man would have remained in Athens."

"But Panayiotas and you did, and without concern for yourselves or personal safety."

"As I said—a man of God and one who was insane."

We left the church before everyone else. The family of Andreas would remain there for a while, as hugs would be exchanged, photographs taken and stories told of baptisms come and gone. We walked back towards the farmhouse. The sun was already beginning its daily calefaction of the world, even in the shade.

"I'm glad we came, Ion. I was touched by how proud the child's parents looked."

"To witness life's beginning—is there anything more beautiful? Soon, it will be my turn, no, my duty, to make room for another young soul to take my place."

"It's hard to imagine not seeing someone you love, ever again," I said, trying to skirt the subject striking at my deepest anxiety.

"I fear something worse. I fear that I will lose myself before I am lost to the world—that I will no longer be in control of my fate, much less the manner in which it ends."

"I suppose none of us has a choice about that."

"That's the consummate definition of slavery, isn't it? Perhaps a man need not see his final breaths as an act of submission."

"How?"

"By choosing the time and manner of his death..."

"As an act of defiance?"

"No—the ultimate expression of freedom."

Later that evening, candles softly illuminated Ion's room as we sat and talked.

"Ion, I hope this isn't a bad time to speak about this, I know that Panayiotas' death has been terribly painful."

"He was to tell me something, but his passing has dashed my hopes of finding..."

"Of finding what, Ion?"

"There was a work I never completed, one that my old friend would have cherished. Perhaps I can bring full circle that which life left unattainable."

I kissed Ion good night, blew out the candles and made my way back to my room in near blackness. Exhaustion seized me. I was literally pulling back my sheets when I remembered something very important. It probably could have waited until morning, but I didn't want to forget.

I put on a white button-down shirt and stuffed into its breast pocket a small bag that Dimitris had brought me from town this afternoon. I'm sure he was puzzled by my request. I unlatched my door and within a few moments was standing outside in the dark, but for the faint light of a waxing moon. I moved silently to the garden where Evangelis had been playing earlier, after a few minutes search in the near dark, I found the trowel he had been using. Kneeling on the ground, I went to work unearthing the trench where Evangelis had earlier planted his pebbles. Opening the small bag of seeds, I sprinkled them into the trench. Just a few more minutes, and the thin dry soil was back in place.

Tomorrow, and each day thereafter, Evangelis and I would make sure to water this trench. The seeds of life had been planted—and one boy's precious task would not be denied.

18
ELLINAS! ELLINAS!

"Pheidippides, we have been told of your heroism in running from Marathonas. That is a feat worthy of our respect. You are an honored guest in our city," King Cleomenes spoke.

"Thank you, great King Cleomenes. It is true. I have run a great distance but I have a message of greater importance. For even now, as we speak, the Persians have disembarked on our soil—making camp along the shores of the Bay of Marathonas. I can only pray that they have not already launched their attack on our vastly outnumbered army. Men of Lacedaemon, the Athenians beg you to help them. Do not suffer a most ancient city in Greece to meet with slavery at the hands of the barbarians."

"Barbarian means one who does not speak Greek," Ion informed me. "To them, other languages sounded like *bar, bar, bar*."

"So what of Shakespeare, Milton, Rousseau, and Lamartine?" I asked.

"Barbarians," he laughed.

"I guess that also makes me one," I teased him.

"You speak Greek, you just don't know it yet," he laughed again, not willing to be cornered.

Sure. I still confused *Oxi* and *Nai*. They sound like *Okay* and *No*, but respectively they mean *No* and *Yes*. In high school, I thought that French was hard. Compared to learning Greek, it is easier than finger-painting. Greek's unique alphabet adds another degree of difficulty. Throw in lower case letters, special accent marks, and colloquial demotic versus *kathaverousa*—classical Greek scripture—and I knew I wasn't going to be conversing in it anytime soon.

On Monday morning, Ion and I arose as the cock crowed. We didn't have to meet the Hellas Tours bus until eleven, but I had promised the passport officer that we'd handle Ion's passport first thing this morning. Milos and Dimitris were going to accompany us, having been excused by Father Diogenes from their daily chores about Panteleimon.

I walked across the hall to the bathroom and was greeted by the comfortable warmth of the morning air, so different from the cold assault—whether from winter's lack of sun or summer's intrusion of air conditioning—from which I usually rushed into and out of the shower. Returning to my room, I let the towel drop to the floor. My hair was still wet, and drops were running down my shoulders and over my chest and back. I stepped to the window to take in the glorious sunshine. The breeze blew across my body as I touched my suddenly hardened nipples and goose flesh, caused as the remaining moisture evaporated.

I ran my hands over my body, applying some jasmine infused oil. It reminded me of how long it had been since I had felt caressed. I let myself—hand and mind together—drift into the listlessness of reverie. As I drifted I caught my reflection in the glass panes. My half-closed eyes seemed to look back at me as I plunged deeper and deeper into a trance. I was watching and being watched at once and the sensation thrilled me and enveloped me from crown to toe.

I looked again out toward the sea and no longer saw it as distant or other. It was my own pool, and I felt that I could simply dive into it and wear its aqua silk over my naked skin. Sea and sky, all one moment all being one. Sea and sky and eyes. They were not mine! Another's eyes stared back at me like dark clouds from behind the olive trees, and I was startled. Startled, then frightened. Then they were gone. Intense and dark—I'd seen these eyes before. Dimitris? Milos? I ran across the room away from the window, and hit the table with the violence of my retreat. Had our gazes crossed in an instant or had his eyes been lingering as I wandered into myself?

My body was electrified from the shock of its unexpected exposure. The fact that I didn't know who my observer was, and yet had to face him in a few moments, didn't suppress the anxiety—or my arousal. No harm had been done, yet my hand shook as I held it out before my eyes. I tried to convince myself that it was my modesty that made my body react so, but that virtue had been sacrificed long ago under the strobe lights of Studio 54 and the wild nights of Tea Dances on Fire Island.

A few more minutes to brush my hair, a touch of makeup and my ritual was complete. I took a few deep breaths to steady my nerves, and then walked down the hall to the kitchen.

Eftehea had a cup of coffee waiting for me. It had taken a few days to get used to its sandy texture. When Dimitris and Milos came in, I sank my eyes into my cup. Neither one's mannerisms gave me any hint of who had been the voyeur. When either one of them looked at me, I felt naked again before the window.

"We must be go not later than seven," said Dimitris, snapping me back to the moment.

The two boys—boys, not men—went back out again. Milos said nothing. Was his silence a sign, or was the fact that Dimitris spoke a betrayal of his reconnaissance? I was reading too much into it. Maybe neither one had seen me at all, or if they had, perhaps neither one cared. This was Greece after all. Her islands are renowned for their topless beaches and nightlife defined by veil-like fashions and wild dances.

I took my coffee and went to find Ion.

"Are we ready to go now?" he asked.

"Almost. Dimitris said we're going to leave in about half an hour. Eftehea is in the kitchen as usual, preparing something special for you."

"Oh she is, is she?" he laughed.

"You old fox, you know that she fawns over you."

“She’s just being a gracious hostess, I’m sure that’s all,” he said, unable to contain his smile.

“Gracious hostess? Ha! Don’t get me wrong, that she is, but I can see the way she gets all flustered every time she is near you.”

“Flustered, I don’t...”

“Now Ion, you know more than I’ll ever know about most things, but I’m a woman. I know when another is flustered and the look in her eyes when you come into the room is pure infatuation.” I was teasing him, but there was truth in my observations. Whenever she would hear Ion approaching, or have to go to his room, I would observe the casual primping of her hair or the smoothing out of her dress—the unmistakable preening of a woman who that refused to let the passage of time have the last word over her femininity.

“You’re imagining...”

“Now, now, stop denying it. You’re almost blushing,” I laughed.

“She’s suffered a lot in her life and years of endurance have toughened her. But few in Marathon could once boast such beauty. Of course, she was never as captivating as you,” he said, as if I were jealous of her. I thought it amusing that Ion might think me jealous of a woman in her seventies. I was, but not because she paid particular attention to the man I held so dearly. No, I was jealous because experienced a part of his life that I could not.

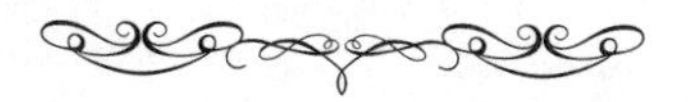

“What are those boxes with crosses on them?” I asked while pointing to several on the side of the road as we made our way into Athens.

“They are *Eklhsaki*, memorials to peoples killed on that place,” said Milos.

“Greek drivers is crazy,” added Dimitris. “Maybe ten thousands killed every year.”

“What vanity and recklessness can do,” said Ion, shaking his head from side to side.

In a little over an hour, we pulled onto Avenue *Vassilisis Sophias*—the location of the U.S. Consulate. While Ion waited for his passport to be readied, I went across the street to the Greek National Library. I wanted to do some research on the obol, but all the titles were in Greek. The librarian allowed me to use her computer for my search.

The most obscure reference was the one that I found most intriguing. It was from a *National Geographic* article entitled “Controversy Surrounds Greek Shipwreck.” The ship sank in the Black Sea during the Crimean War. In 1854,

Czar Nikolas I—head of the Russian Orthodox Church—waged war against the Ottomans to protect Christian sites in the Holy Land. After initial successes, the tide of battle turned against the Russians. In a vision, Saint Peter told the Czar that he needed to make peace with the Pontic Greeks if he was to defeat the Turkish alliance. These Greeks had settled the Black Sea—*Evxinos Pontos*—a thousand years before Christ. The monks of Mount Athos sent a ship to retrieve captives and a bounty the Czar hoped would appease them. The ship never returned—going down in a storm off the coast near Sinope. Recently found records showed that its compliment of goods included "a silver star once enshrined in the Church of the Nativity and a sacred pendant worn by the messenger of Marathonas."

The controversy centered on whether a salvage attempt would violate the rights of those who lay entombed in the vessel's remains. It quoted Dr. Schaffhausen, who claimed that the sighting of the obol in Germany, eighty years later, proved it had not gone to its watery grave. Other experts flatly dismissed his claims as being "sensationalist and lacking in evidentiary foundation."

When we arrived at Omonia Square, the tour bus was taking on passengers. Dimitris dropped us off and then went to park the car. Within fifteen minutes, the door of the bus had closed, and our day of sightseeing had begun.

"Ladies and Gentlemen, welcome to the Hellas Day Coach tour of Athens, one of the most fascinating cities in the world. Our arts and sciences have paved the way of civilization for millennia. My name is Adonis Zarzavatsakis, and I will be your guide today as we see modern Athens, and then step back in time to witness the glory of yesteryear. Where are you from," he asked the group. Several nationalities—German, English, Spanish, Scandinavian, Greek, American—were shouted out.

"Wonderful. Whether you are Greek or foreign, whether this is your first time to Athens, or you are a veteran, sit back and relax in our newest luxury high-deck, fully air-conditioned bus, and enjoy the sights of this timeless city. I will be narrating as we go, and the driver will stop periodically to allow you to take pictures."

I noticed a resurgence of Ion's energy. He seemed to defy time's progression, becoming again the Ion Theodore of my childhood—a man telling mythological stories at lazy summer barbecues as crickets chirped and ice cream melted.

The bus made its way through the sites of Athens as the guide continued his narration.

"Ladies and Gentlemen, we are now going to stop at the world's oldest athletic stadium," he said, as he ushered us off the bus at its entrance. "Please stay together as we will be spending the next thirty minutes outside."

Panathenaic Stadium, designed in the shape of an elongated horseshoe, is open to the air and sky. We passed through a plain wrought iron fence that led directly onto the athletic field. The black ground, made of some elastic composite, felt spongy beneath my feet. Above us, on three sides, rose its glittering white marble seats. So clean and pure, it harkened of an ancient time and its proud tradition. Its simplicity was a reminder that here, glory is won by athletes not architects.

"If you would gather closer for just a moment. You are now standing in one of the world's most sacred and storied athletic arenas," he began. "Do not let its lack of ornament camouflage its grandeur. Many of the world's greatest athletes have competed on this very surface." Our guide didn't seem to be much older than Dimitris, though I fear that anyone under twenty-five looks like a teenager to me these days. He was dressed in gray slacks, and his light blue shirt and dark blue tie gave him an offical appearance. He must have been on the verge of a heat stroke in that outfit.

"The stadium was built in the Fourth Century B.C., and looked very much as you see her today, though modern construction has dramatically altered its original pastoral setting. It holds sixty thousand spectators in seats hand-carved from local Pentelic marble." I tried to imagine how these athletes felt, with their hearts beating rapidly and adrenaline rushing through their veins, as they stood in the center of this vast arena.

"To the ancient Greeks, athletic training had a greater purpose than frivolous or leisurely play. Each event in the games has its origins in military necessity. Men who could run, throw javelins, wrestle, box, and race with shields in full body armor—*Citius, Altius, Fortius*—were more likely to survive the physical demands of the ancient battlefield.

"*Citius, Altius, Fortius*—swifter, higher and stronger," Ion whispered to me.

"Just as athletes used to gather here from the Hellenic world, today, they come from the four corners of the globe to compete in a variety of track and field events." Over here, on the right-hand side of the entrance, is a plaque listing all of the Games and their host cities—please take note of the first name on the list."

It was, of course, Athens.

"On the other side is one commemorating Greek athletes who have championed in the Games. Though they are all worthy of mention, let me draw your attention once again to the very first name though written in Greek..."

"*Spyridon Louis*," said Ion.

"Quite right sir. From your conversation I took you for an American, but you apparently read Greek."

"A little bit," he responded with a devilish smile.

"Who was that," asked the same German man who had spoken before.

"He won the first Olympic marathon," answered our guide. "We will speak more of him in a few minutes, but now, let us walk to the other end of the stadium. For those of you able to climb, we will visit the top row. Perhaps you will feel the spirits of the hundreds of generations who watched their heroes competing below."

We walked over to the wall of seats, which rose above us like a marble tidal wave. There was only one way up, and that was along a steep and narrow pathway between the long rows of stone benches.

"I want to go up," said Ion to me with a muted voice.

"I don't see how..." I trailed off. I watched him look up as if were seriously contemplating an ascent, but he then looked down and shrugged.

"You will reach top, Mr. Theodore," said Dimitris. "We are climb together."

Offering no explanation and waiting for no reply, he came over to Ion and lifted him into his formidable arms and began to climb. The summit afforded a majestic view, not only of the stadium, but also of the hills beyond.

"One of the most memorable sporting events of all time took place here in 1896, the inaugural Games of the modern Olympics. As a Greek, I am unashamedly prejudiced," said the guide with an infectious grin.

"The day of Resurrection," interrupted Ion. He was speaking to me and the boys, but it was loud enough for Adonis to hear. "The opening ceremonies fell on Easter Sunday," Ion continued.

"You are well informed, sir," he said, but I could sense that he didn't like to compete for attention.

"Thank you, young man. I am thoroughly enjoying your stories," said Ion with genuine affection.

"As I was saying, the Games had not been going so well for the Greek national team. The week's events were being dominated by American, English and German athletes. Greece had not won a single first-place finish. The final day of competition had arrived, and one of the last events on that last day was the marathon. The runners began at ..." he paused in mid-sentence because Ion was talking to Dimitris, and had once again interrupted his train of thought. The guide continued, "... began at two o'clock. No one in the stadium knew who was leading the race as there was no television coverage." Several more times he paused to glance over at Ion with a look of impatience as he could hear Ion whispering to Dimitris. "Sixty thousand waited for any news of the race's progress and," he stopped in mid-sentence and finally turned to Dimitris and asked, "Okay, what is it now?"

"He says there were over a hundred thousand people waiting."

"Oh really, is that so? Perhaps he missed the earlier part of my description. The stadium only holds sixty thousand," said the guide with a look of condescension, as Ion continued to whisper to Dimitris. "Now what is he saying?"

"He says the others watched from those hills which overlook the stadium," said Dimitris with a shrug.

"Apparently, we have an expert in our midst today. How fortunate for us," he said with noticeable sarcasm. "And how has your grandfather come to know so much about this stadium?"

Dimitris spoke to the guide in Greek, his voice steady and deliberate.

"Dimitris, please, it is of no import to these people," Ion said, tugging at Dimitris' arm.

"What is he saying to him, Milos?" I asked.

"He is say that Ion is not grandfather, but if he is that, no grandson could be more proud ..."

"Sir, is what this young man told me true?" The guide suddenly asked Ion with a look of astonishment.

"Yes, and I apologize for his impetuousness and my interruptions," said Ion.

The guide came closer to Ion. "Please sir, do not apologize. Allow me to shake your hand. What is your name, sir?"

"Ion Theodore, and he was a champion," said Dimitris with an air of pride. "Mr. Theodore, forgive me, but our uncle is speak of you many, many times."

"Ladies and gentlemen, it appears we are all honored today. This man has competed in this very stadium—in the Panhellenic Games." Several eyebrows raised, and I could hear a murmuring of respect.

"He won the olive wreath here in 1928," Dimitris added to the guide and tour group, several of whom turned their cameras on Ion and began to snap pictures.

"And he personally knew Spyridon Louis," I was happy to interject. Adonis sat down and a large smile came over his face.

"I have given this tour several thousand times, and I have never met a man who competed here. Perhaps you will let me sit and listen to the tour that I have been pretending to give. Please, tell us of the great victory."

"What I can tell is sketchy as age has made fuzzy the memories of that day." I think we all expected a story of Ion's Panhellenic triumph, but he had no intention of orating on that subject—determined to regale us with the feat of his mentor, Spyridon.

"He told me that the race saw many leaders, each taking turns, vying to set the pace. First an Australian, then a Frenchman, then Flack—the favored American. Since this was only the second marathon ever run, there were few strategies and no one could gain from the experience of previous runners—the last one having collapsed dead after his momentous feat. Spyridon, though a sheepherder from Amarousi, had developed great endurance from running up mountainsides with heavy water jugs.

"Throughout the race, runners fell victim to the marathon's grueling demands and began to falter, but Spyridon edged closer to the thinning pack in the lead. As they turned onto *Leoforos Mesogeion*, about six or seven miles from the finish, he felt his pains suddenly intensify—searing his chest and limbs. That was followed by a growing numbness as every impulse commanded him to stop."

"Sounds like he had hit the 'wall,'" offered a younger tourist, I think a Spaniard. He was fit and had the build of a man who was probably no stranger to long-distance running.

"Yes, he had, but there was yet no word for it. And few knew what lay on the other side of this physical barrier. There is only one way to get to the other side, and that is straight through her heart. Spyridon willed himself through the wall of pain with nothing but courage. He took the lead—one he would not relinquish."

"The crowd must have been incredibly excited," said one of the tourists.

"Remember, they were watching other events, unaware of the great struggle being waged on the road to Athens. Shortly after four-thirty, a Royal Hellenic artillery unit fired a cannon as a signal that the leader was a mile away. The crowd grew silent as the pole-vaulting event was temporarily suspended. Observers on the nearby hills couldn't make out his identity, but they could see the colors that adorned his struggling form—white and light blue—the national colors of Greece. Then a cry went out so loud that it was said it could be heard as far away as Marathon itself. '*Ellinas, Ellinas*,'—A Greek! A Greek!"

Ion paused for a moment, breathed in deeply and then continued.

"Try to imagine yourselves in these very seats, at that very moment," he said to us as we sat transfixed, "as the hero approached. The crowd was in a frenzy as that lone figure, clad in that glorious shade of Aegean blue, came running through those gates. A roar erupted as the fans went delirious with patriotic fever. As he ran by the royal seats, Spyridon gave a humble hand gesture of greeting to his country's King and Princes who joined the crowds in their wild cheering. As he broke the string, which was stretched out at the Sphenodone, Spyridon ran into the hearts of his countrymen and into immortality. So overwhelmed were Crown Prince Constantine and Prince George, that they both ran out onto the field and joined Spyridon in his victory lap. Then carrying him in their arms, they brought him before the King—who had broken his naval cap waving it so enthusiastically."

"What did he say?" asked Adonis.

"Nothing. Spyridon told me that when he saw tears in the King's eyes, he turned away so as not to embarrass his majesty. Spyridon had won for Greece, for Pheidippides, for the warriors of Marathon and for every shepherd who dreams of glory. I do not believe that there was a man present who could forget that moment of victory for as long as he lived; nor was there likely anyone in Greece at that time who could not recall exactly where he was the moment he learned of Spyridon's triumph that afternoon," said Ion.

"That is incredible," said the Italian man.

"Perhaps more incredible is that Spyridon almost didn't compete. That morning, he left Amarousi after taking a sacrament from his priest, calling upon the heavens to aid him in his struggle into the unknown. He made it to the starting line just minutes before he would have been ruled ineligible."

"What happened to him after the race?" asked a few of our company.

"That Sunday, dressed in his finest *fustanella*, he joined the other Olympic champions at a breakfast at the Royal Palace. His humility was inspiring to all who were there, but if you knew Spyridon as I had the fortune to, it would have been no surprise. He was a national hero, and many gifts were offered to him by his fellow countrymen. Even the King asked him what he wished for on behalf of a grateful nation."

"What did he ask for?" asked Adonis.

"A cart."

"That's it?" asked the guide.

"That was it. A small cart to bring back to Amarousi to help him carry water for his father."

I do not share the American males' love of sports, but I have overheard enough to know about free agents and bonus babies and walkouts and holdouts and players whining about being paid paltry millions to do what most would still like to believe is a game. And in this world of athletes serving time for drugs and rape in between their sneaker endorsements, it was refreshing to hear of a greater triumph and even greater humility.

Ion continued, "That day, after dining with his King, he was met by his father who embraced him with tears of pride. The two of them rode slowly by in a mule drawn wagon as thousands of well wishers lined the streets to glimpse their God."

Spyridon had chosen his prodigy wisely.

I was not the only one moved by the story. Everyone in the group was silent until they broke into a respectful applause. Several patted Ion on the back. Some took pictures standing beside him. Another had Ion autograph his brochure. While others reached into pockets in an attempt to offer him tips, as if he were the piano player who had just played everyone's favorite song. It was awkward, and I assumed Ion would refuse.

"Please, that's really not..." I started to say.

"Allow them their moment of generous expression," he said as he took the money and rolled it up in his hand. I was surprised. Was he being overly polite, or did he somehow feel he needed the money?

"Mr. Theodore," said Adonis. "I often have tourists who try to show me up with some scrap of information they just read in a guidebook. But today, I have no words to express my admiration for what you have done."

"I did nothing but reminisce about my hero and a time almost forgotten. I admire that you come here every day to keep our tradition alive."

"If I were not on duty, I would offer to buy you a drink."

"If I were not with my young niece, I'd join you. I think you said your name was Zarzavtsakis. Kretan is it not?"

"Yes, I was born there."

"A fine people. I know no prouder," he told Adonis as he handed him the drachmas that he had collected. I thought the boy would cry.

The Acropolis was calling me, no, daring me—to climb higher. To ascend if I were worthy of the hundreds of hand-carved steps.

It floats like a white marble city above a city, set in stone for eternity. I stood there in awe, unable to do anything but aspire to its glory. Though it reaches for the heavens, it was created by men who accomplished with their bare hands that which now requires our best technology. They didn't push limits—they were unaware that limits existed. How in God's name did they build this?

If I thought that it had looked impressive from below, I was in for a humbling surprise on its summit. There are certain things in the world that no matter how many superlatives are appended to their descriptions, we come no closer to revealing their wonder. The Acropolis defines our poetry and defies our logic.

"My God, Milos, I don't know what to say."

"Perhaps that is say all." Only Milos and I had made the ascent, Dimitris having stayed behind in the bus with Ion. We walked through the Propylaea, the entrance to the Acropolis. I was still catching my breath from the ascent. The Parthenon—Athena's sacred temple—rose from the center of this vast plain. Towering at least three stories, she appears as a temple within a temple. Her scale is extraordinary even though she has decayed to a fraction of her original grandeur. Built entirely by hand, it is no wonder Zeus was jealous of mankind—for only a divine hand should be allowed to sculpt with such majesty.

"It's like a ghost," he whispered.

"No, it's alive, Milos. I'm sure of it."

"It is not always empty. Once is enormous statue of Athena, right there," he pointed inside the magnificent structure. "She is covered from head to toe in gold and ivory."

"What happened to her?"

"She is vanished and is leave no trace."

"Perhaps she needed to be free..."

"King Aegeus is jump into sea from here," he said as we came to the very edge of the precipice.

"He threw himself into the sea, from here? The shoreline is three miles away!"

"Good jump, no?

"Now I know you're teasing," came my reply.

"He wait for son to return by sea. Black sails dead, white sails is okay. Son is forget to change black sails. Father is jump."

"Kids!" I joked.

We were stopped in front of a very small temple, which jutted out on its own promontory high above the ancient cyclopean walls.

"Temple to Athena Nike," he said, anticipating my question.

"It's also empty."

"Once is here live statue of Nike, with wings like angel," said Milos.

"Did it also vanish, like Athena?"

"Yes. Even though peoples break off wings to stop," he laughed. "But, Nike is vanish with broken wings."

"You can never hold something that doesn't wish to be held," I said.

"How are you know your wish until you are be held?"

An old woman approached us. She was clothed in shawls even though the heat was sweltering. Her face was withered and had the texture of leather. Her forearm was draped with dozens of chains, which held amulets of all shapes and sizes. She waived them, causing the chains to rattle, glints of reflected light caught my eyes. I was going to shoo her away when Milos summoned her closer. He carefully studied each medallion. After a few moments of browsing, followed by bantering, he had purchased it.

"Here. It is Madonna. Souvenir of first time here. Please, it is bring good luck."

Extending my hand slowly, he poured the pendant into it, its gold-plated chain falling like a stream into my palm.

"Beautiful. Very beautiful," I said as my fingers ran across its raised relief.

I placed it around my neck, my hands shaking slightly, and fumbled with the clasp. I was looking down at the medallion as it fell between my breasts and sensed Milos' gaze but I dared not look up.

"Let me," he said. Before I had a chance to react, he was behind me, and his powerful fingers moved along the skin of my neck. I pulled my hair aside. I felt vulnerable. Whether it was the height or the heat, I momentarily lost my balance and fell back against his torso. His lips seemed close to my ear, I felt his breath against my neck, and I could sense him staring down at the pendant's resting point between the swell of my breasts.

When we got back to the bus, I noticed Dimitris eyeing the trinket.

"I am not remember you wear this morning."

"Milos bought it for me."

"So nice of my brother," he said with his eyes shying away from mine.

Did you enjoy the day?" Ion asked as he leaned back into his pillows. The sun had set hours ago, and all was quiet at Panteleimon. I imagined my fleet-footed poet running in the Panathenaic Stadium, struggling swifter, higher and stronger against the elements.

"I had a great time—I'm so glad we took the tour." I placed my cup down gently on Ion's nightstand. I had made us some chamomile tea. "I'm sure things have changed a lot in your eyes."

"In some ways—yes. In other ways—not at all. I guess that the old adage is true, the more things change..."

"I know—the more they remain the same. Do you think that's true about us?"

Ion paused. Perhaps he was reflecting on a wise answer, or perhaps he knew that there was no answer. His continued silence led me to believe it was the latter.

"It's funny, I used to think Long Island was living in the country, but life here is really simple."

"Is it more meaningful when it is complex?"

"Probably not, but I wouldn't mind it if they had a T.V."

Ion laughed. "Can you imagine Euclid trying to invent Geometry during commercial breaks?" I couldn't, but at that moment I would've paid handsomely for a cable. I looked at Ion, who was breathing easily, almost leisurely. I had worried about him today—this was the most strenuous day that we had shared since I found him in the Home in Queens. He was, in many ways, a new man. But then I remembered that Dr. Riggs had pointed out that Ion's lethargic state in the nursing facility was brought on more by a depression given his vapid existence there. Now that we were in Greece and he had brought full circle his personal diaspora—he was enjoying a renaissance of energy and purpose.

"You seem to be so content here, Uncle Ion. Why did you leave?"

"The first time I left because I had no one. The second time, because I thought I had someone. I never should have left that time; I've paid dearly for my misguided chivalry," he said.

"But at least you've come back," I said after some silence.

"I had to."

"Why?"

"I needed to bring you home."

19

A ROSY-FINGERED DAWN

"Even now Eretria has been enslaved, and Greece is weaker by one distinguished city," Pheidippides continued. "Do not be lulled into believing that Attica is the only prize Darius seeks. The Mede's thirst for conquest will not be satisfied until he has subjugated all of Greece.

"Athens and Sparta have had their differences. We now ask you to put aside ancient enmities and see that we are the same in the face of the barbarian onslaught. If Athens falls, the Korinthian Bridge will be all that stands between Sparta and Darius' armies. How long will he wait until he covets the hills and valleys of the Peloponnesus?

"We implore you to march to our mutual defense."

After I was sure Ion was asleep, I went to the church. I sat admiring a sculpture I had seen earlier. Though the Madonna and Child are one of the most depicted couples in the history of art—this one was fresh and followed none of the patterns I had seen before. One might even say it had the hand of blasphemy as its rounded curves made the Virgin appear voluptuous and alluring.

"I remember Panayiotas sitting just where you are on so many evenings," said Father Diogenes, who had appeared from the room behind the pulpits.

"He must have been a wonderful role model for you, and your sons."

"What is anyone without icons to learn from—to worship if necessary?" I wondered if he responded in the positive about Panayiotas, or was he implying that I was Godless.

"I think Ion holds art in that stratosphere. To him, it is divine," I said.

"It is. Just watch a sunset over the mountains, a tempest at sea, or an eagle swooping down from the sky. All we can do is try to mimic such beauty—to approach with years of sweat what He creates in a single exhale," Father Diogenes said while looking upwards for an instant. "But your uncle has the gift and he has blessed us. And like my uncle, I love this one of our Madonna the most of all."

"Ion sculpted this? Why didn't he tell me?"

"Perhaps he believes that the subject is more important than the artist. It is called the *Panayeia*."

"Perhaps you'll think me a little odd, but I wondered about a mystery your sons told me about that statue."

"It started decades ago. Each year on the Fifteenth of August, an angel cleanses this statue and lays flowers at the Madonna's feet."

"Did you never want to stay up and watch? To see whose hand it is?"

"I suggested it once, and only once, to Panayiotas. I was questioning my faith and his. He warned me not to mock its sanctity. It is an angel and I shall not question Panayiotas or the Supreme Power. The hand that washes the statue may not be known."

"Did he give a reason?"

"When the Episkopos says something is unknowable, it is unknowable."

"But he is no longer watching."

"In the house of God, all things are seen," he said. "I honor Panayiotas by obeying his wishes, even after death. Until the mystery is revealed, we can do nothing but seek His redemption."

"But if you don't know what caused it, how can you know what to seek."

"Panayiotas foretold of the coming of an orphan, an orphan who holds the key."

"Evangelis?"

"The coincidence of his appearance so soon after Panayiotas' death is unmistakable."

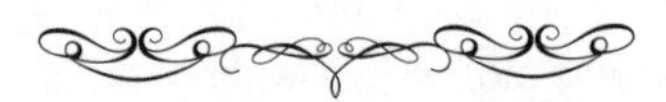

I stayed in the church for some time after Father Diogenes had retired for the evening. My recollections of sitting in church as a young girl, forced to listen to fire and brimstone spewing forth from the pulpits, led me to believe that men of the cloth saw the world within narrow blinders. A few days in the company of Father Diogenes had radically changed my perspective. He gave comfort and a certain feeling of security to his parishioners. The cycles of life would continue, but these people knew that when a life ended or a new one began, they would all come together in this sacred place to help each other through grief and celebrate joy. And they knew Father Diogenes would be there to guide them and provide them the rituals and sacraments of their faith.

I was about to go back to the house when a moving light caught my eye. It was a candle, flickering faintly in the darkness. Whoever had shared my inclination to visit the church so late in the evening was not announcing himself. I paused, unsure of what to do, and then slowly craned my neck to get a better view. He was on the other side of the *Panayeia*. I got as close as I could, while remaining undetected. The viewer stared intently at it, but what was odd was that he examined the pedestal, not the statue itself. He ran his fingers around the base and then tried to move it, but the gesture was futile.

I watched him exit. As his candle left the room, it became pitch black. The eeriness of being left alone in a darkened church kindled deep-seeded fears. I had to feel my way along the walls till I felt the casing of the door. I moved my arms before me, using them as a bumper for objects that my mind knew couldn't really be there. Soon, I was back in the farmhouse. On the way to my room, I peered into Ion's.

He was deep in sleep. The only sign of his mysterious excursion was the dirt still fresh upon his bare feet.

After we had finished breakfast Tuesday morning, I asked Father Diogenes whether he had a telephone. I hadn't seen one since I had arrived.

"It's in my private study. You may make use of it anytime. I apologize that we have no fax or answering machine." I realized how things like faxes and cell phones had changed the way we lived and the way others expected us to live. No longer could we enjoy the serenity of inaccessibility. We were now expected to be responsive to anyone's whim, any time of the day or night. And when we're not instantaneously available—we invite unwarranted irritation.

I entered Father Diogenes' study. Like the rest of the farmhouse, its walls were white and there was the familiar pattern of oak crossbeams supporting the ceilings. But unique to this room was the wood paneling that lined the walls. There were several bookcases, which were packed tightly, and a small wooden desk in one corner. On top of it lay the stationary of Panteleimon, and a pewter mug filled with writing implements. There was a fireplace in the center of another wall. Its smell, and that of the wood paneling made the room very cozy and inviting.

The telephone was an old rotary device. I picked up the receiver and waited for a moment until the telltale European dial tone was audible. I could hear a fair amount of static on the line, and I wasn't sure if the call was going to go through when after a pause of about five seconds, I heard the familiar rings commencing. It was after one in the morning in New York. I did not expect to reach anyone at my office. I was specifically hoping not to. I just wanted to reach my paralegal's extension to leave my number. Clean, efficient and no chance to hear any office problems. A simple voice message and conscience absolved.

"You have reached the offices of Schroeder, Wilkes & Barron. Our offices are now closed. If you know your party's four-digit extension, please enter it now. If you would like a company directory, please enter '1,' if you want to leave a message in our company switchboard, please enter '2,' if you…"

The automated voice continued to drone on as I gazed down at the rotary phone in frustration. Our state-of-the-art telecommunications system had impeded my ability to communicate. I hung up the phone with a less than gentle application. I would be forced to call during business hours.

I dialed the Herodion Hotel.

"Hello, Adam?"

"Yes, this is Adam, is this Marianna?"

"Good morning Adam. There was a message from you at the Hotel Plaka."

"I'm so glad you called me back," he stammered, still clearing his throat.

"They said that you had checked out."

"We did. We're staying in a monastery in Marathon."

"I thought I'd lost you. So what have you been doing the last couple of days?"

"Well, we witnessed a Baptism. Yesterday we toured Athens. We were in Syntagma Square but missed the changing of the guards at the Tomb of the Unknown Soldier."

"We did that yesterday! But the weirdest thing happened."

"What?"

"Well, the monument was very impressive. But when I got really close I could see inscribed on the white marbled tomb the words 'Here lies Murray Morphoupolstein—Greece's Unknown Warrior."

"What? Are you kidding me?"

"I know, I was amazed, so I went over to one of the soldiers and asked him 'Hey, what kind of *mashugina* is this, this is supposed to be your Unknown Warrior, but the guy's name is right on the tomb.' The guard looked at me and said, 'Oh you mean Murray? Believe me, as a warrior he was unknown, but as a tailor, *oy* was he famous!'"

"You're bad Adam," I said, chuckling, "I should have seen that one coming. What do the parents pay to have their kids accompanied by you, two drinks and a cover?" I quipped.

"Touché. Hey, I'd love to bring our group out to Marathon, to see the monument there. Perhaps you and Ion could join us? Your uncle made quite an impression on my students. Several of them have been asking about him."

"Can I get back to you about that? I'll need to check with Ion, and our host."

"Of course."

The drops of water splashed onto the dry earth and then quickly found their way into the pores of the earth. And then it came again like a spring rain, though this water fell not from a cloudy sky, but from an old aluminum container. The thirsty soil sucked down its refreshment so greedily that moments after the container emptied, no trace of moisture could be seen.

"That should be enough," I said, taking the gray can from him. In three days, he had said nothing to me, but at least he hadn't run away. He still said nothing, nor did he seem to have any desire to try. But he looked at me with the focus and concentration that I had never observed in one so young.

I walked with him back to the house. Everyone except Father Diogenes was inside. I suddenly felt his right hand grasp the two small fingers of my left. I looked down at him, but he was looking straight ahead. The object of his gaze quickly became apparent as he pulled me towards a flower. I knelt down and pulled it closer to me, without breaking it from its stem, then put my nose to it and inhaled.

"Flower," I said.

He put his nose to it, mimicking what I had done. The petals must have tickled his nose, because I saw the muscles in his face wrinkle up and he withdrew his head quickly, startled by the sensation. I couldn't help but laugh.

He looked at me laughing, then looked back at the flower. He put his nose back down and inhaled.

"*Glikia*," he said. Then he looked at me and repeated the sound "*Glikia*." I had no idea whether that was even a word, it didn't really matter—we had taken the first steps across the lonely void.

After dinner, Father Diogenes, Ion and I sat in the study, which once was used by Panayiotas.

"Ion, perhaps while you are here, you can help me organize my uncle's papers. There may even be something of sentimental value that you would wish to keep."

Ion was perusing the dusty volumes on Panayiotas' shelves, pausing briefly at one or another, whispering to its aged leather as if it might reveal what it had witnessed in the years of his absence.

I brought up my conversation with Adam. I thought it would be good for Ion to have the children visit. It might make him feel useful in this place even though we were too late to serve the initial purpose of the visit.

"Ion, I spoke to Adam Gittleman earlier. He was wondering whether his class might visit the monastery one day this week. That's if it's okay with you, Father Diogenes."

"I think it's a splendid idea. Provided that they understand this is a working farm as well as a church and that we have many ecclesiastical and agricultural duties every day."

"I am sure that they would be respectful of both. Would it be too much commotion for you?" I asked Ion.

"I would enjoy such a visit. There is much to see here."

Soon, Ion and Father Diogenes retired, leaving me alone in the study. I called the Herodion Hotel, but Adam was out. I left a message that Thursday would be great.

I then dialed SWB and was put through to Tracy Feller, one of my paralegals. I had only wanted to stay on long enough to give her the number at Panteleimon but I felt compelled to ask how things were going with my cases.

"It's been a little crazed this week. The US-REIT case you and Melissa are working on had some kind of blow-up yesterday afternoon. There are some files she can't find—she keeps asking me if you've checked in."

"Shit, she knows where everything is. You may as well transfer me over to her highness."

"She's at a meeting over at Marshall & Simpson. I'll find what she's looking for. Try to enjoy your vacation."

"Thanks Tracy, I'm glad you're there."

"I'm not," she laughed. "I'd rather be on Fire Island getting a tan."

"I don't blame you." I had only been gone a few days and already I felt the pangs of anxiety about my caseload. I hung up the phone. At that moment, I wished Father Diogenes didn't have one. But I had something more important on my mind and the wait was excruciating.

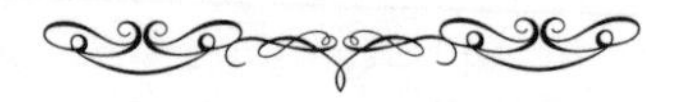

I went back to Panteleimon. The church was dark and deserted, though I was prepared for its ink darkness. By the light of my own candle, I gazed upon the Mother and Child. One could stare at this monument for an eternity and still never have seen it. It was so subtle that at first I thought my eyes played games with me as the light reflected off the contours of the stone. The lip of the statue's rectangular base was not even all the way around its pedestal, it had been shifted off center. I put the candle on the ground and pushed with all I could muster on the side of the sculpture. It did not budge. There was no way I could do this by myself.

I felt so close, and yet frustrated by my own lack of strength. I needed help and I knew where to get it. I blew out the candle before stepping into the crisp night air.

20
A GIFT OF THE GODS

Fergadis was the first council member to respond to Pheidippides. "I join my comrades in admiring your magnificent run, and the sincerity of your plea. But do you believe the Mede is any match for Spartan warriors? Let them march down the Eurotas Valley and attack if they please. The green grass will run red with their blood," he boasted.

"Forgive me, I meant no slight. I am all too familiar with the prowess of your soldiers. I am not born Athenian, I am an Achaean, from the village of Nonakris. My father died under the Spartan lance at the battle of Pheneus, but not before he had satiated his sword's thirst for blood with four of your bravest sons. I do not seek your enmity or sympathy. My father died so that I may be free—just as the Athenians are willing to do so that all Greece may be free."

"Is everythings all right? Father? Ion?" murmured the still dreamy eyed Milos.

"Shh, they're fine. Keep quiet, I don't want to wake them up," I cautioned him, as I held my fingers to his lips.

"Dimitris?"

"Still asleep. I need your help."

"Of course."

"I'll be waiting outside in the hall."

I heard him throw back the sheets and slide from his bed. A moment or two of rustling clothes and he joined me in the quiet hallway. I took him by the hand and led him to my room. I'd have to speak quickly, I dreaded any misinterpretation of our rendezvous. I explained to him what I needed. He said nothing but I could feel his eyes never losing contact with mine.

"So, will you help?"

"Move *Panayeia*? Is serious—no joke? Why?"

"I can't explain, but it's important."

"Why we no wait in morning ask my father? If okay, my brother is also help."

"I wish I could wait, but I have no one else to turn to, and I..." a tear welled up in my eye and then slithered down my cheek.

"Okay, okay. You no cry," he said, moving closer as if to take me in his arms. "I am help you—no cry, please."

"Thanks, Milos, I knew I could count on you..." I said as I sniffled a little bit and wiped my tears away. I really hate to admit this, but when strength, reason and bribery fail—tears work pretty well.

Very quietly, we made our way to the church. I wouldn't let Milos light his candle until we were inside. I wanted him to understand how important it was for no one to discover us. I suppose I didn't need to worry too much; even though he didn't want to be a priest, I got the feeling that Milos felt he was in danger of desecrating something sacred—he had no more desire to be seen than I did.

"Okay Milos, on the count of three. Ready? One, two, three..." I felt the statue grudgingly yield to his power. One more push and the opening in the base was wide enough to snake a hand inside. Then it occurred to me that should something be inside, I wanted no one, not even Milos, to see it.

"Milos, I heard someone," I whispered. "Will you go to the door and look?"

"Now?"

"Please," I said, allowing the monosyllable to linger. "If it is Ion or your father, I'll need you to distract them."

"Okay, I'll watch," he said as he swiftly moved to the door of the church and slipped through it. I knew he was torn between the opportunity for chivalry and the desire to see what I might find.

I reached inside the sacred vessel and pulled out a leather volume. Asleep in its marble tomb, I wondered when it last saw the light or was touched by human hands. My fingers ran along its surface where another's hands had left oily imprints. Milos would be back any minute. I reached in again and was able to pull two more similar volumes out before hearing him approaching. I needed to hide my treasure quickly. I looked around frantically seeking a safe place to stow them. Without time to ponder the practicality of my choice, I quickly slipped into the confessional and stowed them under the oak bench seat. One quick look back at the bench as Milos returned convinced me that they were out of sight.

"Nothing, huh?"

"No, I'm afraid we wasted our time. Sorry to have dragged you out of bed," I told Milos.

"Is okay. Anytime you need, I am here," he said as we prepared to move the lid back into its place.

Milos did not try to light his candle on the way back. He took my hand and led me to the house in the pitch-dark night. He knew the route by heart and his grip on my hand was strong and sure, pulling me under to avoid a low hanging branch and pushing me to the side of bushes. His masculinity was protective, not threatening, but by the time I got back to my room, my heart was still fluttering.

Somehow, the truck with the large red letters didn't seem to fit in here. The cloud of dust it kicked up came closer until it settled right in front of the farmhouse. The letters "DHL" were now clearly visible. I signed for it—it was a two-inch thick courier package—Manhattan to Marathon in less than a day—remarkable, yet so commonplace as to be unremarkable. The driver jumped back in his truck and sped off, with dozens of packages to go before he slept. I looked down at the pouch, it had Schroeder, Wilkes & Barron's pre-printed air bill affixed to it.

I'm not sure why I let Tracy send me this work. It was partly out of obligation to a pending case and partly to fill the hours of *ennui* on the farm. Perhaps I was still compelled by feeling needed, or the illusion that there was an important task before me that only I could do.

And there was always the adrenalin rush of daily crises.

For now, a trip to the warm waters of the Aegean would have to suffice. The documents that Tracy had sent would wait until later. I went back to my room, dropped the DHL Pak on the dresser and grabbed a large beach towel. The sea was calling, and I couldn't say no.

"What have you been doing?" I asked Ion, as I came into his room. My swim had been invigorating and a bathing suit unnecessary.

"Making clay while the sun shines," he said though without laughing or moving his head from his work. Ion was seated in front of a low table, which hadn't been there this morning. It was covered with an old sheet, and on it sat two buckets. One looked more like a small washbasin. In it was a dark reddish-brown mixture that he was kneading like dough.

"The boys were kind enough to dig this up for me. Submit to my will!" he spoke into the basin.

"Ion?"

"Just a little spell," he said, as he immersed his hands in the thick malleable material. He would feel it with his eyes closed, then, like the connoisseur of fine clays that he was, he would sprinkle a few drops of water into it, plying it to optimum consistency.

"Do you have plans for it?"

"Plans? Yes, I suppose. To create form answerable to my needs."

"What are your needs?" I asked somewhat nervously, afraid for the first time of the consequences of taking his hidden journals.

"The need for beauty... the need for beauty that is responsive to my hands."

"Are your hands..."

"My hands are fine, though they are not up for the force of metal chisel against marble. Clay is more responsive to my frailties." This time he looked up from his work then turned his head back down to the rhythmic play of his fingers in the red, fleshy clay. He then continued along a train of thought far deeper than that of sculpting. "We fear death when we have not created something that will last beyond our temporal lives. The Gods have given us the ability to create things that live on after we have returned to dust. It is in these things that we defy Death itself."

I thought of his sensuous creations that had transformed the sterile interior of my Long Island home into a sanctuary of aesthetic delight. It always seemed to me a miracle worthy of only the greatest of Gods—the ability to master the hardness of stone and infuse veins of marble with life. Yet these same Gods that allowed Ion to soar so close to creation also forced him to suffer the indignity of his own decay.

I was just beginning to see what his life had actually been like. I wanted so much to talk with Ion about what I was reading in his journals, but I could never broach the subject without confessing that I had stolen them. I was not ready to admit my crime, not until I had finished reading all three volumes. For now, all I could do was keep to simpler subjects. "Are you excited about tomorrow?" I asked him.

"I'm excited about the moment," he uttered.

"I meant being with the Dalton students."

"Oh, is that...yes, tomorrow," he said in a tone of mannered surprise and with his brows raised slightly in studied detachment.

"Yes, Ion, we've been talking about it all week."

"What time is he coming?"

"*They* will all be here at ten."

"Of course, at ten, of course, my dear."

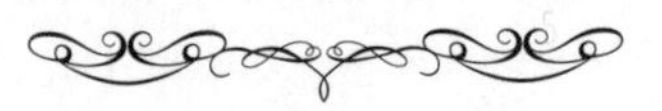

Night is a mysterious place. With nothing to taunt me but my own mind, anxiety and despair are amplified. These emotions prefer the dark, when we are most exposed and vulnerable—helpless to change what happened today, too early to alter what may happen tomorrow. These are the interminable moments when I pray for my mind to shut down, waiting for the cleansing of dawn.

Whatever had brought me to Ion's nursing home was now pointing me towards a strange and wonderful portal. I had something unusual on my horizon, something unspoiled by doubt and cynicism. I gazed out at it as if through a spyglass. Sleep was going to have to wait.

That evening, I had returned to Panteleimon with all the excitement and anticipation of a small child traipsing downstairs on Christmas morning. I struck a single match, letting it burn for a second or two before lighting the wick on the small candle I had taken from the altar. Sitting alone in the confessional, I pulled the first book out from beneath the bench where I had hidden it the night before. Fingering the relief along its binding—I was intoxicated by the smell of the leather and binder's glue. What could be in them that he would have buried them for so long and not chosen to seek help to unearth them? I had to know, justifying that my right to know was for his sake.

I peeled open the cover, delicately, as if opening a treasure box, careful not to let loose anything I could not retrieve. The first entry was from 1936.

The night is still and perfect... I began to read the words that would transport me to another world.

20 July 1936

The night is still and perfect. The sky is illuminated with the starry abundance that only can be seen from the sea or the desert, though the two are often one in the same. The horizon stretches into infinity in all directions, just as it does in those two sacred places, but only one will reflect the moon. I looked out at the path that this lunar light had draped across the blackness, back towards my adopted home. The last man-made lights had faded earlier this morning as we lost sight of the lighthouses along the Newfoundland coast. Now there was nothing but open ocean, its imperfections appearing like ripples across a windswept desert.

We would make landfall in a week, at the French port of Le Havre. The summer breeze felt warm upon my face, and the salt air filled my nostrils, making me feel safe in the womb of her watery expanse. I recalled with some nostalgia another time I had set to sea, many, many years ago.

I celebrated my birthday today. For the sake of those around me, I turned thirty-three years old. I am uncertain of my precise age. Perhaps it is a gift that I may be whatever age I choose, or whatever age I believe. But today was special for another reason. The Torch left Olympia today precisely at noon. After leaving northern Hellas, it will pass through Bulgaria, Yugoslavia, Magyarorszag, Austria and

Ceskoslovensko. It is fashioned from more than two pounds of pure silver, but its importance cannot be measured by its size or composition. It will be carried by me and 3,421 other runners, one kilometer at a time—entering Berlin Stadium sometime after 5:00 P.M. on the 1st. I am pleased to partake of the rekindling of this ancient tradition—one that had once stood unbroken for a thousand years. I didn't know Konstantin Kondylis, the boy who started out today from Olympia, but I knew his father. He could have been a champion in his own right. Today his son has made him one.

I bought myself a gift yesterday morning before we set sail. A book, but one with no words. On each page is an invitation for my pen to put them there. I shall not disappoint my gift by shunning its silent solicitation.

I had never thought about keeping such a temporal reminder of living memories, many of which I was content to leave in nearly forgotten hiding places. But something about the sea, with its tides and currents and distant squalls, has summoned my demons from their refuge and brought them rushing forth like a torrent.

Writing these words forces me to relive their living in some small part. I can only hope such resurrection does not prove too painful and thus fatal to these jottings. It is one thing to carry memories in the inward eye, another to etch them in ink upon the page—a life poured onto white canvases.

21 July 1936

I was thinking about Kalos, an old slave without whom this journal would not have been possible. He taught me to read from an old copy of The Odyssey *that he had hidden from our masters, who barred all things Hellenic. He was a Turk with Greek blood coursing through his veins. He told me that his father could trace his lineage back to the colonies on Rhodes.*

Sometimes, late at night, we would take turns reading passages from its delicate pages. It was the only book I gazed upon until I was a man. No, "book" is far too pedestrian a word to describe Homer's masterpiece. In this divine creation, I felt the Gods speaking to me—a lowly Greek slave-child. The Turks were the descendants of the Trojans who had come from Priam's city to enslave us. I fantasized that Odysseus, Achilles, Ajax and Agamemnon would rise again and conquer these Turks from Troy and set me free.

Kalos had been blessed to die in his sleep. By all signs, his passing had been peaceful, and I recall sitting in the same room as his body until it could be properly removed for a simple burial. He had no family, and virtually no worldly possessions, except for The Odyssey, *a small bronze coin he wore about his wrist and a few items of clothing.*

I wanted that book, but there was no formality in ancient bequeathals. Inheritance was simply a matter of possession and I alone knew where he had hid it. His body was still warm as others divvied up his belongings like bounty. By the time I saw him laying on his bed, still and lifeless, he had been stripped bare but for an old sheet.

I waited until dark; I dared not light an oil lamp for fear of arousing insomniatic miscreants. I went back to his room to uncover the book's hiding place, praying that it had been undiscovered. Lying still, he appeared serene and confident, as if unperturbed by the indignity of the thieves. I paused, wondering whether I too was a thief. Like the others, wasn't I coveting something of his that I deemed mine now that he was dead. I wished that he could send me a sign, even speak just one more time to guide me.

Then I panicked, realizing that my dilemma may have been for naught if the book's sanctuary had already been violated. Kalos had kept it in a small vault he had dug in the ground and lined with stones. It rested under a slab, which in turn lay under a wooden chest that had held his meager clothes. The chest and its contents were already gone, but it didn't appear as if the slab had been disturbed. I pried it sideways. It was heavier than I had imagined. Catching my fingers under its weighty mass, I almost cried out in pain. Cursing my carelessness, I got a small stick to use as a lever. A little patience and persistence finally moved the slab aside enough for me to reach into the dark hole. I felt nothing, but I continued to dig. The sand was a fine dry powder and then my hand touched the hard texture of the book's binding.

My excitement quickly turned to fear as I heard something. It broke the dead silence so unexpectedly that I thought it was Kalos' corpse, which had uttered the sounds. I stared at his motionless profile, expecting at any moment to see him rise with fury in his hollowed eyes. But I sensed not even the slightest trembling other than my own.

Then it came again, the noise, but now I could tell that it came from outside the hut.

Not wanting to be caught with the book, I removed my hand and pushed with all my strength to return the slab to its original position. I jumped through the window, and ran in the opposite direction of the noise without looking back to see who or what it was.

I cried for days, but only in secret, for such sentimentality was not held in universal esteem. I was saddened not only by losing my teacher, but the suddenness in which it happened, depriving either of us the chance to say goodbye. It was during one of these lonely soul-searching nights that I decided that it was time for me to go.

My planning was quite unsophisticated. I would make for the west towards the Aegean. With no map, no idea of the terrain, nor any idea of what I would do if I reached the sea, I set out. My strategic horizon was about ten minutes and a few hundred meters. Nor did I stop to think of what I would do to survive if I managed to escape. I had no skills in any trade, and my entire education was gleaned from 24,000 lines of Homer. Thankfully, my ten year old mind simplified my tactics. I would make my own boat or stowaway on another, anything to set out to sea. I cared little where the winds and tides took me, as long as it was away from here.

For days before the appointed hour, I stole food from the table of my master, hiding the items under my bedding until they could be smuggled out of the house and buried nearby. I chose items which would not easily perish while buried. A runaway slave cannot fret about food encrusted with sand and dirt. In cheesecloth, I wrapped olives, goat cheese, dried figs and dates. I would hunt for what else I needed, which was quite presumptive having never killed. But it is amazing how resourceful one can become when stripped of choices.

I was determined to be free or to perish in the attempt. I only knew the purgatory of the moment. I had originally planned to take my leave alone, but there was one other who I took pity on. Bayazid was several years older than I, but his health was poorer, having what I now suspect was asthma. And he was fat for a young boy. How he managed to become so portly on the scraps we were allotted is still one of life's great mysteries. Like the runt of a litter, he always took an extra share of our master's cruelty. I didn't think him a particularly good accomplice, but a companion would not be bad, especially as I was unsure of what special needs might become vital.

We had timed our escape with the Mevlid Kandili—the festival for the birth of the Prophet. A day and night of celebration and drinking—the latter, and in profusion, was what I was counting on. I would wait until I could see the constellation Lyra at its highest point in the sky. Kalos had shown me how to spot its focal star, Vega, the second brightest object in the heavens.

The wait became days, then hours and then minutes. I imagined what freedom would taste like. Contemplating my prospects, I was too afraid to sleep. My bedding was on the ground in one of the small outbuildings, which stood not far from my master's house. There were no guards, though my master possessed several dogs, used mainly to control the herds and attack any hungry predators. The dogs had no love for the slaves, and they were best avoided.

My first stop was the old hut of Kalos.

22 July 1936

Though The Odyssey *provides little in the way of food, shelter or camouflage—I had no intention of leaving without it. I felt invigorated as the first steps of my plan were executed flawlessly. Undetected, I once again pried open the vault to retrieve my treasure. I tied some twine around it widthwise to keep it closed tightly, then lengthwise through its binding so I could hang it from my neck. It bounced gently against my body as my limbs moved, each moment of contact made me feel as if Kalos were with me, touching me, guiding me.*

I made my way to the far side of the fields, where Bayazid waited in his quarters. En route, I picked up my cheesecloth of stolen food stores. I was shivering—the nighttime temperature in the mountains of Turkey can drop precipitously from their midday highs. I felt myself teetering in the twilight between servitude and freedom, not yet knowing which way I would fall.

At the prearranged time, I made our signal—the low sound of a bleating sheep. But my accomplice did not appear. I made the noise again, and again. No Bayazid. The dogs began to howl as if a wolf or coyote was approaching. The longer I waited, the lower the odds of success. I sensed the plan beginning to unravel, but I could not desert him.

I dropped back to the ground and thought of my choices. I could wait, I could flee or I could return to my own quarters and regroup in the morning. Gazing back across the field, my eye focused on fires coming from several torches. Three or four of them grouped together, flitting about from the direction of my own outbuilding. At first they seemed to move without purpose or direction. Then, the loudening of voices told me that they were approaching. I climbed up the side of the hut, my fingers and toes taking hold in the stone's imperfections. Laying flat on the roof and closing my eyes, I tried to make myself disappear.

Then one voice became clearer than the others. That's when I heard the words, which struck my heart, hurting me more than the whip had ever done to my flesh.

"He said he would be here, it is exactly as I told you, I swear," he said.

"He can't be far. You have done well, Bayazid. You will be rewarded."

The boy I had pitied had betrayed me.

They did not see or hear me, though I thought my heart could be heard beating for a great distance. Soon, I could see the fires retreating. Lowering myself to the ground, I began to run. Jagged rocks bruised and cut my feet, and thorny brushes tore the flesh from my legs. I ignored the pain and ran. Up and down hills and ravines, across creek beds, over flat dry plains, it didn't matter. I didn't slow my pace until near dawn, and only then because it was prudent to run only at night. By day, I hid in caves or high enough in the mountains to be unseen. To encounter any other human would mean an end to my flight. There would be no help and I could trust no one—it was death to aid a runaway.

By the end of the second day, the food ran out. But thirst was a bigger problem. You have never known heat until you have traversed a desert under the scorching summer sun. By the time you feel it, it has already blistered your skin. There is no relief, whether from above or from below as the desert sands melt into glass. I lived as a wild child those days in the Armutcuk mountains. My mind began to deteriorate from the constant hunger, fear and isolation. The line between life and death faded like a mirage on the hot desert floor.

As night fell on the third day, I found myself without the strength to begin my nocturnal canter. I was exhausted beyond any state of fatigue I had ever experienced. And with fatigue, came hopelessness. My limbs no longer felt like the ones I remembered—bounding gracefully over the ground—but now seemed as two leaden weights pulling my torso down. I sat frozen in self-pity. I wanted to throw myself from the height of my hiding place, end my misery in one instant upon the rocks below. Better an end with terror than a terror without end.

To carry out this purpose, I stood on the precipice behind which I had taken refuge. The string around my neck, the one from which Kalos' book dangled, caught on the rocky ledge, momentarily choking me as it grew taut. I sat down and untangled it from the rock where it had snagged.

I unraveled my bundle by the light of the stars, carefully untying the strings that had faithfully held it closed. When I opened the book to gaze upon it one last time, something fell to the ground—it was Kalos' amulet. It dawned on me that he hadn't been surprised by Death. Why else, on the last evening of his life, would he have removed this from his wrist?

Inside the cover Kalos had written only a few words, but they spoke volumes to me. It read A ION, THEOS DOROS—to Ion, a gift of the Gods. *It was at that moment that I adopted the name that I have used ever since: Theodore. If he could only have known how much he gave to me: a book, a charm and my very own name—one that no man could ever take from me. It was fitting that such an intangible should come from him, another orphaned slave.*

My incredible find gave me strength. It didn't bring me water to quench my thirst, but it gave me the resolve to run without it. I finally made my way to the seaside village of Babakale, its dark fortress presides over the sea below. Boats came and went from here all the time from ports in the Mediterranean and the Black Sea. I found a place to hide atop a knoll above the harbor. From there, I studied the boats, trying to choose the one that would carry me from this coast.

23 July 1936

I had chosen. It was a sailing vessel, larger than the scores of boats whose keels were partially buried on the sandy shore. It appeared to be a trader and not a fishing vessel. The latter may take to the sea, but they return with their catch. I had observed its compliment of men scamper down the gangway an hour earlier, headed for some waterfront taverns.

I held my book above my head, and slowly lowered myself into the water at the foot of the harbor. It was warm and filled with floating debris and fish carcasses that had been picked by birds and other sea scavengers. I couldn't find anything to grab hold of, and its railing was too far above the waterline for my arms to reach. I was frustrated to have come this close only to see how helpless my hands looked as they tried to grasp onto the ship's barnacled side. Wading around the bow to get to its starboard side, I had already decided to risk exposure on the gangway. Then I spotted one of the ships tie lines hanging partially in the water. My hands burned as I hoisted myself up to the deck, ever wary of running into any crew members. There was one who had stayed onboard, perhaps as a watch, but he was snoring loudly atop some cushions he had strewn on the stern.

I lowered myself into a hatchway, and found a tight space in the forward hold. I covered myself with an old tarp. I was soaking wet, miserably uncomfortable and sleep was impossible. Whenever I would drift off, some movement near me would waken me in a panic. The fact that my tormentors were rats and not crewmembers was small consolation. Eventually I heard the men staggering back aboard ship.

For the better part of the day they moved about deck. Supplies were loaded, lines were secured and other gear stowed and unstowed as necessary. I heard their voices, and there were moments that they came so close to my hiding place that I imagined I could smell their alcohol-laced sweat.

Suddenly, I felt movement as the ship jarred sideways—pulling away from its moorings and making its way towards the harbor's mouth. Though I had been to sea once before, on my childhood voyage to Turkey, I had never had a chance to study her until the previous evening. I must inform you that she is a liar. She tells you that she is calm and flat and easily glided across, and she beckons you to join her for a soothing sail along her surface, but she tells not the truth. As soon as we had left the protective waters of the bay, the ship began to pitch wildly.

I thought for sure that the vessel would sink each time it crested over a breaker and hit the trough below. I thought for certain we were in a tempest and that this vessel could not possibly remain seaworthy given the creaking and moaning as her frail ribs struggled to hold back the encroaching sea. In hindsight, I was the only one not seaworthy, and the terrible tempest I imagined wouldn't have made a true seaman flinch, even atop the crow's nest.

I could not take the suffocation of my confinement any longer. Though it was dark, I was not topside for a minute before I was spotted. Two men ran after me as I scampered for the stern. My flight was an exercise in futility as one quickly runs out of room aboard ship. I was easily cornered by the foul-looking seamen. They yelled at me in a language that was neither Greek nor Turk, and from its tone, I sensed they didn't find any humor in stowaways. I pulled my sharpened stick from my waist and brandished it, only eliciting sadistic laughter from my pursuers. I had heard horrible stories about sailors, and I had no desire to confirm them. So I did the only thing I could think of. I climbed up on the rail and grabbed hold of one of the loose stern lines and slipped into the sea.

I could barely swim, and the seas were heavy. The men were yelling and tried to throw something to me, some kind of flotation device. But I was so frightened that I could not distinguish between them trying to capture me or rescue me. Perhaps they meant me no harm, and who knows my destiny had I trusted them and grabbed the rope. But in a few more seconds it was no longer an option.

I lost sight of them in the foamy seas. What followed was a blur of sea and air and spray. I swam for lights that I prayed were on the shore and not lanterns on vessels farther out. Coughing up the salt water, I was tossed and flipped in the frothy mist. Then all went black.

Washing ashore somewhere near the mouth of the Canakkale Bogazi, I must have been a surprising catch to the old women of the village as they came down to set their nets. Half dead and half alive, I was taken to the home of one of these women—an old widow. It pains me greatly today to have forgotten her name. She showed me great kindness. As I lay in a bed, I felt for the string that now dangled weightlessly about my neck. The wine-dark sea had claimed my book—and with it my heart.

News of a runaway slave travels quickly, and my master was already en route. I shook with fear when I heard the wheels of his cart drawing near. I could see in this old woman's eyes that she didn't want to part with me, but she had no choice. Too many had seen me and I was too weakened to attempt another escape. I heard her making him promise that I would be well treated. He promised, even upon his holy book, but what did that mean to a Turk? He couldn't read it anyway.

I will never forget the sadness in her eyes as I was tied in the back of an old mule-drawn wagon and led away. I so wish I could have remembered her name.

Upon my return to Hamdibey, I was beaten, more savagely than ever before. I recall the eyes of Bayazid in the crowd that watched as a firebrand was applied to my ankle. The mark of a runaway, burned into my flesh as a reminder of how misguided my notion of freedom was. It seared my flesh, but did not diminish my hope.

A quarter of a century has passed since those desolate nights of despair in the Turkish mountains. But tonight, as my ship cut the frigid Atlantic waters on route to Europe, I thought of the deep waters that almost swallowed me. I knew I had been granted another chance, but for what and towards what end, I feel sadly ignorant.

21
THE TORCH

"Fergadis is right," chimed in another council member. "Is Darius not there to punish Athens for her assistance to the Ionians? Why should the Lacedaemon concern himself with what troubles Attica?"

"Wise counselor, your comments are fair, but I ask you—has the policy of the Mede been one of quiet existence within his own territory, or has it been that of a conqueror?" responded Pheidippides. "I am a simple messenger, not an oracle, but if Athens falls, will not the barbarian hold the key to the Peloponnese? We must bury our past rivalries and unite against the barbarian—to preserve forever our Greek way of life, whether Athenian or Spartan."

There was a murmuring amongst the Lacedaemonian elders, and several went to speak at once, but then King Leonidas rose, and all fell silent.

29 July 1936

The world has gone mad. I thought I had already seen such a time. The blood, the shelling and the gas are not yet present, but the madness is. The bitter lesson has been forgotten.

I traveled by train from Le Havre, through Paris, Reims, Luxembourg and Berlin. I have come to participate in a great honor bestowed upon me by my countrymen. But I am saddened by what I see here in Berlin. Touted by its leaders as the new Athens, it is more a reincarnate of the corrupt Roman Empire. Its red, white and black banners stream from every window and street pole. They have no concept of what my ancestors lived and died for.

Yes, the buildings are impressive, the Reichstag, the Lustgarten, the Operahaus, the government buildings of Wilhelmstrasse, the Brandenburg Gates. Wonders of technology and engineering, but devoid of art and spirit. Everywhere I look, I see uniforms, and tall black boots, marching in faultless precision like a thousand brown-shirted automatons. It is a foreboding rhythm that I heard twenty years ago. I would have banished the memory had it not been for the remarkable circumstances of my liberation—and the beauty of one girl.

We, the Greeks, are housed with the American and British teams. I am awaiting Spyridon. He will be here as an unofficial ambassador, to present the host country with an olive wreath of peace. I almost wish he would not witness this, but I have not seen him in many years and I am selfishly anticipating his arrival four years ago he was so disappointed by the governing body's decision. We had trained so hard, he as much as his pupil.

I had won in Athens in '28, no—we had won together—my legs upon his teaching. I was to have represented Greece in the 1932 Olympics in Los Angeles, but my immigration to the States a few months earlier had disqualified me. Alas, it was not meant to be. Now I am considered an old man. I must laugh at that, though in these modern games I am already old. All it takes is falling a step behind or an ache that lingers. Not much, but enough to lose in a competition decided by seconds after forty thousand strides. But I will carry the message as my ancestor did 2,400 years ago. It is a message of victory over barbarity and tyranny—a message that must be delivered, no matter the consequence.

30 July 1936

Yesterday afternoon, I traveled to the village of Potsdam, to await the Torch—my link in the chain. I am receiving it from a Swede—my brother in the great Olympic ritual. For two days I can relax, confident that I am prepared. On Friday, I will perform the deed.

I spent the morning touring Potsdam, accompanied by a lovely young French girl named Sabine, who I met yesterday in Berlin. She's studying Art History at the Sorbonne, but came to Berlin for the summer to intern at the Pergamon Museum. She and I joined some local residents for lunch and several bottles of a pungent Riesling. I don't know how these people can eat so much. Perhaps a little siesta and then some loving. Yes, that is best.

1 August 1936

"Enter the games... there is no greater fame for a man." To a Greek, there is no more honored test of manhood than to compete. When we run, jump, or wrestle our spirits rise above the barbarian, above human weakness and above grief.

What verdant crowns awaited the heroes of my ancestors: the laurel at Delphi, the pine at Corinth, parsley at Nemea and the coveted olive wreath at Olympia.

The games are descended from the ancient rites at Olympia, caused by the jealousy of the tyrant, Oenomaus. Kalos told me that the tyrant challenged all wishing to marry his daughter to a race in the four-horsed chariot—the first challenger to win would receive his daughter's hand. Those who lost would forfeit their heads. Many tried, all lost—the race and their lives. Then one day, Pelop came and fell in love with Oenomaus' daughter. Killing the tyrant, he ascended the throne of Olympia, and at his wedding he organized contests of athletic prowess—our very first Olympic Games.

It mattered little where a man was from, whether he was rich or poor, or of noble or bastard birth. In the stadia, all men begin as equals. Only his courage, swiftness and willpower could make a man victorious over his peers, and win the respect of both men and Gods.

I remember the rows of gray temple columns, which stood amongst stately groves of pine trees. Leading all the way to the crystal blue Alpheus and Cladeus Rivers. Rising from their confluence was the sanctuary of Herakles. There grows the olive tree from which the victors' wreaths are fashioned. In my mind I can see the great arch that we would pass under in procession to the dirt-strewn field and rows of marble bleachers. Near it was a statue plinth which had a list of names inscribed on it. A memorial of shame, not glory, for carved into its smooth white face were the names of those who had disgraced themselves by violating the sacred oath. And beside each individual's name, was inscribed the city upon which such men had also brought shame. Far better to lose with honor than to find oneself listed amongst such degraded company.

> *"We, who gather here at thy sacred altar, Great Zeus, lord of Olympus and of all creatures below, do swear to strictly observe the rules of these games; to abide by sportsmanship in victory and defeat; and to bring honor to thee, to ourselves, to our families and to our peoples. May the world be delivered from crime and killing and freed from the clash of arms."*

All Greeks were honor-bound to observe this peace during the Games, as wars would be suspended so that friend and foe could send their athletes to Olympia. All were guaranteed safe passage, even through hostile territories. I doubt that Chancellor Hitler has ever heard these words, or if so could ever understand their meaning.

It is time to meet the Swede in the village square. Sabine will bring my bag with her to Berlin. We'll meet at sundown in a special place in the Grunewald near the Havel River. As one of the relayers, I will miss the opening ceremonies. Spyridon was to have arrived this morning in Berlin to present Chancellor Hitler with a wreath.

1 August 1936

It was exhilarating. I could have made a much faster pace, but I had to maintain a certain speed, so as not to throw off the timing of my hand-off. My right arm is sore from holding the Torch—it is not the way of a runner to hold such an object. I passed growing crowds—not there to see me, but to line the Torch's path. A very light drizzle persisted but it didn't bother me—nor could it douse the flame, which burned above. They cheered as we passed by. Out they came from homes, schools and storefronts. They stopped walking or riding their bikes—even streetcars paused in their tracks, acknowledging the flame of the ancient Greeks.

For an instant, I thought I saw her in the crowd—a face from my past. I was sure it was her, but I could not stop or change my direction. The image was so fleeting, yet so real. There was no reason she could have been here, in Germany. Though I had no idea what had happened to her after we were forcibly parted by British soldiers of the Tigris Corps. I wanted to look back, but the Torch carried me forward.

I have taken a warm bath. Sabine has gone out to find some bandages for me. It's nothing serious, just a cut I received as I grazed the side of a watering trough in the middle of the village square. I couldn't stop to dress it on my way. I don't think it requires any attention, but women are nature's caregivers, so we do best not to argue.

2 August 1936

Last night's reunion was wonderful. In the Olympic Village, Spyridon and I were joined at a small tavern by several members of the Greek team, as well as a few track and field athletes from the American and British squads. There was a bottle of ouzo, but only Spyridon and I partook, the competing athletes refrained.

"Ion carried the Torch in the relay today" announced Domnitsa Lanitis, introducing me to the group. Dominitsa was one of our athletes, the only female. She was a nice girl from Thessaly and very intense in her sport. She had her hair bunched up under an old hat to disguise her sex as only male athletes were permitted in the village.

"Carried the Torch, eh? Brilliant thing, old chap. Well done," said Ernest, one of the Brits. He ran "the run"—the marathon.

"You were a runner, weren't you?" asked the American, a 1,500-meter boy, they called "Black" Jack.

"I still am," I said. "Anyway, I'm sorry I missed the opening ceremonies."

"It was quite a parade. Your team, as is customary, entered first. And equally as customary, the Yanks snubbed the protocol," said

Ernest, giving Jack a light jab in the ribs as he said the word "Yanks."

"You didn't complain about our protocol when we were greeting the Boche at Chateau Thierry and the Marne River."

"Oh, really mate, were you there also? No? Well, you would have made a fine doughboy. I swear, we'll be hearing about how the Yanks saved our arses for the next century." Ernest announced to the rest of us.

"I've heard that the American team won't lower its flag," I said.

"You heard right, pal. But we also refused the Chancellor's orders that we all salute him with a sieg heil."

"It's just a simple gesture of courtesy to our hosts," said Alexis, another member of the Greek team.

"I don't blame the Americans," I added. "No one can be blind to what lies beneath this ceremonial show of strength."

"You've been living in America too long, Ion," added Alexis.

"I think Berlin is beautiful." continued Jack. "I've never seen boulevards so wide and so clean. And that view down Unter den Linden towards the Brandenburg Gate is breathtaking. They've recreated the beauty of Athens, don't you think?"

"They've copied her architecture, but they cannot create her soul. Something isn't right here. There is a lie beneath this efficient façade. There is anger and hatred, not the love that inspired the art of Athens," I said.

"I think you're paranoid. Look at what he's done to a war-torn country, a defeated one, in just fifteen years since the Great War ended. And look at Athens today, it's been crumbling for over two thousand years." I could tell that tempers and patriotic sentiments were about to flare.

"Is it paranoia that he has remilitarized the Rhineland and reinforces the Siegfried line?" chimed in Domnitsa before I could respond.

"Can you blame them? It's their own backyard, and the Siegfried is defensive," said Jack.

"What's next, the Sudetenland? Austria? Poland? When will his call for lebensraum be satisfied?" retorted Lamnitsa.

"Don't worry, he wouldn't dare cross the Maginot—it would be suicide. If he tries, we'll give him another what for, and send him scurrying back to Berlin," bragged the Brit.

"Yeah, and if you don't think you can handle it alone this time, just give Uncle Sam a call, we'll come over and help you teach the Hun another lesson."

Only the virgins of war speak of it with such ignorance and braggadocio. The initiated know that war has no friends, feels no loyalty and gives no quarter.

"Boys, such talk has no place here and now. We are all bound by the ancient truce, even the Hun who shamelessly parades his military might must observe the sacred Olympian pledge," I said.

"You're right, Ion, but there is a big difference from parading soldiers and fighting with them. He'd be a fool to start anything with the French or Brits, or us, again," said Jack.

"Being a 'fool' is war's first requisite. The second is having amnesia of the last one. And yes, parading is different from fighting. But it is the medals, and the decorative ribbons, and the synchronized drums, and the brass bands, and the brightly colored uniforms marching around like peacocks that make young boys forget that the polished bayonet does not shine when it is stained with blood."

"As long as it's the other fellow's blood..." Jack said with arrogant indifference.

"No, there is little difference. Once tasted, blood begets more blood—yours, theirs, it is the same."

"How would you know, you're not..."

"He knows," said Spyridon. These were the first words he had spoken during the entire interchange.

He didn't speak very much. He was a very shy man, not given to lengthy oration, rather embracing the philosophy that deeds spoke louder. But Ernest turned to him and asked "Mr. Louis, you stood closer to the Chancellor than any of us. What was he like?"

All conversation stopped as eyes and ears turned to Spyridon. All present respected him, for he alone amongst us had worn the olive wreath.

He didn't rush his response, but slowly lowered his glass of ouzo and leaned back in his chair breathing deeply. "I presented the wreath of peace to Herr Hitler. He took it without looking at me, staring instead at the adoring crowds, as if imagining himself a God. Only the one true God may know what Herr Hitler will do with it—and He alone will sit in final judgment."

Spyridon gave me something special after the others had left. We spoke of the earlier conversation, and how flippant the young are about things they know so little. War is so terrible that it cannot be dreamed of, it can only be experienced to be known, and to be believed. And then it is too late.

He handed me the object, which was loosely wrapped in the pages of an Athenian newspaper. I tore the newsprint from it and gazed upon a Richard Lattimore translation of The Odyssey. *It was beautifully bound, and must have cost him two weeks' wages.*

"My friend, it is too magnificent."

"And yet such a small token of my friendship."

"But why in English?" I'm sure it was not an easy thing for him to procure in Amarousi.

"So you may learn your new language from our old words," he said.

It was as if Kalos himself had reached into the deep Aegean and had rescued my book, returning it safely to me. Before Spyridon bid me leave that night, he asked me if I had a quill and some ink. I handed him a bottle of India ink and the very quill that I have used to write these words. He opened the front cover and wrote me a pledge.

"There. Now it is unique. Befitting its owner," he said as he and I bade each other goodnight. How lucky I am to know such a man.

8 August 1936

The Games closed today. Sabine and I met at the Pergamon during her lunch. Afterwards, we sat on the steps of the Altar. Its frescoes depict the battle between the Gods and Giants. Like the spoils of Lord Elgin, it had been uprooted from its birthplace and caged far from home. It made me think of how out of place I was. A Greek figure in a sea of fascism is as far from demokratia as I suppose one could imagine.

Yet, in the midst of this Nazi pall, the athletes and their accomplishments cannot be overshadowed. How little these politicians understand the Olympic spirit. I will never forget what happened between an Aryan long jumper and that Negro fellow Owens.

I dined with the American track and field team. Metcalf and Robinson were there; Williams and Owens joined us a little later. All of them had medaled, but Owens was the talk of the village. I admired that he had come from such humble beginnings, being the son of sharecroppers from Alabama. Ran like the wind, and was about as humble as a man could be. He had fouled twice in the long jump. A third misstep would have disqualified him. Lutz Long, a German competitor favored to win, put his arm around Owens. We all watched as Long whispered something in his ear. Owens went on to win the Gold.

That night, after dinner, we asked him if Long's advice had really made the difference. The papers made a lot of fuss about the whole event. Most, including the official ones, cried foul. I'll never forget Jesse's answer.

"It took a lot of courage for him to befriend me in front of Hitler. You can melt down all the medals and cups I have won and they wouldn't be worth the plating on the 24-karat friendship I feel for him at this moment."

Spoken like a true Olympian.

I put down the journals. Even with life left in my candle, my eyes couldn't read anymore. Soon I was back in my bed, sinking into my pillow. The boundary between wake and sleep is a line that I cross every night, yet I never recall having been there. Perhaps it is the one sacred moment that the Goddess Nyx keeps all to herself.

22
SUNSET

"Pheidippides, I am Leonidas, King of Sparta. We respect any man who can stand before his ancient enemy and display such courage. We have all lost many comrades, but the quantity is unimportant, for the loss of even one heroic man is felt by every citizen." Leonidas then gave Pheidippides the Spartan reply. He was touched by Pheidippides' impassioned plea.

Ten years later, in the small mountain pass of Thermopylae, King Leonidas would lay down his life for the freedom of all Greeks—Athenian as well as Spartan. Pheidippides' father's death would not have been in vain.

Pheidippides later stood with Agapenor gazing out through Sparta's Eastern Gate. "I do not envy the run you must make back to Attica," said the commander of the Spartan Gurads. "Perhaps you and I shall meet again as comrades in the phalanx—I should be proud to have you on my right, your shield guarding my life."

Ion was always in good spirits in the morning, but today he seemed purposeful. We were both looking forward to the arrival of Adam and his students, but for Ion it was as if it was an important event for which he had to ready himself. I heard him stirring an hour before we usually arose, prompting me to enter his room.

"You're up early this morning, Ion," I said.

"I have to prepare, my dear."

"Prepare?"

"For class..."

His words, though now spoken in the lucidity of daylight, were reminiscent of painful monologues whispered in the occlusion of night. I recalled with trepidation those other times in Old Westbury when Ion prepared for something that did not exist.

One night last spring, I was awakened by a noise which I assumed was a breeze forcing its way through some open window. Knowing that my own were closed, I got up and walked down the hall following the sound to Ion's room. Stopping just at the door, I heard the intensified sound that I realized was a voice, an articulate voice, punctuated by the singsong sighs of frustration.

Opening the door, I saw Ion standing in front of a mirror, fumbling with an ascot that he was attempting to tie around his neck. Other than a white dress shirt, all he wore were a pair of cotton boxer shorts. Despite lacking the balance of his attire, he turned to walk towards the door.

"Ion?"

"I'm late."

"Late?"

"They're waiting."

I wanted to press him for an explanation, but I recognized that he was in a world of his own and that there could be no reasonable response. There I stood, the sole audience to a monologue, and Ion did not even know that he was performing.

"Cellini," he continued. I watched him turn and step closer to his bookcase, lifting his shaking hand towards the volumes it held. He ran his fingers back and forth, without them coming to rest on any one in particular. He stopped and turned. I thought he was looking directly at me and that his reverie was snapped. But my fears only increased when he continued speaking as though I were not there. "I must have left it at school."

"Ion..."

"Oh, it's you," he spoke softly in recognition of my voice, yet not really aware of who I was.

"There is no school today," I said.

"No?"

I was able to coax him back into bed. I put his ascot away and as I watched his eyes close, I slowly backed out of the room. Though I was shaken, I calmed myself with the thought that Ion was simply having a dream. But each successive night that week, I was awakened in the middle of the night by the sounds of his preparing to meet his imaginary classroom of students. Each night, I was able to cajole him back to bed. I was torn between ignoring his behavior and the real fear that he might fall down the darkened stairs or leave our home half dressed in the middle of the night. And I wondered whether his conduct was harmless sleepwalking or an indication of a deeper and more insidious physiological problem.

And then I snapped. The next night, after a week of sleep deprivation, I reproached him. He was going through the same motions of dressing and searching for his book, the *Autobiography of Benvenuto Cellini.*

"Ion!" I exclaimed, grabbing his shoulders and looking him in the eyes. "Ion, please, Ion, stop! Stop. There is no class to go to."

"No class today?"

"There is no class anymore."

He stared at me as if I had struck him. I could feel him falling backwards even though his body did not move. His eyes looked at me as if to say he knew why but yet still needed to ask "why?" Ion finally went to bed, but he appeared a defeated man.

I tried my best to forget the episodes, hoping that he would do the same. We never spoke of it and it hasn't recurred. But as Ion prepared himself today for Adam and his students, I could sense the pride of a man who was about to be vindicated.

They were due in a few hours. We had quite a day planned. They would be joining us for lunch, which they would help to prepare. Father Diogenes was a firm believer in purifying the soul through honest hard work, and Dalton students were not above a little purification.

We had arranged to meet at the church. Ion made us arrive early, which was fortuitous, since we were not there long before a large yellow van drove up.

"Good morning, Mr. Theodore," rang out a chorus of teenagers.

"It's great to see you both," Adam said, extending his hand to Ion, and kissing me on the cheek.

"Children," said Ion, "you must forgive me, I have forgotten some of your names. Would you mind repeating them for me?"

One by one, each student called out his or her name.

"Wonderful," he said, rubbing his hands together. "Absolutely wonderful. I'll bet you are the best students at Dalton. A fine school," he added.

The bells of Panteleimon resounded with their ten o'clock chimes. They reminded me of the bells that signal the beginning of class, and as I watched the Dalton students following Ion, I knew that school was in session.

"Ah, Giotto, one of the greatest colorists of the Italian School. His variations from the Byzantine formula are slight, but the change in spirit cannot be denied," said Ion, as we all gazed about us at the colored walls. "Stereotypical forms are replaced by tender humanity. This is what made him and his colleagues more than painters and sculptors—they were revolutionaries. Daring, like the Athenians, to make the human body their subject."

"What made them so far ahead of their time?" asked Mai Lin. She had told Ion earlier that she wanted to study Art History when she went to college.

"They took their commandments from the heavenly Father pleasing the laws of aesthetics, not the whims of their patrons. They had to reconcile the wisdom of antiquity with the teachings of the church, and where better to initiate a revolution but at the doorsteps of the most powerful church—under the watchful eyes of the Holy See."

"It's amazing they had the courage," said Dylan.

"What choice did they have, once they unlocked the power of the art? They took their lessons from nature—the mistress of all masters."

"Were you always an artist?" asked Kira, a very beautiful girl with long brown hair.

"Everyone has always been." He didn't elaborate. I knew he wouldn't. Most would have reveled in being the center of attention. But I could tell that

Ion was slightly embarrassed. For him, art has always been about love, not laurels.

Lunch had been quite an adventure, with the kids participating in its picking, grinding, cooking and filleting. Eftehea had grilled *barbounakia*, sweet red mullets, with lemon and olive oil. We also ate sautéed dandelion greens, saturated with lemon and olive oil, and a traditional *mousaka* with—of course—olive oil. I believe that anything besides olive oil on a Greek's plate is only there for textural variety or to help absorb more of this sacred liquid.

"Do you enjoy school?" asked Ion.

"I guess it's okay, but my math teacher is really tough," said Keith.

"Yeah, he's so unfair. Like, you know, he won't even let us use calculators on our tests," added Kira in a tone of disbelief and indignation.

Ion laughed, a bellowing laugh that came from deep in his belly. "My dear children, without a calculator, you can design the pyramids, describe the motion of the planets and measure the circumference of the earth, from right here on this spot."

"Measure the earth, from here? No way. How?" chimed in Kira.

"Actually, all you need are two things," answered Ion. "A stick and an incredible imagination."

Richard, Kira and Keith moved a little closer to Ion; he had their attention.

The chartered van pulled up just as Ion began his explanation of how a Greek librarian measured the Earth's circumference. It had something to do with this guy, named Eratosthenes, who got an idea while gazing into his well. He noticed that the noonday sun appeared directly in the water's reflection and that the sides of the well cast no shadow. Then there was something about the Sun's rays traveling parallel to each other, and some measurements of shadows he took in Alexandria, about five hundred miles distant. "So, using simple geometry, he was able to calculate the circumference of the Earth so precisely that only Apollo astronauts have achieved a more accurate reading."

"That's so cool," came the adolescents' response.

"Where to?" asked Mr. Georgiou, the van driver.

"To the Tomb," said Adam.

It was hardly visible until we were practically on top of it. Surrounded by tall weeds and wildflowers, it might have been no more than an inland sand dune, or a three-story landfill. The students did not seem to know what to say, their faces registering something between awe and perplexity. I too was surprised and speechless, having grown accustomed to national monuments like the Lincoln Memorial or Grant's Tomb. There were no gates, no tickets booths, no guards, no guidebooks, no postcards and not a single other soul here but our group. Nothing—not even a "KEEP OFF THE TOMB" sign. Just a thirty-foot high pile of dirt. But for a single sign on the main road pointing down this obscure street, one would pass by here and never attach any importance to this weed-covered field.

Adam cleared his voice a little. "This is remarkable," he said, his tone wavering between disbelief and sarcasm.

"What is?" asked Chandra.

"They're in there, aren't they?" said Richard.

"Who's in there? It's a pile of dirt," said Dylan.

"It is a pile of dirt, but it covers the bones of the Athenian hoplites," said Adam with an air of authority and drama meant to impress.

"Are you sure we're in the right place?" Thomas asked.

Adam looked puzzled, and I noticed him looking at Ion, waiting perhaps for a sign that this was a mistake and that nearby, some gleaming white temple of victory awaited our approval.

Ion held my hand, and very slowly knelt down and patted the soil on the edge of the rise. His silence reassured Adam. "Yes, it is," Ion said.

"I can't believe it's been undisturbed, why has no one touched it?" asked one student.

"They all rest in the field where they fell—everyone knows not to move them," said Ion softly.

One student, with a thin face and intense blue, inquisitive eyes, asked or rather stated suddenly, "Why did they throw them all together, why not give each one his own grave and marker?"

Adam attempted an explanation that seemed plausible. "It was the aftermath of a great battle and no doubt it was difficult to transport bodies and dig so many graves."

"Was this intended as a memorial at all?" asked one student.

"Maybe this was just a mass grave," suggested another, who had surely seen such images in documentaries of war in the twentieth century.

At this point, I watched Adam look at me, half smiling at the skepticism of his very bright students but somewhat disappointed in his own inability to justify human sacrifice and such a modest memorial.

"*Dulce et decorum est—pro patria mori*," said Ion speaking clearly. "It is sweet and fitting to die for one's country," Ion translated as I noticed Adam wince slightly.

"Why? What is worth dying for? Vietnam, Somalia, Grenada?" said Allison.

"Or worth killing for?" asked the same blue-eyed student who had spoken before. These students grew up in the liberal and socially conscious New York City. They were well read, well informed and trained to question authority.

"There is a difference between killing for something and dying for something," Adam pointed out.

"Of course, there is, Adam," Ion began as if to agree, "but not in this case. No, these men and their compatriots killed thousands of the barbarians. And they did so in hand-to-hand combat. There was no cover and no sense of protection. They knew there was a likelihood of being killed."

"Was it worth it?" came one student's voice and silence ensued.

"Ask them. Here they lay, all for one, free men, bones pressed together in the soil from which we all spring, in the service not of themselves as individuals but of a way of life—but I think I've already said too much..."

"Look at the plaque," Adam said directing all of our eyes to it. It was a carved stone, in harmony with the uncomplicated nature of the site.

ΕΛΛΗΝΩΝ ΠΡΟΜΑΧΟΥΝΤΕΣ ΑΘΗΝΑΙΟΙ ΧΡΥΣΟΦΟΡΩΝ
ΜΗΔΩΝ ΕΣΤΟΡΕΣΑΝ ΔΥΝΑΜΙΝ
ΣΙΜΟΝΙΔΗΣ

"Ion, would you do the honors?" suggested Adam, as though any one else present might attempt it.

"*Here, the Athenians, in command of the Greeks, vanquished the Medes who were dressed in gold and many in number*," quoted Ion. These words were astounding in their subtlety. Then I realized, this place wasn't created for the approval of twentieth century tourists, it wasn't created at all, it just happened. No staging, no story boards, no photo ops, no perception of how history would be altered in one afternoon—just men having the courage and determination to do their duty. Ion seemed momentarily drifting, his eyes almost closed, a serene look passing over his face.

"Why were they dressed in gold?" asked Kira.

"Somebody call the fashion police," teased Mai Lin eliciting a laugh from the girls.

"Why a pile of weeds for something so sacred? Why not a marble memorial or something?" asked another student, but it reflected the feelings of several.

"What lives—the monument or the deed?" interrupted Ion. "Monuments crumble. Man cannot *build* the eternal, but he can *do* the eternal. For when no traces remain of the monument, it is the deed that resonates throughout time."

"It seems like such a deserted place," said Kira.

"So, how many guys are in there," asked Robert. Forgive the generality, but boys seemed to love the gory statistics of battle, while the girls were still imagining the Persians in their gold sequined uniforms.

"One hundred ninety-two," said Adam.

"At least they are not lonely," Ion whispered. I knew he was thinking of the soldiers as well as of himself. I had rarely seen Ion exhibit anything resembling self-pity and even more rarely jealousy. To see both together in a single phrase was almost painful. Not because I pitied Ion, but because it brought out my own frustration at his beautiful but impenetrable dignity. The more I read his journals, the less I understood why he had never told me his stories. He was so insulated and alone and no secret I had discovered had told me why.

I could see Ion looking at the mound as if into his own future. His furrowed brow seemed a battlefield between his own choice of a long life of teaching and art, and the sacrifice that cuts life short, violently short in the name of something whose future we never live to see. His eyes welled as he walked to the side of the mound. He seemed to fade into the vernal monument as the monument seemed to fade into the background of a blue sky. As I watched Ion, I was aware of Adam staring at me.

As if by some unseen cue, the children drifted towards Ion, following him without plan or motive as he walked to the far side of the tomb. Perhaps they hoped that Ion would further unlock the mystery of how such a small number of Greeks could have withstood the barbarians, so many in number and dressed in gold.

I was about to follow, but at that moment, I felt Adam lightly hold my arm. It was just enough pressure to still my movement.

"Let them go, they'll be fine together," he said. "Besides, I haven't had a chance to talk to you all day."

"He's some teacher, isn't he, Adam?"

"Yes, he is. Some professors teach subjects. For your uncle, life is the subject."

"I wish I could feel the same way about my life, my career."

"You have far too much integrity for your job."

"What are you saying, Adam? That lawyers are lacking in the integrity department? I'm shocked." I teased. I enjoyed the playful banter Adam and I had developed over the brief time we'd known each other. It felt good to laugh. I think it was the first time I had in three days. "This place, it wasn't what you expected, was it?" I asked him after a brief silence.

"Not exactly."

"Even the plaque, it was so understated given what happened here."

"Marianna," he began hesitantly, "would I be out of line if I asked for your phone number, back home I mean. I'd love to call you when we're back in the city, for a cup of coffee or something?"

"Are you asking me on a date, Adam?" I was teasing him again, but he couldn't tell this time.

"Well, not exactly, but sort of." I could feel his throat getting dry from three feet away.

"I'd love to meet you back home for coffee. But I have to be honest with you..."

"Uh oh, the 'honest with you' reply," he interrupted softly.

"I don't think I'm ready to date. Not right now."

"I understand. I didn't mean to be so forward. But I'd love to see you again, just as friends. That is if, it won't ruin your reputation to be seen with a high-school teacher."

"Are you sure you want to be seen with a lawyer?" We both laughed this time.

Adam had a pen and a used ticket stub from the Archaeological Museum sufficed as writing paper. We exchanged numbers and I folded his up and made a point of showing him how carefully I placed it in my pocket.

Suddenly, the sounds of rambunctious laughter were traveling around the tomb.

"Come on, let's see what we're missing," I said, pulling him so that he had no choice but to follow. I could sense a little disappointment in his eyes, but now was not the moment for the weaving of spells.

"But, why don't..."

"Shh," I silenced him as Ion and the children came into view. "Watch," I whispered.

Ion wasn't talking about Greek history, or the Battle of Marathon, or anything pertaining to the *Tumulus*. He was telling them a story about a Varsity wrestling match between Horace Mann and Dalton, decades back. Apparently the Dalton student was on the verge of losing when his athletic cup dislodged and fell from his jock strap onto the mat. The Horace Mann wrestler slipped on it, fell on his back and was easily pinned.

"And every year, to mark its anniversary, the Horace Mann Wrestling coach would send his Dalton counterpart a gold painted athletic cup in memory of that auspicious victory," he finished. The students were eating it up. I could only imagine Ion saying it was not strength but art that wins the prize. Yeah, art and a poorly fitting jock strap.

I glanced over at Adam. He had a profound look of admiration in his eyes—he knew when he had been outwrestled.

Watching Ion, and the way he captured the hearts of these children suddenly reminded me of Mrs. Jung. She taught French at my high school. I never thought much about what teachers did when they weren't teaching, as if they existed only in the confines of their classrooms. But I recalled the last period of the last day of ninth grade. I'm not sure why I watched her closely on this occasion, but I did as the last minutes of class ticked away and the buzzer sounded. Mrs. Jung smiled at us, stepped away from her lectern, then stood for a moment behind her desk. She placed her materials in the desk drawers and locked them, as if they could have any value in anyone else's hands. My classmates exited through the portal that had brought us to her at the beginning of the semester—the beginning of our journey together. The empty echoes of the nearly deserted lecture hall exaggerated the quiet. It was hard to compete with the outside world the coming hazy summer afternoons of picnics, lemonade and lazing in the shade. But for an instant, she held our imaginations in the palms of her hands, molding them ever so slightly, returning them to us changed forever.

My eyes continued to follow her as she went to a door at the back of the room. Her students hadn't seen her coming, and except for me, they wouldn't see her disappear. To us, it was as if she had always been there and would always be. I was supposed to have her again next fall for French II, but she never returned. We learned later that she lost a battle with breast cancer. She had known long before the end of that semester, but she never burdened us with this knowledge. I tried to imagine how she must of felt at that moment, as she took a last look at the stage of her dreams. Did she wonder who would remember the performance after the hall was dark and silent, or did she think about who would be there next fall to greet the new class? I realized now how important we were to her and I regretted missing the lessons that she didn't live to share.

The sun seemed to hang for an extra minute or two on the ridge of Pentelicus as the Dalton students began boarding their chartered bus. It was as if a bell had rung and the students were filing out of their classroom on the last day of school. Ion was tired—he had held nothing back today. In another moment, Helios had driven his cart below the horizon.

23
TO END ALL WARS

He ran once again into the enveloping darkness. The sun had set, taking with it the last vestiges of light, though the sky remained a deep cobalt blue for several more minutes. Pheidippides knew that he had to return as quickly as possible from Sparta—though it was not with the news he wished to deliver.

The aches and pains in his body intensified. Sweat no longer came and Pheidippides' mind began to wander into the realm of dreams as the darkness and isolation disoriented him. He imagined himself home, reclining after a delicious meal of spit-roasted rabbit, figs, olives and warm barley bread coated with fresh golden honey. These thoughts only made him more miserable as loneliness set in. It was worse than any he had ever felt before—even the day that his father did not return—even more bitter than the day he left Leontia without knowing if he would return.

After dinner, Ion and Father Diogenes played chess. The pieces were Greek, with Gods and Heroes waging war on a blue and white marble battleground. Hoplites, with shields at the ready, formed the front line of defense, and the Temples of Athena and Zeus stood on each end as rooks. They played with the unhurried passion of two men who enjoyed the contest for its playing, not its outcome. At the end of an hour, though neither had secured an advantage, they just smiled and reset the board.

Ion was exhausted. Perhaps traveling had caught up with him. Perhaps it was the exertion of a day with the Dalton teenagers. Or maybe it was the emotional resurrection at the Tomb of Ion's ancestors. He was in bed soon after darkness had descended. I wiped a dampened washcloth along his soft and wrinkled brow. He wasn't sweating though he was very warm. I wrung out the cloth into a small water-filled basin and let it soak up some cooler spring water for another pass over his thirsty skin. Ion reached up and held his hand to mine as it passed again over the horizon of his forehead. Its gentle squeeze told me that he was ready for sleep.

"Your touch is rejuvenating, my dear. I have felt that touch just once before. You are so much like her..." he trailed off into slumber. I was pleased that he had retired early. Not only did he sorely need the solitude, but I too longed for the seclusion of the confessional and the continuation of Ion's saga.

12 August 1936

I arrived in France yesterday by rail, and had one last afternoon to play in the streets of Paris. Sabine saw me off at the Gare du Nord—she was going to look for a new flat for the fall semester. We parted on the train's platform as the steam from its engines sifted around us. It would be the last time, but there were no tears. We both knew our meeting would fade into a beautiful remembrance of a magical week—nothing more and definitely nothing less.

I am on board the S.S. Normandie, *bound for New York. The ship hoisted anchor this morning—by nightfall, land and Sabine's warm body were a distant memory. A school of porpoises are running before our bow. It is a majestic sight, and far more pleasing to a sailor than the white-capped fury of a battered sea. The ship's gentle rocking, and lack of any responsibility for the next week, should give me ample opportunity to finish the tale of my emancipation.*

Whatever part of my life I consider as childhood ended at an age that most still consider as youth. In some terrible and ironic way, it would be death from which my life would spring. Two bullets, fired by a Serb nationalist, changed everything. Apparently, the war started with one man killing another. The assassin was then executed and nine million more would die to avenge their respective deaths.

I had no knowledge of, or interest in, world politics. All I knew was that the Ottomans had allied themselves with the Germans and Austro-Hungarians—forming the Central Powers. Boys from as far away as France, England and eventually America would come to fight other boys who didn't speak their language. I was almost thirteen, most soldiers were a few years older—but we were all children. God surely must weep.

For the world, the outbreak of war meant tragedy, for me it was serendipitous. It was just months before the ritual was to have taken place. As a male house servant in a Turkish home, I was to be castrated upon reaching my thirteenth year. It was but one of the indignities to which young boys under Turkish rule had to succumb. I began to see my desire, fueled by my burgeoning virility, as a curse. The thought of becoming a eunuch, of being desexed, was almost a relief.

The siege of the British garrison at Kut al-Amara had commenced a month earlier. With a soft cloth hat serving as a helmet and clothing fitted like a potato sack on my undernourished body, I boarded a train to join the regiments that had repulsed the enemy at Gallipoli. I had neither the physical nor mental preparation necessary for the carnage I was to witness. I learned that war is ordained by those who sit safely in distant palaces, while boys with no understanding of the causes hack themselves to pieces in slaughtering fields.

Which brings me to a perplexing question—and that is "why." Why write this? What have I accomplished that is worthy of these pages? I am now thirty-three years old. By that age, Alexander had already conquered the known world, Jesus had given himself for man's sins and Mozart had written forty symphonies. What does a fugitive have to say to the future?

13 August 1936

Al-Kut is a lonely desert outpost about sixty miles south of Baghdad, springing up from the sands where the tributary of Shatt al-Gharraf branches off into the wide desert. It is said that this valley was the site of the Garden of Eden. Now, it is nothing but parched earth, interrupted by marshes, man-made trenches and craters formed by bursting artillery shells. And into the cracks of this once fertile crescent the blood of a civilization oozed away.

The terrain is a paradox of burning sands by day and cold lifeless nights. Aridity to scorch the soul and torrential rains, which make the ground, swallow a man. And when it rains, the marshes are a breeding ground for mosquitoes and all manner of vermin. Fog and mist and mirages are common. And though the Tigris flows in abundance, it is brackish and saturated with indescribable filth, yet she beckons the thirsty like a Siren luring men to drink her, leaving those who do writhing in intestinal misery.

I had no idea of the significance of what I did, or what value lay in spilling life over this piece of desert. Blood for sand seemed a poor exchange. My feelings for my masters, and the dubious manner in which I was volunteered, made fighting for them repulsive, whatever the cause. There was no bigger picture or grander scale beyond my own misery. I fought only to escape my dreary life and to be set free, one way or another.

I had little chance of taking another man's life. I was in the front-lines, but not as a combatant—I never carried a weapon—they were far too scarce to waste on a slave turned soldier. I was assigned to the 32nd Regiment of the Turkish Sixth Army, a servant in a supply train supporting the Sultan's army in the northern desert.

I could tell about the battles, the attacks and counterattacks, the advances and the retreats. I could write in detailed chronology about the Tigris Corps' operations against us. I could reel off the statistics or speak of the strategies of attack and the gun placements and supply routes and how the Mesopotamian Valley affected the outcome of the theatre and the war. But that would be the view of the historian—writing from the comfort and safety of time and distance—not the view of a soldier who was there.

I eventually did read the history, several versions as a matter of fact. Some were pretty good, all were accurate about dates and troop movements, but others—I wondered if they had witnessed the same war I had experienced. A war looks very different on a map than from the ground, or a few feet below it, which was my usual vantage point.

14 August 1936

Terrified, I huddled in a trench, which quickly became saturated with blood and mire, a grave for hundreds of hapless souls. Our diet was appalling: tins of preserves, unleavened pita made from the brackish Tigris waters and spoiling cured meat. Scurvy became common. Flies swarmed around rotting corpses and the runoffs from the crude latrines.

Foraging amongst the enemy's dead was not uncommon. We meant no particular disrespect, but clothes and ammunition were always in short supply. On one such mission, Abadin, Solmaz and I came upon several British corpses. They were of His Majesty's 2nd Light Horse Regiment, though they were recently and abruptly retired. We searched them, telling ourselves that we might find some intelligence of value, but we could not have cared less about their papers. The first few times you do this, you are timid, and hold your nose. Soon, it is no different than performing some unpleasant household chore. Solmaz found a week's supply of tobacco. None of us smoked, but it made valuable barter. Abadin found several tins of cured corned beef—a favorite of the Brits. I helped myself to a compass and a letter from one man's overcoat. I kept it, depriving his widow of her last communication.

Folded in the binding's crease was the letter in question. It was perfectly intact, but it had a discoloration on the envelope that I hoped was dirt—but suspected was dried blood from the dying soldier's wound. I opened it and read what were most likely the British soldier's last written words.

"We had to attack a trench which was only a few yards away. This thing was the cause of a lot of trouble. Everybody was jumpy and they kept on firing, rapid firing, all hours of the day and night to prevent us. Anyhow, we were badly knocked back and between our two trenches it was just literally thick with dead people and they were blown to bits with erratic shells and firing. The bodies were in all states of decomposition and the place was worse than a slaughter house. We

were on the windward side, so the stench blew into their trenches with the result that they asked for an armistice. It was granted and we all gathered our dead—the place was just an awful mess. I can only pray that the Lord grants me the good favour to return home to you and the children soon."

Ion's entry of August14, 1936 continued.

My English was not proficient enough for me to read it for many years. But I knew what it said—the experience of the trench was the same to all who suffered in these hellish self-dug graves. I often wonder how I could have behaved in such a cruel and insensitive manner, especially at an age when boys should be playing games and climbing rocks and daydreaming about images they see in the clouds. I still carry shame of how easily I succumbed to a despicable way of life and how survival clouded my judgment. I thought nothing of watching another starve, or of stealing something off a dying man. This is the true crime of war: it steals the souls of those it does not kill.

I saw a stain on the page that could have been a tear. I touched my fingers to the spot and thought of the pain that this admission must have exacted from the confessor. I took a few deep breaths and found the stomach to continue.

The garrison of Al-Kut was manned by 12,000 British and Indian troops. We were told that the garrison would surrender after a few weeks. One lesson of war is that arrogance is rarely rewarded. The fools, did they not remember Constantinople 1453? It took them five weeks to defeat a Byzantine army one-tenth their size. Starvation had set in and the British suffered more than 23,000 casualties in failed relief efforts. Five months from the day of investiture, the British commander finally realized his position was untenable.

The Turks celebrated with wild reverie. I did not celebrate, though I was pleased to have avoided the long lists of the wounded or dead.

24
A FISHERMAN'S ARIA

He gazed down over the Plain of Argos, and in the soft moonlight, he could make out the city of Mycenae rising in circles on a hill. Cyclopean walls of yellow and gray were silhouetted in the distance. Its inhabitants slept soundly, regenerating their bodies and minds for another day of hard work in the fields and on the slopes. Flocks of sheep grazed these rugged hills. When they moved en masse, it appeared as if the earth itself was shifting. He could hear their chorus of bleating, as his footsteps made them cry out their staccato song.

Feeling as if he were going to die alone in the mountains, he began to imagine Death as a relief, as a welcome friend coming to end his torment.

Shadows moved about him and the wind echoed off the canyons, creating sounds unlike any he had ever heard.

Then came the voices.

"To friendship born in strange places," said Adonia, as she raised her glass of red wine.

"Strange and very high places," I added, touching my glass to hers. She smiled, and I watched her take a healthy sip of the dark red liquid.

"I knew that we would meet again," she said, taking my hand for a brief moment.

"I had hoped so too. Your invitation was so generous. Ion sends his regrets, but sitting on a stone bleacher for a couple of hours, even with a mat, would've been too much for him."

Adonia had tickets to the Athens Festival, which packed the Herodeion each season with plays and concerts. We weren't eating dinner yet—that was reserved for after the show. My digestive system was slowly adapting to a different gastronomic schedule—Greeks eat supper late. It was not uncommon to be dining at one o'clock in the morning and still see people coming in seeking tables.

The Herodeion, or Odion of Herod Atticus, was a massive amphitheatre carved into the southwest cliffs of the Acropolis by the Romans in 160 B.C. Originally enclosed under a roof, the technology of which I could not comprehend, its open-air stage now lay partially in ruins. Decaying stone walls rose three stories in the air behind the semicircular stage, which itself gave way to an equally high and steep rows of marble seats. The crumbling façade only added to the mysticism of the place, and as if in concession to modern science, hidden lights illuminated the stage's backdrop, through which the evergreen-covered hills beyond could be seen.

We sat about halfway up, towards the left of center stage. Though smaller than the fossilized amphitheatre of Dionysos, which rested dormant a few hundred meters away, the Herodeion still held over five thousand people. It had easily surpassed its capacity tonight, as people who could not find seats seemed happy enough to stand during the evening's performances. The night's program was comprised of the works of several composers performed by the Greek National Opera and the London Symphony Orhestra. The featured symphony would be Moldau's *Smetana*, but first we'd be treated to an opera composed by a contemporary Greek artist based on Aeschylus' *Prometheus Bound*.

Coincidentally, I had just recently purchased the book. It was one of those books I was supposed to have read, but being so familiar with the story, I'd fooled myself into thinking I had. At home, I had shelves of great books, most of them left to me by my parents. I used to love reading for pleasure, but when I came home from work the last thing I wanted to do after a day of stressful concentration was to focus on more words regardless of how artfully constructed. On the rare occasions that I had any energy left after my long day and equally long commute, corporate breeding left me no choice but to read only those things which would further my professional success.

"I hoped our last conversation didn't make you think I was a bit neurotic," I said as we took our seats.

"Not at all. I found it most refreshing, and all too real."

"What do you mean?"

"You search because you are uncertain. Life is good and comforts abound, so you assume it must be right, but still you feel lost. Somewhere in your dreams—the ones unscarred by expectations unfulfilled—you wait to be rescued. Just as I waited for my Captain to return from the sea."

"There's a story in there, Adonia," I said. But I'd have to wait for her response, as the lights dimmed and the orchestra began its entr'acte. The program, which fortunately had an English translation, informed me that *Prometheus Bound* was the only play that never used the stage. The entire cast, including the chorus, clung to sides of the towering wall to simulate Prometheus' precarious perch atop the Caucasus Mountains.

As the sound of strings and reeds filled the starry night, I recollected with amusement the experience Ion and I shared a month ago as we browsed the stacks at Barnes & Noble. He led me to the section on drama and said, "may I suggest we proceed right to the master?"

I smiled at him and instinctively fingered the spines of several Shakespearian tragedies.

Ion laughed, "A clever newcomer, my dear. He imitated the rhythms first recorded in the Fifth Century B.C. by the *sine qua non*—Aeschylus. Anything that has been said or could be said about man's tragic nature, his heroic aspirations and his comic failings, was cast in Aeschylus' fine hammered lines. He transformed the language of ordinary life into the descants of the Gods. Because of them, young swains like Shakespeare could elevate 'I was thinking the other day,' to '*When to the sessions of sweet silent thought / I summon up remembrance of things past*.' Ah, here's his masterpiece." Ion slid a thin book from the middle shelf. The volumes were packed so tightly the others quickly swallowed the niche it had just vacated. "He fought at Marathon."

"I thought he was a poet, not a soldier."

"Without freedom there is no art." Ion proceeded to tell me that after a lifetime of achievements, Aeschylus wished only one deed memorialized in his epitaph, "*How tried his valor, Marathon may tell*."

I loved Prometheus and everything he embodied of the Greek Gods, their divinity and their humanity. Nearly unlimited in power, they were vulnerable to every human passion including a passion for mankind. The Greeks worshipped their deities so free of piety—they did not sanitize them—they paid homage without overlooking their sins.

"The Gods create man and then forsake him; in turn Prometheus chooses man over the favor of the Gods," Ion said, bringing back memories of his passionate story telling. "Refusing any compromise with Zeus, he roused our reason and accepted eternal torment rather than serve in a heaven of slavery. Listen to these words:" he said as he found the page he had been scanning for.

"*Thou firmament of God, and swift-winged winds. Ye springs of rivers, and of ocean waves that smile innumerous! Mother of us all, O Earth, and Sun's all-seeing eye, behold, I pray, what I, a god, from gods endure*. Like Prometheus, we all carry a flame, Marianna. Magnificent though the torches of some souls are, they grow conscious that their lives burn red, then white... then out."

During the intermission, I turned and asked Adonia to elaborate on what she had said at the show's prelude. She was usually so composed, yet there was something vulnerable in her words.

"Hearing your words reminded me of my younger, more naïve days when dreams never had to end."

"And what of this '*Captain who returned from the sea*'?"

"He's dead. It will be ten years on September twenty-ninth."

"I'm sorry, Adonia, I—"

"I cannot imagine life before Niko."

"What did he do?"

"He was a fisherman. Every single day, in calm seas or raging tempests, he set out in search of his catch. It was a hardy existence, and when he caught no fish, we did not eat. My Niko fought in the resistance during the war, using his fishing boat to run guns and supplies to the allies on Crete."

"That must have been extremely dangerous."

"He was fearless, even when he was captured and brutally tortured. When they realized he would sooner die than betray his comrades, they left him to die. Though he had saved me before—I could do nothing to help him then."

"Saved you? From what Adonia?"

"From the hell that was my life." I felt as if she shouldn't be telling me, a perfect stranger, these things, but I could not resist hearing what could possibly follow.

"I was born in the small fishing village of Galaxidi. During the war, whole villages, or what was left of them after the Nazi occupation, were lost to disease and starvation. We had no running water or electricity for months at a time. What I ate for lunch today would have fed my whole family. Two of my younger sisters did not survive that time."

"What happened to them?"

"One died from malaria, the other diphtheria. Just names, they even rhyme, like a nursery tale."

"How devastating for you and your family."

"Our daily struggle to survive was so overwhelming that we didn't have the luxury to mourn them. They were buried in communal graves—hastily bulldozed over without any markers. Nothing of theirs remained to show that they had ever lived. Can you imagine having to trade their clothes for a quart of milk, or burning a favorite rag doll in the fireplace for warmth on a bitter cold night?"

"No, I can't," I said with great sadness. "Adonia, I've read about it in books, but I won't ever fully comprehend the suffering that went on in Europe during that time." Adonia nodded and looked at me as though she appreciated the honesty in my admission and was touched that I was aware of that which I would never really know.

"My father was a very proud man, and he lost everything in the war, including his dignity. It changed all of us forever, but I think it changed him more than any of us. He was no longer the warm and loving father that I remembered from when I was eight or nine. Only on his deathbed did he try to make peace. He cried when we spoke about Eleni and Amalia, my two sisters that had died. He hadn't mentioned their names for decades—I thought he had forgotten them. Those times had hardened his heart. Some things are hard to feel." Then a smile came over her face. "And then there was Niko."

"How did you meet him?"

"After the war I used to see him when I would go to a market near the wharf. I don't think he noticed me at first, but I would watch him setting his lines, or making repairs to his boat. I was being courted at that time by the son of a wealthy merchant. He was arrogant and lazy and incapable of loving anyone but himself. But my father had arranged it. He was more concerned that I marry a man with money than one with a tender heart. This boy's father had made his fortune during the war. I can assure you, any man who became rich under those circumstances, did so in money stained with blood. His son was no better. He thought that his position entitled him respect, but I would sooner have respected a jackal.

"I met Niko one day in the village church. We only spoke for a few minutes, but it was enough for me to know my course. I expected him to be intimidating, but he was so shy that he could barely look at me. My father had seen us talking, and all the way home I felt his displeasure. The next time I went to market, I worked up the courage to find Niko. And then i found him again, and again

When my father discovered that I had been meeting Niko in secret, he forbade me from seeing him ever again. Needless to say, I found every opportunity I could to disobey my father, and our love blossomed under the most difficult of conditions. I gave Niko what no other man could ever have again," she said with a tender look in her eyes that told me all I needed to know.

"One day, Niko came to ask for my hand. My father flew into a rage and insulted Niko to his face. My darling lover stood his ground and never returned the anger or the indignities that were hurled at him. My father wanted me to marry a man with means and Niko had none."

"I had no idea. Well, you just seemed to be so elegant and..."

"Niko was most successful by what he gave—not by what he had. He lived life as he chose—who can ever hope for more? We could afford few luxuries, luxuries to us, though probably insignificant things to most Americans. I have often observed that the more material possessions you have, the more you become a slave to those things and the temptation for more. But is that not the Great American Dream?"

I wasn't sure whether or not to defend our way of life, but a part of me was becoming less and less proud of our obsession with material accumulation. There is so much pressure to amass wealth and I was certainly guilty of being a player in that game. I thought of Ion—paralegals in my firm make more in a summer than he ever made in a year. Then I thought of Adam who had given up everything because he saw that it really amounted to nothing at all. "I know it seems we often forego our passions to fill our pockets," I said, opting not to waive the red, white and blue.

"Perhaps one should be greedy about one's passions not possessions," she said.

Adonia pulled out an old clipping from her purse. It was an obituary from a local Greek newspaper. Above the text was a picture of a man dressed in formal evening wear.

"He's so handsome."

"And he had a voice that would make the wind stop to listen. When the waters were still and the fish could not be seen, he would sing an aria. The fish would draw near and become so hypnotized by his melodic voice that he could catch them with a net. He became a tenor—his dream was to sing in Vienna—but he never..." her voice trailed off, and she put on her reading glasses to focus on the small article.

She translated it. Its headline read, 'Tenor Dies at 64.' Besides his tenure at the Royal Hellenic Opera, it also mentioned his being a hero in the *ELAS*—the Greek resistance. It went on to state that he was survived by a wife, Adonia, but there was no mention of children.

"I would love to have heard his voice," I said.

"When I close my eyes, I still can," was all she said as she folded up the clipping and put it safely back in her handbag.

"I see that you two didn't have children either. But you had such a wonderful marriage, it seems a pity. You would have made such good parents." But as I said this, I realized that I may have inadvertently offended her. She immediately looked at me with uncertainty in her eyes. I was about to delve deeper when I stopped myself. I'm glad I did, though the answer to the question I dared not ask abruptly followed.

"When the *communistos* left him to die, they had already killed a part of him. No one would have made a better father than Niko."

The resurrection of buried memories had fatigued her. I was also tired, but our conversation left me both invigorated and drained. I admired her courage to love, even against the will of her father and the destruction of the world around her. She chose love over any other consideration, and I envied her for it. She had been through so much, and she could speak about it with me, a stranger, with no shame or fear. There was so much I wanted to tell her. Why was I so hesitant, so afraid? I longed for the freedom that was so naturally a part of her being.

I lived in a world where people talked incessantly about their grievances. What were my stresses but the results of a life lived too easily, an abundance of luxury and freedoms without responsibility—and without true knowledge of how these things had been earned?

Ion had fallen asleep long before I arrived back at Panteleimon. I too should have retired, but the next entries in his journals beckoned me.

25
THE SIDE SHOW

The rim of the approaching sunrise had turned night's blackness to indigo. The trail he had been following for nearly ten hours had disappeared. Running through endless mist, he was lost. Slowing to a walk, he began to cough harshly. His lungs felt as if a vice had clamped around them, and was being twisted tighter with each forward step.

"I cannot make it. It is futile." Pheidippides sobbed uncontrollably—though his tear ducts were as dry as the sand.

"My son, what hast caused thou to weep so?" A voice filtered into Pheidippides' mind. It shocked him, for it did not seem to be his imagination and yet it could not be.

15 August 1936

It was May of 1916. A few days after the British surrender, we were ordered to accompany the captured officers to Baghdad. Though defeated, the Tigris Corps was a proud and formidable host. The enlisted men were separated and marched a thousand miles overland to Anatolia. I would later learn that two-thirds of them died on that barbarous march.

I had no idea what Englishmen were like. Except for their battlefield cries for help, I had never heard English spoken. The one word a soldier hears more than any other is 'mother'—in any language one knows it as the last groaning sounds of the dying.

*They were different-looking. Much paler. Many had moustaches, which were well groomed, even out here in the field. As soldiers, they were far more disciplined—their uniforms neater and more consistent: dark khaki shorts with suspenders; ammunition belts slung across their shoulders, tall socks pulled up to the knees and beige helmets that looked like canvas covered tortoise shells held on by thin chin straps. They had laid down their Lee Enfield rifles, and empty scabbards dangled without their long knives. The Gurkhas, brigades from Nepal, were distinguished by their soft floppy hats and long curved khukuris. We feared these knives more than their rifles. If you have ever heard their shriek of '*Ayo Gorkhali*' and lived to tell—consider yourself lucky. Their motto—*Kaphar hunnu bhanda marnu ramro*—better dead than to live a coward—are more than mere words to these desert warriors.*

We built a temporary P.O.W. camp in the outskirts of Baghdad. The prisoners from Al-Kut joined others who had been there since the beginning of the war. Among them were wives and children of officers and diplomats who had been stationed in Mesopotamia.

Soon there became little distinction between prisoner and guard. We both had little water and subsisted on scarce rations, we both slept on the unforgiving ground, we both endured the merciless extremes of hot and cold, and neither of us could leave. Trying to avoid misery was like spinning in place to escape the noonday sun. I felt as much a prisoner as those I was ordered to guard—perhaps even more so, as they would ultimately be released, back to their homes, and lives, and freedom. I had no such hope to sustain me through the desolate nights—nights in which I lay shivering, searching desperately for reasons, any reason, to live.

16 August 1936

Let me see if I can describe the Great War. We killed a lot of their boys, then they killed a lot of ours, then we killed more of theirs and they killed even more of ours. Some were killed with bullets, some with bayonets, exploding shells or gas. Some died from good old-fashioned disease and the wrath of God. Many went home intact, but many others went home missing an eye, a limb or their testicles, and everyone gave up a part of his sanity.

Some battles were fought by day, others by night, and others day and night. Sometimes we gained ground, other times we lost it, then counterattacked and reclaimed it the next time only to cede it the time after that. Brutal death became unremarkable. We were privileged to experience every glory of war: frigid cold, sweltering heat, blisters, trench rot, shock, agony, loneliness, terror, nausea, starvation, thirst, vomiting, constipation, dysentery, deafness, lice, sadness, boredom, and utter despair.

I didn't hear the phrase "the war to end all wars" until long after the war had ended. Today, as I look around me, here in Berlin, I can only pray that such noble words will be more than a slogan.

It would be several months before hostilities resumed in Mesopotamia. It was ignominiously called a "side-show," and "no man's child," of the real war. Believe me, when boys barely twenty are dying or losing limbs all around you, war seems real enough no matter where you are. Perhaps it was a "side-show" if one looked at it on a map. But to me, it seemed like the center of the world, and that world was collapsing in on itself. As far as it being "no man's child," war's lineage has no better description—it is a bastard in every sense of the word. And like a bastard, all men volunteered to plant seeds, though once the ugly child is born, no one can be found to admit being the father. And what remains for the mother after the father has fled—a raped body and scorched soul?

I performed the daily routine of guard duty. The only respite I had from this drudgery was when I ran messages to other outposts. Because the desert was heavily mined, it was dangerous duty even if not encountering enemy patrols. It was here under the desert sun and over its burning dunes that I honed my craft.

I began to take pity on the prisoners, especially the women and children. They were filthy and hungry—even more so than we. We weren't trying to starve them, but in war, food is scarce, and a soldier must eat first. There had been outbreaks of trench fever, dysentery and typhus. Abadin and I were sent in to remove a corpse that had to be burned. No funeral, just immediate cremation. It is the way of war. There is misery here, on both sides of the fence.

We were directed to the tent that contained the deceased. The living had no choice but to share the quarters until the body could be removed. I didn't know his name, nor did I care. Abadin and I rolled him in a large sheet to make it easier to lift his body. Today's victim was just like the dozen others we had disposed of and I felt nothing but the desire to finish our task.

Amidst my morbid labor a pair of brown eyes stopped me. Though thousands of eyes had crossed my sight, this pair held a life I felt sure I had known forever. They belonged to a girl of not more than three or four years of age.

I wasn't sure of her relationship to the dead man. Her face was stricken but passive, and her lack of tears made me wonder if she knew him at all. And she had a swarthy complexion, much darker than the man we had shrouded. His skin, though starting to ashen, was lily-white. But her hair was another matter. Though unkempt, it was thick and lustrously golden, matching the deceased's waves of bright blond hair. The same colored stubble spiked his chin and jaws.

A woman, in whose image her facial features seemed to have been created, knelt next to her as if in prayer. Abadin and I unceremoniously dragged the body out of the tent and attempted to heave him into a wagon. Misjudging its height, we dropped him with a thud. I turned my head just in time to see the woman's eyes widen and her mouth gasp at the crude handling of her beloved. On the second try, we managed to get him over the lip of the wagon.

Though I was merely doing my job, I dreaded confronting the woman. Our orders were that all clothes and personal effects of typhus victims had to be burned. She clutched his overcoat as I tried to take it. Her eyes narrowed in hurt and anger the harder I tried to separate it from her grasp. I felt she would have shot or stabbed me if she could.

I was about to cry out for Abadin, but my head snapped back suddenly at a tirade that first seemed foul and almost immediately transformed itself into the sweetest music.

"You are savages, lower than dogs, you filthy Turks. You have made me a widow, must you also plunder me?" What made the words so lyrical was that they had been uttered in Greek.

"Ellinas?" I cried out, not having heard my language spoken since Kalos was alive.

She looked at me with equal surprise, so much so that she let go of the article we had been struggling over. Abadin entered the tent, asking me if I needed help. As the woman stared at me, I told him that everything was fine, and to wait outside while I finished my search. I felt as if some of her anger was dissipating though she never took her gaze off of me.

"Here," I said as I handed her back the garment. "If it is found, you do not know me." I turned to leave the tent.

As I got to the flap that led outside, the little girl spoke for the first time to me, saying in my native tongue, "Please take care of Papa."

I did not get halfway to the wagon before I vomited in the dry sand.

17 August 1936

In this hellish landscape of extinction, there was a pinpoint of beauty and virginal innocence. I could not stop thinking about the Greek woman and her little girl. I wanted to see them again, to find out who they were, how it happened that this mother and child could be here in this camp, and what their relationship was to the dead Englishman. I wanted so desperately to hear her voice again. I had never heard my native tongue spoken by a woman.

Fraternizing with prisoners was grounds for punishment. But I watched her whenever I could from my side of the barbed-wire fence. Even behind this twisted steel she moved gracefully and swiftly.

Every once in a while she would glance at me with compassion. I would always turn away, embarrassed at being caught in my voyeurism. I wondered if she knew the effect she had on me.

One day, she spoke to me. "Who are you?" I heard her soft voice.

"I don't really know," I answered.

"Have you a name?"

"Theodore." I proudly spoke the name that Kalos had inadvertently christened me with. I wanted to know more about her and to say how sorry I was. But I was so disarmed by her eyes that seemed to blaze like the flames of lit matches. Instead, I froze, afraid to speak.

"Elektra. Elektra Leontokardis," she said, sensing my shyness.

"Your husband, he was Greek?"

"He was English, but he was not my husband."

"You were not married?"

"When you look around you, does that detail shock you?"

"No, I just assumed that you were."

"I wanted to thank you for your kindness—I knew you weren't like the others—I saw it in your eyes that day."

"How did you meet?" was all I could stammer.

"He was the British Attaché in Athens, I was a nurse. He could recite the words of Milton and Shakespeare—I was young and could listen to poetry all night long. We made music, then we made love." I was scared and excited by her frankness.

"Why were you here?"

"He was transferred to Baghdad a year before the war. I brought our daughter Alexandra to visit, then it was too late to leave and we became guests of the Sultan."

"This is no place for women or children," I said, attempting to sound noble.

"Or boys pretending to be soldiers," she said, harshly at first, then more softly added, "Why don't you run away?"

"To where? Killing is all around."

"You won't live to be a man this way." I felt as if I had suddenly seen truth and beauty fused together in one person and in one moment. She made me believe that there might be better. I looked around to see that no one was watching and walked to the fence. She snaked her hand through and touched my face. I felt wetness, and realized that she was bleeding slightly from catching her hand on the wire.

"How can I help you?" I asked.

"Go. Run. Escape this."

"And what of you?"

"I've already lost everything."

"But Alexandra."

"Look where I've brought her," she said with bitter self-reproach.

"No. You can't give up. I'll save you."

She suddenly recoiled, spit at me, and screamed, in Greek, "Pig!" Before I could comprehend the violence of her rejection, I felt the blow of a rifle butt between my shoulder blades knocking me to the ground.

"She's too fucking old for you, you little mother fucker. She needs a real man," said one of three drunken soldiers from the Pasha Vehip regiment. They made crude gestures at her but she turned her back and walked away. Soon, they lost interest and left us alone. As I got up, my hand wiped the spit from my cheek. She glanced back at me from a safe distance. I realized that she had acted the part she knew would protect me. Turks cut throats for less provocation than jealousy over a woman.

I would speak with her only one more time.

I was morbidly intrigued. I usually attributed talk of war to men and their testosterone-driven motives. Here was a boy thrown into the maelstrom of violence, and like Evangelis, stripped of a child's rite of innocent passage. At thirteen, Ion should have been exploring the woods behind his home, learning algebra, and finding the courage to ask the girl in pink if he could carry her books home. And the only guns he should have seen would have been at shooting galleries at county fairs. Here he was teaching me about something that I had little ability to grasp.

I recalled some advice that Ion had once given me. He told me, "never try to solve the world's problems when you lay down to sleep." He was right. Small problems only intensify into great crises in the solitude of night.

Besides, I had picked up the scent of a trail that might lead me to Alexandra—Ion's lost love.

26 FALLEN ANGELS

"Son, can you hear me?" asked the voice that could not be.

Pheidippides looked all around him, but there was nothing but wretched darkness. "Do not bother to look for me in the flesh for thou will not see me."

"Are you really here, or do I imagine your voice in the howling of the wind?"

"If you believe me to be here, then I am here."

"Then you have come to witness my disgrace. I have failed."

"My son, is there another amongst your comrades who could have made it this far? It is only important that a man have the one skill required when his moment of destiny has arrived," continued the voice of Pheidippides' father. You, and only you, have that skill—and your moment has arrived!"

On Tuesday morning, Father Diogenes and I drove into Athens. We pulled up to the wrought-iron gates of the *Orfanotrofio ta Angelouthia*. The architecture of the place was out of character with what else I had seen of Greece. It was almost gothic with its large red brick towers and concrete fascia. Though it was an elegant structure, surrounded by manicured hedges and flowers, it had the look of a fortress.

"This shouldn't take long. I'm meeting with Father Anagnostopoulos, he's responsible for accommodations. Would you still care to join me?"

"Yiannis, would you think it rude if I didn't?" I felt a sudden urge to remain outside the imposing iron gates, saddened by Dickensian images of hungry and unwashed children begging for an extra scrap of food and by the thought that this is where Evangelis would end up. If I didn't see how bad it was inside, perhaps the idea would not haunt me.

While I waited for him, I walked once around the block. I'm not sure if I was looking for anything in particular—maybe just something to show me that some beauty existed in this home of the forsaken, some small corner of happiness that Evangelis could cling to while waiting for a real home. I thought the children may have some area outside, and I might spot them, but there were none to be seen. The thick stone walls hid from the world its fallen angels.

Father Diogenes returned in less than twenty minutes. He wasn't smiling but he had the look of having accomplished what he had set out to do. Telling me that a spot would be available within a few weeks, he didn't elaborate further. When I suggested that some lucky child must be finding a new and permanent home, he passively agreed. But the silver lining in a hopeless cloud quickly dissolved as I learned that the departing child had incurable leukemia. The new and permanent home Father Diogenes referred to was the Kingdom of Heaven.

"I know the Lord has some purpose for these children," he said.

"It must give you comfort to have such strong religious beliefs."

"Do you see it as comfort—something to catch us when we feel ourselves falling, or failing? In a world crying out for help, my faith is not a shield—it is a sword through which I can make a difference."

"I was not brought up with that faith."

"Each person must find his or her own God," he continued. "Nothing else is real." I was surprised to hear a priest say that. My recollections of sitting in church as a young girl, forced to listen to fire and brimstone spewing forth from pulpits, were that men of the cloth saw the world within narrow blinders.

I walked in the direction of the Achillon Gardens. Father Diogenes had dropped me off as close as he could, but many of the small streets of Plaka can only be negotiated on foot. Though I had been here the week before, finding the cafe again wasn't easy—our tour bus had come from a different direction. The streets were crowded, mostly with tourists moving in and out of gift shops like swarms of bees searching for pollen. I paused for a moment to browse a rack of postcards. To my amazement, there was a whole series depicting toga-clad men and women in very intimate poses with unrealistically exaggerated equipment. I was flustered especially that a seemingly harmless family run shop would openly display what would have easily been labeled as pornography in the States. I was about the turn and leave when one in particular caught my eye. Completely embarrassed, I bought it to sent to Tom.

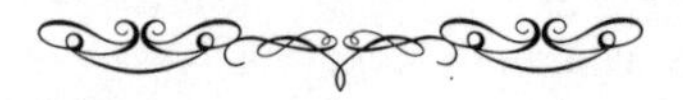

"I'm glad you were free on such short notice," I said to Adonia as we raised our glasses of red wine.

"Short, long? What difference to me now?" I loved her ability to live as she chose, not by the standards set by others.

The café was nestled high in the hills of Plaka on the terrace between several old houses, and was shaded by bougainvilleas and grape vines. If it weren't for the tables and umbrellas, one might walk by and never know a restaurant existed here, or the dozens of other tiny cafes, which fill every nook of this district.

We talked and drank some more wine, then ate a little food, then drank even more wine. We were like two friends who had known each other a lifetime, but had not seen each other in almost as long.

"How did you get into Athens?"

"Father Diogenes drove me. He had to meet someone at an orphanage here in Athens."

Adonia closed her eyes for a moment. "Places like that hide our evils," she said. "Why did you two go there?"

"To see if a space was available for an orphaned boy named Evangelis."

"Is one?"

"Soon. Oh, Adonia, another child is dying. That's why there will be an opening... They deserve so much more."

"You know that I didn't believe you on the plane."

"What?" I said, somewhat astounded at her bluntness, but also not sure of what she meant.

"You told me you didn't want children because they would interfere with your career. Why did you really never have a child?"

I was speechless. This woman saw me as if I were naked, as if she could just wave her hands and my protective shield would be swept away.

"Oh, because I'm sentimental about some orphan, you think I want to have kids?" I laughed, but it didn't come out with the flippancy that I had intended it. "Anyway, it's a long story. I'm not sure you'll want to hear it. I'm not sure I want to hear it."

"It's a great bottle of wine, isn't it?"

"Yes it is, but..."

"It takes a long time to unlock the flavor of the vine. Drinking it quickly is to do injustice to the patience of the winemaker. Let's savor his handicraft as you tell me your story." She filled our glasses, I was entranced by this woman, and I needed to unlock something that had aged far too long.

"I once loved a man I believed in," I began.

"Your ex-husband."

"We met while I was at law school. I walked down the aisle having faith in the unbreakable bonds of our marriage."

"You were very young, and love is wily..."

"We started out happily enough, riding the mystique of new romance. Peter was a successful business manager with one of the largest telecommunications companies in the world—a rising star. I had just received my law degree and I took a job as a staff attorney for an environmental advocacy group. On the surface, life seemed perfect, meeting everyone's expectations."

"Whose expectations?"

"I don't know. My parents, my friends, articles in *Cosmopolitan*."

"What about yours?"

"I thought so. Within a few years, we had bought our first home in a Long Island suburb. I thought that I had 'arrived.' I had a husband, a nice house, owned two cars and had plenty of money in the bank. I had what you referred to the other night—the Great American Dream. Everything seemed to be going according to plan, but as you know, perfect pictures can be deceptive."

"Ah yes, the best laid plans of mice and women... You're preaching to the converted, dear," Adonia nodded her head.

"At first, not having children meant freedom for both of us. We could devote our energy to each other and our careers. Though I loved children, we had decided to wait in order to create a more stable environment—which really just meant more money. At twenty-five, I didn't see myself at home with a baby while Manhattan social life beckoned. Then I passed my thirtieth birthday. We had a lot of money, but it never seemed enough. And Peter seemed to have lost interest in becoming a father. He was now a senior vice president, making incredible money, but the demands of the job were also steadily increasing. Whenever I broached the subject, he would tell me, 'soon, now's just not the ideal time.' Eventually, I realized that 'soon' had no meaning to him, and I became anxious that there would never be an 'ideal' time."

"Ideal..." Adonia let her words drift into oblivion as she listened, yet I could tell that something about my story was causing her mind to run in different directions.

"Children went from being a sporadic discussion, to an almost daily subject. The more he avoided it, the more I fixated on finding out why. I began to doubt myself. Was I losing my allure? Did he no longer love me? Everything in our lives centered on him, his career, his travel, his stress. He no longer seemed to know or care who I was anymore. On the infrequent evenings that he was home for dinner, we sat in awkward silence. And if there were any conversation, it usually was about something that had happened to him at work, or some deal he was working on. Or else he was receiving a business call, leaving me alone while he would spend the evening on the phone."

"What a selfish sod."

"Wait, that was the happy part of the story," I said. "The more successful he got, the less he would be home. Our problems made me fantasize even more about having a child—not because I thought it would save my marriage, but to fill the void left by my absent husband. I imagined that a child's unconditional love would make up for the emotional estrangement. I was so lonely, Adonia."

"When did you know it was over?"

"It was over long before I could confront the truth. The option of being married and miserable seemed to win out over the anxiety of being single and alone."

"It sounds like you hit bedrock. I know what you must have been feeling," Adonia looked into my eyes, and I believed that she truly empathized with what I was saying.

"Adonia, I had only hit the clay that lies a few feet below the surface.

Bedrock still awaited me."

"What happened after all this?" she asked me as if she could anticipate what was coming.

"One day I went to my doctor and verified what I suspected. It was as if my prayers had been answered. Peter was out of town, so I waited patiently with my exciting secret until he had returned."

"How did he receive the news?"

"As if I had dropped an anvil on him. I will never forget his reaction. He only viewed it in terms of himself, and how it would impact his business schedule. There I was, all dressed up to go to the Prom and he had poured a bucket of mud over me. I kept my cool, and he did make a feeble attempt to backpedal and feign excitement—but it was too late—the damage had been done. I cried myself to sleep that night as he lay with his back to me."

Adonia sighed. I knew she wanted to speak, but she also knew that I needed to finish my story.

"Regardless of his callousness, the pregnancy brought a ray of hope into my life. I did everything alone—Peter never even came to the doctor with me. His disregard surprised my doctor, who asked me if Peter was even planning to be there for the birth."

"And if not?"

"Did I know anyone who could," I said as my voice faltered. I was close to tears.

"Are you all right? Perhaps we have delved too deep..."

"No, I'm all right. It feels good to get it out." She took my hand and waited patiently for me to continue. "I carried a boy, Adonia. I thought of names for him and began to decorate his room. For the first time in a long time, I felt purpose. Picking out the sun and moon wallpaper, a crib, a stroller—I was alive. I still hoped that Peter would come around, that something would make him want to share this experience with me."

"Nothing did, did it?"

"It turned from awful to worse. Peter had always been a social drinker, but then he began drinking more heavily at home. And I do mean heavily. He became more hostile and he would say the most unspeakable things to me, then in the morning, feign no recollection of what he had said."

"Did you leave him?"

"Not before one last indignity. Peter was out of town again. I had some flu symptoms, but they didn't improve. I was running a high fever and I was afraid. I called the hotel where Peter was staying, but he had checked out the day before. I became frantic and tried desperately to reach him, but not even his office knew how to locate him. All I could do was leave a message and wait—he didn't call until the next day."

"I can only imagine how frayed your nerves must have been."

"I feel so foolish now, but I was actually worried that something bad may have happened to him. What a total fool I was."

"No, you were not a fool. Saints would have had less patience with this man," she said.

"When he finally did call I was hurt by his nonchalant attitude. I told him how worried I was about him and that I was sick. Looking back on it, I don't know why I expected his sympathy. He implied that I was creating my 'illness' in order to get him to cut his business trip short and that I was always trying to sabotage his career with my selfishness."

Adonia let out a soft moan and shook her head.

"He got defensive when I questioned him about where he was and why he had checked out of his hotel without telling me. His excuses were lame. I knew that he was lying to me, but I couldn't confront him. My heart was suppressing what my mind knew was the real reason for his behavior. In the midst of my pleading with him to come home, he abruptly told me that he had to get off the phone and that he would return as originally planned.

"During that night, my abdominal pains got so bad that I had to call an ambulance. I was taken to St. Lukes Hospital. Though there was an obstetrician on staff, I couldn't reach my own until about 8:30 the next morning. By then, it was too late."

Though I had kept my composure up to that point, I could not stop the flood of tears. Embarrassed, I tried to turn away from Adonia. She slid her chair next to mine and held me as I sobbed like a child in her mother's arms.

"Hush my child. Shhh, don't try to speak."

I am not sure how long we sat like that. I had waited so long to release the suppressed pain. I never would have guessed that someone I had so recently met would be the one to pry open the bars that I had constructed around my heart. Then again, Ion always told me that certain souls can never be strangers to each other.

"What you must think of me. I bet you're sorry you asked me anything," I laughed through my tears.

"I'm not sorry at all."

We sat quietly. The sun was no longer overhead and the wine began to wear off, but not the spell that Adonia had cast in comforting me. I'd been single, and alone, for a long time. It wasn't that I hadn't received my share of romantic offers from many men who desired my company—I just didn't desire theirs. Better to be cold than hurt. Better to be alone than betrayed. That had become my credo since Peter, but its illusion of safety had brought its own brand of pain.

"What time did you say you needed to meet Father Diogenes?"

"Four..."

"Let me walk you there. It's not that far, and a little exercise after eating always helps my digestion."

"You don't have to."

"That's right, and I don't have to buy you lunch either," she said as she picked up the check from the table.

"Adonia!"

"A woman does what she does for love, not obligation."

We were walking arm in arm towards the Mitropoli Cathedral. We came upon a large open area which I thought was a construction site, but as I came to the fence surrounding the square block, I could see that it was a protected archaeological landmark. Dozens of marble columns were arranged in orderly rows around other carved outcroppings.

"It's Roman," she said. "It's their ancient forum."

"Roman? Why would the Greeks honor a place of its conquerors?"

"Were we conquered? An author once said, *even if the Greeks are annihilated and only one Greek is left, he'll teach the conquerors Greek and make Greeks of them*."

We continued making small talk but my mind was still churning over our earlier conversation. Though Adonia's concern was genuine, there are few, no matter how sensitive and caring, who could truly understand what I had experienced. To lose my child so devastated me that I questioned living. I was guilty of the greatest sin a mother can commit—I failed to protect my baby. My feelings of self-incrimination were only matched by my deep resentment of Peter. There was no reconciliation, he moved out within a week. I drifted day to day in a trance—mired in a bad dream from which I could not wake up. At night I would peek in on the little blue nursery before slipping into my own empty bed I gave away his crib and stroller to a charity, which assured me that these things would get to a mother in need.

The day the court papers were signed, I vowed that I would never, ever rely on a man again. Not for money, not for security and never for love. I pursued my new-found independence with a vengeance. Work became my sanctuary.

There I could purge my demons. I was distracted by the acquisition of power in a male-dominated business, and the financial rewards bought me independence from love.

"Peter remarried," I told Adonia. "She had children from a previous marriage. It's funny—two children for the man who never wanted one. So there I was… alone… then lonely. I knew I couldn't rid myself of my flaws or my desires but I had hoped that they would merge and soar with those of another. Now I no longer bother to dream."

"There is always hope that tomorrow one may find all the happiness in the world," Adonia said, as we reached the doors of the church where I was to meet Father Diogenes.

"But why is the price so terrible? I still imagine what my son would have looked like, what he'd sound like—the color of the eyes I will never see. Some nights, I dream I am falling into a pit, falling with nothing to grab onto. Then dawn comes and I find myself back at the top of the pit, to live another day on its precipice..." I stopped. I didn't want to cry again, I couldn't—I had no more tears.

"I know, child, I know..." She hugged me again. Her compassion ran deep, but I knew that she couldn't really understand.

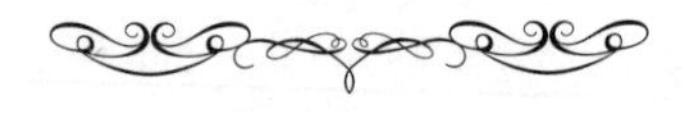

I sat quietly as Father Diogenes drove us back to Panteleimon. I was happy he wasn't in the mood to talk. The wine, the hills of Plaka in the midday sun and the uncovering of painful recollections had sapped my energy. I was relieved yet also frightened that I had unburdened myself to Adonia. It helped that she was still a stranger, lived far away, and couldn't possibly run into anyone who knew me. There was also the likelihood that I would never see her again—my secrets safely buried. How often do strangers part exchanging phone numbers, which are soon misplaced?

We got back to Marathon in the midst of a power outage. A fire at a nearby generating station had shut down the grid, so we would go without until electricity could be rerouted from another power station. At first, the blackout was a minor inconvenience, and the thought of food spoilage seemed someone else's problem. But as dusk settled, the lack of light became more apparent. I anticipated an evening of dark adventure as if I were a child again preparing to sleep in a tent pitched in my backyard. Back home, when the power goes out, I'm basically screwed. Lights, television, stereo, refrigerator, stove—all electric. My hot water heater is gas, but its circulating pump needs electricity. And I'd rather swim with sharks than spend a summer's night on Long Island without air conditioning.

In Old Westbury, there are street lamps and lights glowing through neighbors' windows. Tonight I experienced a darkness that I never have before. I was dizzied by the intensity of the Milky Way's dense cluster of celestial bodies arcing from one horizon to the other as if wrapping the Earth in a cloud of luminescent dust. So virginal was this view, I had to remind myself that it was always there, but for the layers of natural and man-made occlusions.

The temporary sensation of blindness allowed me time to think. Something I assumed I did all the time, yet like the obscured Milky Way—I allowed daily routine and anxiety to cloud my vision of what is really there. I wasn't very good at being contemplative, and I could not shake the desire for constant crisis. Even when I met a wonderful man, like Adam, I found fault. What was his? That he earned less than my starting salary out of school? And why? He was an unsung hero in a world of overpaid celebrities, rock stars and attorneys.

I wasn't depressed about any one thing, but felt myself in a state of inertia. I hated to label my growing melancholy with the cliché mid-life crisis, but I realized I didn't need a change of pace or of venue—I needed to change my life.

Before I slipped back inside the farmhouse, I took one last glance skyward. Recalling Ion's words of the Sistine Chapel, I suddenly felt humbled, staring upward at the face of the Almighty.

Ion was sitting on the edge of his bed when I peeked in to say goodnight.

"Mind if I join you, Ion?"

"It would be my pleasure, my dear," he replied.

"What were you up to?"

"Just contemplating."

"A drachma for your thoughts."

"I was thinking of a decanter of fine wine."

"Would a glass do?"

"Probably not, I am interested in emptying a whole vessel."

"Are you that thirsty?"

"Wine assuages less thirst than desire."

"Desire?"

"Desire to speak. You know, *in vino veritas*."

"Oh, what truth?"

"I am like the grape after the juice of Bacchus is pressed from it. From these pressings, a richer, more potent drink may be distilled. After all the pressings that life wrings from me, a richer spirit may yet be drawn from the spirituous residue—leaving all but the body of the grape."

"What made you think of this tonight?"

"I want your oath," he said, sidestepping my question.

"For what?"

"That you will not mourn me."

"Ion..."

"Life is in Death—and Death breeds Life. From the dead leaves of autumn is formed the garment in which the seed invests itself."

"Ion, please, you still have..."

"Precious little time."

"Let's not talk about that—it makes me sad."

"Sad? It depends on how you choose to finish."

"Finish?"

"The race. One can choose to limp or one can choose to run brilliantly—expending all the soul's energy—holding back nothing. Remember, the coal burns brightest before it is extinguished. There can be great beauty, even glory, in dying."

27
THE MESSENGER OF ILL TIDINGS

"Why should I go on? What is one less soldier in the phalanx? Besides, I have no good message to return with—and there is no one to return to."

"There is the woman who loved you."

"You know of her? But how? We met after you..."

"I am in your mind."

"Then you know that I do not need her."

"I know what is in your heart as well as your mind. Few deaths are timely. Do not let yours come without telling Leontia how you feel."

Everyone has bad days. The car won't start, you miss your train home, you spill food on your suit during a business lunch. But I'm talking about the kind of day that you would sell your soul to do over again. Imagine that helpless feeling as you watch your life spiraling down so fast that all you can do is pray that it's only a bad dream and that your alarm clock is going to rescue you from a reality spinning out of control.

Yesterday was such a day. And it isn't over. Well, yesterday is, but not the descent. The alarm clock would not ring, nor could I coax its hands to move backwards. What's worse is that if I had the chance to relive the day, to undo my sin, I'm not sure I would have done anything differently—I enjoyed it so.

The day hadn't started badly, giving no indication of the tempest that lay ahead. Even the evening was pleasant as we dined at a local taverna. Eftehea stayed home with Evangelis.

"Yiannis, please, let me. You've been overly generous," I said as I reached for the check.

I could see he remained hesitant to remove his own hand. Here, women were presumed to be the weaker sex and men were expected to display traits of machismo and dominance, and priests were not above these stereotypes.

I couldn't tell him that I made fifty times all of them combined. I doubt they could have grasped the magnitude of our economic gap. In New York, I may have been offended, but I nodded my head and withdrew my hand from the check in deference to an ancient culture.

When we got home, a little after ten, Eftehea was in the kitchen. I'm sure she spent more waking hours in that room than anywhere else. She spoke hastily to Father Diogenes.

"Marianna," he turned towards me and said, "Mana received a call for you about an hour ago."

There were only two, no three, people to whom I had given this number. My office, Adam and Vivian should there be a problem at my house. I had a two out of three chance of it being bad news.

"Was it a man or a woman?"

"Mana says it was a man."

That eliminated Vivian and Tracy. My odds had increased. "Ion, let's get you squared away for the evening."

"Are you sure you don't want to call him now?" he said with a smile that told me he too thought it was Adam.

"He can wait," I tried to say with an air of indifference. But butterflies were already beginning to take flight in my stomach.

"Adam, hi, it's..."

"Marianna! It's great to hear your voice. You just caught me, I was about to run out. What's up?"

"I was just returning your call."

"I didn't call."

"Oops," I said, feeling embarrassed. Would he believe it was a mistake? I quickly narrowed the mysterious caller down to one other possible source, and nothing good could come of it. We chatted for a few minutes, but my mind was on the next call I had to make.

I dutifully dialed SWB's main number and asked to be transferred to Tracy's line.

"Tracy, it's me."

"Hold on a second, let me get off my other line." It was only a few seconds before she returned. "I'm back," she informed me.

"Was anyone there trying to find me?" I said, clinging to the hope that no one was.

"It was Steve," she said, putting an immediate end to the mystery.

"I know he didn't call to see how my trip's going. What's up?"

"The Braxton depositions. They're on. We couldn't get them postponed."

"You're joking. Please say yes."

"Melissa went before Judge Margolis. He wouldn't grant the motion, remember, there've already been three delays."

"What about Spelling, Ambrose. Didn't they agree to a mutual stipulation?"

"They wouldn't budge. They said they were ready."

"That's a crock and they know it."

"You're not going to get sympathy because you went on vacation with a court order pending."

"Damn it. Can't Steve..."

"No chance, and you know it. You're welcome to speak with him, but he's been wrapped up in the Credit Suisse closing all morning."

"But my return ticket—it's…."

"He had me book you on the Delta flight to JFK on Sunday. If you have a pen, I'll give you the ticket number."

What choices did I have? I knew about the deposition and I had promised to cover anything that came up while I was away, but they really didn't need me to do it. Steve was calling my bluff. How was I going to break this to Ion? Right ahead of me was a rock. I didn't have to look behind me to see the hard place—I knew I was between them.

"Ion, something has come up, and I need to go back to New York."

"Trouble at the office?"

"There's a case pending, a deposition to be precise. I tried to postpone it but it wasn't possible."

"And what of our trip?"

"I don't know what to say. There's nothing I can do, I've got to return."

"I am not ready to leave yet."

We spoke of the choices, and the logistics. I wasn't sure it was the right thing to do, to leave him here—but I saw no other solution that he would agree to.

"There is something I need to tell you," he said after we had made our decision.

"What, is it, Ion?" I had no idea what was coming but I half dreaded it.

"Why we came to Panteleimon..."

"I know why and I'm not..."

"... And how I found you."

"Found me? I found you. Remember, the photo you sent Abraham and Christine, the art exhibit, the nursing home?" I could not tell whether he was being mystical or forgetful.

"I remember well. But it is late, let's leave this till morning. Things will look different then."

Ion was asleep. Dimitris and his father had gone into the study, the wooden door closing softly behind them. Milos had run into some of his buddies at the taverna and stayed behind. I was too tired to sleep, and craved a cup of coffee. Many people will not drink coffee at night. I have a simple rule, if I am awake, then I will drink coffee. Of course, this extends the time I am awake—a delicious and vicious cycle.

I took a walk. Even without the caffeine, my mind raced at flank speed. The hearing, leaving Ion, the meaning of life. I had wandered into the fields behind the house. The night air seemed to carry with it the energy of a thousand invisible creatures. Moths flitted about the outside light, fighting I supposed, over who might reach its center and so be burned first. I heard the choir of crickets, present all around me, yet invisible. Fireflies danced and disappeared in the distance.

Rows of trees like crosses disappeared into the dark. In the distance beyond I could see specks of moonlight glancing off the satin black sea. And nearer, rising just above the horizon was the copper-domed church of Panteleimon, its solitary cross barely visible against the velvet sky. I felt life stirring around me and through my body. Standing between dusk and dawn I felt I was in a state of limbo, seeing myself as a spectator watches a drama.

I felt them upon me again—and then saw them. Eyes! Those eyes! His eyes—then him. I knew it was him, coming straight for me out of the dark, his presence heralded only by soft crackling of the dry grass beneath his feet.

"You startled me!"

"I am not try to. I am see you leave house, want talk with you, alone..."

"It was you, wasn't it?"

"You are always know this, no?"

"No, I didn't."

"I am know you did. Know by way you are look me." He walked closer, staring down into my eyes and smiling arrogantly.

"No, no...What do you mean? How did I look at you."

"Everywhere. At dinner table, in church. I feel you are want say many things."

"I can't think what it might have been. Why were you watching me?" I said, trying vainly to maintain control of this strange dialogue.

"Why? You are why. Because you are so beautiful…and sad."

"Sad? How do you know what I am? Just who are you to..." I said while taking a step back from him.

"Of what are you scared? Is it that I am find you beautiful?" he said, moving forward and re-closing the distance between us.

"I'm not afraid of anything, or anyone..."

"Nai, excited maybe, it's okay."

"You don't know me..."

"I am want to very, very much, and I am think you are need too," he said touching my shoulders. I grabbed his hands to push them off, but they overtook me, running first up to my neck beneath my hair, then down until they were wrapped around my waist. He pulled me into him and kissed me softly, then more intensely. I felt the craving for tenderness and the ache of desire wash over me like a warm wave, taking me helplessly into its strong currents. I let myself go for a moment, then stopped.

"Please," I said, pulling from him, "you must go. This is wrong. I think you had better leave."

"Why?"

"A hundred reasons, not the least of which is that this is mad. I can't handle it..."

"I am think you are want me."

"No! I don't know anymore, I —"

"I am a man."

I tried to speak, but before I could part my lips he was upon them, again and again. My hand instinctively shot across his face, stinging my palm as it met his cheek. Its loud smacking noise pierced the silence around us. He didn't flinch, and his eyes never left mine.

I awoke in the middle of the night exhausted and insatiable.

His eyes, those eyes, were closed. I thought he was asleep. I ran my fingers down his chest. Suddenly, and without opening his eyes, I felt him take my hand and draw my fingers to his lips. And just as suddenly, I felt his warmth as he curled behind me. I felt movement like the surf breaking along the water's edge. The waves subsided only to regain strength, build to a great new one and then crash again. It was no longer possible to resist the tide that I felt, and that I knew that he felt it too as our bodies gently collided.

I awoke again—but this time light streamed through my shutters. Father Diogenes' voice was calling out for his son. I'd overslept.

Jumping out of bed, I went to the door, placing my ear against it.

"Ion, have you seen Dimitris?" I heard him saying next door.

I looked back towards my bed at the naked torso barely covered by a sheet. The outside world was intruding on us, but dreams have to end. And this was one dream best left in the wilds of last night. Dimitris bolted upright as he heard his father's voice, calling out, louder this time.

"What is happen..." he began to exclaim, but I had already placed my hand firmly over his mouth.

"Shh, no time."

Understanding the predicament we were in, he rose quickly, pulling on his jeans. I was torn between guilt and desire. When I looked at him as if to ask how he could expect to leave my room unnoticed, he merely glanced at the window and nodded. It's not the way I envisioned a lover leaving after a night of intimacy, though I was happy that we would have no time to talk. In the light of day I was beginning to feel ashamed of myself and I didn't want to be with anyone.

He came over to kiss me, but I backed away. Unfazed, he smiled at me and stepped to the ledge of my window, the window through which he had first spied me nude. One last look and he jumped down to the side portico, and I pretended that my troubles were over with his hasty exit. That was until I heard Milos' voice coming from outside.

"Dimitris! What are you doing in there? Oh my God!"

28
NOMAN'S LAND

"Father, tell me again about the wrath of Achilleus."

"Indeed I will, but let us run together while I recount the tale."

"But which way?"

"There, into the mist."

"But I cannot see," Pheidippides said.

"Follow my voice," he replied to his son, who had started to move his frozen limbs again. As Pheideppides ran, his mind heard tales of concubines abducted, lovers mourned and armor forged — soon five stadia became ten, and then twenty.

"I must go now, my son."

"Will I see you again?" But there was no answer. The winds grew intensely, then dissipated as quickly as they had arisen.

The next few hours were torment. I was too embarrassed to leave my room, yet I couldn't stay there. I had no idea what consequences awaited my rash actions, but I knew they wouldn't be as pleasurable. I dressed in my running gear. I had to get out to the freedom of the mountains—I had to punish my body for its indiscretion.

The terrain was hostile. From afar, it seems green and smooth, like an inviting carpet. But where the sole meets the ground, it is anything but smooth or forgiving. Several times I nearly fell or twisted an ankle. Somehow I kept my balance, though it was more from luck than athleticism. My heart was pumping and sweat poured from me until there was no more to yield—penance for pleasure without discipline.

I wondered what would be waiting for me at Panteleimon when I returned. I hoped that nothing would have changed though I knew everything had. Would Milos tell his father? Would anyone tell Ion? Or would sins be quietly told, acknowledged and left in the sanctity of confession?

I fell back upon what I was good at—being an attorney. I braced myself as if I were walking into Superior Court, anticipating my opponents' arguments and readied counter-arguments to any avenues of attack. I processed all of the scenarios and prepared myself for every contingency. No matter what the law or the facts, my client must be vindicated—as if her life depended on it. But the attorney who represents herself has a fool for a client.

The clay tile roof finally appeared through the groves, its front door anything but welcoming to me now. Eftehea was the only one there. Still clothed in my sweaty athletic gear, I went out to the porch and looked for Evangelis. His eyes were red and swollen, and I could see the traces of salty tears on his cheeks. But he didn't look sad. He seemed indifferent, apathetic to whatever was the cause of his tears. I don't know whether he had overcome some temporary crisis, or whether my presence had made him cease any outward display of emotion.

Father Diogenes walked out onto the portico. Before I could say anything, our eyes met. I knew in an instant that they were not the same eyes that I had seen yesterday, they stared at me with a look of hospitality betrayed.

"Good morning, Father Diogenes," I said, forgetting his request that I call him Yiannis—though I noticed that he made no attempt to correct me. "Do you know where Ion is?" I asked.

"In church," was all he could say.

"Great," I said, trying to maintain my composure.

"Mana needs Evangelis." Father Diogenes took the youth by the hand, but the boy tugged at it for an instant in the direction of his garden, our little garden. Father Diogenes and I must have noticed it at the same time. All the little seedlings that had sprouted like magic in the past few days were dead. A tear rolled down Evangelis' face, and Father Diogenes picked him up and held him.

I felt crushed as I gazed at the dying garden. What had gone wrong? Too much water? Had Evangelis himself accidentally killed the seedlings? Was the pall that I had cast over Panteleimon reaching down into the very roots in the soil?

As the two of them turned to walk away, I felt the need to say something.

"Father Diogenes!"

He stopped short and turned around and looked at me with intense eyes. There was no anger, and yet neither was there sympathy.

"Yes?" he asked. But the moment was lost, and I couldn't think of what to say. I merely shook my head from side to side.

"Oh, nothing. It can wait."

He nodded his head again as if he telling me that it was too late for words, or perhaps too early. They left me to myself. Abandoned by a priest and an orphan—my day was not off to an auspicious start.

I showered and hastily dressed and then went to Panteleimon to find Ion. When I gazed inside I was grateful that he was alone. He knelt before the sculpture that he had crafted for Father Kyriazis a half-century earlier.

"No matter how many times I see this, it never fails to move me," I said, attempting to initiate the conversation, and keep it within safe boundaries.

"Yes, she moved me too, very much so. Such clarity, and truth, too young to die."

I looked at the child held in his mother's arms. It could have been any mother and child, it could have been a child like Evangelis, or Ion, but I knew the fate of this one. "Crucified for his clarity and truth," I said.

Whatever I had said made Ion suddenly turn and to look at me, a hint of surprise in his expression, but then just as suddenly he turned back to face his handiwork.

"You slumbered in your Pentelic tomb, tight sealed your lips," he began to speak. "Your breath securely locked within your marble vault while Adam sinless and alone wandered in Eden the girth of eons. And in his stride your mortal maker has come, not only with his chisel did he fashion thee, he breathed into your nostrils and gave you of his life. Touched your grooved eyes and lit there an eternal light. Through countless years of storing rain and sun and snow and ever changing winds. You were born to be my masterpiece." Though he let me hear him, he spoke not to me.

"That's beautiful, Ion."

"You had trouble sleeping last evening?" he asked without turning around in any way, his gaze still fixed upon the cool white marble.

"I couldn't sleep... I took a walk, in the fields behind the house."

"It's beautiful at night—a time for discovering things which do not show themselves by day."

I didn't know whether to keep silent and conceal my ignominy, or fall to my knees and expunge myself of guilt and pray that this man could absorb one more affront upon his goodness. If he already knew, then hurt was unavoidable, but if he didn't, confession would only serve to transfer the pain from one soul to another.

"Ion, wasn't there something that you wanted to share with me today," I said, recalling our conversation the night before.

"I used to love walking in these fields at night," he said, avoiding or not hearing my question. Whichever the cause, I realized that it wasn't going to be my choreography, which determined the course of the dialogue. "Perhaps I am grown too old for such adventures."

"Ion, you're..." but a quick glance from him left my sentence unfinished. He wasn't going to hear any false compliments, and he certainly didn't seem to be in the mood to be patronized.

When I returned to my room, I felt that someone had been there. My eyes quickly fixed on a small cup of freshly picked flowers that sat on my dresser. Under the cup was a folded piece of paper. I closed my door and unfolded it, my heart beating more rapidly, my stomach in knots.

> *Am not stop think of you or last night. I am need speak with you, please. Eyes all around now, but am alone this night after ten. Meet me at...*

I was frazzled. On one hand, Dimitris was young, handsome and Greek and lived thousands of miles from my home. On the other hand, he was young, handsome and Greek and lived thousands of miles away from the judgmental eyes of my world. These things intoxicated me, but I knew it was meant to burn for only one intensely heated night.

I crumpled the paper. I was afraid to confront him, afraid of my own weakness. I imagined myself behind the wheel of a car racing down a highway in rain so intense that it hit the windshield, not as drops, but as entire sheets of water—while I desperately tried to get the wipers to work. Somehow I knew that I couldn't just pull over to the shoulder and wait out the storm—it was not going to abate.

I helped Ion to bed as I always did. He was quiet, and could not be coaxed into small talk let alone the important subject he had raised the evening before—and I was in no position to force the issue.

I wasn't sure if this was a good idea, but I felt as if I had no choice. I entered Panteleimon for the second time today and at first I couldn't see him. The only light was coming from a series of burning candles that lined one side of pews. It was as if they were illuminating a path. I followed them to the back of the church until it dead-ended into a thick red curtain. I stood with my back to it, gazing at the altar. If Saint Panteleimon were true to his name, then I would need him now.

I heard the curtains stirring and a hand clasped my mouth.

"Hush," he whispered and drew me back into a room that adjoined the main chamber of the church. "We must to be quiet. If father is find here together, he is to be very disappointed."

He let go of my mouth.

"Dimitris, there is something we need to talk about."

"Do not speak just yet, then not break spell. I am want look at you and pretend it is last night and we are be like one."

I did as he asked. This smaller room was aglow with dozens of candles. He reached for my hand, but I pulled away, terrified of going too far down a path neither of us could resist.

"Oh, I see..." he said.

I looked into his eyes, they appeared larger than usual, and the flesh around them was swollen.

"You've been crying?"

"Yes. My father and me have very big argument."

"Because of..."

"I am quit my studies and not become Papas."

"What? Why, Dimitris? You've spent so many years working towards this. How could you quit now?"

"For me it's okay. Not problem. I am in love."

His words stung me. I should have been flattered, but the idea of this boy falling in love, not with me, but with some dream of love, made me very uneasy. And what terrible thoughts his father and brother must be thinking of me now. No doubt, they saw me as a woman corrupted by the vices of a degraded civilization now becoming the temptress and corruptor.

"Dimitris, what happened last night was a mistake." No sooner had I uttered this word then I could see that I had struck him in the heart.

"How can be mistake—such beauty?"

"You're right, that's not fair. Not a mistake. It was beautiful," I continued, and I watched his eyes look up at me as I said this. "Nothing can take away from the night."

"But?" he asked.

"But what?"

"Is always a 'but,' is not?"

"In most things, Dimitris, in most things."

"Can you tell truth you are not feel ground tremble as we are make love?"

"I did, Dimitris. I did feel it tremble, but ..."

"Again it is 'but.'"

"There is flesh and there is reason."

"Can not reason and flesh be live together? Is possible, no?"

"Sometimes, I suppose."

"What then. I know you are feel somethings. Last night can no be accident."

"There is another," I said knowing that it hurt but was often the only excuse that would dissuade a man. But it was just an excuse. "Besides, you cannot love me. There is so much more to love than what we experienced, so much more pleasure and pain. You cannot give up your dream."

"And who is have this dream? Me or father? I am not sure anymore."

"If you're not sure, then why quit? Why make a decision until you are certain?"

"Because I am not certain. Not sure is not worthy of being Papas, and church is not accept the color gray—it is black or it is white—and I am stain my white garments."

"You have been given a rare opportunity—and you have a gift—to help people. Look at your father and Panayiotas before him. See how many lives they have changed, the difference that they have made."

"What you are do to help others?" He paused, but I said nothing. "Is noble idea when someone else's life, someone else's problem." Like last evening in the garden, I found myself losing ground to this young man—why was I so powerless in his presence? It was hard to reply to his stinging comment.

When he left, I felt hurt, and sad that I had hurt him. I retreated to the solitude of the confessional and to a world far from the reality I had spun.

19 August 1936

News of the British advance on Baghdad made its way around camp long before the official orders to prepare for the enemy assault had arrived. Buddhoos brought word of the English massing men and artillery at Basra, and their movement of gunboats up the Tigris.

When the first shells began to fall that March, I was inside the Al-Khadhimain Mosque. She is a magnificent site, her gold-capped domes and minarets surrounding an opulent courtyard. Built in the 16th Century, she has survived centuries of desert storms, both God's and men's. The steel projectile approached without warning. It pierced the roof rafters and smashed into the floor. But there was no explosion. The existence of these journals is adequate proof.

Making my way back to my trench, I passed a battery of captured British 75's. Men were loading the giant red and khaki shells into the rear side of the long barreled guns—they were of such weight that it took two to lift and slide them into the open hatch. A third soldier pulled a long cord—the ensuing explosion jerking the gun backwards. I nearly lost my balance from the shock wave that was followed by the most deafening roar. While my body reverberated from the blast, the soldiers were already reloading another salvo.

It is hard to describe an artillery barrage to anyone who has not experienced one. It is like being in both an earthquake and a thunderstorm at once, with incessant lightning strikes. The Earth rumbles and shakes and you can feel the vibration in your bones. By day, the sky fills with dark, acrid smoke from airborne bursts, which can make your ears bleed. At night, it is the opposite—darkness is eradicated, lit up like an aurora borealis, sometimes appearing brighter than the day itself. It is not unusual to lose track of whether the night is illuminated or the daylight obliterated in this strobe-lit hell.

And bombs approach with an eerie sound, like an airplane nose-diving on the spot you occupy. By the time you hear the noise, there is no time to move. After the first few times—you don't bother. If it is going to hit you, it will.

Intermingled with these horrendous sounds is the crying of scared soldiers, from the cowardly to the courageous—all cry at some point.

Try to imagine this persisting day in and day out, night after night, as the enemy hurls every piece of hot metal he can muster. It is a mechanized and impersonal war—all the easier to absolve Cain for spilling blood when he need not peer into his brother's eyes.

I remember one soldier, an Ottoman, from Ephesus. Several times we had to pull him back into the trench for fear that he was attempting to climb out and run. By the time we noticed him missing again, a shell had exploded and his leg was blown off—a fact we would not learn until morning. He was in no-man's land, not alive and not yet dead. Ahead of him lay a night of agony for which his reward would be death. There was nothing we could do to could save him. Perhaps I could have tried, but I was too frightened to move. As our penance, we were forced to listen to him scream, then cry, then moan as the life slowly oozed from his body. May your ears never hear the slow song of the dying.

During these weeks of constant bombardment, I had no idea how Elektra and Alexandra fared. There were explosions near the pens, but that was true anywhere within 15 miles of Baghdad. Places would become "hot spots" until the British artillery units would change coordinates and shell another target area. Bit by bit, this once great city was destroyed again. Long before the Mongols and Ottoman Turks, long before Islam itself—the Babylonians, Assyrians, and Chaldeans had marched their armies through this valley. Even Alexander the Great conquered and died here. Now it would be time for a new dynasty—the House of Windsor.

General orders to retreat had been issued. Our regiment was to prepare the prisoners for the march north. For many of the POWs, this was as good as a death sentence. Abadin, Solmaz and I started toward the holding pens, but they appeared sparse. At first, I thought that the prisoners had taken cover but I soon realized that many had already been evacuated. I scanned the rows of faces looking for my beloved. My cohorts were shouting to the prisoners to gather close together. I screamed too, but in a daze, and Abadin yelled back at me, "Hey, who are you looking for? Get on with it."

"I'm looking for no man." I answered, using the ruse Odysseus had spoken to Polyphemus.

"What? Are you nuts?"

I was nuts, and intent on finding Elektra. Abadin yelled again, "If the Captain catches you, he will make you bleed, you know that fool." It was the last Abadin and I ever saw of each other. I think back on him as a friend. In any other place and time, we may never have considered ourselves as such, but adversity nurtures unusual bonds.

Ion had scrawled a poem in the right margin. It was written at an angle, and its last lines wrapped around and ran vertically along the side of the journal.

Bright orbed Helios shakes night's mantle free of stars
And rings a drowsy Earth within myriad spears of pulsing lights
Off in the shattered east soft stalking Dawn
Grasps in her pale, soon rosy, hands a fire-tipped spear
And pursues her approaching prey, Polyphemus of the Cyclopean eye.
As Odysseus' men lash the steeds of night to mad retreat
Singeing the dawning sky with fiery breath
And Dawn approached branding fire tipped spear,
Turning deep into the lone cyclopean eye
"Noman, Noman," its vaporous frenetic cross.

I continued reading from the text.

I had become desperate, looking for her amongst the long khaki line of prisoners. Coming to the last stragglers I exclaimed, "Elektra? Elektra?" hoping that they knew of her. They looked ghastly, pale, emaciated, staring ahead at nothing in particular. I felt I was shouting at ghosts who could not hear me. Then one, almost waifish, young soldier turned and raised a shaking arm and waved it in the direction of a solitary field tent.

I started to run for the tent when a Turkish officer yelled "Stop, or

I'll shoot." I turned and saw he had trained his rifle on me. I had decided to disobey his orders when we were interrupted by an exploding shell from a British Howitzer. Disappearing with the smoke from the blast was any trace of the officer who would have done me harm.

I rushed into the tent, which was being used as a makeshift medics' station. Elektra was assisting a British medical officer as he attended to a dozen prisoners too severely wounded to evacuate.

"Elektra!" I yelled striding up to her. "Thank God I found you. We must leave now." I noticed the medic looked over at me with indifference and turned back to his patients.

"I can't."

"It's not safe here." I caught sight of Alexandra huddled in a corner, watching her mother. A priest was whispering in the ear of a man mangled beyond comprehension. The others seemed to moan as if longing to be next to die.

"I cannot leave them."

I looked down at the soldier she was comforting. With one hand she held his and with a moist cloth soothed his dry brow. His eyes looked up at her as if he were viewing a saint or one beloved with whom he knew he would soon be reunited.

"But your child?"

"They're all my children."

A sudden blast of heat and light tore through the tent, and I felt myself lifted and hurled before all went blank.

Just then a gust of wind blew out my candle, leaving me in the dark and unable to finish this entry. I felt that I was not alone.

"Dimitris?" I cried out.

I could distinctly hear someone on the priest's side of the confessional.

"Dimitris, is that you?" I said again through the grating.

"No."

"Who is it?"

"There are no names here in confessional. Are you here to confess, my child?"

Shit. It was Father Diogenes. Why else would he think I was in here? Just great! I could imagine it already, Forgive me father for I have sinned—let's see—it's been three decades since my last confession. I'm sitting here using your confessional booth to read someone's private diaries without his knowledge. Oh, and did I mention that I slept with your son and made him quit the priesthood? Yeah, that should go over well. I was in deep, so what harm would one more lie do?

"Forgive me father for I have sinned. It has been... three... three months since my last confession..."

My confession took about twenty minutes. I avoided any mention of events here in Marathon—choosing instead to drown Yiannis' priestly ears with all sorts of sordid things I did at work. When I felt I had expunged enough, I stopped, and he had no choice but to let our session end. I knew that he was not pleased—I could feel it even through the supposed anonymity of the wire mesh that separated us in the darkness.

I had brought discord into the harmony at Panteleimon. Its soothing rhythms had become a cacophony of discontent and betrayal. I was guilty and angry with myself. Had I broken a trust with Ion? I didn't know. Perhaps that was the problem; I wanted it to be clearer. But it was wrong, if not for Ion, then for Dimitris' sake. I was turned on by his arrogance, his self-assuredness, but after the bravado was peeled away, there was a vulnerable child. For me, it was one night of unbridled passion and I could leave it that way. But I had played with a young man whose emotions did not match the strength of his body.

But I wasn't just angry with myself—I was angry with Ion.

Angry because he was so much what I dreamed of in a man, yet he had the audacity to be unavailable. How dare anyone believe that I should feel shame? I was a free woman. I could do as I pleased. Ion was not my lover. No promises had been exchanged, or broken.

Yes, I was angry at Ion, but had anything really changed? Ion was who he was, and the fates had chosen the hours of our respective births.

Yesterday, at this time, I was dreading leaving. Now, I felt compelled to leave—almost relieved to have time and distance to reflect on what had happened. I wanted to run as far as I could from here.

I lay awake that night staring at the ceiling as my demons danced and played before my mind's eye—taunting me without mercy. Where can you hide when there is nowhere left to run?

29
EXOMOLIGISI

Pheidippides knew he had wronged her. His penance was to find his way home through this grueling ordeal. He could not make out anything recognizable on the ground, but there was something familiar about the mist. It was not fog brought ashore from the sea, but a layer of condensation that lingered between the mountain ranges flanking him. To the left it seemed that the mist was thinning, to the right was its thickest density. He veered deeper into the thickening mist until suddenly an incline dropped before him. Rock and soil turned to sand and a vast expanse of water revealed itself.

He knew this place. It was here that Herakles slew the Stymphalian Birds, but his knowledge was gleaned from personal experience—running here from his village as a younger man. There could be no mistaking this body of water. He was off course, but now he was no longer lost. His father had led him to safety.

Pheidippides broke the perfect mirror of the lake's surface. The chilling water at first jolted his body and he felt the abandon of losing himself in its frigid purity. Wading ashore, his body shivered, but the chill revitalized him. Orienting himself between the Olygyrtos and Kylene Mountains, he propelled himself forward—water streaming from his hair and body.

My flight departed Hellenikon at exactly noon. Dimitris wanted to drive me, but I thought it best to take a taxi. It was incredibly cheap—an hour ride for twelve dollars. But that wasn't the reason. I couldn't be alone with him right now, though I saw that he wanted desperately to speak with me. There was another reason I opted for a taxi. I had made hasty arrangements to meet with Adonia. I needed to see her.

The taxi entered the city, and then drove up its winding roads toward the Church of Saint George on Lyccabetus, the highest of Athens' seven hills. The last quarter mile one must walk up hundreds of hand-cut steps. I made a business deal with the driver. He would wait for me—I would pay him a day's wage—almost eighty dollars. It was a fortuitous decision. Hailing a cab from there would have been impossible.

It was ten minutes to nine o'clock. I was early, but as I reached the summit, I spotted Adonia standing on the far side of the church. At first, neither of us spoke. Then, we spoke at once, laughed and she gestured for me to go first.

"Adonia, thanks for coming," I said as I embraced her.

"I feel as if we're old friends."

"What are they doing in there?" I asked about the people who were coming out of St. George's. There were too many, and they were too orderly to be tourists.

"What does anyone do in a working church? Pray? Confess? Propitiate?"

"Adonia!"

"Do I blaspheme?" she smiled.

"I'm one to talk, I've been to church more the last week than in the past thirty years."

"Do you feel enlightened?"

"I'm not sure... Do you believe in original sin?"

"Ah, an easier question than 'what are they doing in there,'" she laughed.

"Well, do you?"

"What is sin?"

"Doing something immoral."

"Whose morals?"

"One's own. I suppose."

"Then how can there be original sin?"

"I guess there can't be. But why do we do things that make us feel so..."

"Guilty? It's arbitrary."

"Perhaps, but I am sometimes afraid to act."

"Afraid? Why, my dear? You seem so in command in your career."

"I do what is expected to be done. What's sensible and safe for me to do."

"Then what do you live for?" she said.

"I don't know. I wanted to live for something but I've lost so much."

"Lost? So much? You seem too young to say that."

"I embarrassed myself, disrespected my host and I think I deeply offended Ion." I looked down but I could tell Adonia's gaze was still fixed on me. I don't know what came over me. First he startled me. Then he was kissing me, I couldn't resist him, and the next thing I know it's morning and he's..."

"Ion?"

"No. Dimitris. One of Father Diogenes' sons. He's only twenty-two years old, and he was studying to be a priest. Now he's thinking of giving it up because of me. He's fallen for me, and his father's pissed. His younger brother, who also has a crush on me, caught us. And I don't know whether Ion knows or not but he was acting funny yesterday and what he must think of me..."

"My God—take a deep breath." I did. "That's better. So, how was he?"

"Adonia, I..."

"Now, now. You're not in church, and it is way too late for an *exomologisi*—a confession."

"Well, what do you mean, 'how was he?'"

"You know exactly what I mean. You're a woman and he's a man, and you can't be forgiven for your sins until you've committed them. Was it exciting?" I blushed, but then I felt suddenly unencumbered—a temporary reprieve from the cynicism and disillusionment of adulthood. I felt as if I could say anything, from profound to the profane, and I would be neither reproached nor rebuked.

"Okay, you asked me! He was hot, he was young and virile and insatiable. We ravaged each other until dawn until I realized that I had screwed up everybody's life. We would have stayed in bed until a lack of food became life threatening! Is that what you wanted to hear?" I said it loud enough that a group of parishioners stopped and stared at me.

"Well, that's a better tragedy than the last one you told me. But you still don't walk away with much, do you?"

"I'm walking away with my tail between my legs—that's all."

"You know, I think this was a good thing. You are human and after all your heart has been cold and alone for too long. Maybe this boy is not meant to be a priest and you did him a favor," she said reassuringly. "But this is what you Americans call a quick fix."

"I want to feel love, but I've been hurt too much." I knew that Dimitris was safe. There could be no love, and thus the inevitable hurt was not remotely possible.

"You have to ask yourself how close you let love come to you." I felt her words like a knife and I think she saw me wince. "You still think about your son, don't you?" she asked.

"I try not to, but he never leaves me. Can you imagine mourning a person you never met? I have no picture of him—no images—except the fuzzy outlines from a sonogram. Though I touched him, felt him, lived with him."

"You cannot blame yourself for what happened," she said sincerely. While the words echoed the advice of self-help books and were well-meaning, they did not sound cliché coming from Adonia. They sounded like the truth.

"Do you believe the soul is immortal?" I asked suddenly.

Adonia reached out and drew me toward her.

"Of course I believe."

"How?"

"There is no 'how' otherwise it would not be belief."

"I feel cast out from any faith."

"Like Eve?"

"I don't take Genesis seriously."

"The worst thing about Genesis is that people take it literally. And that isn't the fault of the story. But of course, it's true."

"Including the need to blame the woman and through childbearing make her suffer?"

"She sees more, understands more—she's more susceptible to grasping the ungraspable and forbidden."

Adonia had me smiling for a moment, taking my mind off the hurt. The white elephant between us was what kind of faith she had. It seemed more mystical than religious, more inviting than dogmatic. I wanted to dance around it.

"What did the ancient Greeks believe?" I asked.

"Many things, but the durability of the soul and its glory were rarely in question."

"Why?"

"That's just it—some things aren't about 'why.' You just can't confuse science and faith."

"I wish I had the faith to know that I hadn't caused his death."

"I understand what you felt."

"How can you? I mean, I know you couldn't have children because of Niko, but I carried my baby eight months. I felt so ashamed, and so responsible for what happened. It is too much to ask anyone to understand."

"I lied."

"What?"

"I led you to believe something that wasn't true because the truth was too painful."

"You mean, Niko was able to—"

"No, he couldn't. But his misfortune helped me to believe that fate had chosen for us, helped absolve me of my solitary guilt."

"I don't understand. What happened, Adonia?"

"I told you that my father had never liked Niko."

"He wanted you to marry someone else, if I remember it right."

"For that I could have easily forgiven him."

"It must have been frustrating that he never liked your husband."

"He did."

"You just said he never liked Niko."

"Niko was never my husband."

We walked arm in arm to the far side of the Lyccabetus Hill. I wanted for her to unravel the mystery that she had spun. But I couldn't ask. I just walked with her and waited.

"Niko was my lover," she finally said. "My first and my last. And though there was another who took me, in my heart Niko is the only one. But our love was hidden in the shadows."

"But why?"

"You cannot compare a woman's life then to the freedoms that we have now. I was barely more than a possession to be bartered for like a piece of furniture or livestock. My father knew how much I loved Niko, but he had already decided that I would marry the son of the businessman I told you of—that entrepreneur of blood and misery."

"What was his name, the son?"

"I never utter it...I was forced to marry him. On our wedding night, he tried to take that which I would never have given him freely—even if it had not already been given to another."

"He knew?"

"Yes. If not from my body, then from my eyes. He beat me savagely until I bled, but it was not the blood of marriage's consummation. As was the custom, he hung the bloody sheets from the balcony as a ritualistic proof of his conquest and my submission—but I had to hide inside for days so that none would see my bruises."

"My God, Adonia."

"There were no hotlines to call back then. I told my father of the beating, but I dared not speak the reasons for my husband's rage."

"And?"

"He told me that we all suffered, so why should it be different for me. He assumed that whatever the reason, that I had brought it upon myself."

"But he was your father! He should have done something."

"I was raped every night. This vulgar swine was undeterred by my apathy. After a year or so, his interest waned, no, it increased—but for others. He did little to hide his cavorting, but I was not jealous or mad—I was relieved. The thought of him, or of any man, touching me made me wretch."

"You had no one to talk to, no friends who could help you?"

"No one."

"How did you keep your sanity, I would have lost my mind..."

"Maybe that's how I survived. And then one day, Niko changed everything."

"What happened?"

"I couldn't sleep. Sometimes I would walk the streets—often finding myself at the cove where the fishing vessels lay beached. The sea seemed inviting because it was absent of anyone that I knew or anything that I could remember. One night I allowed myself to linger until dawn. Soon fishermen would arrive to ready their boats, and I would be drawn back to my home like the fish that would soon be ensnared in their nets. Instead of going home, I waded into the lapping waters—trying to swim to safety—as if I would find peace in its unknowable depths. Deeper and deeper I penetrated its black velvet embrace. A sudden ripple startled me out of my sleepy drifting. For a moment, I thought it was a fish that had broken the surface but when I looked up—there was Niko. He too had waded in but he seemed strong and cheerful. He asked me whether I was cold and I told him 'no' but by that point I was already numb. He laughed and I laughed too—the first time in so long—he had snapped me out of myself. Putting his arm around me, I found myself lifted up and carried to his boat. I lay for a while wrapped in a blanket in the berth as he prepared his ship for the sea. We cast off and headed out towards the horizon. And there, in the gentle swells of the Aegean, we enveloped each other in the full warmth of the morning sun. A month later, I realized that it had been the beginning of a new life and not just mine—though I could tell no one."

"I see."

"I was in a panic. My husband would know that the child was not his. I knew he would not have the courage to confront Niko, but his father was powerful, and life, and death, were cheap then."

"What did you do, Adonia?"

"I went to my father and threw myself at his feet, begging him for help. He was ashamed of me, saying it would bring disgrace upon him, but what he really feared was the possibility of a divorce. That would have dried up the food chain that my father was now feeding on. I had sinned, there was no doubt, but it paled before the one I was yet to commit."

"Did he force you to…"

"He would have, but I wouldn't let any man touch my child. But what I did, I did to save the man I loved. I knew that the baby was already as good as dead—I couldn't lose them both."

"Didn't your husband find out? Didn't he wonder why you went to the doctor?"

"What doctor? I couldn't go to one. There were none who didn't fear repercussions."

"Couldn't you have gone to some other village, found a doctor who didn't know you or your father-in-law?"

"Travel to another village?" Adonia looked at me as if I had suggested she seek out a Planned Parenthood on Mars. "I was alone and I knew what I had to do. There was no one to help. The bleeding became so bad that I passed out. For a long time I believed that dying would have been more merciful than the reality that I woke up to."

"How did you ever get away?"

"It was a few months after the incident." I thought about her use of the euphemism 'incident.' "My husband came home from one of his extended binges of drunken fornication. I have no idea why he decided to hit me, it doesn't even matter now. It would usually stop when he got tired or passed out. But that night, he wouldn't stop. He would be stopped."

"Niko?"

Adonia simply nodded.

"He had come to my house. From just outside the door, he heard my cries and burst in. I remember seeing my husband reaching for a revolver and aiming it at Niko—who set upon him. Things happened in a blur, and I almost felt as if I had left my body—observing a surrealistic scene of violence and brutality. Niko must have carried me to my bed, because the next thing I could recall was him tending to my bruises. When the police arrived, they could barely recognize the scum who had beaten me."

"Was he... dead?"

"Death would have been too merciful."

"And what happened to Niko?"

"He was arrested and charged. It was self-defense—but judges could be bought. Fortunately he escaped."

"How did he manage that?"

"One of the guards fought with him in the resistance. He was careless locking Niko's cell one night. When he fled Galixidi, I thought I would never see him again."

"Did your husband beat you again?"

"Never. Before he left, Niko swore to that scoundrel that if he raised his hand to me again, he would cut his throat with a fish knife and use his innards for bait. My husband knew that Niko would have risked his own life to make good his threat."

"You must have hated your husband."

"I hated him, and his father too, but it was my father I loathed even more. I loathed him for giving me to this man and then doing nothing to save me. Even as my husband raped me, I saw the eyes of my father—the eyes of his indifference. I never thought I would know happiness. And seeing so much misery in the world, I had no reason to believe I was entitled to any."

"Until Niko."

"Yes, my Captain."

"How did you find him?"

"My husband wanted nothing to do with me after the incident. His father, fearing a scandal, sent me away with enough money to last for two months. It took me almost a year, and life wasn't easy after the money ran out, but I knew that my Niko would follow the sea and the fishing fleets. I found him, and our first night together was as comfortable as if we had never been apart. It took Death to separate us again."

"You and Niko never married?"

"I was never divorced from that awful man. But what did it matter?

Had Niko been my husband, I still could not have loved him more.

30
BEFORE THE FALL

"Thank the Gods that you are safe, Pheidippides," said Erebus, one of Callimachus' aides. "The Mede hasn't advanced, but his scouts become more bold each day." Militiades and Callimachus had come into the tent where Pheidippides lay. He immediately sat upright when he saw them enter.

"What news from the Spartans? Will they march?" asked the Athenian archon.

"Not until the full moon has passed."

"Fools! Do they really believe the Mede will wait until the waning moon?"

"I am sure they don't," replied Militiades. He then unsheathed his sword. Running its sharp edge along the thick part of his palm, he drew blood that trickled onto the ground. He calmly stooped to pick up a handful of the crimson stained soil and let it run through his fingers back towards the earth.

"It is settled. We stand alone..."

My problems seemed to be amplifying. The flight back to New York was unmercifully boring. Besides fighting the headwinds of the Westerlies, flights heading west tend to be in the middle of the day when one isn't predisposed to sleep, so I had too much time to think. To make matters worse, I had my period. Since my miscarriage, my cycles alternate in severity, every other month is mild, but this wasn't the "good" month. Fortunately it doesn't linger for days—it's intense for about twenty-four hours, then it passes. But in that day, I can blow a case or lose a friend. I checked my purse. I've learned never to be unprepared. One miscalculation in summer whites or while sitting on a friend's couch cures one of forgetfulness. I know that the only thing men are less comfortable talking about is that exam when the doctor asks them to cough or bend over. I don't think men find that subject funny, yet they possess a wealth of jokes on the subject of menstruation. I usually don't mind them, however unfunny, but I am pissed when they imply that we exaggerate the symptoms. A man should only imagine spinning in a circle until he's ready to heave, kicking himself in the groin, feeling like he's urinating in his pants and then strutting into that all important board meeting without a care in the world.

That about summed up how I felt as I went straight from the airport to my office. There were several things to do which were vital to my preparation.

I was only there for an hour by the time I felt I had to get out of the confined space. I decided to walk all the way to Penn Station, so I changed into some workout clothes that I kept in the office for those days that I went to my gym. The old rules seemed to be falling like a house of cards in a gust of wind. I had become a squatter in a prefabricated world built by someone else—my own ideas remained in blueprints. I had been drifting dangerously on the assumption that I have plenty of time to find a life goal more fulfilling than postponing death.

I went to bed without dinner, my clothes lay strewn about the floor where I had lazily dropped them. As I lay there, staring at my walls, I remembered Ion telling me about Hypnos, the God of Sleep.

"Each night," Ion would tell me, "Hyperion concedes the heavens to the Goddess of the Night. That is when Hypnos leaves his home on Limnos, flying over the earth carrying a large eucalyptus branch. Whomever he touches on the head with its leaves is powerless to stay awake."

Mercifully, Hypnos' branches quickly found me and kissed my forehead.

At Penn Station, where I transferred from the LIRR to the "E" train, I was treated to a sea of diverse humanity. Strained make-up, wilted suits and morning smiles turned into determined scowls as each made his or her way through the throngs. Commuters waded three deep, pushed right up to the edge of the platform which hung over the darkened tracks, ready for a rugby scrum. Passengers trying to get off trains have to establish their presence, or chance being trapped inside as the doors close.

Normally, I would have been among the "fittest" that made the first train, but today, I waited for the next and less crowded one.

I knew that the crackling voice over the P.A. system must have been announcing the 50th Street Station, though the conductor sounded like he was eating a box of Ritz crackers. I never listened to these garbled announcements since my subway commuting was limited to a few lines that I knew by heart. I stared at a graffiti embellished map, which was as easy to decipher as the Codex Leicester. My stop was next, but reading something in the crowded car allows one to avoid the straphangers' taboo—making eye contact with other human beings.

By the time I had arrived at Rockefeller Center, I was looking forward to my battle in the air-conditioned offices of Spelling, Ambrose, Marshall & Hellman.

"I'm with Schroeder, Wilkes & Barron," I informed the headset-wearing receptionist, who seemed to be speaking to me while simultaneously fielding a barrage of incoming calls. "I'm here to see Richard Cooper."

"They're already in Conference Room B. It's the second door down that hallway on your left," she said politely as she transferred another phone call.

I walked past their main conference room, which could seat over forty people. Conference Room B was about a quarter of its size, but much better for our purposes today. I was here to depose Drew Urbach, the Chief Operating Officer of Continuum Corporation. They were suing our client—Braxton Enterprises. This room had a large oval glass table upon which yellow pads and water glasses had been laid out. A court reporter was making her preparations to record the deposition that was about to occur. I set my briefcase down in one corner of the room and greeted my adversaries.

"Good morning, Rich," I said as we shook hands. I had met him several times on previous cases.

"Morning, Marianna. Let me introduce Mark Fielding, one of my partners."

"Nice to meet you," Mark said, as he extended his hand to me.

"And you must be Mr. Urbach," I said, as I looked over at the well-dressed man seated between his two attorneys. He nodded at me, but didn't say a word.

"Don't worry, I won't bite."

"That's not what our scouting reports say about you," Rich interjected.

"I'm flattered."

I poured myself a cup of coffee and made small talk with Rich and Mark. Serious economics would be at stake today, but that was no reason not to observe the niceties of polite coffee conversation. Mark and Rich exchanged awkward glances, as if they wanted to broach something and were looking for the right timing. But this was like a war, and I had read Sun Tzu.

Let your rapidity be that of the wind, your compactness that of the forest. In raiding and plundering be like fire, in immovability like a mountain. Let your plans be dark and impenetrable as night, and when you move, fall like a thunderbolt.

"I say we get started with the deposition. I've got a lot of ground to cover here today with your client," I said with a certain forcefulness which let them know I meant business.

But it was Rich who cut to the chase. "We've reviewed the documents you've provided and frankly, we think your case is weak." In lawyer talk, that means, 'we really hate the fact that your client documented things.' "You've got a tough case to prove, and pursuing our client will take a lot of time, money and luck." I knew exactly what Rich was doing, and he knew that I knew, but it was a necessary ritual.

Security against defeat implies defensive tactics; ability to defeat the enemy means taking the offensive. Standing on the defensive indicates insufficient strength; attacking, a superabundance of strength.

"I beg to differ with you, Rich. I've got reams of precedence supporting our position. We're ready to go to trial," I said, as if my client was invincible, and unwilling to negotiate.

"As are we," fired back Rich. He was pretty good. "And we have reams of cases showing the opposite, as well as two thousand dollar a day experts who will contradict your two thousand dollar a day experts..."

"What are you getting at?" I loved this part.

"Even though we're confident that we will ultimately prevail, my client would be amenable to discussing how to resolve this matter more expeditiously."

"May I take it that you're ready to discuss a settlement?" I asked.

"We think a settlement might be in the best interests of both parties." Read 'my client has nothing to gain and everything to lose by being deposed today.'

It was a different language than the fiery rhetoric at the beginning of every case when each side swears to fight to the finish. There must have been something in the documents we provided, or perhaps something Mr. Urbach's attorneys had detected in prepping him that had prompted the urge to settle. Whatever it was, I held the upper hand. I had been around long enough to see such an advantage turn on the happenstance of a poor deposition or an unfavorable ruling on what might appear to be an important motion—the time to strike was now.

"Do you wish to discuss this now, or after Mr. Urbach's deposition," I said, knowing the answer.

"Why incur the expense and time if we come to terms?" asked Mark. Every attorney knows there is nothing to gain and everything to lose when your client is deposed. I could have pressed them, but my client's case had its own glaring weaknesses.

He will win who knows when to fight and when not to fight.

"Well, gentlemen, I'm happy to hear your offer."

"Drew, we'll be in my office. Ms. Stern, will you excuse us for a few minutes," Rich said to the stenographer. She'd seen this happen scores of times just as she was about to begin recording. It didn't really matter to her one way or the other.

If you know the enemy and know yourself, your victory will not stand in doubt; if you know Heaven and know Earth, you may make your victory complete.

They must have had some particularly dirty laundry that they needed to bury rather than chance its exposure in discovery, or worse—in open court. Our preparations had shown the weakness of their case, making me all the less pleased to have been called back from Europe to handle a no-brainer.

"I'm not sure it'll fly, but I'll relay what you've offered." They allowed me the final movements in the game. I wouldn't press every advantage. In a future case I could be on the other side of this equation, and I'd want them to give me room to breathe.

Before I left, I telephoned my client and informed him of the offer. We agreed to meet in two hours at my office.

A silver Lincoln Town Car from SWB awaited me in front of 4 Rockefeller Center. As I sat back into its leather-upholstered seats, I felt uneasy. For so many years, I had lived for moments like this one. The big wins. The accolades of my bosses. The congratulations of my clients. I had won but there was no elation, no adrenalin rush, no glory. Nothing. I had flown twelve hours for this feeling. My firm would get paid its fees. The client would swear how great we were then privately resume cursing lawyers. No one would care that I had left someone who needed me thousands of miles away. I knew that. But just how little they cared would become more apparent later that day.

"I strongly urge you to take their offer," I told my client, Paul Braxton of Braxton Enterprises. I was surprised that he was balking. Perhaps the suddenness with which the defendant had offered to settle had made my client cocky—more sure of his case than the facts warranted.

"Marianna, I can appreciate your desire to bring the case to a close, but if they were willing to go this far, perhaps we haven't found their limit yet."

"Paul, do I have to remind you about our conversation of just a few minutes ago? We're fortunate that they couldn't find the memorandum they say was lost. It would have been pretty damaging."

"You mean the one sitting in my briefcase?" He said with a slight chuckle, though I saw nothing funny about the situation.

"You have that document? The one I've staked my reputation on by denying it existed?"

"So, you didn't lie..." he said with indifference, as if that technicality made it justifiable.

"I'm just..."

"Is your *conscience* bothering you?" he said sarcastically.

"Yes, yes it is. Is that a problem?"

"No, I admire people with consciences, but not when they're billing me $400 an hour. Why the sudden attack of morals?" It hurt me that he said that.

"Sudden?"

"You took this case over from Phil McKinnon. He never had ethical problems with it." I took a deep breath. I was on the verge of losing my cool.

"Paul, you intentionally withheld key documents from the defendant—and from me."

"And your point is?"

"What's my point? It's not right."

"Then, come to think of it, I'm mistaken. That document never existed."

"Paul, come on, is that your position?"

"Hey, whose lawyer are you anyway? Do you want to search my briefcase?"

We both knew that I wasn't about to call his bluff. "I'm sure you were mistaken about what you thought you had found. But I still want you to settle." I suggested with a demanding tone.

"Don't you think they'd have done the same thing? Hell, two of them blatantly lied during their depositions, you know, that Foster guy, and his assistant Guardini."

"I'm not arguing with you, Paul. But that's something their lawyers will have to live with..."

"Like they give a shit?"

"Be happy, I got you an offer that was well above what you wanted."

I sat in my office after Paul had left. I was disturbed at the turn our conversation had taken. Now I was the one who needed a little advice.

James Barron had interviewed me when I was hired, and I remembered him saying that his door was always open. I had never felt the need to take him up on his offer until now.

When his secretary escorted me into his office, he was on the telephone. James Barron was in his mid sixties. He was wearing an olive green suit, though he had removed his jacket. Fitting underneath a white tab-collared shirt was a brightly colored Paul Stewart silk tie, which contrasted with the braces over each shoulder. On his left wrist, I spotted a very elegant and very expensive watch—a gold Girard Pirageaux with an alligator leather strap. He was certainly not fat, but the clear manifestations of years of fine dining, first class travel and sitting at boardroom tables were very conspicuous. Though it was the dead of summer, he wasn't tan; rather, he was reddened along his forehead and neck. His totally whitened hair was slicked back and meticulously combed.

I made a motion to suggest that I would wait outside until he was finished, but he said to the listener on the other end of the phone, "Hold on a second Tim," and then waved his arm for me to come closer. "Come in, come in, this will only take a minute or two. I'm wrapping up a call with Senator Murtaugh.

Sit down," he said, pointing to one of the red leather seats near his round conference table. "I'll be right with you. Can I have Estelle get you anything to drink?"

"Some water would be great."

"Estelle, please bring two waters, I'll have sparkling with some lime," he told his personal secretary. There was something patrician about the way he spoke, he had the intonation of a man who was accustomed to giving orders, and having them obeyed, though he did so with charm rather than force. I studied his office as he continued his telephone conversation. I was impressed at the ease at which he addressed the Chairman of the Senate Banking Committee. James Barron was a rainmaker, one who brought in the clients and whose stature lent credibility to the firm. He hung up the phone and came over to the small table and sat down opposite me.

He noticed me looking behind him. On mahogany console was a scale model of a boat of the size that takes a crew to sail. I could see its life-sized counterpart in pictures on the wall.

"She's beautiful, isn't she," he said with an inflection of longing. For a moment, I sensed Jim's mind drifting in hazy sentiment. His eyes followed the sensual form of her sleek hull. "She's dry-docked up in Greenwich. God, I'd love to…" Then, like a man caught by his wife eyeing another woman, he suddenly snapped back to look at me, and it was back to business.

"Paul Braxton stopped by to see me after your meeting this morning," he said with a hint of concern.

"I see. He wasn't happy with the settlement offer?"

"He intimated that he was receiving very little cooperation from you."

"Really? I'm sorry he felt that way," I said. I was sure that Jim didn't know the details, and when he did, he would clearly see that I had done the right thing. "You don't know what had happened, Jim."

"He told me."

"Do you know that he withheld…"

"Yes. I'm aware of the situation."

"Then surely you can see why I was forceful."

"Marianna, Paul's father, Gerald Braxton, was a client of this firm when Lloyd Schroeder was alive and practicing law. Last year, Braxton Enterprises had had revenues of over $750 Million, and after expenses, they had pre-tax income of nearly $128 Million."

"That's impressive," I said, trying to soften the tone of his lecture.

"I really couldn't give a damn about their profit margins. What I care about are their expenses, specifically their legal expenses. They help pay for these offices, and for your salary, and the salaries of paralegals, temps, administrators and mail room staff. Don't get me wrong, no one is asking you to do anything illegal, or unethical, but we don't get paid to argue with our clients for minor oversights."

"Is hiding documents a minor oversight?"

"Okay, so his judgment was a little clouded. In a perfect world, both sides would be absolutely forthright and would strive to find truth and assume responsibility, but we don't practice law in a perfect world."

"That sounds like a justification."

"Schroeder, Wilkes & Barron doesn't make the ground rules, we only play by them—and we play to win," he said. It reminded me of the line from the Godfather, the one which excused any behavior, *it's only business*. "Any lawyer who says he's never entered the gray zone is either naïve or lying. Do you think you're the first attorney who's ever faced a moral dilemma? We all try our damnedest to stay the course, and use good judgment. It's like doing 30 in a 25 mph zone, we've all done it."

"What happens when 30 becomes 45, and 45 becomes 60 mph—and you're in a school zone?"

Jim slid his chair a little closer to mine, and he leaned towards me. Then he spoke in a lowered voice as if he were suddenly taking me into his confidence. I noticed how weathered his hands looked. They were not what one expected to find on a lawyer, or of a man who had spent the better part of his life seated in a leather chair behind a mahogany desk. They were hands tempered by the wind and sea and rope. I thought about the difference between the two lives that he lived. One Jim was content to be seated, driven in the back of a limousine, the other Jim happy only when standing on deck, driving through the wind. Did Jim still yearn for the sea and its promise of freedom and challenge—or had he conceded to the sirens of capitalism?

"Let me share a piece of advice that I once got from old man Schroeder when the firm was just Spencer & Schroeder. He told me to remember that no lawyer has a saint for a client. Everyone always assumes it is the lawyer who manipulates, but just as often, we are the ones manipulated. The first twisting of facts takes place when I first meet with a client and he explains to me what a victim he was. We're the face of evil until they're in trouble—then we're their heroes—transformed from Satan to Savior. And our clients pay us for results, not for lessons in humanity."

Jim stood up and walked back to his desk, reaching for a folder on it.

"You're familiar with the class action suit against Trident Energy?

"A little."

"We're considering turning the case over to you. They're one of our more important clients, and several of the senior partners thought you would be the best suited to take the case. But we can't have a repeat of what happened today. Don't let us down."

"I'm flattered, Jim. I'm sure I won't."

"They've got deadlines coming up. You'll need to get up to speed immediately. Read what's in this folder and I'll have Dave Hammill brief you this afternoon."

"Jim, I can't start it yet."

"I understand you were on some sort of vacation. So you cut your trip short. We'll make it up to you at Christmas." That was the euphemism for "bonus time." It was so typical to view money as the all-encompassing salve for all ills.

"Jim, I have to return, if for no other reason than to bring my uncle back."

"Can't he travel alone? I mean, if someone helps him to the plane." We can have a car pick him up at JFK.

"I suppose, but I just don't feel right about asking him to do that."

This Trident matter is going to take a lot of focus. You're going to have to let this uncle of yours know that you might not be home every night by 6:00 P.M. for supper." His tone was becoming more condescending with each syllable.

"Jim, I..."

"You've worked hard to get where you are, don't lose sight of the goal now. I'm sure you'll make the right decision. He looked at his watch and said, "I've got to be at the Harvard Club by noon. I'll get a memo over to Dave telling him to forward all the Trident files to your desk."

"Thank you Jim."

As I reached his door he said to me, "Don't worry about Paul Braxton, I'll handle him. Great settlement, by the way. He's lucky this never went to trial."

Bastard.

I went back to my office and sat down in my chair, leaned back as far as it would go and took a deep breath. I had brought my mail to the office. I quickly went through the bills, paying all of them. As a child, I remember looking forward to seeing the postman. On the rare occasions when something came addressed to me, it was a thrill. A birthday wish, a postcard, a note from a distant pen pal. Now I dreaded his appearance and the never-ending stream of demands for money. I had a long-awaited letter from the Riverdale Home.

It came from one of the trustees of the home, a gentleman named Terence Archer. It informed me that he was holding a spot for Ion. We were lucky to get it, and the writer was not shy about reminding me of that fact. Well, no more need to worry about getting home by *supper*, as James Barron had forewarned. Jim was right. I needed a tougher stomach. I needed to be strong, to attack without fear of consequences and without regard for my adversary.

"Tracy, would you please come in. I need to dictate a letter," I said into my intercom. In a moment, she had appeared at my door. She had a green steno pad, a pencil, and a cup of coffee that she placed on the edge of my desk. She sat across from me and prepared for my dictation.

"What client matter?" she asked. Everything in a major law firm, from hours, to photocopies, to telephone calls to paperclips, is billed to specific client accounts.

"None."

"Then what should I file it under?"

"Resignation letter," I said as she knocked over her cup of coffee.

I hurried home, and repacked my bag. I had no time to eat. I wanted to get to JFK early. I didn't have a reservation on the flight to Athens that night. It was overbooked, so I put my name on the standby list and tried again to call Father Diogenes. There was no answer. It had been quite a day. I woke up as a highly compensated partner in one of the most prominent law firms in the world, and by dusk I was unemployed. Or, as I preferred to euphemize, I was *between jobs*.

My stomach was in knots. I checked with the airlines staff every ten minutes, always with the same response, "Please have a seat and wait for your name to be called." It wasn't looking good. The lounge area was teaming with people, all headed to where I needed to be. I had arrived fairly early, but I was still the seventh name on the list.

There were so many things I wanted to tell Ion that I couldn't before. Once I reached him, I could fix everything. I was used to taking charge and making things go the way I wanted them to. I had just overlooked one lesson—that pride always cometh before the fall.

"Papadimos," announced Mr. Baccardi from behind the check-in counter. I had gotten to know his name from my frequent inquiries, which, while making me feel proactive, got me no closer to my objective. I watched as the first two lucky passengers excitedly claimed their boarding passes, and then worriedly hurry towards the gate as if this unexpected gift could be taken away as easily as it had been granted.

A few minutes later, "Mandrakos," followed quickly by "Androtsakis." He stopped reeling off names and went back to some other work. My heart sank. I wasn't looking forward to taking a taxi back home, especially after wasting an evening at JFK. I had resigned myself when I noticed another staff member handing him a clipboard. He glanced at it briefly, then looked up and scanned the room.

I knew his eyes looked for me.

I was relieved to finally board the plane and head back to Greece. Arriving back at Panteleimon, I didn't recognize the car that was parked outside the farmhouse. Father Diogenes came out quickly to greet me. He must have heard the sounds of my arrival. I was so glad to see him, but as I got closer, I could see that he was not smiling. He had a worried look on his face.

"Everything is all right now," he said. But it was not.

"I have to see him, right now!" I demanded, before Father Diogenes could finish telling me what happened.

"You can see him, but he cannot see you yet. He's heavily sedated."

"Where is he?" "The nearest hospital is in Nea Makri."

I learned that they had called me yesterday, but in my haste to make the last flight out of JFK, I had forgotten to check my messages.

"How did it happen?"

"He complained of chest pains the night you left, but he seemed fine by morning," said Father Diogenes. "Late that afternoon, he was in the fields with Dimitris and Milos when he collapsed. The boys knew that I was out with the only car, so there was only one way to summon help. Dimitris stayed with Ion, while Milos ran the three kilometers to Dr. Constantacopoulos' office."

When I was allowed in to see Ion, it was very disturbing. He had a similar look to the way I found him in Queens, though his eyes remained closed and he had a variety of tubes feeding and monitoring him. I held his hand for a while, but he was, as the doctor warned, heavily sedated. It was perhaps true that the worst had passed, but I hadn't seen the worst, so I was totally unprepared to see my uncle in such a helpless and vulnerable state. Dr. Constantacopoulos suggested that Ion may be able to recuperate back at the monastery, possibly being discharged as early as tomorrow, but we'd wait and see.

"Thank you doctor, I know he's in good hands," I said.

"Yes, he is, but good hands are of one of more power to heal than me," he said, looking skywards. "And do not to forget thanking sons," he said while nodding towards Father Diogenes, "they save his life."

"They're good boys. I don't know how to..." but before I could finish my sentence, I had lost my composure, and words would not form.

I had left Ion, and he had nearly died. I had abandoned him, and what for? A settlement offer? The bad joke was that I had risked everything for something that now meant nothing. I was sick to my stomach.

I couldn't sleep. I was in a state of utter despair. I decided to return to the spot above the sea from where I had watched my first Grecian sunset. Drawn to the precipice, I looked into the darkness beyond the ledge. A question suddenly occurred that frightened me. What would happen if I took that one extra step? It was an insane idea—but it was not the first time I had allowed this thought to surface from some deep and dark place. One tiny step and all anxieties would end. No, it's a horrific idea, stop thinking about it—step back. I tried to move away, but my legs were immobile. I peered again over the edge at the black waters. They seemed so safe and warm—would my fisherman save me as Niko did Adonia?

In the past, that demon thought was part of a game I played to scare myself—and to test the limits of my own taboos. But that night, as I stood at the precipice between death and desire, my mind wandered in a new and more macabre space. What scared me the most was that I actually found myself answering the question of why I shouldn't take that step as if it needed one.

As I stepped back from the edge, I felt the winds whirling and singing. Then a sudden gust knocked me off balance and I felt a frightening disorientation as the sea opened her arms to receive me.

Pride had come and gone—I was falling.

PART THREE

NIKE

31
BEDSIDE HOMER

Back in his tent, Pheidippides was applying olive oil to his dehydrated skin.

"You cannot blame yourself for the actions of the Spartan," said Neotolemus. "It was surely the will of the Gods."

"Whose Gods? Ours or the Medes?"

"Time will tell."

"I know whose blood will tell—it will be ours, not the Lacedaemonians."

"Then our children will remember it so."

"If I had them..." Pheidippides said, stopping short of telling Neotolemus it would have served as little consolation.

I felt the earth beneath me. I hugged it as if molding myself to the contours of a soft mattress. Feeling its warmth, I waited for the inevitable pain, but none came. Its absence made me presume I was dead—a logical conclusion from a logical mind—though it was nothing like what I imagined death to be. Something, perhaps a small animal rustled the tall grass near me, drawing my mind back from its ethereal dream of having departed this life. As I rose, I expected the sharp pain of an internal injury—but nothing. The tempest and the fall from the cliff were a delusion brought on by my guilt-fueled hysteria. I lay on the same spot I had stood on before, having fallen only five feet to the ground beneath my collapsing legs.

Though I was safe physically, my emotional world was in turmoil. When I had journeyed to Greece with Ion, my existence seemed at least copasetic. Now the gentle tides had turned into larger and larger waves cresting, breaking, and threatening to carry me out to sea. As I stood in the darkness, I prayed that I had not squandered my last chance.

My last conversation with Adonia had left me feeling confused. She had challenged me. When Adonia wanted to say something to me—she said it—with or without the accompanying social niceties. She made me see things whether I was ready to or not. But she was real, and she was there when I needed her. That was more than I could say about so many acquaintances whose friendships shifted with the winds of fortune.

I wavered about calling her the morning after I returned to Marathon. Though we had developed an intense rapport, we had just met. It worried me to find myself leaning on her. It scared me that the only one I could turn to was a person I had only known for two weeks. Since we had met on our Olympic Airlines flight, my life spun wildly between adventure and despondency. Ion was semi-comatose. I had strained my relationship with Father Diogenes, and I couldn't even begin to confront his sons, one in love, one smarting from imagined rejection. Evangelis' seedlings would not grow. If I could have spoken Greek, I would have thrown myself upon Eftehea's mercy.

I called. "Adonia, hi, it's Marianna."

"Hello love. Are you back from the States?"

"Yes... yes, but...."

"What's happened? I hear it in your voice, something is wrong. Did he find out?"

"Ion had a stroke. I don't know what's going to happen to him..."

"I'll be there in an hour," she said, and hung up.

The troubles that began with my night of indiscretion, now paled in the light of Ion's infirmity. According to Dr. Constantacopoulos, Ion had suffered an ischemic aphasia—a stroke. I thought it morosely humorous that the doctor had told me if the patient survives the initial stroke, they have a chance of recovering, as if I couldn't figure out that those who die have very little hope of getting better.

Ion had stabilized, and he was brought back to the Diogenes' the next day. Over the next few days, Ion's condition did not deteriorate, but it stubbornly refused to improve. Mine was becoming noticeably worse as I grew more fatigued and less able to cope. He drifted in and out of a comatose state brought on by medication, but also caused by his body's desire to hibernate while he decided whether to live or die. There was little that modern technology could do. It was in Ion's hands now or perhaps in the hands of that Creator that he had always spoken about in defiance of any formal prayer or ritual. He was as comfortable as we could make him, at least in body. I wondered where his mind was. Was it too resting comfortably or was it preparing for a long journey?

In the past two days, I had seen less of the Diogenes. Under other circumstances, I may have read more into this, but given my vigil in Ion's room, our lack of social interaction was to be expected. Of course, each of them in turn came in to sit with us, especially Eftehea, though the coldness that she exuded whenever I was around seemed only to intensify. I had a terrible suspicion that she blamed me for Ion's state.

Where Eftehea went, Evangelis usually followed. He would sheepishly poke his head in and stare at Ion. I could not help wondering what this child perceived as he conquered his initial apprehension and slowly made his way closer to Ion. He came right to Ion's bedside, watching his elder inhaling softly—sometimes with a slight rasp or wheeze—lungs laboring for life-sustaining air.

When Ion and I were in the room with Eftehea and Evangelis, it sounded as if four different languages were being spoken. Besides the English and Greek, Evangelis spoke a curious language, while Ion communicated only by the severity of his struggled breathing.

Father Diogenes would stop in every evening after church. I noticed that he would not change first from his orthodox garb. Initially I assumed that it was because he was in a hurry to see Ion. Then its real reason occurred to me—sending a chill through my already strained nerves. He wore his priestly garments as he would upon visiting any parishioner who might require last rites at a moment's notice.

I don't know how I would have found the strength to navigate through these days and nights without Adonia. She was selfless. Sitting with me until sunset each day, returning each morning, never with despair in her eyes. That first night, she stayed at Panteleimon, but it wasn't necessary for her to find a place to sleep as neither of us did.

I left several urgent messages for Dr. Riggs. He was whitewater rafting in Colorado. Even if he had received his page, he was probably out of cell phone range and miles from any landline. I told his office that he was to call no matter the time. I didn't care whose feathers he had to ruffle, I was going to get the best specialists I could muster from five thousand miles away. Not that I didn't trust the well-meaning Dr. Constanticopoulos, but at that moment, if the Pope had gone to medical school and been Ion's physician, I'd have asked for a second opinion. It sounds cruel—I'm sure Greek physicians are highly skilled, after all, they are the literal children of Hippocrates—but right now, good wasn't good enough. I wanted to speak with doctors whose office walls were decorated with Ivy League Medical School Degrees not pictures of Santorini.

Towards the waning hours of that night, I finally received a call back from Dr. Riggs.

"You'll have to speak up, I can barely hear you," his crackling voice filtered over the airwaves on its weak signal.

"A stroke," I found myself raising my voice into the telephone. He could not help reminding me that he had advised against this trip. "Quick, before I lose the call, get a pen," he barked authoritatively.

"Got one."

"After we hang up, I want you to call a colleague of mine, Dr. Ken Baruth, at (212) 305-2500. He's Chief of Neurology at Columbia Presbyterian. Tell him I referred you and asked if he'd confer with Ion's attending physician."

"Thanks, Dr. Riggs."

"Do you want to try to transport him?"

"I don't think so," I said. I'm not sure if my thoughts were foreboding or optimistic. *H TAN H EPI TAS*."

"What was that? You were breaking up."

"Oh, nothing," I said, but I knew that Ion was going to return with his shield or lying on top of it.

Once I had reached Dr. Baruth, there was a flurry of calls between him, Dr. Constantacopoulos and Dr. Riggs' office. I had what few of Ion's medical records there were at the hospital in Nea Makri, faxed to New York.

I managed to participate on one such call from Dr. Constanticoupoulis' office. Dr. Baruth informed us that without personally examining Ion and getting Magnetic Resonance Imaging, that there was little he could determine from where he was sitting.

One look at Dr. Constantacopoulos told me that in Greece I was more likely to find pieces of the Great Wall of China than MRI equipment. Dr. Baruth concurred that moving Ion was not an appealing option, and that he was best off right where he was. He didn't seem to be in need of any immediate medical procedures, and he was stable. I was grateful, but I could tell that my being an attorney made him to choose his words carefully.

"So what do we do?" I asked.

"Nothing," answered Dr. Baruth. "It sounds like his attending physician has done everything he could have done under the circumstances. There is really nothing else to do for him except make him comfortable and let him rest—the desire to live is in his hands now."

"How can I just sit here and do nothing but wait?"

"You can pray," interjected Dr. Constantacopoulis.

"It's not a treatment they teach in medical school, but it can't hurt," added Dr. Baruth. "With a little luck, your uncle may recover without complications." Complications? As if being almost ninety isn't complicated enough.

Sainthood requires three miracles—I would have given my soul for just one. I needed a sign, no matter how small, something, anything to make me believe that I had not come all this way just to bury Caesar.

Adonia couldn't come that Friday, but she called me several times to check on Ion, and me. That evening, I was once again alone with my patient. I had been alone with him virtually all day. It wasn't only because I didn't want to leave his side; it was also to avoid other contact.

Ion was still on an intravenous drip to insure hydration and minimal nutrients. I looked over at my withering warrior, watching his labored breathing and glassy eyes. I began to speak to him, not expecting any answer, but bolstered by the false sense of a dialogue. Like a placebo, it kept me busy, so as not to dwell on the moment that I now shared with this man who so precariously clung to life. I remembered how he looked that first day in Queens as he sat in his only chair and stared vacuously across the dreary urban landscape.

So many "what ifs" ran through my mind. What if we hadn't come to Greece, what if I hadn't given in to temptation, what if he had never snapped that photo—and what if my parents hadn't saved it? Too many permutations for me to comprehend how he and I could be here, together, now. How little I could have realized on that first visit—the unexpected turns in the road. I recalled Ion invoking the words of Xanthos, Achilles' steed. Did Ion know that this would be his last great campaign?

My mind drifted to my afternoon at Horace Mann, and to Bill and Ion in their boiler room sanctuary. Then I remembered something else about that day, something that Bill shared about the time he had lay in a coma. Ion had stood vigil by his bedside and read him passages from *The Illiad*. I almost had to laugh. The odds of finding an English version of this book in the middle of the night in Marathon were about zero—unless one traveled with Ion Theodore, who never traveled without it.

It took me a few minutes to find the passage that Bill had said was his favorite.

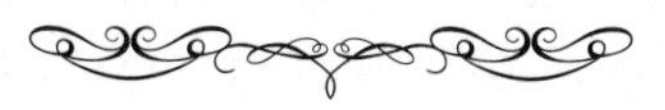

> *... ringing as the note of a trumpet that sounds alarm then the foe is at the gates of a city, even so brazen was the voice of the son of Aeacus, and when the Trojans heard its clarion tones they were dismayed; the horses turned back with their chariots for they boded mischief, and their drivers were awe-struck by the steady flame which the gray-eyed goddess had kindled above the head of the great son of Peleus...*

I read aloud to Ion, just as he had to his pupil so many years ago. I thought of Ion, like the great son of Peleus, readying himself for battle. The armor that he had lent to his lover and best friend, Patroclus, had been stripped from the fallen hero's corpse by Hector—Troy's greatest warrior. The night before,

Achilles' mother had enjoined Hephaestos to forge her son a new set of armor—even more magnificent than any ever worn by a man.

Looking down upon my vulnerable hero, I wondered whether this was what he had meant when he spoke to me of Xanthos? Was Ion preparing to fight or to say goodbye?

"Ion, come back to me. I know that you can," I found myself speaking to his listless form as I held his warm but limp hand. Then I paused and pondered my own words. If he could hear me, was I motivating or tormenting him? What right did I have to ask him to return? He was eighty-eight and had just suffered a stroke. Was it really for his sake that I prayed for him to regain consciousness, or was it for mine? Why could I not summon the courage to let him go, now while he rested in comfort? Would my longing cheat him out of the peaceful death that he deserved, which now seemed to embrace him? Would an even more painful and less dignified one await him should he struggle and refuse to surrender now? Was I resuscitating a nearly drowned sailor so that he may starve to death, marooned on a deserted island?

I needed to rest, to close my eyes for a few minutes. I was about to remove my hand and take up my position on the chair opposite his bed. Had I not held his hand for one added instant, the gesture would have gone unnoticed. But at that last second before our flesh broke contact, I felt a slight squeeze. It was so faint that it could have easily been missed. But I didn't miss it. I held on, waiting for a sign that it hadn't been my imagination, or some reflex in Ion's hand which made his fingers slightly contract. Then it happened again, this time twice in succession as he turned his head slowly towards me. I brought his fingers to my lips and kissed them—letting him know that I had heard him loud and clear. He closed his eyes, exhausted from this, the slightest of meditated movement.

"I will be here with you, Ion. I will not leave you again," I said, but he had drifted away again.

It was a small blessing, hardly registering on the miracle scale, but it was the first—and I needed it so badly.

My body and mind called out for fresh air and open space after being inside for three days. I had lost my appetite and ate only when my body demanded sustenance. I barely saw anyone else, and when I did, the intervals were brief and polite.

I saw Eftehea walk by the room, and I motioned for her to come in.

"Eftehea, can you sit with Ion. I need to walk," I said, though the words were for my sake, with an abundance of hand gestures meant for her. Once I knew that she understood, I prepared to leave, letting her know I would be nearby if Ion awoke. I slipped out of the side door of the house, happy to see no one else. I headed for the orchards.

I walked alone and then sat on the stump of a fallen tree. It was covered with soft green moss. From where I sat, I could see Panteleimon. I watched as Father Diogenes, bedecked in full priestly garments, walked out behind the church. I went to the edge of the grove and called out for him, but when the figure turned around, I could see that it was Dimitris, not Yiannis, who stared back at me from those long black robes. When he saw me, he slowly made his way to the top of the hill and calmly walked over to me. I recalled those eyes, and the way they looked at me that night we found each other here in the orchard. They still burned with passion, but not the way they did that fateful night.

"Dimitris, look at you!" I said, somewhat astonished.

"What are you mean?"

"I don't know... that last time we spoke, you seemed to be hanging up your robes, for good. What made you change your mind?"

"You."

"Me?"

"You are surprised?"

"Frankly, I'm totally surprised."

"I am in doubt and you are allow me taste somethings that my lips are never touch," he said as he held me in his arms. I stared at his lips, remembering them as they caressed me. He closed his eyes and relaxed his grip. Even in black robes he looked sexy.

"Are you sure it wasn't the apple?"

"Perhaps. But like the apple, it is also bring wisdom."

"I'm flattered, but there must have been others..."

He said nothing, but he stared at me with a look of absolute incredulity, his eyes widening fully, as if the sheer absurdity of my unfinished sentence was unworthy of response.

"Dimitris! Wait a minute. Are you going to tell me that I was your..." but his fingers on my lips stilled my voice and I was embarrassed at my ignorance.

"There is only be one first. And this first is help me find way."

"More likely led you astray," I teased. He smiled, and a knowing look passed between us.

"And, how are you say, my flesh was willing. But if not for your words, I am never find right path."

"What words?"

"About make difference, about my father and Panayiotas. That night, your words are hurt, it is sound like polite voice that is say 'have a nice life,' until it is happen."

"What, what happened?"

"As I am alone with Ion, this day in field..."

"You were a hero Dimitris. I could never find a way to appropriately thank you."

"No, you are not understand...I am do nothings," he continued but almost stammered in his response as if unsure of his words and thoughts.

"You're too modest, Dimitris. You were a hero. Ion's heart had stopped—you resuscitated him, the doctor told me..."

"No—I am do nothings," he repeated.

"He had no pulse?"

"No. Milos and I are sure he is dead."

"So you did something, mouth-to-mouth, CPR..."

"I am pray. When nothings else is work, I am just pray."

I ran back to the farmhouse. I ran as fast as I could. There was no reason really. I wasn't any more worried about Ion at that moment than any other since my return. I knew he wasn't alone since I had left him with Eftehea. I just wanted to run. It wasn't brought on by fear or joy, but a desire to breakaway from the inertia of being stuck between them. I wanted to sweat, I wanted to hurt, I wanted to feel my heart pounding. I wanted to know that I was still alive.

When I got there I saw her. If I hadn't taken such a circuitous route, I wouldn't have.

"Adonia, what in the world..."

"Shh," she immediately gestured. She was standing at the back of the house, leaning slightly towards an open window—the one to Ion's room. I could tell from her calmness that there was nothing wrong, but I had no idea why she stood there and listened. Was Ion speaking? And why the need to eavesdrop? I was intrigued at the possibility of clandestine discovery.

I quietly approached until I was next to her. She put her fingers to my lips and pointed into the room. Ion was on the bed. His eyes were closed. He may have been sleeping, but I'm not sure. Eftehea was in the room and Evangelis was playing on the floor, but what was most remarkable was the position that Eftehea had assumed. She wasn't sitting in the chair or on the edge of the bed. She was kneeling on the floor, as if in prayer, though she spoke lucidly to Ion. The floor was stone. I could see her shifting slightly from one knee to the other, distributing the discomfort that showed in her wincing expression.

I ducked my head back and stood on the far side of Adonia, who closed her eyes so she could hear the barely audible words. I hoped that Adonia would be able to decipher some of what Eftehea said. My curiosity and anxiety had risen. I wondered what strange episodes had transpired between them decades ago under the hot blue skies and dark cool nights of Marathon. I remained perfectly still, I could feel my heart pounding, the thought of bursting into the room and forcing an explanation crossed my mind, and then reason replaced jealous impulse—barely. I had no reason to fear ghosts, but it reminded me of how little Ion had shared with me about his life, especially the time here at Panteleimon.

This strange episode was abruptly ended by Father Diogenes. Entering the room, he said something to Eftehea who quickly rose from her knees. He must have told her he'd stay for a while, because she took Evangelis by the hand and left Father Diogenes in the room with Ion. I led Adonia away from the house, through the paths of olive groves, into the field where I had played with Dimitris. It looked much different in the sunlight than it had on that wildly sensual night.

"You must think me awful for sneaking about like that," she finally said.

""What happened there?"

"When I arrived, I knocked, but when there was no answer, I walked around the back of the house to your window, and then Ion's when I didn't see you. I heard talking, and I assumed it was you sitting with him, but as I got closer, I realized it was Eftehea. She was kneeling, just as you saw her. Perhaps I should have made my presence known, but there was something about the way she was speaking with him that made me too curious to interrupt."

"What was she saying?"

"She loved him."

"I knew it. Were they...?"

"I don't know," said Adonia.

"She was asking forgiveness."

"For what? What happened between them that would make her seek forgiveness?"

"It was not for her self that she begged..." Before I could form the obvious question of whom, she shocked me by revealing one I would never had suspected. "...it was for her brother."

"Panayiotas? Father Kyriazis?"

"She never mentioned him by name. Do you know who he was?"

"He's Father Diogenes' uncle. He was the *Episkopos* here and the reason we came to Greece." I took a few minutes to bring Adonia up to speed on the letter, the photo, Alexandra, Panayiotas' death and what little I knew of his relationship with Ion after the War. Adonia gave me a long almost blank stare, seemingly unsure of her own thoughts, pausing before she spoke, as if to foresee the consequences of revealing what she had never been intended to hear.

"There was some sort of rift. A rift between Ion and Panayiotas. They didn't speak for years."

"I think it was over this woman, Alexandra."

"She didn't say, but whatever it was—it drove a spike in the friendship of these two men."

"We need to speak with Eftehea. I need to know what she knows."

"Neither of us can speak with her of this," said Adonia firmly.

"I don't understand..."

"She was confessing to Ion as if he were her priest. Her words are sacrosanct. Inviolable." I was going to try to dissuade her and frankly I was surprised at her adherence to such a principle given how blatantly she scorned most restraints. But, I was also inspired by her resolve to honor the penitent conversation into which we had irreverently stumbled.

The odds of my ever unraveling the riddle that Eftehea had spun were slim to none, but I could not stop thinking about it. Before Adonia went home that evening, she said something that startled me. We were sitting together in Ion's room—his eyes were slightly ajar but he lay still and detached from our presence, and our conversation.

"What if you find it?" she said, seemingly pulling this line out of thin air. We had been discussing job prospects, places we would love to travel to and whether Greek fishermen were sexier than New York City firemen.

"Find what?"

"What if you find it?" she repeated her same words without dignifying my ruse with any further explanation.

"Then I find it."

"What if it is not meant to be found?"

I thought more carefully this time, and then sadly said, "then it will not be."

"How are you feeling tonight, Ion? There, there, don't try to speak," I said as I wiped his brow with a damp cloth. He was warm. It was warm everywhere, but I was very careful to monitor his body temperature. I was fearful of him developing a fever. He had enough to fight without worrying about some opportunistic infection. His pulse was slow, but it was steady. I reached for *The Illiad*, which sat on his nightstand—a red ribbon attached to the spine marking the place I had left off the evening before.

> *...accept from Vulcan this rich and goodly armor, which no man has ever yet borne upon his shoulders. As she spoke she set the armor before Achilles, and it rang out bravely as she did so. The Myrmidons were struck with awe, and none dared look full at it, for they were afraid; but Achilles was roused to still greater fury, and his eyes gleamed with a fierce light...*

32
EMANCIPATION

"Neotolemus, something strange occurred on my run from Sparta. I saw a bear stalking a defenseless lion cub that lay near its dying mother," said Pheidippides. "Before it could strike, an eagle streamed from the sky and clawed the bear. The bear struck the eagle and then, ignoring the lion—whom it knew could not escape—it turned its attention upon the bird which backed itself to the edge of the cliff. Sensing the inevitable kill, the beast lunged forward and the two fell over the precipice. I presumed them both dead until I saw the eagle rising from beyond the cliff—feathers torn and bloodied—but flying. I saw no more of the bear."

"It is clearly an omen. We must bring this news to Militiades."

"What if its meaning sings disaster?" asked Pheidippides.

"Is it not best to know the truth, no matter the ending of the song?"

"If I am ignorant of its ending perhaps I can change the melody," said Pheidippides.

"Perhaps you only believe you have altered it, but life's consonance remains unchanged."

I went to the church at least once each day now. It wasn't to participate in services, but I wanted to pray. I envied the comfort that so many find in their Gods. I wanted to believe at that moment that there was something or someone divine and just, one with the power to make Ion immortal. I felt strange about invoking a dialogue with the Judeo-Christian God of my upbringing, and of this temple. Where had my faith been all the years before? I was sure that God would see that I only paid homage because I needed something.

All my adult life, God had been an afterthought. I neither strongly believed nor disputed His existence, preferring to hedge my bets by paying lip service to Judaeo-Christian traditions. To concede to His ultimate authority now would also be admitting that I had doubted all these years. I knew I could no longer continue along a path of ambivalence.

Hypocrisy and heresy aside, I still prayed silently. At least I felt safe here in the church. Here I could have a respite from sitting by Ion's bedside and yet still feel close to him. So much at Panteleimon spoke of him and his past, a past I wanted so desperately to share. And I needed to retrieve the journals. I wanted to get them out of the confessional that no longer provided me with the privacy I had earlier enjoyed. My wait to be alone was excruciating. Someone always seemed to be coming in or out of the church, and Sunday was clearly a bad day for ecclesiastical clandestine activity. Eventually all became quiet, save the beating in my chest. I entered the booth, which had served so well as my private reading chamber. Removing the journals from beneath the seat, I hurriedly returned to my room. The risk of Ion finding them still existed, but I took solace in the positive circumstances under which he might stumble upon them—that of him regaining enough strength to walk into my room.

When last I left the man-child Ion, he was lying in a state between life and death on the killing fields of Mesopotamia. I continued reading from his entry of August Nineteenth.

19 August 1936

I could not breathe as I struggled to utter what I was sure was true, "I'm dead," but no words passed my lips. There was no sound but a hollow ringing like the wind, and I could feel blood oozing from both ears. I tried vainly again to breathe and to speak, "I'm dead, I'm dead," the words realizing themselves in my mind the way the letters on a headstone begin to appear on a grave rubbing. I was on my back and staring up. There was no tent any longer, and the sky was whirling black smoke punctuated by flashes of sulphurous light. The acrid stench of burning flesh filled my nostrils and choked me. I turned on my side, and felt a sharp pain shoot down my spine. Small fires were roasting bits of black charred wood and twisted metal. But for the pain, I would have thought I was dead and crossed into hell. But then, it occurred to me I was in hell, just still alive. I was myself utterly alone, a piece of burnt material in a world now devoid of life. I felt the shells bursting nearby as the earth trembled but I was too numb to move to save myself.

What I wanted most at that moment was to die, and I closed my eyes to assist the inevitable, hoping a British round would find its mark and deal me a swift end. With my eyes closed and drifting, I felt something touching my face. I smiled, thinking it was the hand of my mother come to gather me home. I felt distress as it stopped and then started again but not so gently. My eyes opened, angry at having my sweet death so interrupted only to find brown eyes staring back at me.

I stared at her and forced my mind to catch up with the revelation that she too was still alive, in this waste, and I knew her. Her smooth tan skin was caked with mud and soot, and her clothes were soaked in dark blood. I could see that she was not bleeding but had been drenched by the torrent that had decimated the others. At that moment, I felt like one submerged in water, barely able to breathe but knowing my task. I had to swim swiftly to the light, to the air, and to life again.

"Elektra?" I mouthed the word, still not sure if sound came out or if I had yelled the name at her. Alexandra shook her head. I knew her mother was gone.

I knew that there were choices, none of them good. I acted immediately on one. I was going to take Alexandra with me and head for the British lines. It was her only chance—mine no longer mattered.

The pain I felt as I pushed myself up was too intense to describe but my sense of urgency to get Alexandra away from this place enabled me to bear it. Alexandra could barely stand—I would have to carry her if she was to survive. I looked around and found a bloodstained swatch of canvas from the shredded tent. It was what I needed. I pulled it around my shoulders and was relieved to see that it was long enough. Tying the two ends so as to make a wrap across my chest, I pushed out against it with my hand to make sure it was secure. Staggering over to Alexandra, I could see her look up at me quizzically. With nothing said, I knelt down before her and motioned for her to climb onto my back and into the harness. She seemed to know exactly what to do, and I felt her mild weight shifting down my shoulders as she slid into it. It felt good to feel her wrap her hands around my shoulders. I never wanted her to become lost and that anxiety jabbed me at that moment like a hot piece of shrapnel. My amulet bracelet, the one that Kalos passed on, would be hers. If we were ever separated and I didn't make it, they would know her to be Greek, and not the enemy. I untied it and slipped it around her wrist and tied it securely—we were now bound by this simple piece of string and bronze.

It was easy to know where to go—right in the direction of the oncoming shells. They existed for me only in their flashes of light and earth stirring vibrations. At first, I walked slowly and deliberately, attempting to fix just the right spot on the horizon toward which to aim myself. Picking up speed I broke into a jog, dodging the patches of flame, twisted metal and twisted bodies. Nothing could be alive in this no man's land. I had to look down but also to look ahead at the same time. We were exposed and vulnerable to everything. All I could feel was the hollow rhythm of my accelerated breathing and pounding heart.

A couple of strewn bodies just beyond the edge of our encampment told me I had entered the minefield. Having been an instrument of planting them, I knew roughly how we had laid them out, but randomness is hard to remember. Several dead horses and one overturned armored artillery truck had already done some of the work of locating them for me. I moved faster and faster, aware only of the precious cargo I carried. Soon enough I was in open wasteland with nothing above me but the silent display of shells bursting, little aware of how utterly destroyed the landscape had already become.

The horizon was soon interrupted by the berms of the British trenches—trenches that we had dug a year earlier. I knew they had snipers but I couldn't stop—that would have made matters worse. My vision was acute, perhaps intensified by my loss of hearing, but the only light came from the exploding howitzers and the periodic flares, which the Brits fired over the landscape to aid their snipers. I could make out men scurrying along a barbed wire fence, my only evidence of them the occasional glint of their bayonets, and shadows cast by their helmets.

I tried to shout but it had all the effect of a scream in a nightmare. Two men sprang out of what must have been a small, makeshift trench and headed straight for me. I raised my arms at them to show them I was unarmed. They kept coming, their blue steel bayonets fixed. In night's silent avalanche of heat and dust, I could see them changing to a dance-like suspended motion and then stopping dead in their tracks as I neared. I felt myself stopping and staring at their raised weapons.

Suddenly, the man on the left pushed his comrade's rifle aside just as a flash of light and smoke flared from its narrow mouth. I felt a slight disturbance of air near my head as its projectile whizzed past me, cutting a hollow path through the dense air around me. I was too stunned and fatigued by all that had already happened to even be aroused by this latest of threats to my life. The two looked at each other with puzzled glances and approached me cautiously with their weapons at the ready. I could see the one who had hesitated look behind me to confirm what he thought he had seen in the shadows.

Though they kept their muzzles trained on me, they would not fire again—they had seen Alexandra. I had navigated the abyss of the battlefield—but it was she who had saved us both.

I tossed and turned all night long. So little happened during my long day of sitting vigil with Ion, yet so much was draining me. Adonia arrived before lunch the next day, as she had every day. I watched as she took out her purse to pay the taxi driver. I went to bring her money.

"What in the world are you doing?" she said with surprise.

"You're spending so much on taxis this week, may I..."

"I think I might have to put my hands over my ears," she said, pretending to cover them.

"Please Adonia..."

"Not a prayer. Think of all the money I save every year by not owning a car in Athens," she laughed.

"All right. But you must promise to come to visit me and Ion in New York."

"It sounds like a splendid idea. How is he doing today, love?"

"I think a little better, but I don't know anymore."

"I'm sure he's improving. Yesterday, I noticed a little more color in his cheeks."

"Really?"

"No question about it." If she were fibbing, I was too grateful to find out.

"I'm starving by the way, but I didn't know if you had eaten yet or not."

"I haven't."

"Perfect. Let's sit outside." I loved the absence of mosquitoes here—on Long Island in summer, they hunt in packs.

We sat in the lazy afternoon sun after consuming a light, delicious meal, we had prepared together.

"Another glass?" she asked me, holding up the bottle of wine. It was made from grapes grown on the island of Thira, or Santorini, as it is more popularly known.

"If I do, I'll probably end up napping like a child all afternoon."

"And why not? Why should children have all the fun?"

"Was it hard... all those years not being able to make love with Niko?"

"True enough, he was...changed—but we never stopped making love. He stroked my hair at night when I'd awaken screaming. He'd wipe my tears when my heart was sullen. And he'd sing away my fears when all seemed hopeless. No man could have made love to me more."

"Did you ever think you'd find someone after him?" I asked, almost apprehensively, still unsure of how deeply I could delve into her personal life, and wary that at any moment I might tread upon some sacred memory.

"Yes, at least I hoped." One thing that I learned to predict about Adonia was that she was always defying prediction. I usually imagined several answers to any question I asked her, any good attorney does that by habit, but often she would find the one response that had eluded my speculation.

"Really?"

"Does that surprise you?

"Well, yes, a little."

"Why?"

"I don't know why. Perhaps it's because you were so in love."

"Ah, I understand. You expected me to say something like 'I know I could never find another like him,' or 'how could I ever find love after what we had shared.'"

"Yeah, either of those would have sufficed."

"Well, I probably will never find another like him, and I doubt I will ever feel again the kind of love that still burns within me for that beautiful fisherman from Galaxidi."

"I don't understand..."

"It doesn't mean I can't try to. Why shouldn't a woman always be a woman?"

"I'm sorry, Adonia, if I've pried into a sensitive area."

"My non-sensitive areas are not worth prying into," she smiled. "They bore even me."

"It just seems hard for me to imagine finding someone else."

"If I had died and Niko lived, I would wish him the happiness that he brought me every day."

"If you could have looked down, would you really be happy seeing him with another in his arms?"

She thought about my question for a moment, then spoke, very deliberately, "If not me, I would hope he'd have found someone like you."

Ion had taken some solid food last evening. He was still weak but his vital signs had stabilized. It was difficult for him to swallow. To keep him hydrated, I would place small shavings of ice on his tongue, letting the warmth of his mouth melt it.

"Good morning, Ion."

No answer. I wasn't concerned, I hadn't really expected one. Our dialogues of the past days had been short one voice, but I could feel his thoughts.

"I hope you slept well. It's a beautiful day outside. Maybe later we can get you some fresh air." I knew he wouldn't be moving anytime today, but I liked to keep his spirits up by speaking only of simple things, small steps, and never a horizon beyond a few hours. I continued my chatter, straightening up the room a bit as I rambled on.

"Ion, are you awake? Can you hear me?" I said, whispering into his ear. I was resting my cheek against his and whispering when a voice from behind startled me.

"Oh, I'm sorry Marianna, I didn't realize that you were in the middle of something," said Father Diogenes, as he came into the room. I rose and spun around.

"It's okay, Yiannis. I was just straightening Ion's pillows."

"How is my favorite athlete doing today?"

"He's quite a competitor."

"How are you holding up?" The way he asked me made me feel that he was more concerned for the nurse than the patient. I hadn't looked at myself for days—I guess the frayed edges were beginning to show.

"I'm fine, really I am."

"Good, I'm glad to hear that. Remember, you need rest too."

"There's no time for..."

"You'll be much more helpful to all of us healthy," he said. "The stress you're under is showing. You need to slow down."

"I will."

"Even here in Marathon the office hasn't seemed far behind you."

"Oh, it's far behind me now!"

"Really?"

"I tendered my resignation the day I returned." As I said these words, I thought I saw Ion stirring.

"That took great courage," said Father Diogenes.

"I hope you're right, Yiannis. I hope I didn't just lose my cool and ruin something I had worked towards my whole life."

"Do you think you lost something?"

"That's the funny thing. My rational mind tells me that I was crazy to quit, but my soul feels unburdened, as if I am finally free to look ahead to the future."

"And the present?"

"All I can feel right now, lies here in this room."

"I understand."

I opened to Book XXIII and continued my reading:

...So long as the gods held themselves aloof from mortal warriors the Achaeans were triumphant, for Achilles who had long refused to fight was now with them. There was not a Trojan but his limbs failed him for fear as he beheld the fleet son of Peleus all glorious in his armor, and looking like Mars himself...

In mid-sentence, Ion reached his hand out towards me, gesturing me closer.

"You quit?" he uttered.

"Yes, Ion. But don't you worry, everything will be fine. I've got plenty of savings and I know I'll find something better soon, I'm sure of it. So don't you worry about me."

"I'm so proud," he said, but his words did not come easily. They squeaked out of a contorted mouth. But he had spoken. Miracle number two.

"I guess you have known me longer than any one else alive."

"Always, Marianna, always, since a thousand ships were launched, I'm sure."

"Shh, don't try to speak anymore," I said as his eyelids slid lower and closed—though I knew he was struggling to stay awake. I waited until he had fallen into sleep. In that state, I could see more readily the perfection of his countenance and its stoic indifference to time.

I too must have dozed off, snuggled in the chair that had been moved into Ion's room for me. As the only piece of upholstered furniture in the entire house, it was a godsend. Ion was sleeping. I think he had pushed himself too hard today. I needed to return to my room, but I was wary of him being all alone, especially now that he was becoming more lucent. I tied a small pewter bell to his right wrist so that I could hear its ringing should Ion suddenly stir or need to summon me without using his weakened voice.

I rejoined my young hero in Mesopotamia.

20 August 1936

Commencing the Spring of 1917, I would spend fifteen months in a British prisoner-of-war camp or, as the Brits would quip 'as a guest of His Majesty.' The gatekeeper turned inmate—how fickle are the fortunes of war. But far more ironic was where I was taken. Of all the places that detainees could be moved, I was brought back to Limnos, to the military base at Mudros. I left as a slave and returned as one, though to a different master. On the whole, we weren't treated that poorly, but beyond the barbed wire fences I could see the hill underneath which the British and French had buried their dead from the failed invasion of Gallipoli.

21 August 1936

I became sick, and languished for several months after arriving back on Limnos. Compounding my weakened state were the rations we were prescribed. It wasn't that the food was especially bad, certainly no more spoiled or tainted than the rations I ate as a Turkish regular, but my digestion wasn't used to the higher fat content of a British diet.

I won't describe to you the dangers of being a prisoner of war. My greatest threat came not from my captors, but from within—from my fellow prisoners. I kept mostly to myself, befriending a rather large and burly prisoner named Ozbudun. I worked as his servant. It seems a funny concept now to have been a slave within a prison camp. Fortunately for me, his preferences did not lie with young boys, though I cannot say he was the rule. In return for my chores, as unpleasant as they were, he kept me safe.

I had not seen Alexandra since the day we breached the battlefield's inferno and crossed the British lines. We had been immediately separated and I fear that her last view of me was my brutal welcome to the enemy's camp—though I felt no more their enemy than a mule does. But I had the misfortune of striding in wearing the wrong uniform. I would have been better off entering their sights naked for all the uniform meant to me. I was beaten, kicked and verbally abused. The blood-lust ran high from the sting of battle, or perhaps from the absence of it, and these young men needed to exact retribution for the march from Al-Kut.

23 August 1936

Real news reports rarely reach POW's, but rumors do. And they are often swifter and more accurate than that which appears in the papers. For days, rumors had been circulating about an armistice between the Ottomans and the British. It was years after the war that I learned the Armistice ending the Ottoman reign had been signed in the Bay of Mudros, aboard a British Battleship named the Agamemnon*—as if in remembrance of the fall of another Turkish Empire.*

But in the absence of this knowledge, I found myself, with hundreds of other prisoners, on a ship bound for the Suez Canal. We were disembarked in Palestine, and then taken by rail to Damascus. My English, though beginning to take root, was not sufficient to comprehend the circumstances of my recent uprooting. A prisoner, like a slave, learns the ebbs and flows of his environment, and adapts to them to maximize survival. Change means uncertainty, and uncertainty is a slave's worst fear.

Not long after my arrival in Palestine, I was brought into the commanding officer's tent. At first I was worried. Behind the Ottoman lines, being called before such a high-ranking officer never brought with it good tidings. He made me sign something that I could not read.

Nor could I write, but an "X" apparently sufficed.

My clothes had become unwearable, and with Ozbudun's help, I had acquired some simple khakis. So there I stood, in my terribly ill fitting clothes like a beggar, flanked on both sides by two perfectly groomed soldiers of His Majesty's 19th Hussars. They escorted me to the large wooden gates protecting the fort at Damascus. Upon a crisply barked signal from one of the guards at the gate, it was opened and I walked through alone. It was 1918. Fifteen years old, without a country, I was an orphan of the world.

In an instant, the large doors closed behind me and I stared across the unbroken desert—a free man for the first time in my life.

33
A FORTUITOUS TRESPASS

"Militiades, there is news from our scouts," said the messenger who had come into the archon's tent. "Darius' ships begin to take on provisions to sail."

"And his men?"

"Some begin to embark, others remain as they were. Perhaps he chooses to withdraw," said a hopeful messenger.

"This is the move I had feared most. You have done well, Telys. Now, go quickly, summon Callimachus—there is little time to spare."

"What is it Militiades?" asked Aristagoras, one of the General's most trustworthy advisors.

"He divides his force, Ari. One to pin us here, the other to sail towards our city."

"What can we do?" continued Aristagoras. "If we remain, Athens is unguarded, if we march, he will crush us from our rear. What choice is left to us?"

"Attack!"

9 September 1936

I thought about her a lot. Both of them, actually. Elektra and Alexandra. Both had kept me going when I thought that all was lost. Now they were both gone. One to the underworld, the other to another world.

Without any currency or notion of what my future would be, I made my way to Athens. My odyssey would first lead me through Palestine, Alexandria, Tunisia, Sicily and Crete. It took me nearly three years, and in that time, I survived by working any jobs I could find. I dug trenches for railroad lines, I worked in mines, I cleaned stables and latrines. No task was beneath me. I finally made my way into Greece through Macedonia, traveling on the same route that Philip, and then his son had taken in their conquest of Attica. I had never been to any part of Greece except Limnos. I had been so removed from my ancestry that I felt as out of place amongst my own people as Moses did upon returning to his Levite family.

I entered Athens with the pride of a conquering hero, though not even the lowliest beggar noticed me as I made my way through the noisy and congested streets. I brought nothing with me but the clothes on my back and the knowledge that I could survive anything.

Greece is surrounded on all sides by water, and fishing villages dot her thousands of kilometers of coastline. There is work for an energetic youth who loves the sea, who works until his fingers are raw and numb, who doesn't complain of the exhausting hours and is willing to risk his life. I had no problem with the latter three, but I had never developed a love of the sea. She and I were like lovers who squabbled when together—preferring to admire each other from afar. To Odysseus, the sea meant troubles. On land he was a king of men, but there, in the greenish-blue froth, he was a pawn to the whimsical moods of the Gods. I had no place in the realm of Poseidon—my destiny lay on the land, reliant on my own feet and their ability to carry me wherever I chose to go.

One day I happened upon the farm of Stavrakas Demosthetiges and his wife Katrina. They lived, with their only child, Filologos, in Kephisia—northeast of Athens. I think Stavrakas was skeptical of my ability to work when he first laid eyes on me. I had lost weight from a body already thinned by nature. I offered to work for one year with my only pay being food and a dry place to sleep. I think his wife was even more skeptical, but then Stavrakas said, "Why not? Let's give the boy a chance. Let's see if he can handle a hard day's work on a farm. Chances are he'll disappear like a ghost after the first few days in the fields—if he can bear the activity that long." I thanked him profusely. Plowing fields to plant life was hard work, but far more rewarding than digging trenches from which to take life or digging graves in which to bury lives we had taken.

I soon became invaluable not only to the farm, but also to the Demothestiges' household. I was performing many of the same tasks that I had done for my masters in Hamdibey, but it was as diifferent as the taste of the bitter root is from honey. I was a free man, free to come and go as I pleased, and the sweat of my brow was appreciated, not presumed. After a few months, Stavrakas said he wanted to pay me, but I insisted on our keeping the original terms of our agreement.

As a slave, I had watched men taking what was not theirs. Filologos, too, seemed to enjoy living off the hard work of others. He barely participated in the working of the farm, and I never felt a warmth from him, if anything, the more affection that his father displayed towards me, the more enmity he harbored. He left Kephisia two years after I had arrived on the farm, pursuing a woman he had fallen in love with. He appeared back home only sporadically—never offering help—always seeking it, usually in the form of money to feed his dilettante lifestyle. Stavrakas' disappointment was evident, though he bore his shame in silence.

I had never thought of my stay in Kephisia as anything but temporary, though I had no idea of what may lay after this, or what path I may have been on. Perhaps I was afraid of any sense of permanency, given the instability of my life, and the fear of becoming attached—everything I had ever touched had proven itself to be fleeting. Life itself appeared as unstable as wispy clouds, easily dispersed by the changing winds.

One day, I had to run an errand into Athens. Stavrakas had an old vehicle, but I had never learned to drive. Besides, the few roads that existed were highly unreliable. I needed to retrieve some medication for my employer, so I took off over the hills on foot. It was a distance of only 20 kilometers, and by leaving at dawn, I would be able to return by nightfall. I hurried, not driven by any sense of emergency. I just didn't want to be traversing the uneven route in darkness. This was not the first time I had made this journey, and as I ran through the neighboring villages and farms, many waived at me as I passed. I saw a man that I had never seen before. That he was unknown was not itself unusual, but the way he looked at me as I crossed his vision perturbed me greatly. He eyed me carefully, almost studying me, as I ran across what I assumed was his farm. I feared that he was bothered by my trespass, but he said nothing.

Later that afternoon, after I had secured possession of the parcel, I began the long trek back to the home of Stavrakas. I contemplated avoiding the older gentleman's property altogether, but doing so, given the unusual terrain, would have added many kilometers to my journey, and it was already getting dark. I assumed that the twilight would aid me in slipping through his property unnoticed. I did not desire any confrontation.

All seemed to be going well. I saw no one about, and smoke rose from his small hut in the distance leading me to believe that he and his family were inside having their supper, or better for me, retired for the night.

"You are quite sure-footed on these rocky paths, my son," came a voice from behind me, almost causing me to loose that sure-footedness. It was he, the man I had hoped to avoid. He was following me, stride for stride, dressed in nothing but shorts. I guessed him to be in his fifties, but his body was as lean and fit as any athlete of twenty.

"I am so sorry, sir. I didn't mean any disrespect by crossing your land without permission." I was about to inform him of the details of my mission, assuming that its medical nature would assuage him from being angry. But he did not seem to be interested in why I ran, only that I did.

"How far?" he asked.

"From Kephisia to Athens and back," I answered, being unsure of the exact distance and not knowing why he had asked, but comforted that his tone was not hostile.

"That's a good run. May I join you for a while?" I didn't know what he expected of me, but the calmness of his voice reassured me, and I was happy to have some company.

We ran together, bounding over the earth, sidestepping rocks as they appeared in our dimly lit path. He made the exercise seem fun, and soon we were laughing, though nothing had been said.

"You are a good runner," I said, without realizing how patronizing it sounded. "Did you ever compete?"

"Once. A long time ago."

"Did you..."

"Win? Yes."

"That must have been a great moment..."

"I have had greater since."

"Greater?"

"As will you."

"What do you think of when you run?" I asked him after a few minutes of silence.

"Of how soft the earth is."

"The ground?"

"No, the whole Earth. She lets me escape from her embrace for a little while when I run—knowing that I will return to her." I felt as if he understood me like no other could have—that feeling of freedom from everything, even from the earth herself.

"It's one of the only things that has ever come easily to me," I said to him.

"You have the feet of a runner and the heart of a champion. Perhaps you will be a future Olympian."

"My patron told me that a Greek has not won since Spyridon Louis in 1896."

"Then you will have to run like him, won't you?" he said as he ran past me again. For some of the way, we ran side by side, but in places, the path narrowed or disappeared completely. In those stretches we would trade off sprinting one after the other through sharp and unexpected turns. Granted, I had been running longer, but I could barely keep pace with him, he moved about the rugged hills like a jackrabbit being pursued by a fox.

"I doubt that will be possible," I said.

"Why not? I see his younger legs in you now."

"Be careful that he doesn't hear you insult him like that," I laughed. He was about thirty paces ahead of me, but I was gaining on him. "The only similarity between my legs and Spyridon's is their quantity."

"He learned to run in these very hills, on the very ground you are now crossing," he said to me as I passed him.

"Running on these hills is about the closest I will ever get to him, or his ability. I doubt I will ever follow in his footsteps," I said to him over my shoulder.

"Then make your own."

After about three kilometers, the older man said, "I wish I could run with you the entire way, I feel as if I could keep going all night. Thank you, you've let an old man feel thirty years younger again."

"That's funny, you made me feel thirty years older," I said.

"We are both of an ancient breed, running is in our blood. Next time you pass here, I insist that you share a meal with me. I have little to offer, but you will be welcome in my home." And with that, he veered off and began to run back in the direction from which we had just come. I turned to watch him. His body knew no age. It seemed lighter than the air around him, moving fluidly through space.

By the time I had arrived home, Stavrakas was asleep. In the morning, I gave him the medication, which had a favorable effect. I told him of the strange man I had met on the way. Stavrakas listened to the story not saying a word. But after my tale, he went to his desk to retrieve some old newspaper clippings. On the yellowed page, of the dried paper, was a picture of the man I had encountered. He was much younger in the photo, but there was no mistaking it, it was him. The headline of this ancient paper merely read, "Olympic Hero Returns to Amarousi."

I would eventually return to break bread with him. It was a chance meeting that would change my life. Spyridon was my inspiration. He trained with me, sweated with me, and was with me in defeat and in glory. His tutelage forged my self-confidence and this skill would lead me far away to a new land—America.

But my plans to move on from Stavrakas' farm would have to wait for many years. He and his wife fell ill in the winter of 1925. She would not see the spring, but he recovered. He would live for many years, but his illness weakened him and prevented him from performing many of the duties that maintaining his lands required. I had become like a son to him, in many ways more so than the one born of his seed. This fact angered Filologos, who visited infrequently, ostensibly, I believe, to keep an eye on his inheritance. Once, while his father lay sleeping in the next room he said to me, "Don't count on getting the farm. I am his blood, don't ever forget it."

"I think only of his life, not his death, and I make no claims on him in either world." What he could never realize is that I never envied him his farm; I envied his having a father. I never thought about profiting from Stavrakas' death. But I made a vow to myself to remain in his service as long as he needed me—which turned out to be the remaining few years of his life.

As I had expected, his son, who had by now become estranged, showed up to collect what was his "due" as the only heir. It didn't matter to me at all. The kindness that his father had bestowed upon me was worth more than all the acres of land on the farm. As if to clear his conscience, Filologos offered me a thousand drachmas for my years of service. I was no longer needed on the farm, as he had decided to sell it as soon as his father died. I took it from him, but as I left Kephisia, I stopped off at Agios Constantine and gave it to the Papas. I knew those few drachmas would be the only part of my benefactor's estate to go to good use.

In the spring of 1932, I bid him and my homeland farewell. Six weeks and six thousand kilometers later, I saw the Statue of Liberty for the first time—becoming one more in the vast sea of immigrants seeking a new life on America's shores. At Ellis Island, I spoke Kalos' words with pride as the name "Theodore" was written on my immigration form and I was allowed to pass, a new chapter in my life about to begin. As I paced the deck tonight, I thought about that moment. By tomorrow afternoon, her weathered form will present herself to me again—appearing out of the fog that blankets the sea before us.

I put down the thin volume. I was beginning to see my life from a different perspective. When I thought about Ion, and how much he had overcome, and how easily it would have been for him to quit in despair—my own problems seemed more trivial.

I had lost track of the time, only realizing how long I had been reading when the sky above Panteleimon began to lighten. All was quiet. Ion's bell had not tolled for me.

34
HADRIAN'S ARCH

"Attack? He outnumbers us by three men to one," replied a startled Callimachus, who had entered the tent and stood beside Militiades.

"Precisely why the Mede will be surprised. He will surely think us mad for contemplating it."

"Yes, and with good reason—it is mad!"

"And our only hope." said Militiades.

"How do the others vote?" asked Callimachus.

"We ten Generals are divided evenly. Only you can now decide whether to lead Athens to slavery or to freedom. Heed my advice and we shall celebrate victory with all of Hellas. Attach yourself to those who would remain passive and you will surely condemn our race to slavery."

When Militiades and Pheidippides were left alone in the General's tent, the older man turned to Pheidippides and said, "Have faith in the Gods and the man to your right. Now, tell me of your run from Sparta, and of what you saw during your journey."

Now that my time was my own, I spent as much of it as I could the next day reading excerpts from Ion's journal. He was making progress and we would have much to discuss when he was feeling better. I needed to finish his story so that I could understand what he wouldn't tell me before I went back to New York—why we had really come to Greece.

According to the dates, the second journal was written during 1948. Ion recalled his earlier observations on Hitler and the Third Reich, and mentioned again the words of Spyridon when he had prophesized that only God would pass final judgment.

Ion had acclimatized himself to life in his new home. He had settled in Astoria, Queens, a logical starting point for a young Greek immigrant, especially one without a family. He had taken a job with E.F. Hutton, as a runner, though the longest distance he would have to travel was confined to the narrow streets below Trinity Church. He delivered trade blotters and stock certificates long before the days of electronic clearing.

By night, Ion studied at the Actor's Studio in the west forties near Hell's Kitchen. Side by side with unknowns who would one day become household names, he studied the thespian arts, offering himself as a dancer when roles demanded that particular talent.

31 July 1948

I haven't written for so long. The world had become impossible to describe. The entire world, I am loathe to call it civilization, has been torn apart by a cataclysm that chroniclers have called "World War II." These same pundits, to keep the pretense of orderly nomenclature, renamed the "war to end all wars" the First World War, demoting it from its noble title as the "Great War." If the first one revealed the fault line of the world, its successor shattered it. The century into which I was born and will most likely die has seen more human carnage than all previous centuries combined.

The world at the beginning of my life was hardly innocent or civilized. In fact, it was on the verge of moral and spiritual bankruptcy. Was the world really ready for a new birth of freedom? The so-called crusaders for the volk, the fascists on the right and the communists on the left proved worse than the royal tyrants. And the promises of democracy through capitalism had turned to festering wounds of dust bowls, shantytowns, and soup kitchens. And from the chaos arose two powers, immersed in a cold war of hate and suspicion. One of them still looming over Europe like the dark clouds of an ancient barbarian host.

And at the epicenter of this titanic struggle was Berlin. It is painful now to remember how I stood with others in a ritual of competition and friendship that supposedly would link us to the highest ideals of Athenian civilization. Instead, it turned out to be an omen heralding one of the most horrific tyrannies since Caligula. I remembered the only time I had been in that city—which had advanced the arts and sciences to new heights—now laying in smoldering ruins. It was exactly twelve years ago from this night. I thought about my evening at the Hofbrau with those brash young boys who predicted that Hitler was bluffing, and if he weren't that they'd personally "kick his arse" back to Berlin. Hitler would be sent back to Berlin, taking his own life in a bunker—but only after causing the deaths of over 30 million people and destroying the homes, lives and bodies of countless more millions. The world sat on the precipice of a new and more dreadful dark age—staring into the eyes of Hades himself—he just happened to blink first

I thought of Ernest Harper and "Black" Jack Cunningham—two of the athletes I had met the night of the opening ceremonies. Young and cocky and in their physical prime, accustomed to the precision of competition, though ignorant of how imprecise war is—and how naïve the concept of winning and losing is in that most terrible of human endeavors. They both took home silver medals in their events, but I wonder what happened to them. Did they enlist? Was Ernest killed above the cliffs of Dover dog-fighting the Luftwaffe? Did "Black" Jack fall on Omaha Beach? Or perhaps they are home right now, having summer barbecues with their families because they were able to kill the sons of others who still mourn at empty tables.

It was at this point in this second volume that the emphasis shifted from painfully culled anamneses to a more extemporaneous account of his experience.

1 August 1948

I arrived here in Athens for the first time in nearly seven years. It may as well have been a hundred, or a thousand—anything before the war now appears like a different universe. There is so much misery all around me that sometimes I feel like I have returned to the hopelessness of the desert and a trench along the Dyala River.

I am here to participate in an alumni gathering of Panhellenic athletes. It was organized by local and Greco-American groups to help dedicate the new sports facility at the American College of Greece. They have asked me to be one of the speakers at the ceremony, a task I do not relish, as I am very shy if more than one person is listening to me at a time. My anxiety was furthered by the fact that I wondered whether some in the audience would see me as having fled here for the comforts and safety of America, while they bore the brunt of the Hun's wrath.

Despite the war-torn landscape, and these fears, I feel quite good, more than that, I feel a growing excitement. But it is not because I have come back to visit my adopted city or the Panhellenic reunion. It is because of a letter I received in the mail just three days before I left New York. It is amazing that she had the tenacity to find me. I had thought about trying to locate her many times, but never had the impetus to search, certain that my efforts would be in vain. I knew her mother's surname—Leontokardis—but that was as useful as trying to find a drop of rain in the ocean.

The letter said she would be in Athens when I arrived, but whether she lived there or was just passing through was a mystery to me. Her tone was almost apologetic, as if she wasn't sure that I wanted to be reminded of her and that brutal time. She suggested that we might meet for a café or a short walk. I wondered how well she remembered that time. How could she not connect me with the violent death of her mother? Would meeting me open wounds or mean closure on that terrible episode?

I couldn't be sure of what she wanted, or what she was feeling, but I wanted to see her, even if for just a few minutes. She was the only person I knew who had witnessed that extraordinary time.

I telegrammed her that I would arrive on the first, but would be occupied for two days with the event for which I had been invited. I suggested a time and a place that we could meet, but having no way to receive messages, I could only hope she would be there when I arrived. I wondered what had brought her back as I too found myself drawn to a rendezvous with my past—or perhaps with my future.

I traveled alone, but this had not been my original plan. I had hoped that my wife, Genevieve, would accompany me. Things are strained between us, and I viewed this trip as a chance for her to learn something of that past. She got a part in a summer stock performance of "The Taming of the Shrew."My disappointment in her decision was tempered by the anticipation of seeing Elektra's daughter once more.

4 August 1948

Fifteen minutes had already seemed like hours so great was my anticipation or, rather, my anxiety. I did not know what to expect but I had known in some dim way that I was playing with fire. This was a relationship that had been forged under the most painful circumstances imaginable. She had seen me first in the uniform of her captors, the uniform of the executioners of her father. Though I had rescued her, from her perspective, the experience must have only been terrifying. Being carried through killing fields and into the waiting guns that had, ironically, killed her mother in one swift explosion. What was I trying to recapture? A relationship that wasn't there but that somehow I wanted to be there. We had, after all, been each other's salvation but that was something one could only see long after the fact.

So many years had elapsed since then, and I so much wanted to recover something from that rapidly disappearing past. Fear had overtaken me, fear that perhaps this meeting was wrong, and could lead either to the reopening of old wounds or, at the very least, disappointment. There was also the vague fear that although she had initiated contact, she was still angry about what happened then or was suffering even worse now. While I mustered the courage to follow through with this meeting, I felt panicked as I realized that more than half an hour had passed. Perhaps she had succumbed to the sane realization that this meeting was a mistake.

The perimeter of my gaze widened by the minute, as I stood there under Hadrian's Arch scanning the crowds. On one or two occasions my heart jumped as I imagined her form coming towards me, only to be disappointed and even a little embarrassed that I had stared with such longing for someone who was no doubt indifferent to me. I knew that there could only be three reasons for her not to be there: she was still on her way, she had never received my telegram, or, finally, that she decided not to come.

I heard the church bells of Agia Ekaterini chiming nearby, signaling to me that the noon hour had passed. It was time for me to go, and I stepped into the shadows now being cast by these Roman ruins. Shifting between disappointment and relief, I could not help feeling unnerved. I wanted to escape the scene quickly but somehow also , wanted to just sit and collect my thoughts.

I walked through the gardens and chose a bench, unoccupied either by the old feeding pigeons or the young feeding each other's desires. As I sat, a flock of pigeons wandered up to me hoping that I too had something to offer. But I had nothing, and I was too distracted to shoo them away. I listened to their whimsical cooing and the ruffling of their feathers as they strutted ever closer.

With a burst that stunned me, they all flew off at once and where they had once been, I saw a figure obscured by the sun behind her head. She stepped forward and reality outran anything I could have imagined. The woman who stood before me was framed by the same golden tresses that had haloed the soot-covered face of a young girl I had seen over three decades before.

"I assumed you wouldn't make it," I spoke first, unsure of what to say.

"I am here."

"How did you find me in the park?"

"I had been watching you under the arch for almost an hour."

I was so taken aback, that I hesitated before responding. She didn't have to tell me that she had been considering aborting our meeting. I motioned for her to sit next to me.

"It's incredible isn't it?" I asked.

"It is?"

"Yes, the arch. Built so well by the conquering Romans."

She laughed, and I was relieved—for laughter is the mark of a full-souled human being.

We spent several hours in the park, divided between sitting on the benches and walking the park's bridle paths. I was far too distracted to remember time. Silences were broken by intermittent conversation that circled the horror that had thrown us together. We began to fill in the gaps between us.

Finally we came back to where we had started, and once again took to the same bench. Long shadows on the ground and the setting sun's light through the trees was the only indication that any time had elapsed. We had been bonded forever in one single night in the intense fires of survival, and yet we were complete strangers to each other. Though we strolled as lovers might through the flowers and trees of the park, we did not hold hands, though several times I was tempted to embrace her, resisting for fear that she would misinterpret my actions.

"How did you find me? I didn't think you ever knew my name."

"I saw you, once, twelve years ago."

"That was you? There in the crowd as I ran with the Torch?"

"Yes. I wouldn't have missed you for the world. I even took this," she said as she produced a photo of me in mid-stride. She also unfolded a newspaper clipping which showed a picture of me taken in 1928 at the Panhellenic Games as I stood barefoot before Episkopos Athas—receiving the cup of victory. The headline of the article read "Former Greek Marathoner to Carry Torch."

"I saw that mark on your ankle," she added, referring to the scar I received when I was branded as a runaway slave. She had only seen it one time—the night I carried her, bare legged, through no man's land to safety.

"I can't imagine you being in Nazi Germany."

"Shh. We have shared so little tranquility—let us not break the serenity of this moment by speaking of such unpleasant times."

As we sat together, I felt her head rest on my shoulder. The tenderness of her gesture emboldened me. I wanted to talk about that night as if it was a locked door that we needed to unlock before we could move forward. I didn't know if the moment was yet right, but I reached out my hand to test the waters.

Taking her left hand in mine, I felt her fingers curling softly until they were interwoven with mine—my heart beat faster in anticipation of peeling back her emotions, buried under layers of sand, blood and time.

"You still wear it."

"Always," she whispered as she took her other hand and fingered the now darkened leather strap which looped around her wrist, held

fast by a knot tied by a terrified fourteen year old as the heavens crashed to earth.

She lifted her head and as I looked into her eyes, the deep brown of her irises burned intensely. I shook my head to remind me that we were here in the safety of Athens, and not back in the hellish landscape not even Dante could describe. There was such pain and beauty in these orbs. I saw decades of scars and disappointment. For an instant, I saw them calling out for me to take them—to shield them from the burning lights.

We were as if in a dream and the world around us seemed to float in silent and graceful movements. Her eyes gradually softened—I watched as she moistened her lips, making them glisten in the fading rays of an Athenian sunset.

Like a bursting shell, the high-pitched screech of an automobile's tires and the sounds of smashing glass and metal crushing metal jarred us from our reverie.

"I have to go," she suddenly said, jerking her head back.

"So soon?"

"I'm sorry, I have to go. It's getting late."

"Will I see you again?"

"I'm not sure, well yes. Yes, I think so."

"How do I reach you?"

"I can't...Where are you staying in Athens?"

"Odos Kyristou 23. The flat of Spinos. But, wait, what about you?"

"I have to go," she said, as she took a step back from me. She ran out through the Xenofontos Gate and to the edge of Syntagma Square. I panicked realizing that I had no way to reach her and no way of knowing whether she really wanted me to. I ran after her into the Square and looked around for her telltale golden hair, but it was nowhere to be seen.

6 August 1948

No contact. I felt helpless, not believing I had let her walk away without first giving me some way of contacting her. What if she had forgotten my address? What if she came by when I was out? The possibilities were killing me as much as the real chance that she had taken my address knowing full well that she would never avail herself of it.

I stayed in the apartment of Constantine Spinos, the cousin of a friend who lived in my building in Astoria. He was also a police officer in Athens. I tried to take advantage of his position to search for any official traces of Alexandra, but he came up empty. I found myself imprisoned in the flat, afraid that she might come if I ventured out. Soon I couldn't take the wait anymore, and forced myself to leave. I had so looked forward to seeing Athens, but finding Alexandra now dominated my desires.

I don't know why I thought of her so. She was beautiful, but that was not why I couldn't get her out of my mind. There was a sadness in her voice the other day in the gardens, and I wished that she would let me help her once again. So much had not been said, yet desperately needed to be spoken. Now I walked the streets of Athens alone with no choice but to wait for her touch upon my face—the way she had woken me from my dream of death in the desert.

7 August 1948

Went to see a performance of "Antigone" at the Theatre of Dionysus. No word from her.

8 August 1948

Constantine was promoted today. We all went out to celebrate with his fellow officers. No word from her.

9 August 1948

I am thinking of cutting my trip short. Athens is lonelier than I remember her. The sights, the monuments, the cafés—they are dull to me now. I am beginning to wish she had never written.

10 August 1948

Checked on flights back to the States. Transcontinental & Western Air had a flight to New York via Paris and Washington. It departs at 7:00 A.M. on the morning of the 12th. BOAC has their flying boat service to LaGuardia's Marine Terminal, but I couldn't get a proper connecting flight into London to catch it on time. I have to let Trans World know by tomorrow if I want the seat on their Lockheed Constellation.

It was quiet today. I took a walk in the National Gardens. It was a bad idea. I'm too tired to pack right now. I'll get up early and start tomorrow.

11 August 1948

I came back from the laundromat with my arms full of just-washed clothes. I could not have been out more than thirty minutes. When I opened the door to the flat, the small piece of paper blew into the hallway. I almost didn't see it.

"Sorry I was out of touch. Café Kolonaki, tomorrow night, eight o'clock. – Alexandra L."

I tossed my clothes on the floor, the suitcase with it. I would not need to pack today. By the time I had folded up the note, I realized that my hands had been shaking.

35
THE GIRL FROM LIMNOS

"Neotolemus, is it hard to kill?" Pheidippides sat with his captain after the others had settled in.

"I have no doubts that you will hear some say that killing is of no great consequence. Those braggarts are either lying or have never done the deed they boast of. No man takes life without killing a small piece of himself."

"Then how can you do it?"

"I pray for his misguided soul, and realize that it is more imperative for him to visit the Underworld than it is for me," Neotolemus said with a grin.

"I am ashamed to say that I am afraid."

"Pheidippides, only the brave acknowledge their fears, and no man is without them. Remember that the Mede's heart is gripped with more dread than yours, for he has nothing to win. He fights only to preserve his own life, we to remain alive and free."

Pheidippides covered himself with his tunic. He had made himself as comfortable as possible on the hard ground. He would need all the sleep he could manage tonight; tomorrow would be a long day.

11 **August 1948**

It is after two in the morning, so I suppose that the above entry is incorrect—though it still feels as if it is part of the same day.

Alexandra and I dined, but neither of us ate much.

"All these years I thought you were dead," she said as we began our second bottle of red wine, the burgundy liquid warming both hearts and tongues. "I had no way to find you."

"Dead?"

"I thought they had killed you."

"Experts have tried and failed."

"I'm glad," she said with a sly smile.

"Did you come straight here, after the..."

"No. I lived for a while in Gibraltar. My father's sister took me in."

"You were lucky."

"I suppose. No one else in his family would have me."

"I can't believe that."

She looked at me, as if to say, "you, born a slave, you of all people should understand." I did, but I still couldn't believe it. "It was duty—not love. They did what their honor demanded of them, but they never could love me." I looked at her as if to speak, but she continued, "Do you know that my mother and father were never married?"

"I know. She told me. But what does that matter."

"What does that matter?" She broke out into laughter, but it was a laugh meant to mask the hurt. "Apparently you haven't lived amongst good and proper Englishmen—they are so bleeding pompous. In that society, such circumstances are poor breeding."

"Was that why you left there?"

"Yes, and to search for something, some history, something to make me feel attached to something real. I came here, to Greece, to seek my ancestry. But it has not been easy."

"I've heard that work is hard to find."

"Yes, it is, but at least it is not based on the prep school my great granddaddy attended, or whether I wear a coat of arms on my jacket.

Don't worry about me, I'll survive," she said defensively.

"I don't know how they could have ever looked down on you. If I could have had a daughter, Alexandra, I wish she were just like..." she put her fingers to my lips to suppress the rest of my sentence, though its meaning had already escaped.

"I almost didn't have the courage to meet you last week," she said.

"Why?"

"I don't know. I was afraid of you."

"Afraid... of me? But I saved you."

"That's why I'm still afraid of you. And why I've never been able to find someone else."

"You're so, so beautiful, and passionate. How could you not find anyone?"

"There have been many lovers, but no one to love."

I walked her home. She lived in a flat on Odos Stratonos.

"You look so different in the night. It brings back so many memories, so many that I don't want to recall," she said as we stood near the vestibule of her apartment building.

"I'm sorry, I don't..."

"Shh, you're the only one I want," she said as she leaned into my chest and held me tight. I felt her body trembling, its involuntary spasms brought on by her crying. I held her as tightly as I could, even tighter than the night she clung to my back as we ran for our lives.

"I was so angry with both of them."

"With whom?"

"Mother and father. Her for bringing me into that hell, him for leaving us there."

"It was hard for everyone, it was virtually impossible to help yourself, let alone another."

"You did. I have thought of you so many times, though I barely knew you. You were the only one who had ever risked everything for me."

After a few minutes, I felt her body relaxing, her tears replaced by long, slow breathing. She moved her face away, and in the soft moonlight, I could see where the tears had run unobstructed down her tanned cheeks.

"Sometimes, I just want to run away, I want to run to where they will never find me. Not the cruel Turks or the Brits with their facade of civility—no one."

I had an idea. It amazes me what can appear in one's mind when one stares into the soulful eyes of a beautiful woman.

"Pack a small bag. I'll pick you up tomorrow morning at ten sharp." I was surprised at my boldness, and prepared to apologize for its presumptuousness when she shocked me with her reply.

"I'll be ready by eight." In an instant she had disappeared into the shadows of the vestibule. I ran all the way back to the flat of Constantine—I could have run all the way to Sparta.

12 August 1948

We stayed at the home of Haralambos and his wife, Kyriakiza. He was a great short-distance runner whom I had met in my days of competition. We were also joined by two other guests—a younger man named Mormanis, and his girlfriend, Delphina, a beautiful woman from Santorini.

At lunch, Haralambos and I caught up on old times. Afterwards, the others lay down for an afternoon siesta. I did not sleep, instead, I looked out at the vast, and untamed Limnian terrain towards Hephaestia and knew exactly what I had to do.

Footwear for runners had improved since the 1920's, but I was used to running barefoot. The bare foot on the Earth, like touching a woman, must be flesh against flesh. It was exceedingly hot, but Spyridon taught me that the time to train was not in the cooler edges of the day, nor on soft sandy trails, but in the intense heat of the midday sun and on the most inhospitable ground one can find. "Then, and only then, will you know your mettle as a true long-distance man," he would say.

I unbuckled my sandals, and taking one last glance back at the comforts of Haralambos' home, I set off towards a place I had not seen since being taken from Limnos as a slave.

Hephaestia is the site of the ancient kingdom of Vulcan. It was here, on the Island of Limnos, where an enraged Zeus flung his lame son, Hephaestos. We are told on good mythological authority that he took the whole day in falling to earth—landing as it were on the island of my birth. And there, on a level plain by the sea where he landed, he set up his anvil and forge upon which he made the armaments of the Gods and heroes. It was here that the Nazis had placed their armaments, terrible guns of steel, which they pointed towards the sea to stop the Royal Navy. The German guns are silent now, removed or rusting half-buried in the sands. It was here, on this flat plain that I made a great discovery.

I was born near the sanctuary of Hephaestos. This was just one more reason that I have always related to the one cast out of Olympus. Though my memories were faded and at best, only as reliable as a small child's can be—I could tell that nothing had changed here in millennia, let alone in the span of my life. In those four and a half decades, I had traveled thousands of miles and witnessed two world wars, and in the midst of these tragedies, I had seen the best and worst of human nature. Today, coming full circle to the place of my birth, I realized that Alexandra was the only person who could relate at all to what I had experienced. It was strange to think that one event, thirty years ago, could bind us forever, and yet we each knew so little about each other.

I was in the ancient amphitheatre when I had noticed telltale green spotting the brown parched earth. It was near the center of the arc formed by the theatre's seats. Investigating the spot with my pocketknife, it beckoned me deeper until I had created a circle about six inches in diameter and about a foot and a half deep. I worked patiently until the earth loosened her maternal grip on some adopted object. Finally, I managed to pull the cumbersome thing to the surface. Whether it was a weapon, a statuette or a utensil was unclear.

Here 'neath skies shorn of vaporous breathings, you slumber,
Dampness in thy tomb from all the rains of yesterday.
Thy beauty-seeking eyes seek no more,
Once beautiful thou givest
To all, ancient beauty wherever thou breath'd
And over thy stilled young heart—a flower
Stranger to the night's misty veil.
Now unfolds her petals to the western sun.

The brown earth, formed by millennia of volcanic ash piled upon ash, formed a tight shell around my treasure. It clung to whatever it was holding with the tenacity of twenty-five years of possession. The sweat was pouring from both brow and body and the summer sun scorched my bare back, but that was nothing compared to the excitement of the find. Dusting off my prize, I thought about its fate. I felt the need to protect it from the centuries of thieves that had destroyed the earth's bounty. Looking across the plain, there was not a human soul to be seen. I knew that no one was about who might have observed me, bent over, struggling to pull something out of the womb of the earth. Though it was with some apprehension that I searched the horizon for prying eyes, nothing stirred in the noonday heat.

A sigh of relief left my parched lips, as I relaxed in the belief that no one had seen me in my unlawful pursuits. But now the problem was where to hide the find. Examining the bundle carefully, and measuring it with the span of my hand, I realized that it would fit snugly in my airline bag that I had left back in my room.

I then decided that the safe thing to do was return the bundle to its hole and cover it over with some earth and rocks until I could return for it safely—and then try to get it out of the country. And so I did and headed back to Haralambos' hut. My throat was as dry as it had been when I crossed the Sinai on my trek to the Monastery of St. Katherine. I took a drink and then sat under the mulberry tree to await the awakening of Alexandra and the others, who slept inside the coolness of the stone cottage.

As the sun approaches its setting, the air begins to cool the brow of scorched day and it is then the siesta ends. I heard someone stirring. I knew I would never retrieve my find, leaving it once again in its earthen refuge, safe from the intrusive eyes and meddling hands of men who knew not her purpose. I reveled that I alone knew the secret that the earth had chosen to divulge.

13 August 1948

It was a wonderful day by the sea. The waters sparkled under a sun that saves her best for the Aegean islands. Alexandra had brought her bouzouki, and Mormanis had an old klarino he had acquired in Tangiers. Delphina sang—she had a voice that could have lured ships to their graves. We spent the afternoon swimming, feasting and singing. We played with the lyrics of the folk song Samiotisa—The Girl from Samos—to suit our locale.

Girl from Limnos, when are you going to go to Limnos?
I'll throw roses on the beach, when I'll come to pick you up.
I'll set golden sails on the boat, which will bring you,
And I'll send you golden oars, girl from Limnos, to pick you up.
I love you even when you're wearing black clothes, or tattered ones,
And even in your working clothes
You drive me crazy, girl from Limnos.

Alexandra looked lovely and more carefree than I had ever seen her. I suppose the latter was not so surprising given the few circumstances under which we had shared memories. It was easy to forget that she had I had buried her father and she had witnessed her mother torn to pieces by a British artillery shell. I tried to put such thoughts out of my head, preferring to let the images of her dancing on the beach of Limnos replace those of war torn Mesopotamia.

One look at her was almost enough to make me forget. It made me cry with joy that something, someone so beautiful could have risen from the depths of such profound loss.

14 August 1948

Alexandra and I had found two old and rusty bicycles and we were riding towards the village of Moudros.

"Wait a minute, slow down," she called from behind me. "I've never had your stamina, remember?" I slowed my pace. "Where is my knight leading me this time?" she asked.

"I must run an errand in town for Haralambos."

At one point, as she laughed and pedaled ahead, I was paying more attention to her than the road and launched myself headlong into a sand dune. I wasn't hurt, except for my pride. The cause of my distraction was not lost on her, though she couched it in a more delicate manner.

"I see that my champion is always looking out for me."

"Some champion," I said, as I extricated my bicycle from the sand. She dropped hers and we sat for a moment against the dune and shared some water.

"It's okay. I love to watch you, too. That day in Potsdam as you carried the torch, I could not take my eyes from you. I rejoiced in thinking that of all who watched you run by, I alone knew who you

were—and where you had come from. I secretly hoped you would see me."

"Why didn't you find me? You knew where I was staying," I asked, uncertain if I wanted to know the answer.

"I couldn't, I was always watched. I was not alone during those years—I was with a man... Or at least, I was with him when he so desired. You wouldn't believe the lies I had to tell to venture that day outside of Berlin."

"Then he was not with you in Potsdam."

"No, but whenever he was not with me, I was escorted by his henchmen. He called them "bodyguards" and insisted it was for my safety, but that was a lie. He was insanely jealous. Ha! A man so blatantly committing adultery, yet jealous whenever his mistress spoke to another man."

"Please, Alexandra, I hate that word."

"Can a word so easily offend one who once was numb to stripping the dead?" Her truth stung me. "Would you prefer concubine, harlot, courtesan, or perhaps whore?"

"How could you say that? I won't believe you..."

"That I could what? Be seduced by money, power, comforts? Can you be so naïve about the way things are—the way men are?"

"Not all men."

"True, not all. There is one, still brave and noble. One who still sees me as a frightened little girl," she said cupping her hands over my eyes. I stumbled and we fell to the sand in a twisted heap.

"I am not blind."

"Are you sure? Who was that fellow you befriended when you were a prisoner-of-war in Palestine?"

"Ozbudun."

"How many men did he kill in cold-blood. How many women did he rape?"

"He kept me alive. My other choices seemed worse."

"As did mine."

"But how did you end up there, of all places, in the heart of the Third Reich?"

"Third, second, tenth, who cares about such labels? I was not even twenty years old, a poor refugee living in Gibraltar. An outcast from my own family who never viewed my blood as being English

enough. Eric was rich and handsome and refined. I was invited aboard his yacht for a party. I had never seen such opulence. I didn't care if he was betrothed to another, or how he made his money or whether his class had social conscience. All I knew was that he was carefree—a feeling I had always been denied."

"If he loved you, why would he marry another?"

"He was aristocracy—they may love women like me, but they never marry us."

"He used you."

"We used each other—I had no expectations of love. My poor Ion, don't look so hurt for me—I never loved him."

"Then why be with him?"

"Has America's ease made you forget? I will not apologize for surviving. Oh yes, the horrors of those times still haunt me. Do you really believe that only chains make slaves?" She had begun to weep, and I rolled her on top of me and held her close.

"I'm sorry, Alexandra. I didn't mean to..."

"It's all right, Ion. I've already sat in harsher judgment of myself than any one else could."

"Those times are behind us now. No one will ever hurt you again."

"Are you sure?"

"I'll never let anyone else hurt you," I repeated.

"It isn't others I am worried about."

Alexandra browsed in the waterfront marketplace, while I went to see Haralambos' friend the atelier. Haralambos had the artisan craft a pair of earrings for Kyriakiza. Each had a dozen baby pearls arranged to appear as a bunch of grapes, with even smaller emeralds forming the leaves. The old man asked if I wanted something for Alexandra, but I had no money for such gifts. Undeterred, he fashioned a chain to replace the leather string, which held the pendant I had given her. Metallurgy is in a Limnians' blood—the result was both functional and aesthetic—a duality that Greeks demand in their art. As payment, I chiseled into the face of an ancient sycamore that stood in the courtyard of his studio, a small figure of a lion.

We ate lunch in a taverna overlooking the harbor. Before we left Moudros, I gave her the chain. Alexandra untied the leather strap and slid the pendant off, pausing to hold it in her hand.

"I wear this all the time and yet never see it."

"Some things are easier to feel than see."

"Especially when they are right before our eyes."

"Especially," I said, as I cradled the bottom of the palm that held the obol.

"Sometimes things escape our vision. I almost didn't see the small letter beneath his legs. It's the sign of the Spartan, is it not?"

"It is not. What men do not know, they create. It was for the ancient warrior's loved one. She was so much like you, so very beautiful—but he failed to grasp what was right before his eyes."

"Her loss is my gain?"

"Now its lambda is for Leontokardis."

"Will it bring its wearer a happier ending than her predecessor's?"

We returned to our friends at twilight. Haralambos had a new camera. He took a few pictures of our frolicking, and we rewarded his photographic work by hurling him into the sea. By the time the sun had set, we had made a huge bonfire on the beach, roasting a lamb that Efstratios had bartered a local shepherd for. We washed its savory flavors down with an ample supply of kalambaki—a red wine made from a grape Aristotle called the Limnio. In the light of a full moon and the embers from our fiery blaze, we stripped naked and swam our last swim of the day, then danced around the fire until limbs and arms could barely move.

Gradually, all began to bid their goodnights and retire. As I watched Haralambos and Kyriakiza, walking arm in arm to the hut, I realized that Alexandra and I stood alone, warmed and illuminated by the embers that still smoldered. Sparks from its dying flames still crackled and rose into the dark night sky that shrouded us. I had wrapped her in a large extra shirt that I had left strewn on the ground, and I was covered in a towel that I had retrieved from the hut. She sat before me, her back pressed into my chest as my arms wrapped around her—I felt her shiver slightly.

I felt a lightness of being that I had known rarely in my life. She turned her head, and I gazed into her eyes. She moved her head back, nuzzling it into my neck. I felt the warmth of her breath as she exhaled, and then the wetness of her lips as they pressed against my flesh.

Our faces met, and she was forceful, almost wild with her mouth. She pulled back suddenly, and I could see her looking at me with something between disappointment and concern.

"Last night you didn't take me either. Still playing the gentlemen," she giggled nervously. But I wasn't playing anything. I felt uneasy because I didn't know whether she loved me or was in love with nostalgia for the hero of Baghdad. But worse, I could not love her the way I wanted to.

"Alexandra, I am bound to another."

She sank back into the sand on her hands facing me with the look of one who had been slapped. She was beautiful in the fading firelight, the smooth flesh of her legs stretched out from beneath the shirt and curled under her invitingly. Her breasts rose seductively from the top of the shirt.

"I know, but you're not happy. I know you're not."

"Does that make me any less bound by my pledge."

"Bound—yes, that is the word. Bound like a Greek boy was to the Ottoman. Has she, too, branded you?"

"Now that's not fair, and you know it."

"Fair? You speak to me of 'fair.' Remember who you are speaking to."

"I'm sorry. You and I were dealt our hands, but I made a choice and honor binds me to it."

"And what of her—is she worthy of that honor?"

I paused, probably giving away my feelings in the delay of my response.

"That's not the question."

"Then what are you doing here, alone with me?" she said, almost indignantly.

"I have no answer." I looked into the fire as I spoke. With my wings of wax, I wanted to see how close I could get to the pleasure of its warmth before its flames burned me.

15 August 1948

I awoke the next morning to bright sunlight and clear thoughts. I wanted to see her right away, to hold her, and tell her what I now knew in my heart—that everything would be well, everything would be won-

derful. I knew that she could still be happy, and that I could chase the dark cloud that followed her. Bolting from my sleeping chamber, I called her name as I entered her bedroom.

The wind from the door's movement blew out the candle. I caught only a glimpse of its flame as it was extinguished, then its trail of smoke wisped upwards. Its once tall form had melted onto the hard plaster surface next to her bed.

For a moment, I thought the tangled pile of sheets and pillows harbored her still sleeping form. But she was not there. I turned, about to call for her again and then saw the note on the wooden dresser. Opening the folded paper, the pendant I had given to her fell to my feet. Picking it up, I realized that the chain that clasped it was only half of its original length. She must have used the flame of the dying candle to sever the middle link. It could not have been easy. The heat from the glowing metal must have burned her hand. Last night we loved by the fire, this morning the fire had severed the last vestige of what we could not consummate.

I read what I should have realized was inevitable, fixing on the last lines, "I love you too much to restrain my heart. I return the treasure, for only you know its value supercedes all the riches in the world. When the two halves of the chain are together again, perhaps we too will be together and free to love—without chains. Until then, farewell my Achaean prince." I felt crushed. She knew that I was not free of my desires and certainly not free of her.

Once again, the pendant had passed between us at a parting of our destinies. That symbol of victory had now become a talisman of misery, for the love that it once held was gone.

It was with much sadness that I packed my travel bag. I would catch the three o'clock ferry back to Athens. Before leaving, I would retrace my steps back to my find of days ago. There I would bury the pendant in the amphitheatre, for I am a fool who has strutted and fretted his hour upon the stage.

When Haralambos asked me where Alexandra was, I hid my pain, and answered cheerily, "She had to meet some people. She left early this morning."

"I wouldn't let that one get away, if I were you."

"Yes, my friend, she's really extraordinary."

But I knew I had indeed let her slip away.

36 GREAT IS THE TRUTH

Helios had finally bade his sister, the moon, farewell and taken his rightful place in the early morning sky. Pheidippides knew that this was going to be a day like no other.

He had only managed three hours of sleep—keeping watch and tending fires had necessitated short rotations. He donned his heavy breastplate, leather flaps below the midriff and bronze greaves to protect his chest, groin and shins. On his head, he set a heavy bronze helmet with high crest, making him look substantially taller. Heaving his wooden and bronze layered shield upon his shoulder, he reached down and picked up his long wooden pike.

The air was crisp. Traces of dew still coated his helmet. This beautiful field, covered with sweet lilies and golden wheat, would soon be stained with the blood of thousands of men—its radiant whites and yellows turned crimson red.

3 September 1948

I am home. Genevieve is still on the road. She telegrammed that she should return by mid-September. The show had gone well. She is a talented actress, and God has blessed her with all of the charms that a woman could hope for. Our marriage had started, as I suppose they all do, dining and dancing under the stars—though our stars were the glittering lights of Broadway and Times Square. A whirlwind romance on an immigrant's budget.

But my thoughts were on a shore thousands of miles away from New York City.

I saw you in a dream before I found you lying there
Silvered pin adorning your golden hair.
Bright rosy red the flesh you wore
When first I met you by the Morphean shore.
Sadly you spoke, "Four stadia distant from where you now sleep,
Over the river's waters a meter deep
Down by the wine-dark Aegean Sea
Where echoing waters finger their sandy rosary
There on a fingered strip of land I waiting lie—
Two browned gaping holes, each one an eye.
Come now and free me from time's weighted sigh
Thus in my sleep you hush'd spoke
Thus quickly from the dream I woke
Bright rosy red the flesh you wore
When last you fled me by the Morphean shore.

There was so much in these entries, that my mind needed time to absorb what I had learned. Here, in my hands, was evidence that Ion had indeed possessed the Obol of Pheidippides. Eric was the German Count that Dr. Scaffhausen said had been executed by the SS. The mistress that the Nazis searched for had to have been Alexandra.

I checked on Ion. He was sleeping, but when he swallowed, it was a slow deliberate action as if even the simplest of bodily function required forethought and careful execution. I rearranged his blanket, though it was already fine—I just felt I had to busy myself doing something to comfort him.

Coming back to my room, I re-read the poem Ion had written for her, each time feeling more of its gentle rhythms. Ion's words were so beautiful that they made me sad. I could feel the love that burned within him on these pages, yet there was something fatalistic—knowing that I had found Ion alone and lonely. He had never spoken to me about what had happened to either Alexandra or his wife, Genevieve.

I imagined Ion writing these words, his strong knuckles grasping the delicate quill. I could tell it was an ink-dipped pen from the inconsistencies in the calligraphy and the fading, then darkening of the words as the ink ran out and then was replenished. It reminded me of how life ebbs and flows, fades and is restored. And just when we think we are falling, the quill is refilled and we rise again to another crest.

28 December 1949

Getting ready for New Year's Eve. There's a big party at Nancy and Hank's downtown loft. It'll be an all-night affair. Their parties usually are—even on occasions of substantially less notoriety. The end of a decade. For some reason we reflect differently on it than the typical change of a calendar year, or the change of one solar day, which is all that any midnight really signifies. But as I step back and think of the events of the last ten years, it certainly has been quite an era—one of both pride and shame.

Christian arrived today by Greyhound. He's going to spend the holidays with us. I met him months ago on the road production of "A Streetcar Named Desire." He's a strapping lad of seventeen, proclaiming himself to be twenty-one, or older, depending on the part. He's going to get typecast as a young "pretty-boy" with his fair hair and chiseled good looks, but he'll have to discover that for himself.

In from the Midwest, he's here in the city to find fame and stardom, though unprepared for the brutalities of New York's gritty streets. I'd like to help him. A struggling actor in this city can use all the help he can find. I know what it's like to have no one. I hope Genevieve likes him.

I've gotten him into Susan Bonner's class, to study acting technique. She uses the Paramount Theatre during the days when there are no matinees, so it will make it easier for him to get to his various "go-

sees," though I prefer call them "go-aways."

There were several other entries prior to the next one, but they were lackluster and without the spark that Ion used when speaking of Alexandra and his time in Greece. I only skimmed these entries. The ones that followed would yield the answer to the fate of the wife for whom Ion had preserved his honor.

14 February 1950

I came home today early to surprise my wife. Flowers are at the ready, a beautiful bouquet of roses, interspersed with similar colored carnations and snapdragons—the red and whites of Saint Valentine. I have been out of town for the past week, rehearsing in Pittsburgh with Max Schonfeld and his troupe for a performance of "Bus Stop." The show opens on Friday night, but I wanted to be home for this day—a day for lovers. I took the 11:37 out of Pittsburgh last night, arriving on Track 28 at Pennsylvania Station at precisely 10:42, the exact time on the schedule. I love New York Central's Pacemaker, always reliable. Genevieve doesn't get home until about three, so I'm here at Lindy's having lunch by myself.

I have rehearsed all week, and my feet and limbs are sore. The day off will do me good anyway, though if all goes well, I shall be put to a physical test of a different kind this afternoon. Things with Genevieve have been hillier than a Coney Island ride, but I'm hoping that the worst is over.

We've fought a lot, a clear sign of growing apart, but lately, things have started to improve. Her career is moving along at a brisk pace, more and more work, better and better roles. She's even talked about television or motion picture work. I'm happy for her success, but it has come at a price to our relationship. It's a stressful business, and the pressures on a marriage are extraordinary.

I'm going to stop by the Belasco before heading out to Astoria. Christian should be there. I got him a job on Monday, Tuesday and Thursday afternoons building sets. It's not a glamorous assignment, but it's work, and in this business, you take work when it's offered. I want to catch him before he heads to Queens to give him a few dollars for the pictures. It will afford me some privacy with Genevieve this evening. Maybe he'll take Doris, that script girl. I think he's had his eye on her, though a handsome lad like Christian has his pick of many. Even the flits throw themselves at him, but his interest lies with the ladies. He's a good kid, I just hope that the city hasn't corrupted or jaded him.

At first, Genevieve had given me a difficult time about him being with us, but then she warmed to the idea. That was lucky for Christian. If she hadn't liked him, he wouldn't have been able to stay with us. If he couldn't stay with us, he would not have been able to afford to remain in New York, and he would have traveled back to Wisconsin with his tail between his legs. I admired that he had a dream—even if his only rainbow turned out to be found in the oil-stained puddles of Broadway's alleys.

There is nothing like an afternoon of romance, and I want everything to be just right for when she gets home. I figure I can beat her there by at least an hour and a half—plenty of time to set the mood. Given Christian's situation, it wasn't often that Genevieve and I were alone in our apartment. It had actually been a while since we were alone anywhere.

I have to catch the 8:22 back to Pittsburgh in the A.M. I'm really looking forward to seeing her; I know we can make things beautiful again. She's really going to be surprised to see me.

3 March 1950

Never trust a politician. Never trust a merchant who tells you he loses money on every sale but makes it up in volume. And never, but never, trust a woman who seems particularly concerned about what time you are coming home. I went to hide her flowers in the bedroom. I opened the door, flowers in one hand, my foolish heart cupped in the other.

I'm not sure when it started. The only thing I could tell by the embrace I caught them in that day, is that it wasn't the first time that they had broken that commandment. It would have made a perfect Valentine's Day card, with all the requisite kisses and caresses, but for the fact that she was in the arms of another. I am not sure who was more surprised by my unexpected appearance, them or me—I only know who was more devastated.

Were it not for me, he'd have been back in Wisconsin dreaming of the lights on Broadway while working in some corner soda shoppe or pushing a plow—now he was caught sowing the wrong field. Christian, Judas, Brutus, Bayazid, treachery has many names—but its face is always the same.

I can't bear to write anymore tonight, my temper is still too inflamed, and my hand is starting to shake.

I read about Ion confronting her. He gave her another chance. Christian moved out, but Ion later learned, from others, that their affair didn't end with his departure from the apartment. Nor was it her only indiscretion. He desperately tried to salvage their marriage, despite all that he had discovered. I know what it felt like to try to salvage a sinking vessel. There is no way to analyze the heart rationally. It can be so fragile, so easily bruised, and yet it can endure the most brutal of human treatment.

11 April 1950

I wrote to her today. Seeking redemption, seeking another chance. I was desperately searching to find a way to rekindle what had once burned so brightly—hoping it wasn't too late. I even went as far as walking to F.D.R. Station for the postage to carry my message upon its wings across the Atlantic to her flat on Odos Adonis.

It was wedged, still sealed, in the journal's binding. Ion must have sent the letter—its postage stamps had been postmarked, but across its face were red letters stamped: return to sender, addressee unknown.

18 August 1951

The last few days since my arrival have been so hectic, I barely had time to sleep, let alone write. I am here in Athens with a branch of the International Red Cross. Our mission is relief work, but my motives are not altogether altruistic. I came here to escape one life, and to see if it is not too late to recapture one that I have lost.

I am finally free of the ties to Genevieve. There was so little accumulated during our marriage that there was nothing to fight about. She granted me the divorce without challenge. I was a fool, and my heart is paying for it dearly, twice.

21 August 1951

Today I dined with His Holiness Andreas Athas. He and I talked briefly of the war, but afterwards, in his study, we reminisced about the Games of 1928 when he personally presented me with the wreath and cup of victory.

I never ran for the wreaths or the cups or the glory of Nike. I ran for the harmony that I felt with the universe around me, and for the joy that I was free to run. Whether for a few hundred meters, or the sacred marathon, the purity of spirit is the same. Mind and body becoming one, perfect balance, the freedom that only the feeling of the raw dirt beneath my feet, the sun at my back and the wind filtering through my hair.

What really defines a slave? It is not merely a man who wears the chains of another. No. It is a man's perception of his own limitations. A man in chains perceives that he cannot go where he wants to because another man prevents him, thus he is not free; nor is any man who creates his own boundaries and then believes he cannot overcome them. That man is every bit as much of a slave—the chains are unseen but are as debilitating as if forged of iron. When I run, I transcend my limitations, pushing myself across boundaries I thought impenetrable. Alone to commune with myself and with the Gods, my burdens are temporarily lifted. Each day, the mountains that surround this city call to me. They call me to run, to escape the misery that enslaves her people, and the misery that still enslaves me.

30 August 1951

His Holiness arranged temporary accommodations for me at Agia Apostoli near the old Agora. I am rooming with a priest named Panayiotas Kyriazis. He is a little fellow, but sturdy and very spirited. His upbringing was as different from mine as two Greeks can get, but we hit it off rather well, becoming close friends in a time normally insufficient for such a relationship to develop. Living and working together nearly twenty-four hours a day, and in such conditions as we found ourselves, left no room for anything but cooperation.

You would be amazed at how fast social pretexts fall when a man inadvertently wears the other's skivvies.

2 September 1951

A bust was to be commissioned of the Patriarch Athenagoras. I had been selected by a committee of Greek Americans, who were to fund the work. I had sculpted some, mostly to augment what little I made acting. There were certainly more talented artists, but I was Greek, available, and very affordable. His Holiness objected, there being no precedent for a living Patriarch to be so honored, but the Americans were insistent. His Holiness agreed to at least meet with me privately. He invited me to his sanctuary and made us some demitasse. Sitting across from me, he said nothing while staring at me. It would have been disrespectful for me to initiate the dialogue so I sat still and stared back, all the while contemplating how I might best sculpt him.

After half an hour, he said, "Please come here tomorrow at the same time." I returned the next day and then again at the same time for the three days after that. Except for salutations, the whole time we sat in silence.

On the fifth day, he asked me, "Do you know the difference between a priest and an artist?" and without waiting for a response, he answered, "An artist must have more patience." As I kissed his hand to beg his leave that afternoon, he asked me to commence my work on the morrow.

15 September 1951

I have let my desires to find her become known to those who might be able to help, but so far nothing has turned up. Fortunately I have the commission into which I can put my anxious energy.

Initially, Athenagoras only allowed me to work from some pictures. I should never have accepted such an arrangement. Working from a photo transforms the two dimensional into three, but life only comes from life. I begged him to release me from this task—saying that if I could not work within eyesight of His Holiness, from some inconspicuous hiding place in the Patriarchate if necessary, that I could do him no justice. His deific smile told me that it was his command that I find such a hiding place and continue to work.

It is good that my days and nights are so filled. The bust progresses, though the aftermath of the civil war permeates life here. It is good to create something in the midst of such destruction.

20 September 1951

Word has come of her whereabouts. She has sequestered herself at a convent on Limnos called Agia Efpraxia. No man, except an Archon, may ever visit such a place. I must be more cunning and send a messenger of the appropriate sex. But whom can I trust to deliver such a message and faithfully return with her reply? I am too apprehensive to think right now, too fraught with the anxious possibility that she will not receive my communication well. I must plan this carefully. She must know how I feel, it is our last hope. Gia is young, but she will help me. Together, we will go together to Limnos, but only she can travel the last mile.

3 October 1951

Panayiotas had come to visit me at the hospital. As he approached, I could see that he was both relieved and angry for what I had done to myself. As he sat on the edge of the bed, I squeezed his hand and said "I will try to get well."

But I doubt I will. I'm not sure I want to be well. Ever since Gia returned to tell me that Alexandra would not see me—and did not love me, I felt myself upon a terrible wave, riding before its crest, spinning out of control into the dark abyss of its trough.

There were no further entries, but at the bottom of that last page was a drawing of a runner. Between his legs was the telltale lambda. To his right, and in the direction he faced, was a woman whose countenance and flowing hair could only be that of his love. The plea that this friend Gia took to her had obviously failed.

After reading the last entry, I felt as though I had stepped outside myself—outside my life and seen it as though it were not my own. As much as I wanted to know of Ion's past, I also wanted it to be left veiled and shrouded, in part out of fear, fear of what one is always afraid of—the unknown. It was not as though I had discovered something horrible. Nothing in his relationship with Alexandra showed Ion to be anything less than what I thought of him—passionate and vulnerable and heroic. But his terrible sense of failure and the intensity of his love shook me.

Who was this Alexandra? How could she have snubbed him—hurt him so. I froze in my own thoughts. Hadn't I behaved similarly, hadn't I abandoned Ion when he needed me most? What was I to him but a palliating endnote to an epic and tragic story?

I thought about the time I first saw Ion in the nursing home. Was he in similar despair, then? Soon scenes from our time together came flooding back—the birthday he threw for me at the nursing home, our talks in the garden, our time at the museum, his nightmares. Though not a different man to me now, he had been changed it seemed, with each journal entry. In that light, my abandonment was a greater failure than I could have guessed.

"Adonia, I have to tell him how..."

"Why?" Adonia and I were sitting in the church's rose garden. It had withered from a lack of upkeep, and its bushes were twisted and windswept. I had told Adonia about the journals. I had no choice. I needed her counsel. "He cannot know that they are missing," she added.

"I don't know. I'm wondering whether he had led me to them that first night here."

"But you can't be sure."

"But I need to know..."

"What? If he meant you to know all this? Does it matter so much now that you do?"

"Adonia, it is a betrayal. I must tell him."

She took my hands and held them tightly in hers.

"If you must..."

It was the thirteenth of August. Our return tickets were for the sixteenth. Two weeks ago, that date represented returning to my career. Two days ago, I wondered whether we would be traveling at all, or whether I'd be alone. Now, the sixteenth is just a date printed on an Olympic Airlines ticket. It held little meaning to me, and I wasn't going anywhere until Ion was ready.

Dr. Constantacopoulos came by the house that evening. He was impressed at how much strength Ion had accumulated in the past two or three days. Though more rest was prescribed, he felt that Ion could be flown back to New York. Dr. Baruth's office had already arranged for Ion to go to Columbia Presbyterian for observation, and though I knew I'd feel better about Ion having access to the most advanced care available, I had grown to really respect this hometown doctor. Constantacopoulos was the kind of practitioner that was common in the States when I grew up—a cradle-to-the-grave caregiver who not only knew the Hippocratic Oath, but lived by it.

Though I had wanted to ask Ion about the journals so many times, I could not. I was intimidated and frightened by his silence and the obvious effort he had expended to conceal their existence. I could not tell whether he knew everything or nothing of my deception. Could he possibly have been indifferent about so serious a matter between us? Or did he intend for me to see the journals all along, and then be left to ponder the complexities of his life in solitude? Was there a tacit understanding the he had allowed me to look under the condition that there would be neither questions nor answers? Or was he now harboring regrets that another had entered his past and his heart?

"Where are we going this afternoon?" asked Ion as I entered his room. This question was all part of a game we played. We weren't going anywhere except to the portico. But in our fantasies, we traveled to Paris, to Rome and to all the places that I have never been and wanted to be taken by him. And of course we talked about the things we would do back in New York, about admiring the foliage this fall and who to invite for Thanksgiving Dinner. I helped him dress. He let me do everything that day, making no attempt even to fumble with the buttons on his shirt.

We took our time to move outside to the portico, reclining on a pair of teak chaise lounges. I covered Ion's legs with a woolen throw. There was a gentle breeze blowing the wisteria-covered portico.

"Well? *El Prado, L'Hermitage... Le Louvre*?"

"Farther than that, yet we will not have to leave our seats," he said, echoing what I already knew.

"How far?"

"It is an important day today, for me, one of the most important ever."

"Help me out, what are we commemorating?"

"Boedromion, the day that good triumphed over evil. Right there," he said pointing out to the plains below. "But it wouldn't come without sacrifice and pain, and no one on this day long ago knew the magnitude of what it would mean until the blood had dried in the sand."

"It is hard to imagine what so small a group must have felt facing such a formidable enemy. They must have been frightened, but maybe I'm just projecting my own meager sense of courage onto their brave souls."

"No sane man faces his enemy without fear. We were scared—any man who says he isn't frightened before battle is either lying or insane."

"What did you think of to give yourself strength?"

"Freedom."

"You attacked at a full run..."

"Yes, and shouting at the tops of our lungs."

"To scare the enemy?"

"To scare ourselves forward and into glory. It's a story that has been told in blood throughout the ages: Marathon, Thermopylae, Valley Forge, the Marne, Bastogne. As long as tyrants enslave men, heroes will lay down their lives for freedom."

"I hope we never run out of heroes."

"When we do, the old ones return..."

Eftehea had brought Evangelis outside. He came over to Ion and put his head on Ion's shoulder, holding his arm. I looked over at Evangelis' garden. There in the midst of the surrounding bramble I spotted several green slivers. It wasn't much—but it was life. Straining towards the sun, they unfolded their leafy structures. It was miracle number three.

Somehow this orphan was supposed to hold the key. But the key to what?

"Ion, you rest for a bit in the shade, I have a few chores to do inside. Can I leave you with Eftehea?"

"Yes, my dear, I am never alone here."

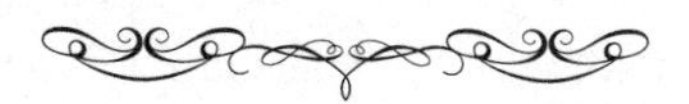

"Marianna, can I come in?" asked Dimitris.

"Of course you may. Please, come sit down," I said, pointing towards the bed.

"Just for minute, I am have errands for father. Are you see grandma?"

"She's outside with Ion and Evangelis."

"I am so very, very happy he is turn corner. It is big miracle."

"I know he felt you and your father praying for him every day."

"And Milos too."

"Really?"

"Yes, my brother is in church every days to light candle. He is still heretic, but is say he do no want to take chances," laughed Dimitris. I envied what these two had in each other. I knew that no matter what paths they followed, no matter how divergent, that they would always have each other. Dimitris would live vicariously through his brother's worldly exploits, and Milos would always have his brother as an anchor for his soul.

"I'm going to miss you," I said, as I sat down next to him. I could not help thinking about the last time he and I had shared this bed. So much had been destroyed in the upheaval of the past week. But destruction always precedes creation, and I felt the genesis of something springing from the chaos I had caused. "We've been more than a handful to you and your family as it is,

Dimitris," I said while caressing his hand.

"You are change my life. Both of you, and I am love you both for it. Before you, I am think that love and faith are two stars that are dwell in separate galaxies. But, no, they are depending on each other—always in each other's orbit. Perhaps things could have been different ..." he began to say, looking straight into my eyes. I didn't let him finish.

"Hush! Thank goodness they weren't. If they had been I would never myself have experienced such a communion of love and faith!" I squeezed his hand, and I saw his lips draw into a large smile.

"Yes. We men of faith are being very, very passionate, are we not?"

"God help your parishioners."

"I can tell you this thing—they are not get same dispensation as you."

"I hope not! Don't ever lose your passion, Dimitris, it's what makes you great. And you will be a great priest. What was between us will always remain between us. Hey, we'll always have Marathon." I said, offering up a really bad version of Bogart, which was fortunately lost on him.

"You are right, I am not wishing things different anymore, I will celebrate what they are. Even father's heart is softening. I had to be reminding him that he, too, is once young and in love. He is falling for older woman who is become my mother."

"Eftehea made something special for us tonight. Would you like a little pastitsio?" I asked Ion.

"That sounds delicious, but could I trouble you for a simple libation, my throat is so dry?"

"Ion, Dr. Constantacopoulos said..."

"You're going to listen to what a doctor said? In twenty years, Constantacopoulos will still be twenty years younger than I am today!"

"Okay, but if he catches you, you didn't get it from me!"

I went to the kitchen and poured Ion and myself a glass of retsina. With a glass in each hand, I idled back to Ion's room where he was staring out the window. He turned and smiled as I set them down, and he immediately lifted his in a wordless toast. Our goblets clinked, and we both fell to looking at their contents, as if to find something there.

"Ion, tomorrow I'm going to be out most of the day. Will you be all right?"

"Where will you be?"

"With Adonia. We're going to do some shopping in Athens. I shouldn't be too late."

"Magna est veritas—et praevalet." Ion said softly, without any explanation, as if none were needed.

"Great is the truth and it prevails," I said, recalling seeing this motto inscribed in large letters in the Horace Mann Library. "It always prevails, doesn't it?"

"It depends."

"It depends? Depends on what?" I couldn't help feeling that Ion was returning irony for irony.

"Do we not sometimes withhold the greatness of truth when its revelation might cause pain to another?" I got nervous that this dialogue was not going the way I had intended it to go, and that Ion was referring to an indiscretion of my own. Was Ion testing me, giving me one last chance to come clean before confronting me?

"I suppose there could be times where silence is warranted," I answered, boxed into a corner.

"I see," he said, and sat quietly for a few moments. Thank God Ion had never become an attorney. He would have been a formidable adversary in any courtroom.

"I suppose people don't always tell the truth because they are afraid what the consequences might be in telling it," he said.

"It's time for bed. I might not see you in the morning; I want to get an early start. I'll telephone when I get a chance." Ion was silent as his gaze never left mine. Ion didn't ask the question I dreaded. Maybe he didn't want to embarrass me, or perhaps he really didn't want to know the details. I could not tell the truth about my not going shopping with Adonia. I was taking an early morning flight to Limnos. I needed to know if she was still alive—perhaps even still there.

"Remember, my dear, to find truth, you must first *seek* it. If you *seek* it, you must be willing to *find* it," was all he said as I dimmed his lights for the night.

37
THE CURSE OF MOUDROS

Pheidippides gazed across the plains stretching out before the village of Marathonas. Here, the flame of Greece would flicker out as a conquered Persian colony—or burn in eternal glory for all the ages.

Men assembled in eerie silence. One thousand Plataens arrived two days earlier and would lead the left. In numbers, it wasn't much—but their show of solidarity with Athens would never be forgotten.

Barely eight furlongs away, was arrayed the vast and deep line of the enemy, archers and cavalry at the ready. The Athenian phalanx began to move forward as if it were one man—one mind—one bonded spirit. It moved slowly at first, as if the new body had to find the rhythm of its thousands of individual feet. Pheidippides looked over the heads of the men in front of him to see the Persian archers raising their bows and loading their deadly arrows.

"Let's have at them, my brothers, for the love of Athena!" shouted Militiades. The hoplites all began to run towards the Mede as the first wave of Scythian arrows descended from the suddenly darkened sky.

The next forty-eight hours would see the irreversible change of a life that had existed for over forty years.

This last thought was not in my mind as I peered down into the thick blanket of clouds. It was uncharacteristic for the Aegean during August, which usually boasts constantly clear blue skies. A twin-engine propeller plane transported me and about a dozen other passengers to the northeastern reaches of the Aegean. It wasn't until we had descended below two thousand feet that anything became discernable out of the rain-streaked window. I was getting slightly airsick from the constant turning and altitude shifts. Limnos suddenly appeared as the pilot banked our craft and headed right for its center.

As the wheels of the plane touched the ground in Repanidi, a drizzle carpeted the tarmac. The drizzle became a downpour—splattering powdery mud onto my shins and the bottoms of the white Capri pants I thought were perfect for the occasion when I left Athens. A loud boom filled my ears. At first I thought it was thunder, but then I realized that it was a fighter jet going supersonic.

Limnos is the ancient home of Hephaestos, the blacksmith of the Pantheonic Gods. Born sickly, his mother Hera tossed him from Mount Olympus into the sea. After a change of maternal heart, she brought him back to Olympus where she arranged his marriage to Aphrodite. Eventually he managed to incur the wrath of Zeus and was once again hurled from Olympus. This time, he crashed onto the rocks of Limnos—hobbling him permanently. As if the cruel indifference of Hera and then Zeus were not troubles enough, Aphrodite betrayed his fidelity. An affair with pretty-boy Ares, the God of War, led to a series of events by which the Limnian women cast Aphrodite's statue into the sea and slit the throats of the island's men.

There was an eerie pall over my heart as I climbed down the steps onto the island of Ion's birth, feeling tossed out from the heavens towards this desolate place.

It was a dreary day, with limited visibility. I caught a glimpse of the island's terrain during the final minutes of the flight. The eastern part was flat, the mountains lay to the west. Its volcanoes were dormant, but so was Vesuvius the day before it leveled Pompeii.

"Rain. Very, very good. Much needed," said the taxi driver as we headed west and north towards my destination. Perhaps he thought it was wonderful, but I'd have preferred another day of drought. Passing the harbor of Moudros, I saw what appeared to be the remains of concrete bunkers and rusting metal barricades buried deep in the sand—both left by the occupying Nazis. In the harbor itself, lay a half-submerged British battle cruiser from the first World War. The driver told me that every few years, divers would still find an unexploded sea mine. He also made a point of telling me, with some modicum of pride, that it was from this very port that the British launched their ill-fated Gallipoli expedition. I surmised that the British forces that besieged and freed Baghdad had also sailed from here. If so, there would have been a poetic justice in the fact that Ion's liberators would have come from the island of both his birth and enslavement.

The final mile of my ascent to the Convent of Epfraxia was accessible only by mule—and then only twice a day. I hopped onto the back of an old frayed mule behind two old women who mounted two others before me. I sat on something resembling a heavy bareback pad, cinched under the mule's girth, with a handle larger than a western saddle's pommel.

White pants—what a great idea that was! But that was not the least of my fashion faux pas. The old women cackled about me like chickens in a barn when a fox is detected near the coop. Without asking for my approval, they had wrapped a layer of fabric around my midriff and chest. Though my breasts were covered, the thin wisp of linen had become wet and transparent—offending their sensibilities.

The mule plodded along with its sure feet up a narrow and winding path that led to the summit. The mountain wasn't that high, but its unusual shape made daunting the thought of climbing it by any other means. It was a clammy heat—and flies swirled around the two-colored head of my mule. He didn't bother to move his head as they flitted about him, but I found myself constantly swatting them from my hair and face. The mule in front of me suddenly stopped on an incline that forced me to lean forward not only to see what obstructed our progress, but also to prevent me from slipping backwards and down the craggy trail. A few moments and a large pile of manure later, and we were on our way. Two more times I saw my life flash before me as I imagined myself plunging headfirst into steep rocky ravines.

When we reached the summit, the old women began to unload the supplies and provisions they had brought. The convent was much older than Panteleimon, dilapidated and crumbling in many places. And unlike Panteleimon's crisp white stucco, the stones of Epfraxia were a sandy color broken by rows of brilliant red and yellow wildflowers. In one arched doorway hung what appeared to be hundreds of large red rosaries which turned out to be bright crimson kumquats strung together on long strings—set out to dry in the hot summer sun.

There was no one to greet me. My expectation of some kind of reception office was far removed from the way things worked here—a light year away from corporate America. There were probably few people to ever receive, and those that came seemed to know where they were going before they arrived.

But just as no one was there to acknowledge me, there was also no one to discourage me from treading anywhere I pleased. No locks hindered my movement. Several nuns passed me, but when I offered a salutation, all they did was look in my direction and nod politely. I stood out as a white elephant yet none seemed to even raise their eyebrows at my presence.

Carved into the side of the cliff, the convent's windows seemed like porous openings in the mountain's white-lava façade. A long path wound away from the sculpted structure to a small plateau on the cliff. I walked to the edge, stared into the open space before me, barely conscious of the hand-carved stone wall and white marble balustrade that held me. Behind me was a large white cross—the first part of the convent visible from the coastal road.

A thick fog blanketed the valleys below, resisting the pull of the blazing sun above. Two different worlds existed for a moment in harmony—the gray one below and the blue one above. It was peaceful to sit between them. The fog's misty cloak was gradually crawling up the side of a distant cliff, branching into fingers, which seemed to reach over the crest. Though it kept moving, it never seemed to reach its goal—suspended in a constant struggle.

I wasn't sure if I would learn anything from this place, but I felt a peaceful calm that I had rarely felt before, anywhere. There was something missing. It was not merely the lack of cars, telephone poles or televisions. It was something else—something untouchable. Absent was any sense that these secular trappings existed anywhere.

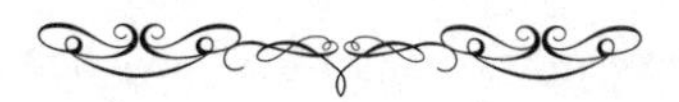

I began to feel her presence and understand her need to come here—away from of a world denuded of its humanity. Somehow I knew she would have chosen to sit precisely where I had. I wondered how she had managed to keep her faith. I had so little while living such an easy life. I had more in my closet than the cumulative possessions of all the inhabitants of this place, yet they possessed a serenity I had never achieved.

"You are welcome here," came a voice from behind me. I was so lost in my thoughts that I hadn't heard her approaching. I gave her a puzzled look. "How did I know to speak English?" she asked, rhetorically. "You dress as an American would. And what Greek would wear those to ascend to our sanctuary?" She smiled, looking at my dust-covered, mud-splattered, formerly white pants.

"I am a little surprised to hear English spoken here at all."

"I am the only one who does."

"So that's why they chose you to approach me..."

"Among other reasons. But I love to speak English. I don't get many chances anymore. My family is from Thrace, but my father worked for British Petroleum. I traveled much as a young girl. Many here have never left Limnos."

"I hope you don't think me intrusive. I mean no disrespect."

"We have few visitors, but those who come to seek truth are always welcome. I am Sister Mary Margaret." She was right, I had come to seek truth, just probably not her version of it. I wasn't sure this was a good idea.

As I introduced myself, I told her I was searching for someone.

"That is how we all have come to be here—searching for one greater than ourselves. You have obviously traveled far. Break bread with us, please. Then you can return to the world you left this morning—it will still be there when you leave. Or perhaps you will find what you seek and the world will no longer look the same to you."

"Sister Margaret, I'm flattered by your hospitality, but perhaps I should tell you why I'm really here."

"Does it matter?"

"Perhaps you will reconsider your invitation."

"You said you were searching..."

"Yes, but not for salvation. I am searching for one who was here—who might still be here."

"Really?"

"Her name is Leontokardis. Do you have anyone here by that name?"

"I don't know," she said, causing me to give her a quizzical look. "We have no surnames here. When we arrive, all worldly possessions are renounced, even our names. We are only known by the saint's name we have adopted."

"Alexandra was her given name."

"Two women here are known by that name."

"She'd be around eighty years old."

"One of them fits that description. She has been here longer than anyone."

"Please, take me to her. I must see her."

"You may see her, but you will learn nothing from speaking with her."

"What makes you so certain?" I asked. "Is she a mute or wary of strangers?"

"Neither."

"Then I'm sure I can make her comfortable enough to talk to me—with your help translating, of course."

"She has not uttered a word in over twenty-two years." Now it was my turn to be speechless.

I sat in the convent's dining room. There were two long wooden tables with equally long wooden benches on either side. A simple meal had been set out in the cooking pots in which it had been prepared. I sat next to Mary Margaret, but my attention was on the old woman who sat across from me. I watched her, but she did not acknowledge me. I studied her features, extrapolating my image of Alexandra across decades of time.

Her eyes were sad, the way I imagined them to be. But I could learn little else about her, except that the other sisters revered her for her piety and self-denial. That, and the fact that twenty-two years ago she had taken a vow of silence. Twenty-two years without uttering a word? How in God's name did she do that? Perhaps that was a bad choice of words—for it was in His name that she opted to close all oral communication with her fellows. I doubt I have ever remained silent for more than twenty-two minutes during my waking hours. Compared to this feat, even celibacy looked practical.

There was an eerie stillness as the nuns consumed their simple meal. No one spoke—even those who had not taken similar vows remained quiet in deference to their more disciplined cohorts. None of the chattering or laughter that would accompany any normal group of two-dozen women eating lunch together. Just the sounds of objects being passed, silverware touching plates, chairs creaking as weight shifted. The silence unnerved me.

I was pleased that their strict religious vows did not include foregoing alcohol as a decanter of wine was passed. It was strong and pungent—Limnos is renowned for producing its own blend of this elixir. I waited patiently for the meal to end, then Mary Margaret ushered me back to the place we had met.

"She will sit with you for a few minutes after chapel. But it is as I have said, she will not speak."

This could not possibly get any more frustrating. A few words with her could unravel so much. I started thinking about the old riddle of a tree falling in a forest without anyone hearing it.

In thirty minutes, Alexandra slowly approached, then sat next to me on the stone bench. There was once a time when I would have reveled in the challenge of making her speak—but I knew by looking into her eyes that no power on earth could make this woman break her vow. During lunch, I had clung to the foolish notion that we could engage in something akin to "twenty questions" with her merely nodding "yes" or "no" without violating any vows. But even this form of asking her questions seemed to cheapen the purity of her devotion.

All I could do was show her the picture I had—the one Panayiotas had sent Ion. Her reaction was worth more than if I could have elicited a thousand words from her. Tears streaked down her timeworn face. She held the picture close to her cheeks as if she could feel the warmth of her flesh emanating from its worn surface. I stared for a few moments at her hands, not sure why I was drawn to them. They were smoother than the rest of her wrinkled skin and very pale—not surprising I suppose, for a nun.

She looked up and stared at me for a moment, as if remembering something long ago lost. I thought she might speak, but instead, she looked down at the photo and back towards me again. Making a gesture for me to remain where I was, she slowly rose and disappeared back inside the convent. I didn't know what to make of her behavior, and after a few minutes I wasn't sure she would return. But soon, she emerged from the doorway.

Alexandra took my hands and wrapped a strand of rosary beads around them. She closed her eyes. I couldn't tell whether she was praying or reading me through my fingertips. Out of respect, I bowed my head and remained silent, unsure of what to do. When she was finished, she released my hands. When I tried to return the rosary, she pressed it into my flesh, letting me know that it was meant for me. I took it and squeezed her hand in recognition of the gift.

I began to say something to her, but she put her ancient fingers to her lips while shaking her head slowly from side to side. I knew the interview was over. I also knew that there was nothing else I could learn from her, or this place—except the fleeting experience of the solitude and peace that she had obviously found.

The mule ride down the mountain was even more frightening than the ascent. As terrifying as taxi rides in Greece are, I was glad to be back in one and off the suicidal mule. This driver was more talkative than the first, telling me about the Curse of Moudros. According to him, and he had it on the authority of his father and grandfather, during the Turkish occupation, Limnians killed several Turks and tossed their bodies into a well at the Monastery at Moudros. Wrongly blamed for the deaths, the monks of Moudros were massacred by the Turks. To punish the Limnians for causing this tragedy, the church put a curse on the inhabitants of Moudros, declaring that they should never sleep.

I was emotionally drained from my visit to the convent, but I had another important destination. Using a guidebook, my memory of Ion's journal, and the driver's knowledge of the island—I was able to find the amphitheatre that Ion referred to in his journals. The seats that he spoke of had clearly eroded, so calculating the center of their arc was quite challenging. I felt an adrenalin rush, as if I were an archaeologist on the verge of an important discovery. But locating the spot where Ion had found and reburied the artifact, and then the obol, proved elusive. I just didn't have the eye that Ion did to notice the subtle variations in what seemed like a monotonous field of dry earth. Nowhere did I see any discolorations or the more obvious signs of upturned dirt.

I knew that whatever he had buried here would not be found by me.

Disappointed, I sat on the stone benches. Looking out at the plains of Limnos, I imagined Ion running here as a child, and yet robbed of a childhood. As harsh as life here must have been, to then imagine him being taken deeper into the heart of the Ottoman Empire was even more frightening. But what chilled me more was to remember how horribly I treated my parents when all I was asked to do was move to sunny Florida.

"I hate you. I wish you weren't my father."

Even now, decades later, the cruel words that I spoke to Abraham, not once, but on several occasions, made me feel hurt and empty inside. If only I could have taken those words back. They were said without thought and by the next day or so, I could continue on in my life as if they had never been said—but how could I have expected him to be so easily cavalier about such spiteful comments. I was afraid to admit that I had been wrong, so I hurt myself by hurting him even more.

I knew I had to tell Ion that I found Alexandra, but to do so would force me to admit that I lied about going shopping, and more importantly, how I had come to learn of this place. I momentarily pondered an obvious possibility: that Ion knew she was here. How could he not have known, or at least assumed so? It was his journals that led me to her, and yet in the entire time we'd been in Greece—he made no effort to see her. Perhaps there was a reason he chose not to and I was meddling where I shouldn't. Then again, perhaps this was the news that a dying Panayiotas desperately needed to tell Ion. No matter the reasons or consequences, I knew that this was what Ion meant by *magna est veritas*—the truth simply had to prevail.

On the way back to the airfield, we detoured again, this time to the beach near Platis. The skies had cleared, though a thunderstorm danced on the edge of the horizon. Its lightning bolts were too far away to individuate, but its brilliant flashes of light illuminated the darker grays of the distant, looming clouds. I thought about Ion awakening in terror on the ground of the Baghdad desert, hearing nothing—sensing only the flashes of light from distant artillery fire, and then wandering through mine-laden fields with nothing but the presumption of death.

At SWB, I had forced myself to believe that I was pursuing a dream. Going to work everyday, I helped only myself and the bottom line of the firm for which I slaved. Straying ever farther from the dreams of youth into an emotional desert—I drove my spirit into burning sands and now, I thirsted for the ideals that once flowed freely from the fountain of my mind.

I spied an old gentleman on the sand, not far from the water's edge. A thin mist still floated a few feet above the surface, and enveloped the man's feet. He was dressed in baggy pants that resembled loose-fitting jodhpurs. Slowly, he began to sway back and forth, causing me to think he was drunk or disoriented. But gradually his swaying took on a more rhythmic pattern as he danced alone in the swirling misty cloud. He was oblivious to me, his face contorted in a mix of suffering and hope. Moving now with abandon, he cradled the air in his arms as if holding a woman he loved—bathed in Limnian moonlight.

38
THE LONG EMPTY THREAD

Two great masses of men collided with a crash. Shields met shields, and swords met both bronze and flesh. Pheidippides had no idea of how the battle was progressing. His entire horizon was no more than the surrounding ten or fifteen feet. All around him, blood and sweat splattered over friend and foe. The fallen, if not dead, would be trampled under the weight of the desperate life-and-death struggle above.

Pheidippides felt himself being pushed backwards—the momentum of their charge had turned. He looked to his left and right, Leotychides and Demaratus were still there. He fought on with a frenzy that only the pitch of desperate battle can induce.

All around, men were in various stages of living, killing and dying. Dust and blood-saturated mud flew up into his eyes, forcing him to squint.

On the flight and taxi journey back to Marathon, I debated which to tell Ion first, that I had read his journals or that I had managed an audience with Alexandra. Ion made me confront my choice as he broached the subject of my supposed shopping trip. Giving me no time to prepare a better story, I blurted out, "Ion, I didn't go shopping today. I went to Limnos." I paused, anticipating Ion's reaction. But he was silent, all the while staring intently at me. "I'm sorry I didn't tell you earlier but I was afraid you'd be angry."

"Angry? Why would I be so with you?"

"Do you know why I went?"

"Yes." I was relieved, yet frightened at what his answer meant.

"I met her, Ion. I sat with her for a while, but she wouldn't speak."

"Who?" Ion asked, and I felt uneasy, as if he clearly knew and yet wanted to play some sort of cat-and-mouse game with me.

"Alexandra."

Ion breathed deeply as if the mention of her name evoked every possible emotion of triumph and tragedy—sadly far more of the latter. I imagined a myriad of Ion's possible responses, even him not speaking to me at all for a while, though none of them prepared me for what he said next.

"That is not possible." Was Ion in some stage of denial, or was he forcing me to state the obvious of how and why I had come to follow her trail to Limnos. I had no choice now but to play out the scenario I had created, though I felt as if I were trespassing in uncharted territory.

"I read the journals."

"I have known that for some time, my dear."

"You saw them on my nightstand?"

"No."

"Then how?"

"In church, I saw the *Panayeia* had been moved."

"You could tell that?"

"I am her creator—I notice everything about her."

"I'm sorry, Ion. I know I should have asked for your permission. I have no excuse. I hope you aren't..."

"It was long overdue. There are things that have remained concealed for too long."

"She went to Limnos..."

"Yes, she always felt a bond with the island of my birth."

"She is still there—at the Convent of Epfraxia."

"It must have been someone else."

"Ion, please, listen to me—"

"Her hands?"

"What?"

"The woman you sat with—did you see her hands?"

"Yes, I actually did. She held mine for a few minutes…"

It was then I realized what Ion meant. I, who was once paid a King's ransom to uncover the most minutiae of details, had missed this one all afternoon. I closed my eyes and thought about her hands—the one's that were pale, and feminine and soft. The hands of the Alexandra I sought would have been anything but that. She had survived the deserts of Mesopotamia, the horrors of Nazi Germany and the depravity of a war-torn Greece. Perhaps time could fade some of the hardship, but not the scars. The woman I met at Epfraxia had none. Ion's Alexandra had burned her hands melting the chain that Ion had given her. I was disappointed. This old woman had fit the description so well. The coincidence was all too frustrating, and more strangely had lead to a place from which I had no idea of where to go next.

"Then what happened to her, Ion?"

"Surely you know these things. You have read the entries. I cannot retell it—it stirs memories too painful."

"They led me to Limnos where Alexandra had sequestered herself at the convent. That's how the third volume ended. There were no more entries, I'm sure."

"Third volume? But, there were four."

I stayed with him until we had talked down the sun. We didn't really say much, which was good, because I couldn't take any more drama today. Never once did Ion ask why I had disturbed his journals and kept my discovery from him. Nor did he ask me what I thought of them. It was as if the journals were a short film of his life, and when the lights went up, I, as the audience, was expected to leave the theatre as the credits were rolling.

Though curious, I knew I had no right to ask why Ion had told me he had lost these journals. If he had intended for me to read them someday, it would have been an odd thing to have told me. But then again, why did he go to Panteleimon that night, clearly leading me right to them? He certainly had not the strength to retrieve them for himself. I wondered if this, like the artifact Ion discovered at the Sanctuary of Hephaestos, was a secret that Ion intended to keep for himself.

The only other awkward moment that evening, at least for me, was when I asked Ion if it would be okay if I retrieved the final volume.

He simply nodded, and said, "I once thought of burning them."

That thought frightened me.

"Ion, they're invaluable…" I began to say, then wondered, to whom?

With Milos' help once again we slid the Panayeia sideways, enough for me to reach in and find the fourth and final journal. I had missed it in my haste the night I had uncovered the others. This time, I didn't try to hide my discovery. Milos' eyes showed his surprise as he saw the dusty leather volume emerge from its dark hiding place. I thanked him for his help, but my mind was on finding a quiet place to read what I hoped would be the full story about the elusive Alexandra.

It resumed in 1952. The first dozen entries were filled with rich details about Ion's volunteer work in Athens, and his growing friendship with Panayiotas, though they made no reference to Alexandra or his recovery. It wasn't until November of that year that she once again appeared in the center of Ion's diaries. Ion learned that Alexandra had left, no, that she had been asked to leave the convent almost a year earlier.

18 November 1952

My search wound me through a maze of people that seemingly had nothing in common, yet they all were attached to a thread at the end of which I prayed I would find her clinging. It was so fragile, and memories were so vague, that only the most serendipitous of circumstances would prevent the thread from breaking—leaving me with a dangling and empty end. Why did I hope her feelings would now be different than the day she crushed my hopes?

Still I searched. Even if in vain, it was better than living within my own mind. First, I visited her landlord, then his cousin who owned the café she always frequented, then a taxi driver that took her to work, and a fishmonger, and the owner of a waterfront bar in Piraeus. So many times, I thought I was so close to finding her, only to have the trail dead-end, making me retrace my steps and start a new search down an equally obtuse path. And when I did find people who remembered her, the information that they imparted was more dreadful than the blank stares of others who knew nothing. But each filled in a piece of a puzzle, her once beautiful soul—a shattered life splintering into chaos.

The civil war that followed in the aftermath of the world war destroyed any hopes that the survivors of that first holocaust may have had. When I was last here, the world was airlifting supplies to Berlin, the enemy now an ally, suddenly worthy of sympathy and support. I suppose Athens has not the strategic importance of Berlin, so there are no parachutes floating down bearing food and medicine. What would Manolis Glezos think now? Did any Berliner have the courage to raze the Nazi flag?

The situation in Athens during the past three years has gone from bad to worse. Disease spreads unchecked, rats roam freely in the streets that were once filled with people—people now hiding from the bullets of snipers that ricochet off the plaster walls, pock marking their once-smooth facades.

I learned that Alexandra had lost her various jobs; seamstress, waitress, even a teacher of the bouzouki. It wasn't that she had been fired, the jobs just ceased to exist, as did so many others. Boarded-up storefronts lined streets once vibrant with commerce. She was forced to take smaller and smaller jobs, anything to make ends meet. No longer hoping for a decent apartment or a chance to buy a new dress—these were already long forgotten dreams—just the chance to eat. Many didn't, and many died. Others, like my Alexandra, resorted to other means to survive, leaving their actions for others to judge.

That's when Panayiotas and I found ourselves walking the grimy streets of Piraeus, looking for a particular bar. It served the lowest form of human life, and alcohol was the least of the intoxicants and pleasures sought by its patrons. Though Panayiotas had insisted on coming with me, it saddened me to bring him to such a place. I prayed that this too would be a dead-end. I could not believe that my Alexandra could have been drawn down into such an environment—a place where the sediment of society accumulated.

We finally found the place. It also served as a boarding house. I shall not describe the types of boarders it attracted, or the temporary nature of their accommodations. The place stank of beer and urine. We entered the smoke filled bar. It would have been a challenge to assemble a more sordid group. It wasn't their filth, or grotesque behavior, which struck me, it was the utter sense of apathy in their eyes. Death himself could have walked into the room and I doubt anyone would have looked up from his drink. Perhaps he was an all too familiar patron. I felt as if this place was the end of the line for these souls.

It wasn't easy to find the man we sought. Strangers didn't go looking for strangers here, and neither Panayiotas nor I looked particularly intimidating, though there was something in his determination that seemed to make even the swarthiest character responsive to his questions. We finally learned that Mitsos, the owner of the establishment, was upstairs breaking in a new hostess.

"Don't lie to me," said Panayiotas. My friend's face had turned crimson with exasperation as the man initially feigned ignorance of what we were seeking. I had never seen Panayiotas so emotional and so aggressive—and so crazy—Mitsos was a good head taller than either of us. Scars, missing teeth and a recent cut above a swollen eye suggested that this was a man for whom brutality was a way of life. "Please, look again at the photo," he urged the man, holding up one of the shots I had of her from Limnos.

"Yeah, I knew her, so did everybody. Couldn't even tell you her name. Why, did she give you something you want to give back?" he spewed out, the nauseating stench of alcohol wreaking from his mouth.

"What do you mean give her something back?"

"Look mates, it's a cash business, there ain't no refunds here. And if she gave you crabs or lice, consider them on the house."

"How can you speak of a woman that way?" I said.

"Woman, ha! A two-bit whore, she was."

"How dare you," I said, feeling my own temper teetering near the point of no return.

"Why, was she your sister?"

"She was no whore," I said to this disgusting creature.

"Oh yeah, sure, you're right, she was a librarian who stayed here cause she like the sea air. Hey look you two, I didn't make her what she was."

"Where is she now?"

"I don't know. I threw her out about six moths ago."

"Threw her out, why?"

"Why? Let's just say she stopped bringing in the rent like she used to."

"What do you mean?"

"Hey, where are you guys from, a monastery? The rent, the paying customers, get it? I'm not the guy who knocked her up—the guy she was fucking every afternoon because he would bring her clothes he stole off the docks. Yeah, I knew about him, never asked her for a cut or nothing. Living under my roof, fucking a guy on the side and not offering me anything—maybe she thought he'd take her away one day, ha!"

"So you threw her out because she was with child? What kind of a monster are you?"

"Look, I run a business, not a refugee camp. All she was to me was a woman who couldn't work and who was gonna add another mouth to feed."

"You'd better remember where she went, my patience is wearing thin," threatened Panayiotas, though I had no clue as to how he intended to back up his threat.

"I swear, I don't know. Ask her priest, he might."

"Is that some kind of joke?" yelled Panayiotas.

"Yeah, a whore from Monday through Saturday, a damned saint on Sunday."

"I'll teach you to take the Lord's name in vain," my friend looked as if he was about to throttle the speaker of the blaspheme.

"Wait a minute, cool it Father. She really did go to the Church of Agios Grigorios. I'm sure they know more than I do. Hey, don't you guys hear everything in confession, you know, just before you wave your cross and save everyone's soul?"

"Let's go Pan, there is nothing more to learn here," I said, tugging at my friend's arm. We turned to leave.

"If you can't find her, come on back, I've got plenty of women who could convert you in no time."

It was all I could do to dissuade Panayiotas from breaking about three more holy commandments, though at that moment, I didn't believe he could devolve any farther. I was depressed, wondering what would be left of my sweet Alexandra when I found her—though I knew more than ever how much she needed me.

20 November 1952

The thought of Alexandra in her current state pulled my world inside out. Images of a young girl in a prison camp rose in my mind, as did a vision of her as a beautiful woman running naked into the sea on Limnos. These scenes became as anguished a riddle as any Sphinx could concoct. What was a life that could have such disparate existences? A beauty that once seemed to permeate her whole being had now become her only currency, but with each day and night of expenditure, its value diminished.

My desire to find her had become an obsession. I felt that time was running out, soon the wellspring of her life would dry out, leaving nothing but dust. I knew that I hadn't saved her that night in Baghdad for her to die homeless on the streets of Athens. On Limnos, she handed me her heart, but I let it slide through my fingertips like grains of sand. I am convinced that if I can just find her I can make her whole again.

21 November 1952

Panayiotas and I went to see Father Kousi late yesterday afternoon at his parish, Agios Grigorios. So many leads had proven false that I no longer allowed my hope of getting closer to her to increase. But of all the people that I spoke to about her, it would be the words of the vile pimp which would lead me closer, closer than anyone could have—right to the heart of the maze.

"Yes, I remember her. Alexandra Leontokardis. What a musical name, and such beauty to match. It is so sad." said the priest.

"So you saw her," asked Panayiotas, his eyes lighting up at this news.

"Yes, I saw her often, the last time was four months ago." Once again, I felt the trail evaporating just when it appeared to come into focus.

"Do you know where she has gone?" I quizzed him.

"It's too late my son, she has left this world. I am so sorry to be the bearer of such news."

I was numb and shaking from the reality that I would never again see the woman I loved. The relief of having found the end of the thread was overwhelmed by the emptiness of its being abruptly severed. I wanted to know immediately where she was and when I asked, all he could do was apologize for her meager interment. I said to myself, as much as to the priest, "Is this all? Is this all?" I wanted him to utter the words that so many others before had—that they had seen her but she had moved on, one step more and I might catch her.

There had to be something else. It was incomprehensible to me that a life could be lived and vanish without a trace—nothing said, nothing remembered. A life, no matter how torn apart, could not be forgotten. I knew at that moment, it was my task to remember. I alone, amongst the living, knew of this life, knew of its promise and of its beauty.

Neither priest spoke for a few moments, but finally, Father Kousi invited us to sit for a few minutes and join him for some wine. We retired to his study, and he had poured us each a small glass.

"Gentlemen, I would fill your cups, but I need the rest for our services tomorrow morning," he said.

"Father, how did she die?" I asked, not sure if I wanted to know, but knowing that I needed to hear it.

"It was tuberculosis, she had it for a long time, but fought it bravely. It finally overtook her."

"Did she pass peacefully?" I asked, but all the priest would say about her dying was that she was at peace now.

"In her last few days, as she traversed a state of delirium, she kept saying 'he will come Father, do not look so sad. He will come for me...' But then she seemed to drift in and out of time, at once a woman and a child."

"Who will come?"

"I assumed she meant our Savior."

"Did she ask about me?" I felt guilty and selfish, but I wanted to know if she had forgiven me before dying.

My one remaining hope was that her recent memory had faded, perhaps leaving her standing in the shadows of the bonfire at the hut of Haralambos.

"Father, we were told that she had been with child many months ago."

"The last time I took her confession, she was not."

"Do you know what happened to the baby?" I respected the sanctity of confession, but felt that it was irrelevant at this moment, that Alexandra's fate and that of her pregnancy should not be mired in the silence of religious ritual.

Father Kousi looked pensively at me, and at Panayiotas.

"A priest hears more than he can say," he began. "I can only tell you that she contemplated a terrible choice, one which I could only give her a spiritual and not practical answer." I knew that he spoke of her decision to abort the child.

I had come to the end of the search, the one true dead-end. I sat dejectedly in silence. My friend thanked the Father Kousi and he then put his arm around my shoulder and said, "Come, Ion, let us return to Athens."

"Wait a minute," said the priest. "She left me with something. I didn't know what to do with it—as far as I know, she has no family. It's in a locked chest in the cellar. Will you excuse me for a moment."

"Why didn't she sell this before selling her flesh? I asked Panayiotas as we stood outside the large brass doors of the church. The skies had darkened, and it had just started to rain. The only thing that remained of hers was the old bouzouki. The pendant that had once bound us was obviously gone. I could not have expected something of such value to survive Pireaus' streets of depravity.

"Perhaps selling this would have meant parting with her last vestige of humanity. It was a thing of beauty, a thing to be saved," he said.

I tucked the instrument case under my shirt to protect it from the increasing drizzle, and we headed down the empty, wet street.

25 November 1952

It was Thanksgiving three days ago. Several Americans held a makeshift banquet. No turkey could be found, so several smaller birds made up the feast. The chef swore they were underweight hens, but I think Athens is missing a few pigeons. It was a reminder of home for my fellow travelers. But I was neither thankful nor homesick. I heard the strains of an old melody, the words of which pierced my already ravaged heart.

I opened a well in my garden to let the birds drink.
You would come in the morning and the evening,
just like a little dewdrop.
One night you came with the wind and my heart was sighing,
Longingly I said "Good Evening" to you, but you said "Good Bye."
Talk to me, I've never kissed you, talk to me,
how could I forget you, my God, talk to me,
I've never kissed you, talk to me, I kiss you only in my dreams.
I planted bushes in front of your door,
so you can have shadow and fresh coolness.
I came here before the moon changed so I could bring you warmth.
I led you on your way up to the sun, to the broad alleys,
but frost and a cold wind came,
And you didn't build me a fire.

O Alexandra, your spirit fled your Earth-moored flesh and found the answers to the questions you sought in vain on Earth.

3 December 1952

Relief efforts continue unabated. It seems that for every person we help, three more show up. It is never-ending, but our work is good, and people trust us. They are so destitute—I wonder if I am making the slightest impact.

I am bothered by the label that had found itself associated with Alexandra. But who that was not here can judge? It often took more courage to live than die. It was easy for scum to use spiteful words like "whore," what did they know of starving slowly while other ate the rations of indecency?

Though I wanted to blame everyone from the pimps, to the Nazis, to the communists, I knew I was as much to blame for her death. And for what had I incurred this pain? To remain honorable to an adulterous wife, while one who needed me died slowly in the gutters of Athens.

Many nights I dreamed of that starry night on Limnos, home of the Vulcan's fire, and how she looked glowing before the fire

Haralambos and I had kindled. She is wrapped in my arms, calling out for me to take her—to save her once more. To save her from demons even worse than those we had faced in Mesopotamia. And in my dreams, I do not resist, and all that followed is different. Then I awaken to endless condemnation.

I thought of Elektra and Alexandra, each trying vainly to save their children.

8 December 1952

Panayiotas has renewed his challenge to me to acknowledge my God. Why? She is dead, the child is dead—what shall I pray for, their salvation, or mine? Where was God when she was shivering alone in her bed at night, wheezing and coughing with the disease that was killing her? Where was He when she saw no other choice but to kill her child? Where was I?

Panayiotas is different from most priests I've met. He sees the gray where his colleagues sense in only black and white. He is able to cope with the misery around us. I envy him for his unwavering faith. He is a good man, but it will take a lot more than his friendly persuasion to make me slip into the waters of salvation—it would take a miracle that I don't think he or his church is capable of.

I wondered about her unborn child. Would he have the dark hairs of her ancestors, or the blond strains of his English grandfather? I wonder whether he would have survived this hell, and what he would have become.

14 January 1953

Panayiotas has taken the posting at Marathon, where 'the mountains look on, Marathon, and Marathon looks on the sea.' I thought of Lord Byron and Greece's independence—though winning it killed him. Perhaps that was his independence...'and musing there an hour alone, I dreamed that Greece might still be free, for standing on the Persians' grave, I could not deem myself a slave.'

I am pleased for Panayiotas, and the parish of Marathon is made richer by his decision. I have been recuperating here at Panteleimon with him for the past few weeks. He caught me sketching on the portico yesterday afternoon. I say "caught" because I did not think my work worthy of the scrutiny of others, so I had been hiding my scrawl-

ings. He has asked me if I wanted to help restore some of the friezes which had been burned by the communistos and vandals. I think he must be desperate to ask me to work on something so important.

What intrigues me more is the large block of Pentelic marble that Tenedos has procured. It was going to be demolished to make way for a road. I have been studying it for days. Its streaks of gray criss-crossing its white surface. It is large enough for two people to fit completely inside. I can almost see them, the Madonna and Child—Elektra and Alexandra—clinging to each other as the exploding shells lit up the night sky. They are still alive, I see them, alive but frozen within the cold sepulchral stone. They live in this state of death, and only I can release them from their marble tomb.

One day I shall get a chisel and a hammer—one day I will set them free.

18 January 1953

I read my journals over the past few days. I realized I had never really read them before. Their words disappeared from my mind as soon as the ink was dry. They opened old wounds and made them bleed again. I wrote them to heal wounds, but in committing them to the page, I made them forever susceptible to being torn open again. I feel the only way to rid myself of this pain is to burn them. Yes, that's not a bad idea—perhaps my memory will be purged in the fires of their destruction.

I went to toss these in the fire, but I could not bring my own hand to do it. Perhaps a Christian burial is more fitting. I thought of the fires, and how much has been forged and lost in them. Where is my Thetis now, where is my armor, all I seem to have inherited is the heel and a one way ticket into the fires. I remember that night so well, the earth, her golden flesh and the fire.

I saw her in a dream, thro summer's haze,
Near the wine-dark waters still and deep,
Golden hair aflame like Helios' blaze,
Awakening my soul from dreary sleep.

Yet, betroth'd was I, and honor bound,
Afraid to finish what I could not start,

Tho her heavenly spark, once found,
Settl'd gently, and singed my lonely heart.

Years of longing, caught in a moment,
Her hand resting in mine, then gone,
The breath of an angel—teasingly lent,
Arousing me like the rosy-fingered dawn.

Wind and sea and sand twas all she wore,
As she danced by the fire on Limnian shore.

I am tired, perhaps I will think more clearly in the morning, but in either case, my hand grows weak from writing. I feel exhaustion overtaking my whole body, and I am grateful for it.

Somewhere out there, across the sea, on Limnian shore she lived, and danced and breathed—now lost to me forever. So close—I was so close. I cannot touch or see her again. I shall never know love.

I had never met this woman, and her death came as no surprise—but the tragedy of her ignoble demise in the gutters of Piraeus was agonizing. Though it was dark, I gazed at the *Panayeia* in a new light, realizing that it was far from what I or anyone else had presumed it to be. It was not that of Mary and Jesus, but of Ion's Madonna and Child—Elektra and Alexandra.

And as for the pendant I had sought, I knew I was initially guided more by the sense of a treasure hunt than what it meant to these star-crossed lovers. It had slipped out of their hands. It hurt me to think of it being traded for sex or alcohol in the alleys of Athens' seedy port—but then again, I have never known such hopelessness. Today—perhaps it rests in someone's possession, someone unaware of its significance—or perhaps it rests at the bottom of the harbor with countless more of ancient Greece's storied treasures.

I sat still, unable to move. I sat for a long time there in the church, long enough for my candles to extinguish into the blackness of the Marathon night. I heard a noise that startled me. I couldn't make out the time on my watch, but I guessed it to be near midnight. The importance of the fact that the fourteenth was in its waning minutes suddenly dawned on me. Tomorrow was the festival of the Panayeia, but tonight I was determined to witness with my own eyes the *Musterion* of Panteleimon.

I huddled in the darkness, irrationally afraid of something I knew could not be true. A dim light slowly appeared, like a halo, behind the statue. The Madonna's bowed head eclipsed the growing brilliance of light that illuminated the pews like a sunrise. Except for the initial noise that had interrupted my reverie, I heard nothing but my own heart palpitating. I was frozen as the spectacle that played out before my incredulous eyes. Finally, the light stopped moving and I heard soft crying coming from the altar. The cry was almost as a child, uncontrollable, and then the weeping became more distinct. A shadow moved around that base of the statue, I couldn't as yet make out whether it was human or spirit as it huddled before the altar.

Above the soft wailing of this apparition, I heard the trickling sounds of water as it cascaded over the feet of the Madonna onto the marble floor of the church. The dark figure, oblivious to its audience, slowly worked the washcloth up the legs of the seated figures, carefully cleansing it of its yearly sin of accumulated grime. Extra care was taken when washing the face of the cradled child. In the flickering light, tears of soapy water streamed down the child's face as the ghostly figure washed its stained features. Even in this dim light, I could see the true colors of the marble beginning to reawaken from beneath its oily residue. And, like the child I had watched baptized here a week ago, the statue seemed to come alive with this watery purification.

39
THE BINDS THAT TIE

A crushing pain sliced through Pheidippides' right shoulder, causing him to drop his sword and fall to one knee. Everything began moving in slow motion. He felt Demaratus lying by his side. His comrade's opened eyes told Pheidippides that he was dead. Looking up, he saw a Scythian sword above him—poised to strike, its metallic surface ablaze in the Attican sun. Pheidippides attempted to raise his shield, but his arm hung limply at his side. He wondered how his scalp would look strapped to his assailant's waistband. He could not see his slayer's features. Death would come face-to-face, yet faceless.

His last thoughts were of a woman and the love he had abandoned.

"Leontia. Oh how I have forsaken thee. If only the Gods will grant me one more chance—I will right my wrongs, Leontia. I will Leontia, I promise."

"Eftehea, what in the world..." I began to say to the shapeless form that drifted in the surrealistic light.

"Marianna?"

"What are you doing here?"

"You must to go from here now! You must to forget you are ever see me!" I was astonished. Not by her words, but that I had understood them.

Eftehea left Panteleimon in a hurry, but her flight was almost comical as I was able to outpace her with ease.

"Wait!" I demanded. She froze in her steps. "You speak English." She didn't answer, though she bowed her head and nodded slightly.

"But Milos and Dimitris told me you couldn't..."

"I never speak it. Once I am learn it for man. For man I think is in love to me. For me, is serpent tongue."

"Does Ion know that you speak English?"

"I am no speak English!" she stated quite emphatically. "No. Him not know," she said a little calmer.

"Why not?"

"It is other man he not know. After Ion is leave Panteleimon. An *American*," she said, emphasizing the last word to show disdain. "For he I am throw away everythings—my brother, my faith—my honor. I am blind by his words, his English words. He is to take me from here, and I am want to go. Him very, very bad man. Him evil man. From America, with big car and big lies. So I no speak English."

"Why are you here?"

"It is as my brother make me. I bring shame to my house and my church and I make him suffer."

"Who? Panayiotas?"

"No, but I am say no more. You must go. Please, leave me in my shame."

"What was your sin, speak, Eftehea. What did you do?"

"I am see somethings I am no supposed to. Here at altar, many years ago. They are hide it from me, but I am see it. It is day of Ion's *raftisi*."

"I know it was unusual. "

"Not his. It is second one in this day—later in evening. My brother is send me to next village to bring food to old friend. It is maybe two hours to there. But when I reach *Odos Marathonas*, Kavakis, son of Giorgios Xaritonimos is ride cart to village. Him take package for me—so I am walk back to church. When I am here, door is locked. Never door locked here. I am look in window on the other side of church."

"Eftehea—I've walked around every side of Panteleimon. All the windows are stained glass—you can't see through them."

"In war, bullets break window. I am look inside but no see altar—but I hear them and hear child. I see Ion is carry baby in blanket. Then I am run to hide. Ion or my brother no say nothings about baby."

"That's it? That's all you know? Your brother never said anything about it?"

"I am shamed! I beg he forgive, but he is say me only orphan can forgive. He say me no more. I must go," she said and disappeared almost as mysteriously as she had entered Panteleimon."

The records of Panteleimon! That was it. If there had been a baptism here, the church records should have recorded it. I wanted to look right then and there, but Father Diogenes was the only one with access to those records. It would be easy to convince him of why I wanted to see them. The night passed slowly, intermittent sleep with longer bouts of restless churning. I thought that I would surely be the first person to see Father Diogenes when dawn finally broke, but he had already left the house by the time I was up and dressed. Given the importance of the date, it was to be expected.

When I got to the church, he was chatting with some of his parishioners. It was a young couple, and I wondered if they were preparing to be married. Their trust in him was apparent, and it made me feel more pointedly the lack of such a community at home. The comfort and affluence of life in America had alienated so many from such spiritual forces. After escorting them outside, he returned and sat down next to me.

"How is he?" Father Diogenes asked me.

"Resting. But he's made so much progress in the past few days. We should be able to make our planned flight home tomorrow."

"It's a mixed blessing. I pray for his recovery, but not to see you go. I know that this wasn't the vacation you had in mind, but I hope that we have been adequate hosts."

"Your hospitality is beyond reproach, I'm afraid we have been less than ideal guests. Father, I..."

"Yiannis."

"Please, I need you to be my priest for a moment."

"Why do I feel a confession coming?'"

"Well, nothing so formal, but I have left something unsaid."

"Perhaps it is because it need not be said."

"I didn't mean to cause you concern, about Dimitris, I mean."

"I overreacted. First, as an earthly father, worried about my son's feelings, then as a spiritual father worried about losing a part of our pastoral community. Either way, it was not for me to choose, it was his, and there can only be one path in the church, the one taken without looking back and without regret. Who knows in what mysterious ways He tests our devotion?"

"I hardly count myself among the devout."

"You are not the one doing the counting," he said, and I thought I caught a wink. "You will always be welcome here at Panteleimon."

"Thank you Yiannis. I am happy things have worked out so well for you and your sons."

"And what about you, the woman they both admire so much? Have things worked out well for you?"

"I really don't know yet, but I know that a new path has been revealed to me."

"God only knows the end of our journey. The paths to our destiny He leaves for our own choosing."

"The choices seem many and difficult," I answered.

"Of course. Until you make them."

"Yiannis, remember you told me that you might be able to find the church records from the early 1950's?"

"It is possible."

"May I trouble you to look, to look now? I think Ion's spirits would really be lifted if I could find some remembrance of his baptism."

"Now? Marianna, I must prepare for the festival of the highest saint."

"Please, it would mean so much to..."

"Okay, I'll look. It should be there. Everything—births, deaths, weddings, baptisms—was recorded in the old registries. They will be musty, but at least the dryness of our cellar preserves them. Come with me."

"Thank you so much."

"Panayiotas is really the one to thank. He was a meticulous record-keeper."

Father Diogenes fumbled with an old iron key ring until he had found the one he wanted. He had to jiggle it a few times in the ancient hardware to get it to turn, one and a half times clockwise, setting the bolt free. The door was about three inches thick, and though made of wood, it gave the impression of impregnability. The vault was a set of two tiny rooms down a flight of steps. There was no wiring down here, and Father Diogenes had brought a six-stemmed candelabra. The air was still and musty. In the vault were wall stones memorializing the dead who had been buried here—though he told me that all the bodies had long ago been exhumed and reburied elsewhere.

"Why do you keep these down here, why not in your office?"

"The current year is, the rest are archived here. I'm not sure why, it has always been this way. Do you recall what year?"

"1953, I believe."

"Let me see, 1956, 1954, 1950, ah, 1953."

He set down the candles and opened the ledger. It was a large ledger book, bound with a folding slipcase and tied with a thick cord. He unpacked the volume carefully, and then drawing out a large handkerchief, wiped his brow of sweat. As I didn't know the month, Father Diogenes had no choice but to start from January. Fortunately, most recordable events, except deaths, occurred on weekends, reducing the number of entries.

"That's odd! This must be a mistake," he said, holding one particular page in his gaze.

"What?"

"There were two baptisms that day." He had barely finished saying these words before I asked him if I could see the log for myself. "Look here. Here's the entry for Ion," he said pointing at it. I could not make out anything but numerals. The rest was written in an idiosyncratic calligraphy—with a little stretch of my imagination, I could visualize the spelling of "Theodore."

"Is that unusual?" I asked.

"I have never seen it happen. The same day he took his holy vows a child was also baptized."

Father Diogenes was now wiping his brow with more frequency. Despite the claustrophobic heat, a chill ran through my body as if I were staring at someone raised from the dead. The hair on my arms stood at attention, and I blinked a few times to make sure I wasn't misreading the entry. The name was written, like everything else, in Greek, but I could make it out—I had seen it in Ion's journals before: Λ Ε Ο Ν Τ Ω Κ Α Ρ Δ Η Σ. I made sure to look upon each one several times, checking the accuracy of what my eyes beheld. No matter how many times I spelled it, it always formed the same name: L E O N T O K A R D I S.

The final proof of Ion's complicity came as Father Diogenes read me the names of the parents. Next to *mother* was Alexandra, her name was followed by the Greek abbreviation for *deceased*. It was Alexandra Leontokardis' child. But this was not what caused my mouth to dry. It was the name listed as the child's father—the name was unmistakably Ion's.

There could be no more doubt, though I lingered, staring at this shocking entry until Father Diogenes said, "We must go. It is often best to leave things where they are buried."

The Fifteenth of August is one of the most venerated of orthodox observances. I would have to wait until after the services to speak with Ion. We were in his room, but not yet alone. Evangelis was playing quietly in the corner. Ion was sitting up in bed watching the boy, moving his hands about as if the child were a marionette.

"That was quite a service, Ion, these parishioners take this holiday very seriously."

"On Tinos, they still crawl to church on their hands and knees."

"Sounds familiar. Didn't you and Panayiotas once..."

"Yes, but only once. The Tinosians do it every year." From my perspective, doing it once was overly zealous.

"Isn't that a bit over the top?"

"It's been passed down from parents to children for centuries." He had given me the opening I sought.

"Ion, were you sad about having no children?" I was almost shivering as I asked him a question bated to trap him.

"Ah, but I have."

"You do?" Could I have misunderstood him all those times I thought this topic had been dismissed before?

"Yes. Many."

"Many?" What Pandora's Box was I suddenly opening? I had visions of dozens of little Ions running around the world wondering where their dad was.

"Yes. Hundreds." Hundreds? How promiscuous had this innocent old man been in his wilder youth? "Hundreds," he said again, but then trailed off with, "But not one of my own."

"Your students?"

"Yes. They are as close as I have come to being a father."

"But none of your own. None of your own flesh?"

"No."

"Ion, Father Diogenes and I found something remarkable in the cellar of the church."

"Some vintage port?"

"The old registry of Panteleimon. I saw the entries on the day of your baptism."

"I see. That was quite a day," was his understatement.

"I can't believe you never mentioned it."

"You've come a long way, my dear, a very long way. And there seems to be no denying you once you set your mind to something. No wonder they coveted you at that law firm. What was their name again?"

"Schroeder, Wilkes & Barron. But you're changing the subject. The child was yours. I saw you listed as the father."

"The real father was found dead in an alley—his throat cut by Moroccan sailors."

"That's awful."

"Don't feel badly for him—not even a rat looked up when his body hit the ground."

"I'm sorry to have doubted you, but why did you have Panayiotas record you as the father?"

"My dear, would you bring us some tea? And perhaps you can take Evangelis back to Eftehea so we can speak, alone, together."

I returned in a few minutes with two cups. I pulled my chair near to his bed, and sat forward on its edge. I waited patiently as he steeped his tea bag, and then added some lemon and honey into his cup. He whispered under his breath as if saying grace before a meal. He looked up from his cup, but his eyes did not meet mine.

"I had given up hope. I had seen so much misery, and my own life was not without its share of heartache. All whom I had loved had vanished. They had died, disappeared, fled, or abandoned me. I did not trust in love, it had only caused pain and disillusionment. I had so wanted to see Alexandra again—I loved her. I felt so ashamed for what had happened to her. It was in my power, once, to make everything right in her life—and mine, but I was blind. When I heard she was pregnant, I was devastated. Another fathered a child that I had always dreamed would be mine."

"I'm so sorry, Ion."

"For whom?"

"For you, of course."

"But I had so many opportunities to set things right. It was I who failed her. I was torn. Should I search for the child—a constant reminder of my privilege denied—or should I forget what I knew and leave the child to wallow in the poverty of a degraded Athens?"

"You couldn't do that, could you? No matter what she had done, you still loved her."

"Yes," he said, his voice trailing off—eyes moving away from mine as pain revisited his wounded soul.

"Why did you falsify the baptism records?"

"It made a legal adoption easier. Both parents were dead. There was no one to speak for the infant. A fate left up to the state? I couldn't have that. As the father of record I could sign whatever papers were necessary."

"Was the child adopted?"

"Yes, by a couple who had tried for many years to have their own, but God had given them an empty nest."

"Did you ever consider adopting the child yourself?"

"A child does not belong with a nomad wandering in the wilderness. The child's painful lineage was best kept buried." I could tell I was chafing a bit against an immovable wall, but I was still confused at how they could have concealed such a thing.

"Ion, didn't you think that someday the child would need to get a driver's license, a passport—you know, to produce a birth certificate someday."

"Forged..."

"Forged?"

"Not impossible for a skillful artist."

"And who might that artist have been?" Ion said nothing, apparently taking a tacit fifth. "Forging a birth certificate. I haven't studied the statutes, but doesn't that sound like a crime to you?" I scolded him, though secretly I was more than a bit impressed.

"I never assumed anyone would understand what I did. But there was another reason besides the legal formalities of adoption. I feared the child would grow up with the stigma of such a lurid origin, with no chance to understand it, much less accept it." I could sense that I had touched a nerve in him. It was not often that I had ever been able to pierce his usually calm exterior. The starkness of his answers both intrigued and scared me.

"Where is the child now?"

"This is better left alone."

"Is the child happy?" I kept digging.

"I can only pray."

"Why haven't you said anything about this to me?"

"As you know from your reading, there is so much I have not said. It is not always necessary to regale another with your tales of woe. Why burden them?"

"It must have been difficult to remain silent. You must have been tempted..."

"Many, many times."

"Uncle Ion, I'm sorry I sounded so judgmental. I can't imagine what those times were like, but you did the honorable thing."

"Honor can be a very expensive currency."

40
A TIME TO HEAL

Something glinted in the sun. Leotychides' sword appeared as a blur. Suddenly, the Mede's arm dangled uselessly, half-severed. A second blow from an eight-foot pike pierced the wounded man's throat, and he dropped to his knees as blood spurted profusely from his neck. Its heat coated Pheidippides' face and began to bring him back into the moment. His sword had been lost, so he took Demaratus', prying it from his dead comrade's tightly clenched fingers. Raising it in his bloodied right arm, he swung it wildly through the Persian host.

The lines of battle had collapsed. A sea of barbarians closed around him and his comrades like a noose. He had lost all sense of which way he faced—such was the disorientation of the raging butchery and the agony of the dying. Its stench filled his nostrils, the stench of sweat and death and disemboweled men. Pain shot through his arms and ribs and he gagged and parried his sword and felt it strike air and flesh and bone as he and his countrymen were pushed to the precipice of death by the Persian bear.

A pile of clothes that needed to be laundered, a briefcase filled with tools no longer used, a plate of food that I had snuck from Eftehea's kitchen—my room seemed filled with things approaching decay and obsolescence. I was restless, wanting to continue my conversation with Ion, but he still slept.

In an effort to keep myself busy, I performed the menial task of straightening his clothes. As I placed some folded garments in his top drawer, I spotted the letter from Panayiotas. It was in its envelope, tucked away at the back of the drawer. I looked at it for a few minutes, amazed that such a light and frail thing as a piece of paper could have so changed my rigid course. The stamps showed the profile of Hermes—the swift messenger.

There was something amiss. Something wrong that only an experienced trial attorney would sense. It was too perfect, and no attorney likes that. One thing I learned in law school about the guilty is that they all leave some clue that inevitably exposes them. Every single one does.

The one thing that kept spinning in my mind was why would Ion have traveled this far to find out about Alexandra when he already knew her fate? He knew more than he had chosen to divulge, and I suddenly felt as if I were no longer the leading character in the story of my life.

I felt the need to run. Away from everything and to everything. So I did, out the door, into the field, and out to the road, faster and faster. Shoes were an encumbrance, an unnecessary barrier between me and the hard earth, and I quickly shed my sandals throwing each, one at time, as hard as I could away from me. The ache of the rough road dirt felt good but insufficient. Just off the road came the sharp pain of sand, gravel, and rock becoming part of the rhythm of my accelerating stride, increasing the frequency of the biting tears against my feet. More and more, harder and harder, until I slowed like an animal suddenly fully aware that it had been wounded, dizzy from the cold, sharp pain. Stopping, I finally dropped to my knees and could see the blood from my feet staining the stones. Who am I?

I was enraged. Rising, I could feel the damage in my flesh-torn feet, but still only wanted to run. I had no will, I thought, and would do only what my feet strangely ached to do—hobble. So hobble I did, until I arrived back at the house where, if for the sake of dignity, if nothing else, I would have to learn to walk.

Limping into the kitchen, I could feel wetness at my feet, and when I lowered my eyes, I could see the small pool of blood that escaped them. Slowly, and almost with somnolent indifference, I reached over to a large washcloth hanging on the cabinet next to me and began mopping the stone floor. The blood wouldn't stop, so I pulled over a high-backed wooden chair, sat down, and attempted to wrap my torn feet with the already crimsoned cloth.

When I looked up, Eftehea stood at the threshold, startled by my presence. I wondered what she thought, but whatever it was, she hurried swiftly to the sink and began filling a large porcelain basin with water. After bringing the bowl to the table and fetching some clean, white towels, she sat next to me and without so much as a word or a question began washing the open wounds.

"I feel so lost, Eftehea—I'm not sure of anything anymore," I started repeating to her, knowing that she could not understand but wanting her to understand. She only looked up at me, shaking her head slightly, and left me for a moment to retrieve a knife and a bottle of what looked like alcohol. Heating the knife she placed it and the bottle on a plate and returned. She held a small cloth to my mouth, and I knew what it meant. Besides the obvious tears to my flesh, and the bleeding, which had not stopped, my wounds were filled with dirt and pieces of splintered thorns.

Biting down on the cloth, I let the searing heat shoot through my body like a cleansing fire. The cloth dropped from my mouth, and suppressed crying soon turned to laughter. There was no humor in my cackling, it was a laugh of self-pity.

"I am sure everythings is be all right."

"That's easy for you to say." I immediately realized how true was the opposite.

"Where are you get this?" she asked of my anklet.

"From my mother," I answered, gritting my teeth in pain.

"Where are you get this?" she repeated. I presumed she didn't understand my answer. But then she began to sob. I began to repeat my answer but she wasn't listening. "I not tell you whole story. About man I love."

"The American who betrayed you, the one who made you hate my language?"

"I am hate him, it is truth. But only love him to escape another."

"You loved another..."

"I am love Ion—but him love another."

"Alexandra."

"Yes."

"You know of her?"

"I kill many soul in one sin. Is too much for me," she said averting her eyes.

"What happened, Eftehea? You can tell me," I asked, almost forgetting that until a few hours ago I didn't believe I could converse with this woman. "Perhaps it is not too late to right the wrongs. Tell me. I will tell no one. Remember, I'm a lawyer. Anything you say to me is confidential..." I stopped myself, stunned at the absurdity of my monologue.

"Is too late... She is dead, and I am kill her."

"Eftehea, you couldn't have. She died of tuberculosis, in Piraeus."

"I kill her all the same, and I kill heart of man who is love her."

"But she was the one who abandoned him. She broke his heart. I know more than you think."

"Do you?"

"I know that Ion sent a messenger to the convent on Limnos. This messenger brought her a sign of his love and a test of hers but returned with the news that she did not love him—that she would not see him."

"Messenger is tell big lie. Alexandra is love him, love him with all heart."

"How do you know?"

"The messenger—it is me."

"How can that be? Ion's writings revealed the name of the messenger... It was someone named Gia."

"*Gia*. It is meaning dark flower," she said with a wistful look that momentarily overcame her sad eyes. "It is old name only he use for me." I was stunned. "To both I am tell big lie—for this I am bring shame to Panteleimon."

"Why?"

"I love him. Him love too, but not in same way... Ion is send pendant with love, but I tell Alexandra that he is return it because he not love her. I am say his heart belong for another—but it is only my hope this true. Her heart is crush, but send back to him with plea."

"What did she say?"

"The same words I am no want hear. She love him, she love him. I can stand no more. When I come back to Ion, I am tell him she love another and is going from Epfraxia. I say she forbid him to follow. They are believing me and my lies. But loss of Alexandra is do nothing to bring him to me. I confess to brother, him very, very sad."

"That explains the letter Panayiotas sent. On his deathbed he was willing to break his vows. He was going to tell him. That's how much he loved Ion."

"Not too much as me."

"How could you have done that to Ion and Alexandra? Especially after they trusted you with so much?"

"I am have big penance—more than cleansing statue. God is making my bed and womb barren. No respect of brother, no Ion to love. And no one to forgive me for my sins. I am wait for orphan and then is come Evangelis. He is need me, make me feel no lonely."

"That is why Panayiotas said he held the key."

"He is orphan and bring Eftehea joy she is not know for very long time—but he is not my salvation."

I took pity on this old woman. Whatever her misguided notions—she obviously did love Ion. I was loathe to cast judgment. These thoughts were welling up inside of me when I abruptly found myself saying, "I forgive you."

She didn't react to my words, appearing absorbed within herself. Then I noticed her breathing become shorter until I thought she might collapse.

"I am know now who is my salvation."

"Who is?"

"I am so very, very sorry," was all I heard her say before she lowered her head and stared at my blistered feet. I almost yelped as the searing heat from the knife cauterized my raw flesh. I knew that we were not going to speak about this anymore. She averted her eyes from mine and set back upon her chore of cleaning and dressing my wounds. She applied a salve and placed some clean gauze and bandage upon my feet. Gathering up the bloodstained clothes, she threw them into the hearth and stood back as the flames consumed them.

She helped me back to my room where I quickly drifted from thinking about the numb throbbing in my limbs to the man who slept in the next room.

"This is take time to heal," she said, leaving me alone. I wasn't sure for whom she spoke. "Wait. I am bring you somethings."

In a few minutes, she returned.

"Here. When Ion is send me with pendant, it is hang on chain. Alexandra is keep pendant, but she is say chain cannot keep. I am not bring back to Ion—I afraid it will tell him something of her love and make him not forget her. Here, is for you," she said as she handed me a chain about eight inches in length. Alexandra had been right, but tragically never knew it. Had the two halves been joined, she and Ion would have known love.

"Why for me? Shouldn't you give this to Ion?"

"I bring to you. You will do what is right. You will know."

"Ion, when you left Father Kousi, you had assumed that Alexandra had..."

"Done the unthinkable. And I would have always thought that had it not been for the Gods placing me in the right place at the right time—and for a stranger." his voice suddenly choked, and his words failed him.

"Take your time, Ion. Would you like to speak later—perhaps tomorrow morning?"

"No! We must...we can...speak now. It is best."

"Okay, tell me now."

"I was unsure of Panayiotas' offer to be baptized. I waited for a sign to guide me."

'Yes, I remember."

"It came—brighter than a supernova on the darkest night. Another American volunteer, a friend named Kostas, was working at an orphanage in Athens. He met and fell in love with a local Greek girl, a dark-haired beauty who lived with her parents. They were leaving Athens for the weekend, so he begged me to cover for him. I could not say no to the opportunity to aid and abet a blossoming romance.

"That weekend, I was in the ward where the youngest children were kept. There were many infants, and they cried out day and night to be nourished. We bottle-fed them a formula the matrons made from what scant ingredients they could commandeer. They were starved for everything, for food—yes—but mostly for love. Even to be held for a few minutes would soothe their constant loneliness and fears.

"I was at the end of the shift, and I was relaxing on the front steps when another volunteer came out to smoke a cigarette. He knew I was an American, which held different connotations to different people. To him, it meant I had money. If only he knew how low I stood on the economic ladder in New York, but to him I may as well have been a Vanderbilt. I had met many like him, always scheming, always looking to barter something. They supplied the black markets with things they'd steal from any jobs they had, hospitals and orphanages were not off limits to their pilfering."

"He wanted money from you?"

"Yes, for something he had found on one of the children."

"What scum."

"I will let him be judged by the great maker; to me he was a savior."

"What was he peddling?"

"A trinket whose value was incomprehensible to anyone but me. I made him show me the child from whom he had taken it. One look into the child's eyes, and I had my proof. I would have known those eyes anywhere."

"What was the trinket?"

"It was from the chain I had given her on Limnos to replace the leather one I had tied around her wrist in the Iraqi desert. She must have given it to her child before she died. The obol it held was long gone. I threatened the swarthy character, but he swore upon his life that the chain was all she had. The pendant was no doubt pilfered before he could defile it."

"There are millions of chains. How could you know for sure it was the same? Even the one I wear is similar—and on Limnos I saw hundreds of them."

"The fires that forgot the bronze were unremarkable, but Hephaestos' flame had left its indelible mark. Here—see how the links nearest one end are different. They were disfigured by the flame that Alexandra used to sever the chain. She told me when the chain's halves were reunited we would be free to love. I sent this one, my half, with Eftehea. The other was given to you decades ago."

"How on Earth could my mother have gotten Alexandra's necklace?" I didn't quite grasp the sudden transition that Ion had made. I removed my anklet and cupped it in my hand, watching his eyes follow it.

"It was always yours. I sent it to Abraham and Christine in a letter."

"A letter?" I remembered the very first clue that led me to Ion. The letter I found in my father's book mentioned a gift from Ion… something "*I would be very glad to have one day*."

"See where your links are worn down by the heat? It is the same chain that I draped around your mother's neck that starry night on Limnos—melted by the same flame that snuffed out our dreams..."

"Ion, what are you saying?" Now I knew Ion was teetering very close to the edge of dementia or at least some unmistakable confusion. "Besides, the entry I saw in the ledger—"

"Maria Anastasia was the name I chose for you the day we were baptized. Christine shortened it—to Marianna."

I was too stunned to speak. Suddenly my brain saw a series of letters. They had started as letters that made no sense, now names were spinning around in my head, and now they had come back to being simple letters, letters that now made perfect sense. I had seen the child's name, Maria Anastasia, but it had meant nothing to me, other than the fact that Alexandra had given birth to a daughter. Maria Anastasia Leontokardis. I always thought my mother had given me the chain, and so she had.

I can assure you, I didn't accept on face value Ion's stunning comments. I suppose there was no way to deliver such a blow except in as few words as possible, but it still hit me with the paradoxical casualness of a memo, "FYI: you aren't you." I made him repeat himself several times, and then several times again, as if hoping some new version would end with "just kidding," or "oh, I'm sorry, I was talking about someone else." But I knew Ion was neither demented nor confused.

I couldn't have known how fragile a thing identity can be. A moment ago I was someone and now I am supposedly the same person but only an act of rational thought allowed me to cling to sanity. The woman at the office, the woman who had taken law school examinations, who had worried and worked herself into a partnership—even the woman who had been married and abandoned seemed someone else, someone I was watching, almost casually, as background on a screen playing in an empty room. The only other thing I saw in that room that was real and had substance was the child I had lost and that child suddenly looked at me with love and forgiveness. That child alone was of my body and of me, and everything else, everything, even my own parents had become detached and fictive images. Spinning became the only motion in the world and what I wanted to do was stop the spinning by trying, by some kind of wild act of control, to connect myself to this new life, but it too eluded my grasp.

"Only Alexandra, rest her soul, knows your real name. The Gods had made me their instrument and had willed me to find you. In you, a part of her lives on."

"And what of Abraham and Christine—what do I call them now—*foster* parents? Have you done their memory any justice by tearing the bond between us?"

"I only wanted—"

"You wanted what? I came to you, to help you, why did you let me—knowing what you knew?"

"You can imagine, now, how I felt when you found me. The child of my dreams had come to me. You know I never sought you out and never intended to burden you with the life mine had become. It was why it was too difficult for me to see you—you were the daily reminder of what I had lost. When you moved to Florida, I could pretend that the distance had made seeing you impossible."

"How could the three of you have hidden this from me?"

"Your birth had come under such dreadful circumstances—they made me promise to say nothing."

"What right did you have to bargain with my life and my identity?" I felt deeply disoriented. To learn that the two people I had always known as parents were merely good Samaritans who took me in to their home was too much to digest. It felt as if I were in a crazy dream that I could not wake from. "Was I ever to be told?"

"When you were old enough to comprehend," Ion said.

"Were they worried I wouldn't have treated them like real parents if I knew the truth?"

"They wanted to tell you, but something happened, something that hurt Abraham very deeply…" I knew what Ion referred to, but I was too hysterical to bear any responsibility right now. "He decided to wait until things got better—he was so afraid that you didn't love him. But things didn't get better, and then he fell ill. He knew he had little time. He wanted you to come, but he was too proud to insist—a foolish notion given the import of this secret that he alone kept since Christine had passed away."

"But he wasn't alone—you knew."

"When you came to Queens, you were grown and strong."

"Strong? Ion, you knew that I was restless and seeking."

"Yes, seeking—but not ready to find…"

"Oh, so philosophical, Ion. So carelessly and beautifully philosophical."

"Marianna, your life had become so centered on… I needed to know you were ready."

"For what?"

"Perhaps you can still grow closer to your father."

"It's a little late now…"

"Perhaps I should have done it all differently, forgive me."

I could say nothing—I was certainly not ready to forgive. We sat for a very long time in silence, until darkness fell upon us. I helped him to his room and readied him for bed, the same as always.

"Forgive me," were his last words to me.

I sat with his sleeping form for a while. After a while I got up and quietly left the room. Going from room to room aimlessly I felt the agony of having lashed out, leaving him there to suffer a little of what I was suffering. He, like Abraham, had done what he thought was right, and I understood for the first time that even our most virtuous efforts can inflict pain on others.

41
THREE STANZAS AND A COUPLET

By the afternoon of Metageitnion 22 in the third quarter of the 72nd Olympiad, six thousand four hundred Persian souls left their bodies in the dusty red plains of Marathonas—carrion for the birds and flies.

"I thought our fortunes lost when our center collapsed," Pheidippides said to Militiades.

"Your vision of the eagle in the wilderness gave me the idea to lure the Mede closer with the false sense of an easy kill," answered the General.

"But you led the center, you were in the eye of the beast."

"Could I ask another to do what I would not dare?" said Militiades, reaching out his hand to help Pheidippides, blood still seeping from his right arm.

"The Mede?"

"He sails around the cape to Athens."

"I must run and warn our citizens."

"Pheidippides, you have already journeyed to Sparta and back, and then been wounded in battle. We will ask Hippomines to deliver the message."

"No! Can I expect another to do what I would not dare..."

It is now late in the evening and I am alone in my room. My earlier run, as the sun set, was more painful than I had bargained for. But through its pain, my mind was momentarily relieved of its anguish. Now I needed time to think, to sort out my feelings. It is deathly still. I can hear no sounds made by man, just the wind sweeping inland from the Aegean as it rustles through the rows of olive trees outside my window.

I cannot sleep. No, it is not that sleep will not come to me—it is that I will not go to her. My consciousness refuses to surrender willfully to the uncertain drift of dreams. And no dreams could ever be as wild as the reality to which I am awake. My mind is alive with so many thoughts, their energy snapping across my brain's synapses like millions of fireflies darting about in a dark cavern. All these streaks of light flit about as if in random motion, while my mind struggles desperately to find their common denominator, to retrace, reevaluate and reshuffle every stored memory in the light of my revelation.

Ion, whose courage sent me into the abyss so that I could find my way, sleeps peacefully in the next room. The past week was terrifyingly difficult. His breathing was labored, and sleep did not come easily. As he hovered between life and death—I teetered on the edge of perdition.

A black phone presented itself to me as a life preserver, and I thought of the wise and soothing voice of Adonia at the other end. Despite the lateness of the hour, I telephoned her. As always she answered the phone without the slightest hint of being annoyed. I told her what had happened to me, and what I had learned—trying to fit each piece of the puzzle into some logical sequence. Telling it, I wanted to believe that I was narrating someone else's story. I told her how angry I was with Ion and the knowledge he imparted. I also told her that the tide had turned, that I knew something that he didn't.

"It sounds to me as if Ion was in a situation he couldn't win," she said after I had finished my diatribe. "He deserves to know."

"Why? He wasn't forthcoming with me."

"Doesn't that sound similar to what you accuse Ion of? Besides, where were we when Ion had to make his choices? Did we give him advice and then make ourselves available to bear the consequences?"

"How do I know that it will help? To know too late that she loved him—is that really better?"

"It is all too tempting for us to judge, especially when we mislead ourselves in believing that our choices existed for another."

"I know, but..."

"There is no but, Marianna. What I shared with you the other day at St. George's had burned my soul for years. I would know happiness one day—but I lived with the silent torment of my secret—that I had killed the flower of my savior. The *communistos* were cruel, but they were too late—I had already done the deed."

"You mean Niko never knew?"

"Never. No one before you. Not even my poor Niko, though he suffered from its cruelty."

"Aren't you happy that he never was burdened by its truth?"

"Burdened by the truth of my suffering? I suppose I was spared the humiliation, but in return, my love went to his grave believing that it was he who had let us down. A lie that I was too ashamed and cowardly to unburden. I should have told him—now there is no second chance."

"Dorando Pietri."

"Who?"

"An old Italian marathoner that Ion told me about. His story reminded me of how sad it is to come so close to something and never realize it. What should I do, Adonia, I'm so confused?"

"We say that life is like a marathon race, but the former can only be run once. Do not wait! Go to him and tell him that she loved him—set him free."

Like all heroes in preparation of a great journey, before Ion would achieve emancipation—he would first be purged in the fires of the Gods. And I was part of that fire that challenged his faith by my ignorance and indifference. I punished him for having been the messenger of truth, unsympathetic to his need to unburden himself of its weight. There was so much that I left unsaid. But tomorrow, I shall right the wrongs.

I long for the sunrise, the first one of my new life. I wonder how it will appear; though the harder I concentrate on it, the more it floats beyond me. I have so much to tell Ion, and so many questions to ask. My desire to know more is becoming insatiable, though I am forced to wait out the long hours before his body once again rejuvenates.

I thought about sleeping. I imagined it to be a safe place that I could retreat to after this day, and all that had happened, leaving my dreams to do the work of sorting out my fears and my anxieties. But for some reason, even though I had awoken with the sun over eighteen hours ago, I was wide-awake.

So much was spinning around me in my newly disoriented state. I felt pain and pressure in my chest. To relieve the pressure, I jumped up and darted frantically about the room. I moved things, touched things, and arranged things with ever-increasing speed, a rage for order building up in me to stave off encroaching chaos.

Nervously pacing on aching feet through the rest of the house, I felt utterly alone and cast off from the life I had once known. I went back to my room before hearing Father Diogenes and his sons come home. They were very quiet, but I heard the van doors closing, and muted whispers as they tiptoed into the house and, I presume to bed. I was relieved not to see them. I wanted to see no one then. No one, absolutely no one, would suffice to save me from the new confinement of solitude in which I had been hurled.

Back in my room, I stared at my walls, studying their myriad cracks and fissures—the imperfections appeared even more spectacular in the flickering light of my candle. These signs of decay are hardly cause to lament. For as Ion always told me *sublime beauty resides in simplicities*. Even in the cracks on an ancient farmhouse wall or in the wrinkles on an old man's face—through them light eventually shines.

The history of my life had suddenly become more vast and more mysterious than ever I had imagined it. This fact pressed around me like suffocating walls and, inexplicably and simultaneously, as though there were no walls at all, nor grass, nor trees, nor anything else but infinitely expanding space and time leaving me, my self, stretched and pressed out of all known shape and dimension.

I long for the stability that a blank page can bring me. There I can articulate what I feel for this man who in a single confession had both destroyed and created my life. Tonight, I shall try to be worthy of him—my teacher who inspired me to see. With a ballpoint pen for a paintbrush, and some torn pages from a travel journal as my canvas, I will paint my thoughts across this empty landscape. I recalled Ion's last words to me as he fell asleep. I was too stunned to acknowledge him at that moment, a moment that he so desperately needed my compassion, but I thought only of myself. I was selfish, but it was hard to be otherwise given the trap door that had suddenly opened beneath me.

But now, I needed to think of him, and not myself, and not look to channel my bewilderment into hostility towards Ion, the man who had risked everything to save my mother, and then her daughter a generation later. He needed to know that I loved him—and held him blameless. He had been drawn into a world mired in inhumanities and he had managed to remain humane, and I had no right to judge him in any other light but his willingness to sacrifice for others.

I wrote an answer to him as the light of my candle danced into every crevice of the room.

My dearest Ion,

You asked me to forgive you. I cannot. I cannot because there is not and has never been anything to forgive. Had you not saved Alexandra in the burning Persian desert, I would never have received the breath of life. Had you not rescued me from the confines of the orphanage, I would never have tasted freedom. And had you not led me to the light of Panteleimon I would never have been able to comprehend the magnitude of these gifts.

I stared at what I had written. I had so much more to say, but suddenly I wasn't happy with it. It was too analytical—I wanted to write something from my heart, not from my mind.I didn't know where to begin. My mind felt as if it wereadrift on a sea so vast that it looked infinite in every direction.

I decided to write him a poem—a sonnet actually—a trio of four-line stanzas ending with a couplet. Though how can fourteen lines possibly do justice to a man's life? Even if it were 14,000 lines, they could barely scratch its most superficial layers. But form is needed to distill the quintessence of so unusual a being.

I will not sleep until it is complete, and I am satisfied with it. And when it is done, I will place it on the dresser next to his bed. I want it to be the first thing that he sees tomorrow morning when he awakens. From this short poem, I pray that he will feel the magnitude of my love.

I only had to write fourteen lines, not even complete sentences, just lines. But the blank page seemed daunting, almost overwhelming. It wasn't that I didn't have fourteen lines in me, no, the problem was quite the opposite. I had millions, and only fourteen of them would make the cut, but which ones? I put my pen down and closed my eyes and relaxed. I imagined Ion's life swimming before me across the waters of my inward eye, and then it flowed.

I made my way back to his chamber. The floor beneath my bare feet creaked slightly, giving and taking the weight of my feet. In my left hand I carried a candle in a small silver holder. It lit my way as I entered Ion's room. Gently placing the poem on his nightstand, I suddenly felt saddened, as if years of straying from my dreams had finally taken their toll on my spirit. Everything was motionless and silent. Half the room was dark, the half that bore Ion on his bed.

Ion was covered in a finely woven blanket, made from the sheerings of the sheep that graze on the surrounding mountains. I noticed that his feet were protruding from the lower edge of this fleece. I stood at the foot of the bed and pulled it down to warm his feet. The soles were leathery with decades of callous formed from running barefoot over inhospitable terrains. Once, these feet had carried him over craggy mountain edifices as gracefully as an antelope sprinting across the plains.

I looked towards the door, but could not leave yet. I didn't think he was awake or able to hear me, but there was something that I wanted to say before I left. I stroked the flowing white hair that framed his tanned weathered face. His chin was coated with coarse stubble growing like silver moss on a diluvian polished rock. His once fine athletic body had withered like a grape that has been left too long on the vine, enduring the first frost, stubbornly clinging to its stalk. Not even for a second did it cross my mind that Ion was an old man in the twilight of death. Only his silver curls and his radiant eyes appeared to me as they might have a thousand years ago or a thousand years hence.

"She loved you," was all I said, deciding to explain the rest in the morning. But Ion suddenly stirred and opened his eyes, though I was uncertain whether he could discern what I had said. He turned his face towards me showing a slightly sad smile. His eyes were shiny disks, and above them his eyebrows curled like light clouds struck over the moon. His gaze was fixed on me as I had never seen it before. He did not look possessed, rather I felt I was seeing Ion turned into a God. Ion's attention felt like that of the sun itself. He appeared an almost veiled figure drawing me toward him, though he said nothing, and made neither motion nor gesture.

I took the chain from my pocket and laid it on his nightstand, next to the poem. He still didn't say a word but I was certain he followed my every move. I bent down and undid the clasp of my anklet and laid it atop the other half. They touched for the first time in forty years.

Standing within inches of his bed, I undid the sash of my robe and let it drop slowly to the floor. I stood before him naked, naked in flesh, in mind and in spirit. Naked as Eve in the Garden without the slightest thought that there existed anything other than the purity of nakedness. But it was not the nudity of sin or lasciviousness—it was the nakedness of a subject before the master sculptor.

His eyes made only the slightest motion, more a dilation, and I saw his hand reach upwards towards me. We never touched, but I imagined the power of his hands on the clay of my soul—ready to breathe life into his creation. My body had never felt more alive, more full of power as it conformed to the flow of his motions. I began to sway slightly with them, dance with, undulating with the rhythms of his aerial strokes.

I felt at once the beautiful and terrible feeling of baring my body and spirit. I drifted swiftly backward as he seemed to fly away from me. But he took something with him that I had never given any man. I gave him all that I am. I gave him me in my most raw and vulnerable state, to do with as he wished. I felt unencumbered, without shame, and timeless. For one brief moment, there was no distance between us, we were one and the same, two souls fused.

I felt that something had been put right for him and we both knew that I was the one to do it. The chains were together again. Somewhere, somehow, after everything that we know passes away, he and Alexandra would be able to love again. That was the reason we had come here and now there could be peace—for Panayiotas and Eftehea, for Ion and Alexandra, and for me.

Leaving his room, I remember his eyes receding like two lights, appearing then fading on the horizon, a vast and dark ocean separating us in the night.

It was well after midnight. In this rural village, being awake long after sundown is like being alone in the universe. But tonight I was not alone, and I never would be alone again. I watched the candles' light and I felt warm, though it had begun to cool down outside. I sat in the small chair I had placed in front of my makeshift writing table and began to write. I wrote in a steady stream whatever flowed from me unselfconsciously in a whirlpool of words. I wrote and wrote, until exhausted in every conceivable way, and I felt the exhaustion pulling me into the penumbra of sleep.

42
CITIZENS REJOICE!

Stripped to nothing but shorts, he took one last drink of water before gazing up at Mount Pentelicus. As he climbed above the plain, he gazed upon the scene of his people's greatest victory—for themselves and for humanity.

Three hours later, Lykavettis loomed on his left as he passed through the Thriasian Gates. The lone runner continued south along the Panathenaic Way, drawing closer to the Altar of the Twelve Gods.

Perhaps it was this kinship that led him past the Statues of the Eponym Heroes, where official decrees were normally posted, to the Hephaesteion—the temple dedicated to the Vulcan blacksmith who dwelled on Limnos. There on the steps before the sanctuary, his head rose above the growing crowd, which drew closer, thirsting for news of the battle.

"Nenikekamen—Rejoice citizens, victory is ours!"

"His last words?" asked the Young Pupil.

"No," answered the Ancient Narrator.

"But the legend said..."

"Legends are stories told by people who weren't there."

I had run a little ways and enjoyed the way the snow fell around me. My gown blew with the wind, it was white like the snow. It was all I wore—yet my body felt impervious to the wintry chill. Barefoot, I was nevertheless oblivious to the bite of the ice crystals that accumulated in my path. Soon though, my movements slowed as the snow rose above my knees. I came to the crest of a small knoll, and as I gazed down into the snow-covered valley, I saw my parents standing in front of the house that I grew up in. Though the rational part of my mind, which still operated on the horizon of the dream, told me that they were dead—it did not surprise me that Abraham and Christine were there.

I wanted to reach them and to touch them, but no matter how hard I tried to run, the snow against my legs seemed to prevent me from getting any closer. And the harder I struggled, the more fatigued I became. I watched as they turned their backs on me and moved towards the front door. I tried to yell to get their attention, to make them stop and wait for me, but they could not hear me. They walked into the house and closed the door behind them without once glancing back at me.

Then the snow became rain, pelting me mercilessly as I stood on the hilltop. But its force also freed my legs so that I could propel myself forward. No sooner had the rains freed me from the grip of the icy drift, than it turned the ground beneath me into a whirlpool of mud. The house seemed no closer. I was scared, scared of being trapped in the suction of the mud as I tried to keep moving forward.

I looked up from my blackened feet, and there was the door. I was relieved and wanted to crawl into the safety and warmth of my old home. I stepped through the threshold and I found myself inside an all-white room. I was frightened that I had entered the wrong door, but when I turned to leave, the way I had come in had vanished. In the center, two large poles swayed with the room, which I realized no longer had solid walls but canvas that billowed in the wind.

I looked around and saw nothing but a cot with perfectly folded white sheets. I turned again to where the door had been, and he was standing there. I slowly walked towards him and he backed away from me. The white hair which I had stroked as he had fallen asleep tonight had turned the dark color of a man decades younger. He was naked but for a simple cloth about his waist and a leather strap around his neck, from which the pendant now hung. I knew that he was still old, but his body was that of a young hero, defined and tanned as he might have appeared preparing for a race or dancing around a fire on the Island of Limnos.

My fear dissipated as I beheld him. His face was fixed in a look of stoic resolution and his eyes appeared to glow with enthusiasm. The sound of rushing wind soon enveloped the tent and sent its white canvas rippling all around me, and my attention wandered from Ion to the tent as it billowed and swayed with the ever-strengthening wind. The guide poles swayed and creaked but held their own as the flaps at front and back and along the sides snapped up to reveal sudden flashes of light. In a panic, my attention snapped back to Ion who stood motionless at the entrance of the tent. He became surrounded by such blinding light that I could barely make out his silhouette. Moving toward the light, I reached out to find him, but he was gone. The wind held me as I tried to rush after him and pushed me back farther into the tent and onto the cot with its perfect white sheets. There was peace for a moment as the wind ceased. "Ion?" I heard it again. 'Ion?' Loud, sharp percussive sounds broke the silence.

I awoke to rapid knocks at the door. It took me a few moments to orient myself in the darkness. I wanted to muster the words "Who is it?" but even a "Yes?" was too much. I was still floating in the state of dreams. I hastily pulled on a t-shirt and dusty jeans. I didn't bother with my watch, but I glanced at its hands—it was almost ten-thirty in the morning.

Stumbling toward the door, I opened it to find Milos, his face sullen and his eyes red and swollen. I felt myself resisting the message with which he was so obviously burdened.

"Marianna...it is Ion."

"No, no..." I said, trying to stave off, even for a few seconds, the inevitable.

"Ion's gone..." I didn't wait for any explanation as I pushed past him towards Ion's door. His bed was neatly made and he wasn't there. I felt my own breathing becoming rapid and short, and heat suddenly flushed my brow. I went back to face Milos, staring at him but unable to speak and unable to shield myself from the meaning of what he had just said.

I sank down in the threshold and leaned against the door, clutching it, as though it were a piece of floating timber after a shipwreck.

"Where is he?"

"About a kilometer and a half from here, on the slopes of Pentelicus. A neighbor, a farmer is hear his sheep bleat more than usual, so he is go out to see if one is ill or is attack by wolf. That is when he is find him."

"Did Ion say anything?"

"He is already gone..."

He wanted to say more, but I stopped him. It was cruel of me not to let him say his piece. He seemed so young and frightened. I felt as though I should be comforting him. But the bearer of bad news is always punished. I was indulging in the fantasy that the country doctor had misperceived Ion's subtlety and that I would show them that he was only resting, meditating, fooling them and fooling Death. The sweetness of the fantasy was almost too much to bear and it was ended by the sound of the rough engine of Father Diogenes' van followed by a pick-up truck as they pulled up to the house. This crude amalgamation of rusted steel and chrome, used to carrying hay or the other produce of farm life, bore now the body of one that had known and suffered so much, but was now on his final journey to rest.

Father Diogenes, as he emerged from his van, looked over at Eftehea who was sitting with Evangelis. She took the boy by the hand and led him away, even though he kept peering over his shoulder. He had seen death before, and he knew that it had come again.

I took a few steps toward the truck, as Father Diogenes rushed over and took me by the arm. I couldn't tell if it was to stop me or to accompany me forward should I choose to go. I watched as the boys silently hoisted him—he was wrapped in the same blanket they had brought to the Plaka Hotel, the day after we arrived, to warm him from the cold morning air. They were handling him tenderly, as if he might feel the slightest bruise if they weren't gentle.

Numbness could no longer hold me back, and I turned to Father Diogenes and wept, hiding my face against his breast covered in the black robes of his investiture. He put his arms around my shoulders and cradled me until my tide of grief began to subside. "Let's get him to bed," I said, knowing no sooner than the words slipped from my mouth that it would be the last time I would say or think them.

"Marianna," said the priest, "Come sit with me for a few minutes. The boys will take care of everything."

"No, I must be with him."

"Please, he knows you are with him," he insisted, as he led me by the hand into his study.

"What happened, Yiannis?" I sat quietly as he poured me some sweet wine from an old dusty bottle.

"He must have decided to take a walk and lost his way."

"Lost his way? Ion knew this terrain better than anyone, how could he have..."

"It was dark, and perhaps he was delusional. Why else would he wander so far, alone and almost naked? It is so sad. He never should have left the house. Where they found him—he was heading up the slope—his body gave out. I'm sure that he didn't suffer."

"Thank you Yiannis, but it's hard for me to see the good in things right now. In my heart, I knew that this day couldn't be postponed forever. I'm just glad that he made it back here one last time."

"Marianna, when the doctor examined him, he found something...something in Ion's hand." Father Diogenes removed a small folded scrap from his pocket. It was the poem I had written Ion. "I apologize for opening it, I had no idea it was something personal of yours." Had it been left on his nightstand perhaps I'd assume he'd not read it, but in this act Ion left me no doubt that he had.

I thought about my letter, then about what Ion was wearing when they found him. He had only two things on, a pair of old running shorts and a chain about his neck. By heating the two ends, he had reversed the process of their separation—fusing them together once again. It was as she had prophesized—when the chains were reunited, so would be the two lovers. In death, they were together and finally free to love.

"Why do you think he was straying so far from here?"

"I don't know, Yiannis, I don't know." But I did know. Ion had set forth on his final pilgrimage, and in his hand, he carried the message just like his ancestor had before him. Ion wasn't delirious. He wasn't sleep walking. He was going out to meet Death on his own terms, to meet him on his feet as a hero, running with torch held high, not lying on his back like a coward. And he most certainly hadn't lost his way—he was looking for the pass, the one that would carry him to Athens, to his beloved city.

"It is not for us to comprehend the great riddle of His purpose," Father Diogenes uttered. I know he was trying his best to be consoling, but it was starting to sound like a cliché and was doing nothing to relieve my melancholy.

"Why does He have to speak in riddles?"

"Perhaps God *does* speak simply, but, like children, we cannot yet understand clearly."

"Yiannis, if I showed you ten bags of coins, and I told you that they were all counterfeit but one..." I proceeded to tell him the riddle that Ion had once challenged me with. I had long ago given up on solving it.

He pondered it, and then a moment or two later, Father Diogenes began his answer. "You line the bags up and number them one through ten. You then take one coin from bag one, two from bag two, and so on, taking ten coins from the tenth bag. You weigh these and how ever many grams the scale registers over fifty-five—that is the number bag with the real coins." It took me a minute to fully grasp the validity of his solution.

"Very clever. But how did you see that so fast?"

"I didn't. Please forgive me for amusing myself at your expense. I heard this riddle from Panayiotas. After weeks of trying to unravel its solution I finally had to beg him for the answer."

"Ion told it to me. I wonder which one of them tried to stump the other."

"Whatever its origins, I know that Panayiotas saw it as a lesson on how difficult it can be to find the right path, the real one, avoiding the temptation to choose the many counterfeit ones that lay ahead. And even though the right path can be obscured, there is always a subtle difference, which allows one to distinguish it. But one must first learn to see beyond one's limitations. Perhaps death is a chance to share with God the answer to all of our riddles."

"Thank you Father." I couldn't believe I didn't see the answer myself. It seemed so simple now.

I could bear to see no one. I only wanted to be with Ion. He had been taken to his room—like a warrior brought back from the field of battle on his shield. We waited for the proper ambulance to arrive—he could not be left there long. I sat by his side and unfolded the piece of paper he had clutched in his death throes.

Born in chains of servitude twas thy destin'd birthright,
Yet thy Persian masters couldst not keep thy spirit down,
Whilst freedom beckon'd thee—for no more gentle knight
Or noble man—hath e'er adorn'd more princely crown.

For burning within thy breast twas the fire of a thousand
Kings - tho history's lineage of royal deeds doth sadly pale
Against thy great compassion as thou fac'd thy mortal end,
O, Ion—indelible is thy Love—and it shall eternal prevail.

From dreary orphan's empty dreams—thou sav'd me,
In ways it is not possible for one to save another.
Thou conquer'd all who wouldst have enslav'd thee,
Ordain'd to shower kindness on my long forgotten mother.

My Achaean Prince—to me a Life didst thou impart,
Once the son of slaves—fore'er the Father of my heart.

I held Ion's soft hand in mine—gone was its self-generated warmth, but the heat from the sun had kept it from growing cold. No one dared to enter and break the sanctity of our final moments. He looked absolutely serene, with his eyes closed, his head thrown back and his mouth slightly opened—yet no more breath would pass through his lips.

"Did you cheat him, my prince? Did you make your own appointment in Samarra? I don't believe for a moment that you were lost, or unsure of your limits." I knew that he had chosen to leave as a hero, doing what he had always done best—running—running for glory and for freedom.

It was time to go now—to move on with my life, with all its renewed hope. I ascribe little to the power of my own wisdom, or even my own will. I have recognized the power of one man to enter my being and reveal to me a way that I had almost lost. Were it not for this one man—a simple Greek shepherd—I would still be wandering aimlessly the landscape of ever-diminishing life. Ion Theodore, my shepherd, had become my moral compass. Born a slave and possessed of nothing—his gift to me was more than any king could have offered.

Finally, Yianns appeared at the doorway, and apologizing for the intrusion, he said, "They're here for him." He waited patiently with two neatly dressed ambulance drivers.

"I understand."

When I was a little girl, my parents took me to Lincoln Center to see Puccini's *Tosca*. It was Maria Callas' last season with the Metropolitan Opera. I remember little of the music or the story, save a vague memory of the costumes and overweight crooners. But I remembered the end.

Church bells were tolling, signaling the coming dawn and the end of a condemned prisoner's life. Tosca's lover, Mario, is awaiting a firing squad. Tosca and Mario have a plan to deceive the executioners. They are betrayed and Mario is killed. Rather than face imprisonment, Tosca leaps to her death.

The chandeliers came on slightly to illuminate the darkened theatre. The orchestra had set down their instruments and the audience was ready to file out.

But they didn't, not yet. They lingered—everyone knew that it was the last time they'd see her. I felt a current of excitement coursing through the crowd. The curtain rose one last time as Callas, alone at center stage, took her final bow. Perhaps the performance hadn't been her best, perhaps it lacked the crispness of so many other nights of her youth when she flawlessly plied her trade—but it was surely her finest hour.

"Be careful!" I said to the orderly who folded Ion's arms across his chest. He and his co-worker moved Ion onto a gurney and took him out the door.

I felt so lost, as if I had no particular place to be. I sat in his room for a while until thirst drew me into the kitchen for some relief from the oppressive heat. Downing two glasses of water, I turned to see Eftehea looking at me tentatively from the doorway.

"Eftehea, tell me more of Alexandra. You were the last one I know who saw her alive. I met an old nun on Limnos, she apparently knew Alexandra well, but she's taken a vow of silence."

"I am remember young girl, friend of Alexandra. She is use same name of saint."

"Yes, that's her!"

"She is sad Alexandra is leave Epfraxia."

"Why? Why leave a place of such serenity for...for Piraeus?"

"Please, pain for me is too great. When she is think Ion not love her, she is lose faith in everythings. Even give rosaries to friend. Friend sad and scared for Alexandra."

"She gave this old woman her rosary?"

"She say she is have no need for them—as she forsaken by her God and by..." she closed her hands about mine. She never finished her sentence though I knew it was for Ion that Alexandra mourned. From that moment on Eftehea never once addressed me again in English. She went back towards her room, as I retreated into mine.

It took me a few minutes to find the rosary. The thought that it was Alexandra's—my mother's—elevated it's importance. I had just assumed that the beads belonged to Sister Mary Alexandra, which begged the question of why she gave them to me. Did she know of Ion through my mother's stories—or did she see something in my eyes that sparked a recognition of Alexandra's spirit? I hoped so. I wanted to feel my mother so badly—to draw in her soul and let her feel the longing of a daughter.

At first, I could not find it. I scoured every square inch of the space to no avail—then scoured the same area over again. I was about to have myself committed when I saw it hanging from the cremone bolt that held fast my shutters. I shook my head at my inability to once again see the obvious. As Ion had said, if you seek it you must be willing to find it. It had taken me so long to even know that I had to search for the truth. And now that I had it, I realized how ill prepared I had been. I plucked the strand from the window and fingered its worn and smooth beads.

The beads for the Hail Mary's were made of a hard wood and those for Our Fathers had been replaced by different charms. I had never prayed the rosary, and I wasn't sure why I felt like doing so now. I didn't even know how to—though I had often seen my mom using the beads for comfort. My "mom," what a suddenly ambiguous concept, almost necessitating a precursor, like "foster" or "birth." Christine would always be my mom, but she was no longer my mother. I ran my hand ritualistically around the loop, as if performing the proper prayer, but it was merely a mimicry of motion. Though somehow it felt soothing, perhaps because I could imagine Alexandra's fingers caressing these same beads. Soon the rosary's centerpiece came into focus and I realized that it was not the typical Virgin Mary or Christopher. She had obviously replaced these traditional icons with one of her own choosing, and in that simple gesture I felt Alexandra as I imagined her. Stubbornly clinging to her dream—refusing to concede—even to God. I could not believe what my eyes told me was cradled in between the rosary beads. I had to be sure before allowing myself to fall prey to some mirage as so many other seekers had.

Beneath the winged runner was the chiseled lambda, the sign of this ancient warrior's love of a woman. I rummaged through my papers until I found the piece of tracing paper. I held it over the object until the edges of the lambda aligned. There was no mistake. It perfectly matched the charcoal rubbing that Dr. Schaffhausen had given to me in my office.

In my hand rested the Obol of Pheidippides.

It had been passed from warriors to emperors, then from an old slave to his pupil—and finally to my mother.

I thought about the incredible find. It had slipped through the fingertips of so many—unaware of its phenomenal value.

Ten million, Twenty million, what were those figures that Viennese doctor threw at me? I had felt relief in leaving SWB, but I knew that this elation would prove temporary as bills came and reality set in. I realized that affluence was a mirage that I constantly chased, working ever harder just to keep pace with an increasingly financially demanding lifestyle. But as much as this one icon could change my status, and my life forever, I knew I could never sell it. Its true value—that of a link between my mother and my dearest Ion—was incalculable.

I sent the following final message to Warren:

From: jumpingdolphin@aol.com
To: wgiles@nyu.edu
Subject: Obol

Sorry Warren. lead turned into dead end. hope you and the doctor find what you seek.

42
ONE WHO FORGIVES ALL

The Ancient Narrator looked around, as if to insure that no one was eavesdropping. He had the look of a man who was about to impart something so sacrosanct that it was known to no one but him. Certain that no unwanted ears were within range, he continued the story of the lone runner.

The crowd let out a spontaneous sigh of shock at seeing the brave messenger fall and lay still before them. All knew there could be no saving him. No words could he utter, but his eyes remained open, searching the crowd for one in particular. She was nowhere to be found.

No one dared approach him, until one boy fetched some water and brought it to the dying warrior, dabbing some on his parched lips. Miles ago, Pheidippides had untied the obol that his father had carried into battle. It was clutched in his left hand, pressed tighter as he ran the last twenty-six miles of his journey. He reached for the boy and placed it into his outstretched palm. He looked upwards, imagining that she stood before him.

"Forgive me..." he gasped. Clutching his breast, he felt the breath flee his lungs for the last time.

As he lay dying, Pancho Villa was reported to have uttered, "Don't let it end like this. Tell them I said something." I thought of last words. What if the words you just said prove to be the ones you are remembered by? How rarely are they poetic or noble or even prophetic. I was sorry that Ion's last words were his begging my forgiveness. A thousand pardons could not repay him for what he did for me and for my mother.

It was Sunday. I had spent a good part of the day in church where Father Diogenes held a special memorial for Ion. As a courtesy, he eulogized in both Greek and English.

"Great Spirit, in whose breath is held the secret of life everlasting, you have brought us together to serve as comfort and solace in this hour of lamentation. You have brought us together to witness the mystery that you alone understand. Again our tears are shed and our grieving hearts are wrung with anguish for those of us left behind, our earthly bonds forever severed.

"For that which is of the earth is to the earth returned—for are we not all debtors to the earth which now claims its just due. And as that which is earthbound is by the earth claimed, so do you now claim that which is spirit, that part of us which is you. You have recalled this beautiful being to that land beyond mortal vision, beyond the need of earthly goods and as he looks down upon us may he send his winged prayers for our imprisoned bodies, our caged souls and our questing minds.

"We pray that this chasm that his departure has caused may be bridged by the memory of his love. And may the memory of that love bind all who knew him in a union that is not only of the flesh, but is invested with his spirit. For he has made manifest that ancient commandment—that we love one another. Amen."

I looked about me at the others gathered in the pews. Faces were very somber. I even spotted a few watery eyes amongst the gallery, even though I doubted they could have known Ion personally. Father Diogenes' words were profound and certainly appropriate, but only Ion understood his own passing. He had casually spoken it to me many times, "My dear, Life is never final, and Death will only be a new journey in my Life." I actually believed, for one fleeting moment of the service, that it was Ion who mourned for us.

I cried, then smiled again, imagining Ion dipping his body in the waters of salvation here, nearly a half-century ago, inspired after a long night of soul-searching and ouzo-drinking with his priest. I realized how vital the thread of forgiveness is in the complicated lives we weave. Pull it out, and the fabric unravels.

"It's not necessary."

"It is, Yiannis. It is."

"The hospital can make all the arrangements and I can send Dimitris or Milos to..."

"No, I'll be there." I had already missed a similar service, and it was one too many.

There are no special preparations for a body that is to be cremated. Father Diogenes was partially right. There was no ceremony over the body, no viewing, just the technical procedure of the cremation. In Greece, someone who knows the deceased has to make a final legal identification. Either Father Diogenes or his sons could have performed this morbid formality, and were clearly willing. But I knew who had to do it as my penance for past sins.

The morgue was in the basement of the hospital at Nea Makris. It was eerily reminiscent of the home that I first found Ion languishing in. Now we seemed to have come full circle. Though Ion's spirit was unfettered by the constraints that his aging body had imposed—I was sad and even slightly frightened as I imagined his body all alone in this chilling place. Thank God I didn't have to watch as he was removed from his drawer-like cubby as if he were a pair of shoes. The orderlies had brought him into a separate room and placed him, shrouded, on a steel table.

Seeing him this one last time was the most difficult thing I ever had to do, but I felt strangely honored that I could do it for him. His mouth was slightly open, and if I did not know any better, I would have thought him smiling. I was glad to know that his final send-off would not be by some indifferent hospital staff members, but by one who loved him more than life itself.

I made the official identification.

"There are just a few papers to be signed," said the hospital administrator. "Perhaps you could join me in my office."

"Yes. I just want one last moment with him. If that's all right..."

"I understand," he said with sympathy, though I knew he witnessed moments like this every day.

I knelt on the floor beside Ion. His hands were cold. I wasn't sure why I stayed, but then it occurred to me that I had come here today to complete unfinished business. I was worried that Ion was not yet truly free—and I alone held the final key. The knowledge of what I had to do for him became immediately apparent. But I knew I had to act before other, more base, emotions swayed my judgment.

I carefully unwrapped the pendant from its secure binding. Since my discovery, I hadn't let it out of my possession. Looking closely at the Obol of Pheidippides, I ran my finger along the "Λ" beneath the runner's limbs. Let the experts believe it was the mark of the Lacedaemon, I knew differently—I knew it was for Leontia. My teacher had told me so, and he was there, somehow he was there. Leontia, Leontokardis—a lioness by any other name...

I held it in one hand, while the other stroked Ion's cheek. I kissed the pendant, and in one quick movement I slipped it into his open mouth and pressed his jaw closed around it.

"For Charon, my love, to speed you on your journey. Your marathon is finally over—and victory is yours."

That Monday, my last full day in Greece, I cloaked myself within the walls of Panteleimon. There was the normal weekday service, but that was not what drew me inside this afternoon. I remained for many hours—long after the congregation had prayed and departed. I stared at the figure of Orpheus, the golden-haired poet. Long and hard, I meditated on the friezes and brightly adorned murals and thought of a handsome young man lying on his scaffolds covered in sweat and colored oils.

I then sat alone in front of the statue I had once called the *Panayeia*, until Ion whispered to me its real name—*Anastasis*—the *Resurrection*. I thought of death and forgiveness and how they touched the lives of my mother, Alexandra, and her mother, Elektra. I had a burning desire to see them, to hear them, if only to help fill the terrible void of their absence.

In Ion's art, I saw my mother cast in cold Pentelic stone. I tried to think of her, not in the form of this petrous material, but in the warmth of her body that I never felt. Now I could see the features I had first gazed upon in the photos of her—taken on Limnos over forty years ago. I studied each and every striation and chisel mark—reaching out, I caressed the smooth parts of the stone where Ion's hands had rubbed and polished its once rough surface. The *Resurrection* was more befitting my rebirth than her death, but perhaps that was what Ion had intended when we embarked for this distant port.

Dimitris and Milos helped me move its heavy slab one last time. I placed the journals back inside the place from which sprang my new destiny. Though tempted to bring them home, I wanted to leave a part of him here so he would forever rest near his image of Alexandra—near the Plains of Marathon.

Late that evening, I sat in Father Diogenes' library. Milos and Dimitris were still awake. Father Diogenes and Eftehea had already gone to sleep. It was fitting, since his sons had greeted me when I first came here, and they would see me off in the morning, driving me to my next destination just as they had carried me to my destiny here at Panteleimon a month ago. Evangelis rested on the couch with his head on my lap.

Everything was set. My flight back to New York was scheduled for the next morning at 11:15 A.M., but I would leave early enough to stop by Adonia's apartment. I wanted to see her one last, no, one more time. I would have to find an excuse to see her the next time, and the next.

With Dimitris' help, I had packed what few things Ion had into a box. I kept only one or two sentimental items, including the few books we had brought and one of Ion's favorite ascots. Everything else would be left here—somewhere, someone would be thankful for his old clothes. I had only one other item to bring home. Sealed in two small urns were Ion's ashes. One of them would be emptied here in Marathon, near a grotto behind Panteleimon, I would sprinkle the ashes from the other urn over the grounds near the old Headmaster's cottage at Horace Mann—the building where Ion lived, sculpted and played. I would wait until spring and life's rebirth.

It was dusk, and Milos had lit several candles. I had grown to prefer this lighting in the evenings.

"Evangelis is ask me where is Uncle Ion go, and when will he see him again," Milos said to me.

"Tell him that Ion has not gone far. He can see him, if he wants to, when he closes his eyes to sleep. Ion will come when he calls." I am not sure if I was saying that for his sake or for my own. The emptiness was too great to contemplate, though Ion had left me with so much—more than I had ever had, or could have hoped for without him.

I stroked Evangelis' head. Soon he would be asleep, and when he awoke, I would be gone, flying around the world to a place that he was not yet old enough to understand. And as I looked down at him, I wished that he could know all about Ion, and I wanted him to believe that his dreams were possible.

A wonderful feeling shivered through my body, and I was prepared to dismiss it quickly. It made no rational sense, yet I knew it was not something that had just entered my consciousness for a brief encounter. It was unrealistic and impractical. I thought about teaching Evangelis English, and in return, he'd teach me the language I first heard but never learned. It was a silly notion of all Panteleimon's residents, I had spoken to him the least, yet I knew I would miss him most of all.

I held him close to my breast as he joined Morpheus in deepest sleep. Perhaps he too would dream of fleet-footed Ion Theodore running barefoot through endless fields of golden wheat—somewhere in Elysium.

"There is no hiding from vanity, is there?" Adonia came to see me off to the airport and I returned a pair of glasses she had left at Panteleimon.

"Adonia, I should live long enough to have half your beauty. Besides, they suit you," I said as she breathed heavily onto her glasses, and then wiped each lens before putting them on. "Will you come to New York again soon?"

"Perhaps, but I think it will be a while. I know I will see you again, Marianna. The first thought on a person's mind when they leave Greece is when they can return."

I was going to say something trite but then the words wouldn't form. I moved toward her and we embraced. "God, Adonia, I'm going to miss him so much. I'm feeling a little lost."

"Hush. What's wrong with being lost? Sometimes the way you discover is more beautiful than the way you came."

"How did you acquire such wisdom?"

"If I am wise today it is only because of all the times I was a fool before. But I still think you overestimate me. Do not leave saddened because of Ion—take the gift he has granted you and honor him in the best way possible—by living your life."

Corfu faded in the distance as the plane's engines carried me westward. It was a long flight—the longest of my lifetime. I was flying home, but a part of me would never return. For that part, home was where I left, not where I was going.

When I had gotten to Athens airport earlier that day, I had to rummage through my handbag to find my return ticket. I felt a deep ache in my heart as

I also found Ion's. He would no longer need his. He had already gone home.

The long trip back to New York was uneventful, my mind preoccupied with what had happened, rather than with my uncertain future. Something fortuitous occurred when I got to my house. My departure from Schroeder, Wilkes & Barron was not official yet, but word had spread along the myriad professional grapevines. One such vine had left a message on my answering machine.

"Marianna, it's Saul Bergman. I heard you've left SWB. Call me before you make any moves." Saul was a former partner at SWB, turned Managing Director at Goldman Sachs & Co. He co-headed their Mergers & Acquisitions Department. When Saul called, you called back.

"Great to hear from you, Saul."

"I heard a rumor, and when I called looking for you, they said you were on vacation, in Greece I believe. But I spoke to J.B. and he said you had tendered your resignation." J.B. was James Barron. "What happened over there?"

"Nothing bad, just wanted a little time to myself."

"I can appreciate that, besides, your talent was wasted there anyway. Now that you've had a rest I want you to consider joining my group over here at Goldman. Long hours, but far greater rewards if you know what I mean."

"I hadn't really thought about it, Saul. I'm flattered." I had made a good salary at SWB, but Saul's people were often paid bonuses an order of magnitude higher than junior partners at law firms. The financial prospects of this situation were beginning to sound very appealing. After all, it was Ion who told me that good things can come from bad if you trust in yourself and never panic.

"Okay. You can cut the bullshit Marianna, I've known you too long. I want you on my team, so don't make me beg."

"All right Saul, you know I'm happy to talk to you."

"Good. I want to set up a conference call with you, Marshall, my co-head and probably Carlos Giametti, another Managing Director. If that goes well, we'll bring you in for a deeper round of discussions."

"Great, when."

"I'm out all day Monday, but I know Tuesday works for all three of us since we'll be together for a lunch meeting. How does two o'clock sound?"

"Perfect."

"Call our main number, they'll page me. Talk to you then. Who knows, maybe leaving SWB was the best thing that ever happened to your career."

I hung up the phone and breathed a sigh of relief. Unemployment sounded better when I was in Greece, but less exciting sitting here in my house with nowhere in particular to go tomorrow morning. I was exhausted, and though I had a stack of mail piled on my foyer floor, I had no desire to sift through it. But one envelope caught my eye. It was a telegram from Father Diogenes with the news of Panayiotas' death. Its timely receipt may have left my life unchanged.

I wish I had met Panayiotas. I imagined him to be a lot like Ion—a well-spring of knowledge and experience. His death made me think of the home that I had rescued Ion from. It's sad that so many of us who feel the pain of the world so quickly forget the suffering humanity so close to home. The elderly, once considered a source of wisdom, now are thought of as doddering old fools.

It was Friday night. I did something I had never done as an adult in my own home—I lit Sabbath candles. This weekend, I'd go to a House of Worship, I just didn't know which one to choose. I had grown up with Judaism and Catholicism, only to discover I was technically neither. I suppose it really didn't matter whether I went to a synagogue, a cathedral or a Greek Orthodox church. Ion showed me, the savior is where you find Him—even on the ceiling of the Sistine Chapel.

Though crooners revered the season, I always believed autumn in New York to be an overdone cliché. Sitting alone one evening in my backyard, gazing at Ion's sanctuary, I looked forward to the final days of summer. I imagined the falling of leaves to be a final shedding of the vestiges of a life I used to live. My nose caught the strong scent of some night-blooming jasmine. I didn't even know my gardener had planted these, but it made me feel for a moment as if I were inhaling the strong fragrance of Aleppo pines.

I suddenly laughed. I was thinking about the first and only time Abraham and Christine had ever been here. Peter and I had looked at homes for two years. Neither one of us were making the kind of money we'd eventually earn, but some savings and a handsome bonus enabled our realtor to take us into the more coveted neighborhoods of Long Island.

"Hurry, a house has just fallen out of escrow… some divorce situation… very motivated sellers," our excited realtor claimed while imploring us to come look with our checkbook ready. This house was a deal, and we made an offer on the spot. Three days later, we were in contract on a home in Old Westbury—a village that I never dreamed I'd be able to afford.

A week before closing, Abraham and Christine came north for the last time. I was very excited to show them the house, the first home I'd ever own.

And though its colonial-style façade needed some TLC, it dwarfed any home that they had ever lived in.

I drove there straight from the airport, and as we pulled into the driveway, I asked them what they thought. Abraham, a man of so few words, was ready with his response.

"Well, I hope the inside's nicer."

Nothing ever seemed good enough to him, even though he had so little. There was no meanness in his words but they were part of a pattern of indifference that I never could comprehend. My recourse was to suck-it inside and work harder to attain the acknowledgement from him that I was always certain would come at the next announcement of some new achievement. I'm sure I could have made his funeral, but years of loathing and self-loathing burst forth in that one moment of cruelty—cruelty to Abraham and cruelty to myself. I knew now that such a flagrant act was hatred for what I had become so good at—shutting off my emotions so I could pretend suffering didn't exist.

"Perhaps you can still grow closer to him." Ion's last thoughts about Abraham returned to me as I searched for the box of his belongings. I felt the least I could do was get to know him better. I carefully laid out its contents on my dining room table. There were boxes of rubber bands, playing cards, combs, penknives and poker chips of every conceivable color—items he brought home from his wholesale candy store. I sifted through his possessions to see if I could piece together something of this aloof immigrant's life. My experience with Ion's journals had prepared me for this task. He taught me to see the importance and beauty of life's smallest details.

There were manila folders of papers, mostly medical records and Social Security statements. There were also certificates from a variety of non-profit organizations thanking my father for his contributions and years of service. I had no idea that he had given so heavily to charities over the years, or that he had involved himself in any organizations other than his business.

I wanted to know more, and more importantly, why I didn't know.

I telephoned Ben Sokolow, the only one of Abraham's friends I knew how to reach. He wasn't exactly enthusiastic to hear from me. It was no secret that I hadn't been at Abraham's funeral, and he wasn't going to let my conscience off the hook that easily.

"So, now you want to know about Abraham?" he said with a guttural accent that came at me like a bat. "You pick an unusual time," he continued.

"I was hoping you could answer some questions…"

"I won't discuss a man's life on the telephone like it's a purchase order."

"But I have no other way, and just a few minutes on the phone—"

"Every one has their own *tzuris*," he said and then abruptly ended the dialogue.

I regretted what I did, and knew I couldn't reverse it. But I apparently had to atone for it, and taking Ion to Greece was not the answer, but rather a key.

I was going to have that conversation with Ben, if for no other reason than to give him a chance to say whatever he would about my transgression to his friend. The mountain was going to have to go to Sokolow.

I would just show up. I wasn't going to let this abrasive man tell me I couldn't come to Florida.

When I arrived, unannounced, at his door, his wife, Gladys answered.

"You can find him at the 'Y' with the other *alta cockers*," said Mrs. Sokolow.

"I thought it was for men only."

"It was until a few years ago. Women can come any day but Thursdays and Sundays. If you want to see him, that's where he'll be all afternoon."

In Brooklyn, Abraham belonged to the Kings Bay YMHA—Young Men's Hebrew Association. When he and Christine moved to Miami Beach, he joined the one on Twenty-first Street and Collins Avenue—across the street from Wolfie's Delicatessen.

I'd never been to the one in Kings Bay, but a classmate of mine had gone several times with his grandfather and he told me that all he did was sit around all day with really old naked Jewish men. And as far as being an organization of "Young" men, any member under fifty is considered a youngster.

I stood inside its front doors. Here I could find men who knew Abraham and who might be able to fill in the blanks of a life I had once viewed only from the perspective of what I expected from it.

I had only met Ben Sokolow a few times. Ben's back was to me as I walked over to the table. He and three other men were playing gin rummy. I waited patiently until one of them laid out his cards, announcing he was knocking. I stepped forward and spoke the words I had rehearsed for several days.

"I am Abraham's daughter and I'm terribly sorry."

I thought Ben's cigar was going to fall in his lap. One man excused himself, muttering something in Yiddish. Ben and the others remained silent for a few moments until the man across from him introduced himself as Max Winograd.

"I'm Marianna, nice to meet..."

"I know who you are," said Max, but his words suggested anything but the joy of recognition. The other gentleman was named Isaac. I noticed a blurred-blue sequence of numbers tatooed on his and Ben's arms. It needed no explanation. They did nothing to hide or draw attention to these telling marks.

The next fifteen minutes were excruciating. They spoke about me as if I weren't there and worse were the sarcasm-laced barbs.

"Obviously, she's too important—a *Gantseh Macher*," commented Ben.

"So *Nu*, what does a father matter? He only sweated twenty-four hours a day for her his entire life," added Max.

"And she missed his funeral," said Isaac.

Which led to Max to conclude, "*Kein ahora*—thank God Abraham wasn't alive to see that. . ."

"In 5753 years, this can't be the worst thing that ever happened," I finally had to interrupt them.

"She knows the Hebrew calendar?" asked Max with some surprise.

"With a Jewish father, what do you expect?"

I noticed the three looking at each other strangely.

"Abraham… Jewish?" Isaac stated as if it were a question.

"Abraham was many things," said Max, "But he wasn't Jewish."

"What?"

"Fellas, it's none of our business," said Ben.

"I have a right to know," I demanded.

"When you chose your career over your father, you were forfeiting that right," said Isaac.

"You can't just say that and leave me in mystery. Look, I made a terrible mistake, but things have changed. I just returned home from a long journey to Greece with one of Abraham's oldest friends from New York. He was the only other man who ever really meant anything to me and now he's dead, too…"

"Ion Theodore is dead?" said Max.

"You knew him?" I asked, and then realized that had I been to Abraham's funeral as Ion had, I wouldn't have had to ask. Neither Ben nor Isaac missed the opportunity to let me know it.

"Why did you go to Greece with him? Vacation?"

"Hardly," I said. "I actually quit my job over it. He couldn't go by himself and… Frankly, I really don't know why."

"It was a *Mitzvah*. A selfless deed," said Ben, but without the castigation that had flavored his preceding comments. "Excuse us," Ben said to Max and Isaac. "I want to show her something, alone."

"What am I, chopped liver?" said Max.

"Max, would a little discretion kill you?" asked Isaac.

"*Feh*," said Max, as I got up to escort Ben to the entrance hallway. On the wall were nailed dozens of brass plates showing the YMHA's past Presidents and benefactors. There, engraved on a plaque fairly near the top, was Abraham's name.

"None of this is making sense, Ben."

"What did Abraham tell you about his childhood?" asked Ben.

"Very little, except that Cossacks raided his village of *Panamunya* and slaughtered the Jews there, including his father. He stowed aboard a trans-Siberian railroad and a few ships and made his way to Brooklyn, where he was raised by a friend of his father's." I searched Ben's face. "Is any of this true?"

"Some," said Ben. "Your father's father was a Cossack who helped carry out the extermination of *Panamunya*."

The blood rushed out of my head, and I felt faint. I, of course, told Ben that what he had just told me was impossible, but I could tell he knew exactly what he was saying and that somehow it was true. After what had happened to me in Marathon, I realized that things were often not what they seemed. What happened to the world that I thought I knew just one month ago? It wasn't perfect, but at least it didn't seem to spin into chaos every few days. For a moment, it seemed that the rock-solid ledge Ion had so generously given me had once again crumbled beneath my feet.

"Your father was not born a Jew."

"How did you find out?"

"It started one day when I asked him why a Christian wanted to join our 'Y.'"

"Just like that—out of thin air?"

"Marianna, in the locker room..."

"I think I get it."

"So he was a gentile—nobody's perfect."

"But the name, Abraham Chaitowitz?"

"That was the name of a boy that your grandfather found alive in *Panamunya*."

Ben shared with me that Abraham's real name was Nikolas and he was born Russian Orthodox. Nikolas had been raised to distrust all things Jewish and this racism ran generations deep. But the genocide in *Panamunya*, and in hundreds of villages like it, carried that hatred to a savage and unforgivable depth. Nikolas' father could not come to terms with his patriotic desire to serve the Czar, and the tragic conclusion of that zeal.

"Nikolas' father hid this child," Ben continued, "But soon his guilt became too unbearable. One day, he calmly killed his commanding officer—the one who had ordered the massacre. He then went out into his barn and hanged himself, leaving your father and this boy alone. It wasn't safe for either child to stay—one was a Jew and the other's father had killed a Cossack officer. Nikolas remembered a friend of his father's who had emigrated to America years earlier, so the two boys set out to escape to America and find that man. The Jewish child didn't make it—freezing to death one night on the Trans-Siberian Railroad as the two huddled together for warmth."

"But why, Ben? Why did he lead everyone to believe he was Jewish?"

"*Kapparot*," said Ben. "Atonement," he added, but I already had figured out what he meant. "When your father was processed through Angel Island, out of guilt or maybe fear of using his own identity, he told the immigration officer the Jewish boy's name. Without any money or the ability to speak English, he made his way across the country to New York and found the fellow Lithuanian. The man's family took him in and raised him, in the Christian faith, of course. But as Abraham grew older, he devoted his life to the very people his father was commanded to destroy. He planted trees in Israel, he gave to Jewish charities, and when he didn't have the money, he volunteered his time—though it always pained him to be apart from you."

"I'm not sure we're talking about the same man. He and I..."

"You meant everything to him. He talked so much about you and what you were doing. We almost started wearing ear plugs."

"Why didn't he tell me?"

"Shame."

"Of what? It wasn't his fault."

"You see these numbers," Ben was referring to those on his forearm. "The 'B' was for Buchenwald. Above the entrance gates were the words *Jedem das Seine—everyone gets what he deserves*. It's impossible to explain, Marianna, but even Holocaust survivors bear a terrible feeling of guilt, wondering what we had done to deserve such a fate." Ben paused. "Abraham loved you, it's now for you to decide what to do with that gift."

It took me a few minutes to digest all this information. In a few weeks, I not only learned that Abraham wasn't my father, but that he wasn't even the *person* I thought he was. I understood what he must have felt, and for the first time, why he had tried to shield me from the truth of my own birth. It took Ion Theodore to point me towards this truth, and the words of this aging Holocaust survivor to let me know the one thing that Abraham had so much trouble in saying—that he loved me.

Ben walked me to the front door. He had said nothing as I wiped the tears from my eyes.

"What can I do now for the way I treated my father?" I asked.

"Soon it will be the tenth day of *Tishri*," said Ben.

"Yom Kippur?"

"She's a genius," said Ben, his face solemn, but his eyes now shining. "Go to *shul*. Go to *shul* and light a *Yortzeit* candle for Abraham. Tell him how you feel. It's the start of the Jewish New Year, the old Book of Life will be closed. In it we leave behind our sins and unburden our hearts. Be true to yourself, your dreams and your God. That's all Abraham ever hoped for you."

As I headed back to Miami International Airport, I unwrapped the food that Ben had insisted I take, "Just in case." The knowledge of Abraham's childhood allowed me to truly see the depth of that unusual and caring man. And even in light of the truth of my origins—I felt closer to him as a daughter than I ever had in my life.

Though I had been home for almost two weeks, I hadn't gone into my family room since I returned. When I finally did, I noticed that Ion had placed the old instrument case on his Morris chair. It reminded me of the end of *Miracle On 34th Street*—the old black and white version with Edmund Gwynne. I always cried when John Payne and Maureen O'Hara find an old cane in the home of their dreams, suggesting that Kris Kringle had led them there all along.

I felt strangely hopeful for a moment that he had somehow returned and just laid this down for a moment. I listened, hoping to hear the sounds of his footsteps treading in the bedroom above. I was aching to go out in the garden and summon him in for dinner.

I'm not sure why I never once, in all the time that Ion stayed with me, ever asked him about this instrument case. The fact that Ion didn't offer up any information was a poor excuse for the fact that I was too wrapped up in my own affairs to have cared.

It was unusually heavy, and not very easy to open. The metal clasps had rusted badly, and one was bent inwards making it hold fast. A little WD40 and I was gazing upon a *bouzouki*, the one my mother had clung to so desperately—choosing deprivation over relinquishing its comfort and beauty. Lifting it gently, I ran my hands along its finely crafted sides. The carved bowl looked like a wide teardrop. The most intricate decorative pattern partially covered its smooth, cherry-wood surface. Its hand-hewn figure defied the advent of modern mass production.

I plucked several strings, I couldn't tell if it were in tune or not, but they seemed tight, and the sound sent a shiver down my back. Knowing that this had once sat cradled in my mother's arms and that her fingers had caressed these same strings brought me closer to her and in a strange way to Abraham and Christine. I wondered if my mother had held me too, before the moment that she and I were separated forever. I would have given anything to be able to play the *bouzouki* right then.

Also in the case, lying under the instrument's neck, were bags of quarters—which explained the case's weight. I presumed they were Bill's monthly payments, or—as Ion liked to call them—his Horace Mann 'dividends.'

Tucked under a flap in the tattered blue velvet lining were several faded sheets of handwritten music, accompanied by text. They were beautifully written.

I returned to Taverna Tony's with the music sheets. Losing myself for a moment as I sipped a cool glass of Chardonnay, I pretended that I was at the Achillon Gardens awaiting Adonia. I wondered how I had missed this part of me, part of my true culture. Always here, surrounding me, yet undiscovered.

I was so happy when I saw Tony's father, Tasos, walk in. I motioned for him to join me.

"Ah, Marianna, it is so very good to see you again."

"I thought you would have returned to Greece by now."

"I have been there and back."

"Me too."

"You have visited my Greece?"

"Yes, and so much has happened to me there—I feel like a new woman," I said, though I wasn't planning on telling him how true that statement really was. "How about you?"

"I have made a pilgrimage to the Holy Land. That's where I first saw *her*. She was in the Garden of Gethsemane. The sun was setting behind her—her fragrance floated to me on the summer's breeze."

"Sounds like love at first sight."

"We sat together for an hour—no words were spoken—or were necessary.

Once I had tasted her fruits, I knew I could not live without her. Would you like to see a picture of her?"

"Sure."

He pulled out a billfold from his back pocket, opened it and withdrew a wallet-sized photo.

"Tasos, it's a tree..." I commented, assuming he had grabbed the wrong shot.

"She is not just a tree. She is over two thousand years old. From her limbs were spawned olive groves from the Kidron Valley to the Sea of Galilee. Do you realize what this means?"

"No."

"When I graft her fruits onto my indigenous trees, I will make an olive like no other. Can you imagine the marriage of such rare species? Mine have witnessed Odysseus' return—hers have tasted the tears of Christ."

We talked for a while longer and I showed him the sheets of music.

"This is written by a woman. She is feeling sicker each day and is afraid she will not finish it. It is meant for her child. I will write it down for you. Like your last letter, this is very emotional. Doesn't anyone ever just send you a nice postcard?"

It was the Tuesday after my return from Florida, but I browsed the Sunday New York Times. That's one of the things I love the most about the Sunday edition—it can be savored all week. I wasn't really interested in the news, or even reading for that matter. I just wanted to bury myself in doing something—the quiet of the house made Ion's absence more blatant. Dozens of back-to-school advertisements fell out from every other page of the paper. *Back-to-school* used to mean a lot to me. The weeks before its arrival churned my stomach, mixing the blues of summer's end with the anxiety and anticipation of the new semester. Lately it meant nothing but moving out summer clothes to make way for fall's fashions. I thought about all those young faces returning to school to face the unknown, the next step up a ladder that could lead them to the stars.

I had lost Adam's number. Not intentionally as I had originally thought I might. But I knew where he'd be next week when the bell would ring—beckoning his new class. Maybe I'd give him a call. I was trying to play it cool with myself, but I knew there would be no maybe.

I went up to my attic to store away my luggage. All morning, I had been thinking about my conference call with Saul and his colleagues at Goldman. I looked at my watch. It was shortly past one o'clock in the afternoon, but here in the attic, one could lose all perspective of time.

It was dark and sweltering. My body had every desire to leave this confining space, to return to the light and air conditioning below. But I paused, looking for a while at the dusty boxes that littered the space. For a few moments, I forgot the heat and its effects on my body, ignoring the beads of sweat that were now forming without constraint.

I recalled how my life's greatest adventure had begun right here—a destiny forged in heat, like the hero's iron in Hephaestos' furnaces on Limnos. Right in the darkened recesses of my own house, it was there all along, but almost not found. How much had changed since that day I rummaged through my parents' relics, finding the photograph of them at Horace Mann, triggering a chain of events for which I only believed I was in control.

I mused about what other paths I may have taken had I opened a different box that day, or perhaps none at all. Then, something drove me forward, into the dark, and away from the light of the stairs. Perhaps I wondered whether light would exist on the other side of the night I found myself entering. I made my way carefully between the haphazardly placed cartons, running my hands along their tops, picking up the years of dust and neglect.

All of a sudden, it happened, again. I hit my ankle on the same piece of wood that still protruded invisibly in the dark. The hurt was intense, feeling more like the poison-tipped arrow of Paris than a clumsily placed two-by-four. It could have struck anywhere, but no, it had to be the exact same spot I had previously injured. I winced, and as the pain intensified and sent its throbbing message to my brain, I started to cry. And then my crying over my wound became an uncontrollable sobbing as the wounds of my heart were stirred.

Why had I returned here, and to what? I had left here certain of my life's structure, now, I felt an orphan, suddenly a Greek with thousands of years of history and generations of ancestors materializing in an instant. I massaged my ankle. It was beginning to swell up and I would need to ice it as soon as possible.

I made my way back to the stairs, this time, making sure not to brush too near any objects that might reharm my stricken ankle. I went into Ion's room. Since I had been back on Long Island I felt as though I were a revenant wandering about in a place I once called home, but no longer quite knew. More difficult for me was re-adjusting to an existence without the life Ion brought into this ordinary dwelling. The walls reflected the powdery blue that I had always meant to change—though its hue now reminded me of the warm Aegean, and Ion's shirt as he carried the Olympic flame. I liked to stand in there though I never dared sit in his chair or on the edge of the bed where I had sung him to sleep so many nights.

I thought about the remarkable coincidence of our reunion. There were infinite permutations under which I never would have thought of him again, and seemingly only one that would lead me to him. Now I believed that one to be the only one possible. Each of us needed the other. Me—to find peace with my life, he—to make peace leaving it. How divinely the Gods interweave our destinies.

I unfolded the piece of paper I had saved from Taverna Tony's. I had read it no fewer than a dozen times since Tasos had translated it for me. Reading her words to me was chilling. They were meant for me, and yet not—in the sense that she did not know me—and what I had become. Or did she? Did she know that I would become a woman devoid of love? Her words were going to haunt me for a long time. I read them over and over, trying to glean her wisdom, imagining her singing me this lullaby as she held me in her weak arms.

Go to sleep, little baby, be not afraid,
Mother's cough will go away, and she'll be just fine,
She's getting ready to go where nothing can hurt her,
Her only pain, that she must leave you behind.
But as she journeys to distant shores, she'll wonder,

Will you even think of her as you blossom into beauty?
Could you possibly think of her if you do?
What could you know of the tormented passion she felt?
Will you believe she abandoned you?

What golden hair will she not teach you to braid?
What dreams will she never see you achieve?
What tears will you shed that she will not catch?
What groom will she not embrace at your wedding?
What grand child will she never cradle in her arms?

She knows you may never understand why it was,
She knows your innocence will be turned to anger
She understands and asks you no forgiveness,

She only wants your path to be better than hers,
But for this lullaby, she has nothing to give you.

She struggles to finish as her days grow shorter,
The winter of her song approaches too quickly,
If you find love—do not squander the chance,
As your mother before you so foolishly did,
In your breath, may your mother be resurrected.

I went back to my room, searching for and then finding my appointment book. I had left it on a shelf, which displayed antique perfume bottles, Lalique crystals and other *objets d'art*. In the center was a new piece—a bronze sea nymph brought back from Limnos. I'm not sure that's what it was, but as its owner, it could be anything I chose.

While retrieving Saul Bergman's number I thought of Alexandra's Lullaby. Suddenly, Ion's words echoed in my mind, "*the Gods have ways of making even the most far-fetched ideas seem commonplace*."

I looked nervously once again at my watch. It was a few minutes until my conference call. I went to the telephone, not quite sure in my mind of what I was doing. I picked up the receiver and dialed the main number. After the automated prompt, I hit the number two and waited patiently while I was soothed with prefabricated music. I ran through what I was going to say, and if it was what I really wanted. I held the handset steady to my ear.

Finally, the music faded and I heard the telltale auditory change which signals that the wait for a real human voice has ended. It was a beautiful voice, soothing and yet, causing my heart to leap as her rehearsed words reached out and beckoned me.

"Olympic Airlines, Ms. Kourkoumelis speaking. How may I help you..."

EPILOGUE
REDEMPTION

"He died? After all that running?" asked the Young Pupil.

"After all that running," nodded the Ancient Narrator.

"That's a terrible story. I don't like the way it ends."

"Come on you two, that's enough storytelling for one afternoon—dinner's ready," the Young Pupil's mother called out from the back porch door.

"Really, how would you end it then?" asked the Ancient Narrator, getting up slowly; his legs were not as supple as they used to be.

"He would have found her again. And when he did, he'd tell her he loved her and she would forgive him."

The Ancient Narrator looked down upon his Young Pupil and smiled—her eyes were so full of the hope that seems to be monopolized by the very young, and in rare cases by the very old who believe they have nothing left to lose. "How do you know he didn't?" the Ancient Narrator said.

"But you said he died. How could he then?"

"Ah, another tale for another time..."

"It's getting cold. Hurry you two," repeated the Young Pupil's mother.

"Wait a minute! What happened to the child with the runner's pendant?" begged the Young Pupil.

"He set sail—far from Athens,"

"To conquer? To win great riches?"

"To find love..." said Uncle Ion as he took my hand and led me into the house.

Movers were coming Tuesday morning. I was nine years old, and I was scared I would never see him again, regardless of his assurances to the contrary.

Despite the short plane ride that separated us, I wouldn't see my fleet-footed poet again for over thirty years. The memories of those hazy summer afternoons of storytelling had faded into the deepest recesses of my mind—reawakening only after the sun had set over a monastery in the shadows of Mount Pentelicus.

AFTERWORD
AN AUTHOR REFLECTS

Trudging up several flights of stairs to the fourth floor of Tillinghast Hall, I first met Ion Theodore as he stood before our Studio Arts class. It was September 7th, 1972. I was eleven years old and a *firstie*, as seventh-graders were then called at the Horace Mann School for Boys in the Bronx. I was nervous, but not so much that I wasn't able to be a wise ass to Mr. Theodore. You would never dream of mouthing off in Mr. Allison's History class, or in Mr. Glidden's General Language course, but old Ion Theodore seemed an easy target for adolescent misbehavior. Besides, every one knew that Art wasn't really one of the important subjects.

Far from the comforts of an elementary school I used to walk three blocks to, Horace Mann was quite an adjustment. This enclave in the Bronx called Riverdale wasn't just far from my home in New Jersey—it was so far, I didn't even know how I got there. There'd be no running home if things got dicey, escape plans involved subways and buses and crossing State lines. My seventh grade teachers were tough; they demanded more of me than their counterparts had in the Tenafly public school system.

Mr. Theodore was an elegant, yet very simple man. It became apparent that he possessed little pecuniary wealth, even compared to other teachers who made far less than they were worth, which in and of itself is a sad statement about our societal priorities. He didn't live in a beautiful home or have an impressive car—as a matter of fact, I'm not sure he ever drove a car at all.

At first I viewed his course as an easy fifty-minute break from the pressures of Reading, Writing and Arithmetic. Mr. Theodore, rightly assuming that most kids in the room couldn't connect two dots with one line, had us sketching the most rudimentary of shapes. I was bored out of my mind.

One day, I took a plastic bust and coated it in a thin veneer of green clay, presenting it to him as if I had sculpted it. With fellow students in on the gag, trying to hold back their guffaws, he at first admired it. Then, detecting the ruse, he said, "Billy, I expected better of you." I wasn't sure why. But I did want to show him how stupid I thought the lessons were, so at home, I took some pencils of varying numbered leads, and drew a picture of the ancient Roman Forum. Bringing it to class, I could see that Mr. Theodore was at first skeptical. Apparently not willing to be duped twice, I had to have my mother call and assure him that I really had drawn it myself.

"A feeling for perspective isn't taught, it lives in the soul," he said.

From that day forth, I was exempt from drawing lines and simple geometric shapes. He let my art expand to wherever it wanted to go. I oil painted, I sculpted, I drew reproductions of Piranesi prints. Mr. Theodore awakened in me an artistic talent that I never knew existed. But it was more than that. He believed in me.

At the end of that academic year, Ion Theodore, already sixty-nine years old, retired. But he didn't leave Horace Mann. He came in every day to a makeshift studio that at first was located in the boiler room in the basement of Pforzheimer Hall. Though students were required to rotate through a variety of art electives and though Mr. Theodore had retired, I somehow won special permission to study one-on-one with him in satisfaction of my art credits. I'm not sure how much this was from a desire to pursue the studio arts, or an attempt to avoid film, theatre and shop classes.

Whatever the motivations, I remember well sitting in that boiler room, toasty warm in the winter, sketching pictures as he chiseled stone or wood. Scratchy old recordings playing on his small Victrola partially masked the boilers' drones as he would cheerfully pontificate about school, history, art, dying and most importantly, about living. The next year, he moved into the basement of Tillinghast, and the year after, to the basement of the old Headmaster's cottage which served as the nurse's office. Sleeping on a cot reserved for infirmed students during the day, and using a hotplate to prepare meager meals, he became Horace Mann's first and only artist-in-residence.

Time with him was an oasis from the academic and social rigors of the Horace Mann School. His stories took me away from the Bronx and lifted me into worlds that I had only begun to read about. Though the focus of his conversations usually revolved around the lives of his students, once in a while, the masonry would reveal a crack through which I could see the depth of his life experiences. Through that portal, I wandered with him through the Mesopotamian desert; I ran over the craggy mountains of Greece and was with him stride for stride in Berlin where he carried the sacred Olympic flame.

I was profoundly impacted by his revelations that he had been born a slave—the property of another man, without the basic human rights of self-determination and dignity. So many of us take for granted the most simple things in life—it's easy to do that in the affluent environs of New York City and the rarified world of a private school like Horace Mann. We ascribe success to skill, when the hand we are dealt at birth is so often the measure of our opportunities and achievements.

I owe Mr. Theodore much of my hunger to see the world and the courage to do so off-the-beaten-path. And in a day and age when parents question the motives of men who devote themselves to the teaching of young boys, he was a beacon of purity. He was a beautiful soul in every sense of the word. Self-effacing and humble to a fault, he never imposed with his own life's struggles—only lending an ear to my travails as I navigated through my teenage years. Mr. Theodore came to my Bar Mitzvah, walking from the New York side of the George Washington Bridge all the way to Tenafly—a distance of over six miles in the bitter cold of a January day.

Over the years, other students joined our Socratic society in the basement studio. Visiting Horace Mann a dozen years after graduation, I saw new generations of eager students working away under Mr. Theodore's tutelage.

Though my other "major" subjects would dominate my academic focus for years to come, I never forgot those days that we spent creating art in his basement studios. Sadly, I lost touch with Mr. Theodore for several years near the end of his life. I have no excuse; I just allowed my own career, first marriage, and other stuff, to consume me. When I finally decided to "track him down," I learned he had been moved from the cottage basement to a nursing home and then to the home of a younger woman named Mary.

This relationship highlighted for Mr. Theodore his greatest regret in an otherwise long and successful life—that of abandonment and betrayal in affairs of the heart. In Mary, he finally found a woman with whom he felt perfectly safe. The Fates can be cruel as well as kind, and they brought them together at the final twilight of his long life. Though the emotional connection was there, it would have to remain forever unrequited. As his body withered, Mary courageously prepared him for life's final journey. She showed me that selfless love exists and that when fate irrevocably binds two souls, no earthly power can erode it.

The last time I saw him, he looked as elegant as ever, and his memories of the many things we did together was as sharp as if months, not years, had elapsed. Mr. Theodore and I sat in Mary's garden and reminisced about old times, and soon we had talked down the sun. He was one of those souls who you just convince yourself will be there forever, though soon thereafter, the inevitable call came. He passed away in Mary's arms.

I saw Mary for the second time at a memorial service which was held at Horace Mann. I had written a sonnet about him, which I read to the gathered assembly. There were current students and alumni of classes spanning from the 1950's through the '90's. Afterwards, Mary and I had a quiet moment together and she told me that she felt she knew me from Mr. Theodore's stories. We became fast friends, if for no other reason than we shared a love of the same man, though in different ways and for varied reasons.

I could tell that Mary had been moved by my mentor in a way that transcended both platonic and physical interpretation. She shared with me her own path of self-discovery and connection to this man that made me realize I stood in the presence of some great love whose consummation, given the Fates' cruel separation of their ages, would never come to be.

At the end of Mr. Theodore's life, Mary learned that she had been born in Greece and been adopted by an American couple—arranged by him. The thought that one's universe could turn so quickly on its foundations startled me, but more amazing was the cycle of salvation. A man rescues an orphan, only to have that child—unaware of her rescuer's deeds—return four decades later to save that same man from the despair of a decrepit nursing home.

Though my revelations were not quite as startling as Mary's, I too was going through emotional changes. I was turning forty and though I had achieved a modicum of success in my chosen career, my life felt empty. It was as if I were trapped in a game of collecting wealth, which by definition can have no end. I wanted to create something other than a larger bank account. I wanted to create something that would mean something special to others, even people I had never met. I hoped to someday put pen to paper (or at least fingers to keyboard) and tell this remarkable story. I also knew that as amazing as my student-teacher relationship with him was, this view through Mary's eyes was even more intriguing, and challenging for me as a writer.

It would have to wait.

Years later, I found myself sitting before that dreaded blank page—the one that I imagine has at one time or another stared back defiantly at every author from Chaucer to Hemmingway. Day after day, I returned and stared at the same page, only to confirm that it was indeed, still blank.

I thought about Mr. Theodore, and his incredible journey from slave to sculptor. I imagined him as a modern-day incarnation of Pheidippides himself, and like the ancient marathoner, he was for me part man, part myth. And as I felt the trials of his long and lonely run, I knew that my potential to write lay somewhere beyond where I had stopped to rest.

So I began to write.

It was the spring of 2001. It seemed anything but an innocent time, but in the aftermath of the tragedy of that September, it has taken on an aura of simplicity. I was glad Ion didn't have to witness this devastation in his adopted city, but his experiences and revelations had enabled me to weather that cataclysm. As I read the obituaries of friends and families of friends, I felt Ion with me, still guiding me as if along a path through the Persian desert on his way to freedom.

And I kept writing.

Ion Theodore gave me faith that no matter how badly one's foundations are shaken—even if reduced to ashes—that life can and must flourish anew.

W. William Winokur
New York City, 2005